MAISIE MOON

Guilt

Nancy Flanagan Chronicles – Book One

MAISIE
MOON

Second edition

Advisor: Angela Thomas
Typesetting by Lorna Reid
Proofreading by Kelly Hambly

This book was professionally typeset on Reedsy.
Find out more at reedsy.com

I dedicate this book to my family, but above all, to my mother,
Nancy Byrne,
who passed away in 2021 at 93.
She was the inspiration for the memoir section, and was a young
Irish Catholic who came to England from Ireland during the
post-war years to train as a nurse.
The book is a work of fiction, but I modelled the character of
Nancy after my mother's determined, feisty, and down-to-earth
personality.
Love and miss you mum x

God creates every single person born on this earth and gives them original sin. They inherit a nature which is inclined to be sinful. There is a dark side to every human, which shows itself during their lifespan. No human being is pure or free from sin.

The Bible refers to original sin in Genesis 3, in a line in Psalm 51:5, and Paul's Epistle to the Romans, 5:12-21.

Contents

Preface

I hope you have had a chance to either listen to 'The Sisterhood', on Spotify and Audible, or downloaded the e-book or bought the Paperback. If you have, thank you very much!

It's useful to read it first, as it's a precursor to the Nancy Flanagan Chronicles Trilogy, starting of course, with this book, 'Guilt'.

I'm excited to say that Guilt will also be available in audiobook format from June 2025.

'Legacy', the second book in the series, which introduces Maeve, is due to be self-published in 2025. 'Destiny', the third and final book in the trilogy, is due to be completed in the latter part of 2025.

I look forward to receiving feedback on these characters and their supernatural experiences from you. I'm only starting out on my authoring journey and am grateful to know what you liked, but also what you disliked. Please email info@maisiemoonbooks.com and tell me!

You can join the Maisie Moon Book club by signing up at my website www.maisiemoonbooks.com, where you will receive a newsletter from time to time with updates. Opt out at any time.

If you have enjoyed any of my work, please do leave a review, it really helps independent authors.

Thank you so much for being a reader.

Much love, Maisie Moon x

Acknowledgments

I just wanted to add a word of particular thanks here to Angela Thomas. Angela was my first beta reader and critique partner, and a fantastic help in authoring this book. She noted inconsistencies, checked plot lines, and became so engaged with Nancy, the main character, she offered notes about what Nancy might think or say.

Her help was invaluable, and if you are ever lucky enough to get the chance to work with Angela, bite her arm off!

It is true what they say, that no one person is responsible for any subsequent success. There is always a successful team behind that person. If any of these books achieve a modicum of success, it's definitely down to the team effort.

Love, Maisie Moon x

Chapter 1

THOUGHTS PASS THROUGH THE mind. Sometimes vapid, other times as emotional as an ageing father at his only daughter's wedding. On this day, my brain was wildly alive, its circuitry taking in the sights and sounds of this unfamiliar environment. Smeared marks on the train's windows from small children's faces pressed up against them, wooden carriage floors worn by passengers' endless movements back and forth, and an occasional waft of steamy, smoky, and oily aroma from the locomotive's engine as it voraciously burned coal to push the train along its preordained path.

Clack, clack, clack went my high heels, the sound reverberating on the polished wooden floor of the Royal Scot Engine as I moved further down its tight corridor. Listening to my new shoes creating a cacophony, I reflected on my situation. Leaving the past behind me, I was beginning anew.

In 1946, the family planned for me to train as a nurse in England, but I didn't, for a tragic and difficult reason. Aged eighteen, a young man took advantage of me, resulting in an illegitimate child. The bitter taste of regret lingered on my tongue. Feeling like an outcast and separated from my family, the following year, at age nineteen, I left Ireland for England to take up nursing training. There was no choice but to leave my child behind during that tough time. Mixed emotions filled me as I embarked on a new chapter with a heart full of sadness, apprehension, but also hope.

My mother was American born and hailed from Philadelphia, Pennsylvania. She was a tall woman with a powerful presence. With a determined gleam in her eyes, she motivated her eight children to pursue meaningful professions. My siblings followed career paths to be nurses, accountants, or teachers. I attended a convent school for thirteen years, reaching a reasonable level of examination.

My sister's friend Elena was a nurse in the army and loved it very much. My older sister Ursula, as well as my mother, thought nursing was a possibility for me as a career choice.

Recruiters from England came to Ireland to attract both qualified and trainee nurses, and mammy pushed me to accept the life-changing opportunity when it presented itself.

Magazines displayed photographs and pictures of junior nurses meeting doctors, falling in love, and getting married as part of their recruitment drive. The trainee nurses were captivated by the scene, imagining a couple embracing under a golden sunset and it encouraged them to take the plunge into nursing. I wasn't interested in romance. Not then, anyway.

The thrill of learning and facing new challenges as a nurse did appeal to my practical nature. Ireland was poor, with few quality job opportunities. Choosing the carpet factory felt unsatisfying, so I looked to nursing as a better choice.

Continuing down the train's corridor, I found the designated compartment on my ticket, opened the sliding door, and made to sit down on the cushioned bench, the one facing the engine. Glancing over at the couple sitting opposite, I gave them my most welcoming smile, tilted my head, and said, "Good morning," as sweetly as I was able.

The well-dressed pair were in their late fifties. However, it was the woman who appeared prim and proper. Their reserved English manner meant the man continued to read his newspaper, whilst the woman's gaze wandered aimlessly, rather than making eye contact with me. Without any response, I felt invisible and expected a long, tiresome journey.

Among the various objects in the compartment, my eyes were drawn to the bright red Communication Cord, standing out against the muted colours. A lengthy chain spanned the train carriage, to alert the driver to a ringing bell in case of emergencies. 'Penalty £5 for improper use,' the sign shouted at me.

Before taking my seat, I placed my suitcase on the corded rack above it. Styled like a hammock, the movement caused a significant amount of dust and dirt to drop. *How often were these racks cleaned?* I thought. The gentleman opposite looked inquisitively over his newspaper and saw me brushing the dust off the seat.

"Soldiers slept on those during wartime," he said rather pointedly.

Did he just scold me for cleaning the seat, implying I should feel lucky to have one?

"I can't imagine it was very comfortable," I replied back to him in my broad Irish brogue. He went back to his newspaper. No more to discuss, apparently.

The sound of the steam train was deafening as its pistons pumped and pushed the train along with all its might. It powered along the rail tracks whilst its vapour hissed and fought against the hard metal. The train jerked on the bumpy route, causing my heart to leap. The thrusting, continuous sound of the pistons straining was one never to be forgotten. Sounding out a mesmerising rhythm, like a hammering on a drum which imprinted on my brain returning in my head.

The train's rolling motion caused passengers to collide with each other whilst navigating the corridor's crowded space. When making my way to the toilet, I fell sideways against a large bespectacled gentleman. He took it in good grace, and I thanked him as he shuffled backwards from the corridor into a carriage compartment for me to squeeze past.

Returning from the uninspiring dark wooden toilet, which was malodorous, I retook my seat. The window in the carriage door slid down with a leather strap to control the amount it opened. Leaning out of the window to watch the engine as it navigated a sharp bend, puffing like an old man smoking a clay pipe, was enjoyable. The train's piercing whistle was reminiscent of a small child's persistent scream as it entered a dark tunnel.

Avoiding the billowing steam, I protected my Sunday best coat from getting messy. Mammy might have killed me if it became damaged. The soot from the train dirtied my face and blew into my eyes if I leaned out too far, but feeling the wind caress my hair as the train sped along was irresistible.

Never doubting the door's security, I leaned further out of its window. A kind man warned me of the dangers of hitting my head on a tree branch and recommended I sit back down for safety. Sitting with a thump, not having considered this possibility, I thanked the gentleman, although not appreciating his interference at the time.

My constant restlessness translated into a perpetual dance and as the journey continued, I squirmed, and shifted in my seat, just like in my childhood.

"Do you have ants in your pants, Nancy?"

Mammy often said it to me during my childhood, as I exuded a boundless energy, which she could not restrain.

The unfriendly couple in the carriage left at Chester Station, and two women boarded. They sat opposite me in the second-class carriage, twin sisters going to Birmingham to visit relatives. As we sat there, I examined their expressions, searching for any hints or clues. Identical, about forty years old, with the same facial features. Their clothes appeared outdated, as though tailored in the 1930s rather than the 1940s. They wore simple brown suits and were carrying brown suitcases, with initials embossed on the front. I wore my Sunday best coat with a fur collar and a form fitting tailored dress, also sporting a hat and high heels, making me feel rather stylish. As children, mammy made sure she dressed us well, and despite the journey causing my clothes to wrinkle, I kept a sophisticated look.

The twin's most striking feature was their platinum blonde hair with distinct kinks, like undulating waves on a choppy Atlantic Sea.

Their hairlines drew my eyes, but they weren't wearing wigs. The hairstyle was such a strong modern contrast to their severe looking clothes; I continued to stare at them.

With friendly and confident voices, Sylvia and Linda exchanged greetings with me. Linda was on the left; Sylvia was on the right. I introduced myself as Nancy Flanagan.

Sylvia noticed my continuous stare and with her eyes meeting mine said, "Oh, I see you like our hair, Nancy," patting underneath the wavy end with her right hand.

"The hairstyle is very fashionable. The Marcel Wave?"

Her sister Linda chortled and said, "Thank you, Nancy. Yes,

we created this ourselves. The texture of our hair transforms with the help of the curling iron. It makes it sleek and bouncy. The hairspray gives it a firm hold. We are quite the fashion plates, aren't we?"

Exchanging glances, they burst into a peeling fit of laughter, reminiscent of an old clock chiming on a mantelpiece.

They told me their wealthy aunt and uncle lived in a grand and ornate mansion and wanted them to work as housekeepers and caretakers because of their declining health. The ladies' eyes sparkled with anticipation, smiles stretching from ear to ear as they explained.

"We used to work for a family with young children. It was chaotic, with toys everywhere and constant demands for our attention, but now we're delighted to be with our aunt and uncle. Right, Sylvia?"

The ladies exchanged glances and burst into giggles, often finishing each other's sentences. Were they both happy and sad simultaneously? It was impossible to tell them apart. In fact, if I closed my eyes, and they swapped seats, I wouldn't have known which was which, they were so similar.

"Do you both have boyfriends?"

The question hung in the air, followed by a momentary silence before they responded.

Linda tilted her head to one side.

"Nancy, we can't waste time on men!"

"Oh, no," replied Sylvia, narrowing her eyes until they were slits.

"We're far too busy. They would just hinder us."

Did they not wish to wed and begin a family? All they needed was each other. I'd heard twins functioned as two halves of the same person, and I guessed they were like this.

"How will you fill your time when not working?"

Sylvia smiled at me saying, "Oh, we like to make our own clothes."

She took the hatpin out of her hat and showed it to me. I inspected the hat.

"Wow, exquisite work. You are talented."

Through our chat, they disclosed their aunt and uncle enjoyed pots of money. The girls held onto the hope of inheriting their wealth when they passed away.

Although their motives for going to look after their relatives weren't moralistic, I found the ladies amusing and I liked them. Connected by understanding thoughts and emotions, they were like two peas in a pod.

Our constant chatter and laughter filled the air, creating an energetic atmosphere during our journey to Birmingham. They were splendid company, and they distracted me from feeling the slightest bit lonely on the last leg of the journey.

Before the train arrived at the station, Sylvia leaned over and whispered, "This is my uncle, Nancy. Everyone knows *his* name."

Linda looked at her disapprovingly.

"Is he famous Sylvia? A film star like Cary Grant?" I asked.

We all laughed at that. But Sylvia shook her head and said, "No, Nancy, he was in the Second World War," she whispered, "But for them!"

She passed to me a faded black-and-white photograph of a severe-looking man in a very smart army uniform. The crisp lines of the German uniform caught my eye, the distinct SS insignia emblazoned on the peaked cap.

Looking at her in surprise and shock, I exclaimed, "Good grief, he was in the SS!"

It was a statement, not a question. The mention of the SS brought forth images of fear, anger, and disgust in the minds of those involved in the war. They were the epitome of evil, having committed unspeakable atrocities.

Linda, noting my horrified response, said, "Sylvia, don't show that around. People won't like it."

Sylvia didn't let her sister admonish her and said with defiance, "His outfit looks dashing, that's all."

The picture shocked me, with no desire for further details. He looked strict and authoritarian.

"Linda's right, Sylvia. People might be sensitive to his background."

We were in 1947, two years following the war. Many people had lost family and friends to the indomitable Nazi war machine. It amazed me that Sylvia mentioned her uncle's involvement in the war, knowing he would be a hated Nazi in England.

Linda tried to explain.

"Sylvia's a romantic, Nancy, imagining our uncle to be a dynamic, heroic type. He's not very well, having sustained injuries in the war, and our aunt has diabetes and needs constant care."

"Being Irish, we didn't enter the war. It's a difficult subject, so I will ask my family to pray for yours."

The ladies, who were not religious types, felt surprised. After a minute, Linda nodded, saying, "Thank you, Nancy. It's appreciated."

I nodded back and I changed the conversation to the weather. *One never knows who one can meet on a train*, I thought wryly. Staring out of the train's grimy window, as we approached the station, the train's iron wheels ground against the metal tracks. Birmingham seemed dreary and filthy at first glance.

The rhythmic chugging of the train echoing through the station as we pulled in. The distant sounds of chatter and announcements only intensified the mixture of anticipation and apprehension growing inside me. Upon my arrival in England the sky was sombre with dark clouds, casting a gloomy shadow over the landscape.

Waving goodbye to the two ladies, I wished them the absolute best. Smiling and waving back, hands swaying in the air, they flounced off down the platform to the exit, with their waved platinum hair bobbing in time to their footsteps. Their heels clicked on the platform floor, sounding out a rhythm, not dissimilar to the rhythmic chugging of the locomotive when it echoed through the countryside.

A strong breeze cut across the platform with an icy chill, and I shivered. *Welcome to England*, I thought. Looking around, the station wasn't as ugly as I envisaged. There were information boards and snack bars, with people milling everywhere. It was a comfortable scene.

Then I remembered the photograph Sylvia showed me on the train and my smile wiped itself from my face. She caught me off guard. *Who was the man in the photograph?*

Focusing on reaching the exit, I tried to forget about the photograph, but my intuition told me I'd meet the ladies again someday. Little did I know what lay ahead.

Chapter 2

LEAVING NAVAN BEHIND BROUGHT an exciting time for a teenage girl, although I felt a stab of loneliness every so often.

You could say Navan in the 1940s was typical of rural Ireland. Life followed a traditional path governed by the land. With rolling green hills, extensive farmland, and cattle and sheep dominating the landscape. There were also the mystical ancient megalithic tombs next to the River Boyne which early settlers made their home thousands of years ago.

To newcomers, the tenements where I lived appeared dingy and intimidating. People may even say dirty. Some called the tenements slums. Yes, there was peeling paint and damp walls, but as a child I didn't view the tenement blocks negatively. Although many felt they were a health hazard, and tenement dwellers died younger and suffered more often from infectious diseases.

Everyone knew each other's personal business in that small town, sometimes to my chagrin. But it was a close-knit community, and I enjoyed fun, mellifluous laughter, and close friendships. Growing up was pure magic.

Mammy was a proud woman and moved heaven and earth to keep a pleasant home. I remember her putting our washing on the long clothesline in the backyard of the tenement block, and the clothes billowing in the breeze on mild weather days.

She hung a picture of the Holy Family in the living room. Every night, we prayed before the rosary hanging from the mantelpiece. Leaving the house each morning for school, we dipped a finger in holy water gained from the pilgrimage site in Lourdes and made the sign of the cross. Mammy was a devout Catholic, and we went to church every Sunday without fail.

Wearing our Sunday best, we attended the immense Catholic Church called St Mary's in Navan. With five pulpits, the architect styled it like a theatre. Imagine five priests saying mass with one leading the ceremony. It was both intimidating and overwhelming for a child.

I tried to behave in church, remembering when Father O'Sullivan, a towering six-foot-three figure, arrived at the crucial part of the mass in that place of worship one Sunday morning. Catholics view this moment as the transformation of the Eucharist by the priest into Christ's body and blood. It is an important and sacred section of the mass.

Father O'Sullivan's booming voice, slowly and with devout seriousness, proclaimed each word slowly, "THIS IS MY BODYEEEEEE."

Our pew shook with our held in laughter. Clamping my hand hard over my mouth, I tried to stop, especially catching sight of our mammy's death stare. Daddy winked at me, and that set me off again. I hope when I reach the pearly gates of heaven, Saint Peter will let me in after having been so unchristian!

In 1940, mammy and daddy bought a three-bedroom semi-detached property in Navan. A massive improvement from the tenement block, with our own long and narrow garden. Laughter and playful chatter echoed through that garden as we enjoyed our time together. Before, we could only play on the streets.

The food we ate was always home-made. Soup made from vegetables grown in the garden, and the kitchen assuaged our senses with an appetising smell of cooking daily. Daddy dug a hole in the garden to store the potato crop to prevent it from rotting.

Although the effect of the Second World War caused rationing and limitations in Ireland, my parents were both resourceful, and being in such an agricultural area, we were able to live off the land.

Mammy cooked rabbits given to her, knowing how to strip off their fur correctly for putting in a pot and cooking. They were delicious. The worst thing we received was the Cod Liver Oil. Mammy gave it to us on a tablespoon, with no water afterwards, every morning, and it was part of our daily routine.

Wherever we lived, though, our house was chaotic, alive, and noisy, with me having at least one fight a day with my youngest brother Leonard.

The third eldest among the eight children, but no good at keeping the peace. I was the main instigator of trouble, getting into scrapes. Leonard called me a *rogaire* one day to my face as we grew older. In Irish, it meant rogue, but I was a lively child, always in motion and full of life, not malicious in thought.

My older sister Ursula, in comparison, was a virtuous person and desired to do wonderful things for everyone.

She said, "Come on Nancy. Let's do something nice for mammy and tidy the house as a surprise."

"No way. I am off out to play. Have fun tidying up!" *What*

an eejit, I thought.

I admit, I was unkind to Ursula and saw her hurt but felt indifferent. She was compassionate and kind, but I resented her constant desire to do what was right. With an unerring belief in myself, there is no doubt I was mammy's mini-me.

Playing football as a girl was considered improper back then, and the neighbours loved to comment on it to mammy, although it was something I loved to do.

"Is it usual behaviour for a young girl, Mrs Flanagan?" said Mrs McNamara, standing at mammy's front door one day. Her arms folded, with her nose in the air.

"I will put the kibosh on her sporting activities, Mrs McNamara. Don't you worry now," said mammy.

Unfortunately, because of demanding situations, my family and the neighbours considered me an unruly child. Usually for ruining my clothes and getting into trouble for it, or for breaking Ursula's glasses. As an energetic soul who loved life, it did not worry me at all.

Many times, mammy roared whilst chasing me round the house with the wooden spoon, "Nancy, get back here right now!" Smacks on the legs from the wooden spoon smarted and stung, but only if she caught me. Sometimes we hid the spoon in a cupboard, and she spent ages looking for it, threatening to use it on us for hiding it in the first place!

Sean was the eldest male of the eight children, athletic and handsome, and I adored him. Then there was Ursula, short, with mousy hair and glasses. Following on from me was Frank, who enjoyed sports, with a knack for questionable jokes.

There was my sister May. With a voluptuous figure, she was irresistible to the boys. Her perfume was floral, which I

13

caught a whiff of every time she walked by, often sneaking out to go on secret dates. Mammy was worried about her safety. The irony. May understood boys and their behaviour. If she only told me, I could've avoided having a child out of wedlock.

I remember a time when a friend of May's appeared one day, saying there was a Black man in town, looking for her. It caused a small commotion. Few ethnic minorities resided in Navan during the 1940s, but we were not racist, just uninformed. I never discovered the story of that connection. In time, she married a publican and proved to be a natural businesswoman.

Pauline, another sister, also became a nurse. With a dry wit, she could cut anyone down to size with her tongue. Then there was Freddy. A constant worry for mammy as he liked a drink and was very independent. I liked Freddy, as he was a free spirit. He became some type of banker and married twice. He did very well for himself though.

Leonard was the youngest child and spoiled by mammy. Short but with bright blue eyes, he got away with murder in my book.

Ita, the eldest among us, held the most power and strictly enforced the family's rules. I kept well out of her way. She was as strong as mammy within the family.

During the war, Navan had something of a relaxed approach. Perhaps because we were not directly involved with the fighting but were neutral. We were supposed to put up blackout curtains, but no one bothered, neither at school nor at home. It would be our own fault if the Germans targeted Navan. Sometimes they made mistakes, dropping bombs in Dublin and Wexford thinking they were bombing England. I hoped the Germans would drop a bomb on my school. In the end we didn't encounter any in Navan.

At St. Augustine's Convent School, I liked to play class clown, enjoying the girls' attention. With cheeks hollowed and eyes shut, I transformed into a comical goldfish, or guppy, flapping for breath. It made them laugh and made me feel popular.

Despite a love for my family's quirks and distinct personalities, jealousy consumed me, especially when it came to Leonard, when arguments erupted. I didn't always start fights but always got the blame for them. A feeling of disconnection from my family endured well into adulthood.

I'd had psychic visions from childhood, but mammy dismissed them. None of my siblings ever mentioned having them. "It's just Nancy's imagination," they would say.

The teacher expelled me from class at school often for disrupting and bothering the other girls. Sometimes the Mother Superior, a terrifying nun, severe and humourless, chastised me for my outrageous behaviour, saying I was bold and bad. Inside, I wondered if I was indeed both.

Chapter 3

LEAVING IRELAND IN 1947, at a young age, made me contemplate my childhood and the challenges I faced. It also made me focus on my family and what my parents went through.

The government rationed us just after the Second World War ended. We called this time 'the Emergency' and fuel was a problem. There was little coal anywhere, and we relied on firewood and turf for heating, but the turf gave us a very nice fire. Ireland enjoyed all the basics, such as meat, vegetables, milk, potatoes, eggs, and fruit. England may not have had access to them. So, we were lucky in comparison.

Mammy made delicious soda bread and vegetable soup, which was available on the stove for a quick snack. She was always resourceful, but her resourcefulness during a difficult post-war period was unmatched.

Ignoring the post-war difficulties, she paid for us to have music and elocution lessons, with high ambition for us all. Our old neighbours in the tenement block nicknamed us 'The Swanks.' Mammy was the epitome of a parent who told you if you wanted something badly enough, you would achieve it.

As an Irish American, she loved the British, whereas many Irish did not. Mammy maintained a deep affection for the aristocracy and defended the royal family from negativity. I think she admired King George VI.

In the silence of our home, I once overheard hushed conversations regarding Daddy's clandestine duties as he relayed messages for the Irish Republican Army (IRA).

'The troubles' in Ireland trace their origins back to the Irish War of Independence in 1921. Since the 1870s, Ireland wanted self- government from Britain.

He was a gentle man, and I don't think he had strong political affiliations, but in that period, if you were a Catholic, you had little choice but to support the IRA. Many children, and adults for that matter, called the protestants, 'proddie dogs'. Just as the world tasted the bitterness of war until 1945, Ireland experienced its own internal political turmoil, leaving a bitter aftertaste.

The family assured me the IRA wasn't a terrorist organisation, but the twenty-one gun salute at my aunt's funeral made me question the truth. In troubled times, you didn't refuse if the IRA asked. Not if you wanted to keep your kneecaps intact!

Most people found mammy's mixed Irish American accent peculiar, but our family was used to hearing her speak it daily. She preferred to say "Tomayto" instead of "Tomaato."

The faded pages of Ellis Island's records hold a trace of mammy's parents' name, revealing their journey from Ireland to America. The first person to pass through Ellis Island's reception centre in 1882 must have felt overwhelmed.

Many Catholics emigrated to America, going on long transatlantic voyages to Boston or New York because of the raging famine in Ireland. America embraced Irish immigrants, despite the social turmoil and prejudice they faced during the 1850s.

Mammy never shared her childhood details, or information about my grandparents, leaving me with little knowledge. I didn't even see photographs of them. My sister May felt a sadness as she told me my grandad, died on the hospital operating table during a routine procedure, casting a shadow over his memory.

I don't know when, but mammy returned to Ireland from America as an adult and met daddy. People knew her as an Irish American because her parents were Irish, and she was born in America.

Her mammy, my grandma, taught her how to dress well. She wore court shoes daily. I cannot remember when mammy did not dress properly for an occasion. She wore a pinafore daily, to keep her dress pristine.

Mammy wore a very elegant Pillbox hat with a veil to church. I wanted one, but my hat was a plain red beret with a bow. I loved the hat made from felt but still coveted her Pillbox hat. She was obsessed with the family attending church and looking our absolute best in immaculately presented clothes. It was super important to her.

Sometimes at weekends, my father joined in poker games with his friends. It was typical for men to play card games in those days. With his exceptional mathematical skills, he memorised each player's cards. He didn't drink, and with a rational mind, my suspicion is he won many of those poker games and bolstered the family's financial pot.

Daddy worked two jobs. When he was twelve years old, the local secondary school offered him a scholarship. Secondary schools cost money in those days to attend, so his parents decided against it, even with a scholarship, and he ended up working in a factory. Undeterred, being intelligent he attended night school to study accounting.

During the day, he worked at the bookies utilising his maths skills. At night, he served as the Secretary of the YMCA equivalent, run by the Christian Brothers. He was a hard-working, honourable man.

He joined the local amateur dramatic society, and I was proud of him. His singing voice was lovely, which I fortunately inherited from him.

My everlasting childhood memory is marching upstairs to bed, all eight of us children. One after the other, swinging our arms, our bare feet padding softly on the wooden stairs. With daddy leading the way, we sang parts from one of his operettas, Trial by Jury.

We continued to sing until we reached the top of the stairs and got into our beds. Then we said the Lord's Prayer, a Hail Mary, and the Angel of God Prayer right before we went to sleep. Daddy explained to us we should say our prayers with feeling, not rush through them like it was a race.

We were chatterboxes, so it took time for us to settle down. His patience seemed endless as he dealt with us.

My relationship with my mammy continued to be fiery, with a heated battle of words. It wasn't unusual for me to stand with my hands on my hips and be defiant. I was emotional and outspoken.

My brothers laughed whenever I did this and said, "You are mad, Nancy."

Mammy was unkind too if she became impatient with me.

"I will send you away one day, Nancy," she said once.

How prophetic was that phrase? Part of me believed she meant it. It made me unhappy and although on the outside I appeared brash, inside I felt unloved.

Sometimes when we were naughty (which was often in my case), mammy threatened us all by saying, "Wait until your father gets home!"

Daddy would approach me, saying, "Nancy, please do what mammy says you should do. She works hard and looks after you."

"Sure Daddy, course I will," all the while nodding and smiling at him, but knowing as soon as possible I was off, playing football, getting into fights with my brothers, and misbehaving.

Daddy was a pushover, never laying a finger on us. I capitalised on it. I wanted my mammy to love me, and she did, but we clashed because I was like her in character. My self-belief verged on arrogance. One might think mammy would understand me as a result, but it didn't work that way. Any fights within the home revolved around me, whether it was with Leonard, my younger brother, over some minor issue, or directly with her, where she wanted to restrain my natural ebullience.

Mammy was the driving force in their relationship. Daddy was only five feet six inches tall; she was five feet eight inches tall, five feet ten inches in her court shoes. Although she was the boss, they enjoyed a wonderful marriage, and every week he brought home flowers and tins of boiled sweets for her.

As children, we thought they were in a perfect marriage. I don't suppose we understood the financial troubles they experienced. Bringing up eight children in those post-war times was both stressful and difficult.

Often at night, there was the faint sizzle of the logs from the hearth fire, and the soft exhale of Daddy's breath as he took a drag. I scolded him for smoking, but he smiled and reassured me it was a relaxing habit. One day, I was certain it was going to be his undoing.

The relationship between my mother and myself took a hard turn as full details of my situation emerged, which shamed me and horrified her. I looked to her for support, and in her own way, she gave it, but not in the way I needed it.

Leaving Ireland gave me time to think about my mother's and father's perceptions of me, my siblings' views of me, but most of all, my perception of myself. Was I good or was I bad? I hoped to find out.

The night before I left Ireland for England was frightening. So often I experienced visions which I knew were unusual, and didn't happen to others, although I never discussed them with anyone else. But leaving my family for England overshadowed the vision.

I tried to explain what happened to me with my best friend, ending up with an unexpected child, hoping my mother would show some level of sympathy, but, as usual, she left me wanting.

I felt it would be a long time before I returned to Ireland, if ever. Because of having had an illegitimate child out of wedlock, it brought shame on my family and left me feeling exiled. I wanted more than anything to go forward in my nursing career and prove I was 'good' person.

* * *

The night before I left for Ireland, I woke up and felt and smelled the fear emanating from a man. An old man, his outline barely discernible. With lines etched on his face, a testament to time and wisdom, or sun-damaged skin. The images came thick and fast, and an outline was rapidly forming in my mind's eye. I was unsure if it was a dream or a vision, but either way, it was disturbing.

His bewildered gasp broke the silence, while his eyes remained fixed on the terrifying aspect just above him. Sweat dripped from his brow. Who or what was he staring at? God, I hated this vision because the scene was just out of my reach, tantalising me. I felt like a starving animal being teased with a carrot on the end of a long stick.

I trembled. Not from the cold, as indeed my bedroom was cold, no matter how many bedclothes I used or wore in bed, as our small house lacked proper heating. No, I trembled because the man's terror enveloped my senses. It wrapped around my body like a cord being slowly tightened. I almost tasted it, metallic and acrid.

Focus, Nancy, I told myself.

I concentrated with all my might, but it was difficult to focus when the air itself seemed to pulse with evil. I heard a disturbing voice this time. Menacing in timbre, taunting, cruel, dark. Disquieted, I shuddered and wrapped my blanket closer around myself. What was the voice saying? I didn't discern any specific words or meaning from the muffled and distant sound.

Then just as quickly as the fearful vision came, poof, it was gone. I blinked, disorientated. *Did I glimpse into another realm, or was it an actual place?*

I experienced visions throughout my life, since forever, but I didn't know the reason why. Mammy said my grandma possessed a gift, a spiritual calling, but when I asked her to explain further, she became silent, leaving me intrigued and frustrated.

"Don't pay any attention, Nancy. It's just made believe."

Mammy said this if I told her my dreams, or visions, or whatever you want to call them. She was a strict Catholic, and the Church disregarded spirituality. But my aunt May said differently when I told her.

"You have a gift, Nancy. Just like your grandma. It's an important gift according to her, so pay no mind to your mammy. She chooses not to understand."

But I didn't really understand 'the gift'. *How did it benefit me?* I thought. It wasn't as if I predicted the winning football pools' numbers or read other people's minds.

Time to get back to sleep. It was a long journey the next day to England. As I fell asleep, my final thought was of the unknown man. I hoped he was okay.

Morning came, and I didn't feel like facing mammy. She was still angry at what had happened to me. But I was furious, being cast out of Ireland, feeling unwanted, like a deflated balloon.

I remembered the strange dream the next morning, but didn't mention it to either parent. Mammy was likely going to dismiss it.

My everlasting memory on that day I left Ireland was of a huge row with mammy, whilst daddy watched on. She stopped washing the dishes and wiped her hands on a towel. Then she stood in the kitchen with her arms folded. She was raging inside and said nothing for a minute. Then she let rip.

"You are a disappointment, Nancy Flanagan. I never expected this from you. How were you such an eejit?"

I sat at the kitchen table, downcast, with my head down. I was hanging on to my sanity by my fingernails, barely holding it together.

"Yes, you did Mammy, you always considered me to be the 'bad' one of the family, the odd one out," I muttered.

Daddy sat by the fireside in his favourite chair, looking sad.

Mammy continued, "No, Nancy, I've been proud of your fire, your spirit, your get up and go. You are headstrong, it is true, but how did this happen? I will never understand."

Mammy paced up and down the dated kitchen in frustration. Her court shoes sounding out a rhythm.

"I didn't understand either, Mammy."

The image of my innocence being taken from me without my consent by Jimmy still burned hot in my brain.

"I want Maeve. She's mine. Don't you think she should be with me?"

I was angry and jealous of a world beyond my reach. Mammy looked at me with a dispirited air.

"You already know the answer to that, Nancy."

Staring directly at her, I said, "What do you expect me to do Mammy?"

I spat the words out and shook my head in despair, feeling stunned by the loss of Maeve. My Maeve.

Mammy walked to the kitchen window and watched the children playing in the street outside. She continued watching as Mrs O'Hara crossed in front of our house, waving to her as she walked by.

"Follow your cousins, go to England, become a nurse. It's your destiny, and you'll achieve it. You need a fresh start."

The situation was unbearable. I knew I had disappointed them, and the Church. My soul suffered an indelible stain, impossible to cleanse. The society and religious community I lived in considered having a child in Ireland out of wedlock as a disgrace and placed immense guilt upon me. I would suffer judgment and condemnation from the community and religious hostility from the Church if I stayed in Ireland.

Some women resorted to killing their babies, while others presented them as new siblings to hide the truth. The mother was of 'poor character', which reflected badly on the parents. All these reasons clearly showed why mammy wouldn't let me keep Maeve.

My pursuit of a career in nursing was pre-ordained, but giving birth to Maeve meant I went to England a year later than planned. They redid the arrangements, as the English recruiters still wanted me.

I hoped my family still loved me, but felt isolated at that moment, and hanging my head in shame, went to pack my bags for the trip to England. Banished from my family and Ireland I endured a broken heart.

Mammy only allowed me to hold Maeve on the day she was born and a few days afterwards. I bonded with her in that short time and felt ripped apart by leaving her. They forced me to leave her behind and give her up for adoption.

Daddy couldn't bear it. He was a soft-hearted soul.

He came upstairs, sat on the bed as I packed and he comforted me, saying, "Nancy, it's not the end of the world. You are doing the right thing. Everyone will eventually forget."

I shook my head.

"I won't forget her, Daddy, I can't. Someday, I'll come back for her."

He patted my hand and said, "We love you, Nancy. Enjoy your new life. Make the best of it. It will all be fine."

"I've let you down Daddy, I'm so sorry."

I felt nothing but self-hate and regret at that moment.

We went down the wooden stairs and he helped me with my

bags into the local taxi, which was quietly waiting.

"Will mammy ever forgive me?"

He nodded and, giving me a bear hug, said, "I will say goodbye to your siblings for you. Write to us often, Nancy."

I saw him wipe away a tear as the taxi left and he waved goodbye.

Chapter 4

I FELT DOWNHEARTED at the scene unfolding before me. No more the beautiful green scenery of Ireland, the mellow sound of the trickling brooks of the river, and the children's cheerful voices at play. I shook myself.

Now that you're here, just get on with it, I thought. A different life called, and I tried to stay positive. This was what I craved, surely? An opportunity to live my own life, the way I wanted to live it.

In my head, I could still hear mammy saying, "She's a good for nothing, she'll never amount to anything, unlike her sisters and brothers."

She could be so harsh, and I never understood why. I was more like mammy than any of my siblings.

Ursula always stood up for me. She had such a good heart and soul, and I realised now, as I looked back on my childhood, that I treated her so badly. Always taunting her about how she looked, or how she behaved. Underneath it all, I think I was just jealous. Jealous of her ability to always put others first, to know how others felt and act accordingly.

I did have a level of empathy, but it was always towards animals first. I was able to understand them, in a way not many others could. I repaired broken wings, or injured limbs.

People brought their pets to me, as a free alternative to the vet. *Perhaps I should have pursued a career helping animals?*

Bringing my thoughts back to the present, I made my way out of the station. War-related camouflage and webbing clung to nearby buildings and factories. A reminder of battles fought, and lives altered. Everywhere I looked was a drab grey or brown, in stark contrast to the panoramic green fields of Ireland.

I saw a myriad of soldiers, sailors and military personnel circulating in the condensed streets. They were in the throes of demobilisation. The whirlwind of people unsettled us all.

World War Two meant the government conscripted men of a certain age to contribute to the war effort, thrusting them into chaos. Now they were re-entering civilian life and resuming their pre-war jobs.

Their sense of confusion was palpable as they milled around. I knew the trauma of war changed these soldiers forever. Their eyes were hollow and haunted. Was a regular nine to five job possible after what they went through? With gunfire and explosions echoing in their heads, I felt it must be difficult for them.

Being alone in this tumultuous city, a sense of foreboding washed over me. I felt isolated and uneasy.

Ireland's neutrality during the war made it especially unusual for me to see so many soldiers in one place. I felt uncomfortable. My heart contracted and missed a beat because dreary streets and crushing strangers surrounded me. It was terrifying and I experienced loneliness among the plethora of people.

I stared at the different uniforms, each with its own unique colour and design. Other men who did not wear uniforms wore ill-fitting demob suits supplied by the government. These were designed to help soldiers start over, but to me, they made the men seem disorientated and worn out.

It wasn't unusual for soldiers returning home to discover a child who was born whilst they were away in the war. The child and father were complete strangers to one another. It must have been very difficult.

The wives, unsung heroes, worked for the war effort in factories, building armaments, or worked in the fields on the land. The women held the household together whilst their husbands were away. Following the men's return, it left the women to an uncertain future. The war caused chaos in their lives, and they strived to return to normality. As the women returned to family duties, the country's economy suffered as well.

Men affected by the war in their homes must have been peculiar to them. They were different from the men they knew before. War changed them. I imagine it was like having a stranger in the house. All the natural boundaries differed from when they were first married. The women became accustomed to making daily decisions, whilst the men became withdrawn and insular.

The estrangement experienced by these post-war families must have been isolating. I understood their feelings all too well. Being part of a family but feeling distant from them. Mammy advised me, "Nancy, brace yourself for meeting unrest in England. Families will try to adapt to living together. The people will be very unsettled."

England was having to rebuild itself. The bombings not only damaged buildings but caused physical and emotional harm to people and families. There was scaffolding and construction equipment everywhere, disrupting and upsetting people's lives.

"Out the way, bab!" A soldier stepped around me as I blocked his path to a side street. Despite being young, he appeared exhausted and haggard. He wore a beige-coloured uniform with a cap, black toe-capped boots, and a web belt. I cannot say he looked smart, more as if he'd slept in his clothes.

"Oops, sorry," I said, as my cheeks reddened with mortification. Smiling, he walked away, leaving me feeling awkward about getting in the way.

The recruiters chose Birmingham for me for my nursing training. Never having been there, I had no idea what to expect. Birmingham, not London or Dublin, remained a bustling city with everyone occupied doing their own thing.

I asked a friendly-looking lady if she knew where the trolleybus stop was. The lady wore a large woollen coat, with a matching black hat, black patent handbag, and black suede boots.

"Pardon me dear?"

I put the lady's age at seventy, with grey strands in her hair and wrinkles etched on her face. She was small and stooped in stature.

I asked her again, "Do you know where the trolleybus stop is, please?"

Her eyes twinkled. "Oh, you are Irish. I missed what you said earlier."

She leaned in, as if sharing a secret. "You'll see it just around the corner, love."

She beamed at me. Despite her friendliness, my Irish accent made me feel out of place and uncomfortable.

Will I fit in and feel at home here? I wondered, thinking of my family in Ireland. The weight of guilt from a year ago still clung to me, a shadow I couldn't shake off. My chest tightened and tears welled up. I stroked my hair in agitation and my temper flared.

How dare she comment on my being Irish? I thought angrily. I was as decent as anyone.

Despite projecting an image of boldness and self-assurance, I harboured deep-seated insecurities which caused me to become defensive. I so wished one of my siblings or my cousin Patrick was by my side at that moment.

It was not unusual for me to feel detached, like an observer watching a scene play out. I believed my struggle to fit in was because of growing pains, yet there was a deeper underlying cause. My internal guilt at what had happened to me only a year ago, and the continuing belief that I was 'bad.'

The old lady directed me to the stop, and I followed her directions. There, nestled against a graffiti-covered wall, was a wooden bench. I sat down on the bench and read its inscription. *'To a loving father, brother and son, Frederick Jones, from all his family. May you rest and be at peace.'*

There was a heart engraved next to the phrase. It was a high quality, decorated memorial bench, with solid wooden arms to rest upon. It seemed odd to place a bench near a trolleybus stop. Frederick, whoever he was, must have regularly caught the trolleybus. This was his favourite spot. *It is not mine;* I thought. It was a dingy area.

Out of nowhere, I sensed I was not sitting on the bench alone. Glancing to my left and right, I saw nothing. Closing my eyes, in my mind's eye, I saw a small man wearing an army uniform. His shape was hazy, yet unmistakable.

I estimated him to be in his thirties with a moustache and dark hair. Concentrating as hard as possible, he tried to say something to me. His lips moved, forming words, but I could not hear him.

Then I felt it. An undeniable sadness which filled my heart with sorrow. The wave of feeling overwhelmed me, bringing a tear to my eye. I caught the sound then, a whisper. It was faint, but I heard it.

Emotion cracked his voice, "Tell Hilda I love her, please. I miss her."

There was an urgency to his plea. I blinked, disorientated, so surprised to see the man, but felt his message was impor- tant. Just before sleep took over at nighttime, faces emerged in my mind's eye, but voices were rare.

As I was pondering this, not five minutes later, a tiny lady appeared in an old overcoat and black suede boots. They were worn, and she looked tired. I smiled at her, and she smiled back.

Then I conceived a notion, and compelled to speak to her, I said, "Pardon me, but is your name Hilda?"

She looked startled, and her eyes widened in surprise, "Yes, I'm Hilda, why dear?"

I couldn't believe she was the wife of the man in my vision, but felt it was important to give her the message.

"Do you often come to this trolleybus stop, Hilda?"

"Yes, dear. This was our spot, where Frederick and I came whenever we ventured into town before the War. My husband and I were inseparable. We were married for twenty years, but he died from artillery fire."

My voice carried a tinge of regret.

"I am so sorry. This is your bench, then?"

She nodded. "We all clubbed together to buy it. His two brothers and me."

She lowered her head. "We all miss him so much."

I put my hand on her sleeve, "Hilda, this might sound strange, but as I sat here, just before you arrived, I received a message. I think it was a message meant for you."

Her head came up. She looked at me with curiosity.

I described my vision of Frederick, her husband, and she said, "Yes, dear, that's him to a tee. The family will never believe it!"

I reached out and touched her arm.

"He wanted me to tell you. He said, tell Hilda I love her, and I miss her."

The little old lady became overwhelmed. Her face lit up and her joy was clear. The happiness in her eyes confirmed her delight at the message.

"Freddie," she whispered, "My Freddie."

"It was a lovely idea to put the bench here in his honour Hilda. He's here with you every day, you know."

She gave me a radiant smile.

"I am so grateful to you, dear. Sometimes I thought I saw him. Just a shadowy outline at the bottom of our bed and have been so down without him. Now I feel happier. Just knowing he's around, I won't feel alone anymore. Thank you so much!"

I beamed back at her. The psychic vision was a strange experience for me, but I felt glad it gave Hilda some joy.

We sat in silence, waiting for the trolleybus to come.

Hilda, lost in her thoughts, gazed into the distance. She stood up, caught the trolleybus, and waved to me as she left, with a joyful expression upon her face.

It was an uplifting experience. Helping to make up for the loneliness and isolation I was feeling. Sitting there, huddled in my Sunday coat, watching for my trolleybus to arrive, it was freezing cold, and I hoped it was going to arrive soon.

On catching the trolleybus, sat down on the cushioned seat, and thought, *Dear God, what have I done?*

Alone with no family or friends, I was fearful, but part of me was super excited, as this was freedom, and contemplated my new life with the world at my feet.

There were butterflies in my tummy, certain exciting adventures lay ahead of me.

Chapter 5

NOW I WAS AWAY from Ireland I had time to reflect on what had happened to me. Looking back at my terrible situation, I realised the close friendship with Jimmy Dawson and my naivety caused some of the trouble. He lived three houses away from us and was fun. It was an innocent friendship, at first.

We scrumped apples together; played football together and got into trouble together.

Early one evening, Jimmy came to see me. He invited me to join him in the grassy area where local kids often gathered. He suddenly grabbed me and pulled me into the bushes.

"Whatcha up to, Jimmy?" I asked, confused as to the secrecy.

"Sure Nancy, there's no worry here. I've got some Poitín, that's all. Do you want to take a slog? I got it from Tommy." I shook my head with vigour.

"No Jimmy. I took the pledge for my daddy, remember? I'm not allowed alcohol, especially moonshine. Mammy might kill me!" But Jimmy didn't drop it. He challenged me to try it. He said I was a lag with no backbone.

"I thought you were my best friend, Nancy Flanagan."

His face registered such disappointment. I didn't like it, so

I rose to the challenge. Since I was known as the bravado kid, the outspoken one, the 'bad' one, I was expected to do it.

Taking a few swigs of the disgusting drink, it made me cough, but soon enough I was unbalanced, feeling strange and quickly becoming incapacitated. I was banjaxed and Jimmy took full advantage of me.

He pulled me down onto the dirt floor, still in the bushes. The situation muddled me. Giddy and confused, I felt his face buried in my neck as he rummaged roughly in my underclothes. Soon enough, he was on top of me, panting heavily with excitement.

"What are you doing, Jimmy? Stop touching me!" And I tried to push him away, but it was in vain. He was too strong for me.

I will never forget what he did. Almost immediately, I was at his mercy. Unable to breathe with his full weight, pinning me down, pressing my body into the unforgiving, dusty ground.

Unresponsive, he eventually got off me, irritated because it all happened in a matter of minutes and wasn't what he wanted. Afterwards, I remember feeling hollow and dirty inside. Looking back, I understand I was traumatised and in a state of shock.

"You are no fun, Nancy Flanagan," he declared and ran off home, leaving me with dishevelled clothes and feeling very sore.

There were spots of blood on my pants. In my ignorance, I just thought it was from a cut somewhere, perhaps because of the stony ground. I did not know its significance. Making my way home, I got to my room, cleaned myself up and went to bed, claiming I was suffering from an upset stomach.

Mammy was busy with dinner, so Ursula looked after me.

"Nancy, you smell odd."

She voiced this loudly and leaned over me to wipe my sweaty forehead. I threw up. The terrible experience and the alcohol, which I wasn't used to, had made me sick.

"Shush, Ursula. I don't want any fuss."

She nodded.

"Okay, Nancy, I'll let you be."

She scurried off to help mammy with the dinner.

I didn't talk to Jimmy ever again. I'm not sure if he felt any guilt for his actions towards me. *Did he just think I was a stupid girl?*

The Convent School I attended didn't believe in sex education, and I thought babies came into this world out of the umbilical cord, even when I first started my nursing training.

My stomach became rounder over time, but it was never large. I assumed I had a bloated stomach until the end of the pregnancy. I didn't have morning sickness. It seems incredible to realise there was a baby growing inside me, but I showed little.

Suffering from terrible stomach pains one day, I told mammy I didn't want to go to school. She wasn't a nurse but she quickly recognised the signs of being in labour. After all, she herself gave birth to eight children. My situation flabbergasted her.

"Ursula, I need you now," she shouted out. Mammy was not happy.

She said, "I bet this is because of one of those boys you play football with."

I looked at her in surprise, completely ignorant of what had happened. It was only with mammy constantly asking me who the father was, I realised the only physical interaction which occurred with a male was with Jimmy.

Together mammy and Ursula brought in a hot bowl of water, and organised towels. After hours of very painful labour, I gave birth to a beautiful baby girl.

Ursula asked me how I became pregnant, but I still didn't know. The baby was gorgeous, with curly black hair and blue eyes. I named her Maeve. Mammy cut the umbilical cord. There was blood, but mammy said it was normal.

Pushing Maeve out, my face turned red from the exertion. I vowed never again and was angry at the pain I suffered. But when mammy put Maeve in my arms, something shifted deep inside of me, and I wanted to keep her forever.

Holding my daughter tightly in my arms, I shed a tear. A tear slid onto the baby's face. She stirred from her slumber but didn't cry. Maeve was such a wonderful baby. I felt she was special. New mothers typically feel that way, but there was a certain magic surrounding her.

Mammy said, "Don't get used to her, Nancy. She can't stay."

Daddy glanced through the door and checked if I was okay. He was so gentle and concerned.

I said, "I'm fine Daddy."

He didn't glance at the baby aware she would not be with me for long. The thought of no medical intervention made me go cold. I may have died; the baby may also have died if there were complications. But mammy maintained a complete faith in God and said to me she'd given birth to her babies at home, including me, and there was no need to worry.

She was on friendly terms with the local doctor. He liked a drink. He was an old soak. Mammy convinced him to visit me discreetly at night and examine me. She gave him a bottle of whisky for his trouble. His nose was red from endless drinking, and I smelled the whisky in his breath a mile away.

He said because I was athletic; I pushed the baby out without tearing the Perineum. I was lucky, as this was my first baby, and sometimes the area needed stitches.

Mammy emphasised, "First and last baby, doctor!"

Of course, they didn't allow me to keep Maeve. I trembled and sobbed as they removed her warm body from my loving arms. My family never agreed to let me keep her. Only Ursula knew about the family secret, while mammy kept my brothers away. My siblings briefly believed I was unwell. Glandular fever, mammy told them. They were busy in their own lives; they didn't question it. The neighbours never knew a thing either.

I shared the abusive incident with mammy, and she expressed her disappointment through a shake of her head. She told me we would never tell Jimmy or anyone, Maeve, was my baby. A secret we would never reveal.

She never once made a negative comment regarding Jimmy's behaviour. There was no recrimination of his actions towards me. I was the 'bad' one. He was seen as feckless. He came from a large, uneducated family, not like ours. His daddy was an alcoholic, and his mammy never seemed to care. I felt betrayed by my mammy's lack of support during my awful experience.

She visited the Nuns at St. Augustine's Convent School. They took little Maeve in, and I hate to think what happened to her. It is likely she ended up in the Magdalene Laundry. I hoped it wasn't true. As a pupil at St. Augustine's Convent School, I knew the laundry existed but like many, ignored the fact. It took in illegitimate children and fallen women, using them as free labour for profit. The best possible outcome for Maeve was adoption by a loving family.

From the first day I left Ireland for England, I sent mammy letters asking after the family but also asked about Maeve and how she was doing. She mentioned my siblings and what they were up to but avoided telling me anything else. Mammy visited Maeve initially, but then silence followed, leaving me unaware of her fate.

As a pupil at the convent school, I saw chilblains on children's fingers who worked in the laundry, noticing their clothes were dowdy and in disrepair. Sad to say, I thought nothing more of it at that time, as it was an accepted institution within Ireland. They kept those children separate from the rest of us. Now I prayed Maeve didn't grow up in servitude with the nuns, but it was the most likely scenario.

Every day, thoughts of her filled my mind. *How was she? What was she like? Was she enjoying her life?* Every day, I lived with this sin and guilt.

The unexpected birth caused a ripple in mine and my family's world. I loved my mammy, my daddy, and my siblings, but I was never returning to the same life again.

Chapter 6

ONCE I SETTLED IN at the Nurse's Home, I got to work. In 1947, when I started my fever training at Little Bromwich Hospital, not only did we face food rationing, but fuel was also scarce, making travel or visits difficult. Then we suffered from heavy flooding which damaged the harvest. Everyone wondered when the economy would recover from its depressing time.

People were miserable, and I tried to maintain a cheerful outlook. Homesick for Ireland, I threw myself into my training, as it was a pleasant distraction. Although I decided long before on a nursing career, I didn't want to dwell upon the reason why I left Ireland under such a dark cloud.

We carried around our sugar and butter ration in little baskets in the hospital when we went to meals. The Government rationed sweets, and we gorged ourselves on the entire month's ration in one go. We could not help ourselves.

Besides providing board and lodgings, I received a small stipend from the hospital as payment, but not much money to mention. We often went to the local children's playground to sit on the swings and roundabouts to amuse ourselves for free. It was a time of invention and finding affordable ways to have fun.

I was always trying to produce ideas for cheap entertainment. We went to the cinema, sneaking in without paying. I loved the cinema and saw 'Green for Danger' with Alastair Sim. He always made me laugh. We regularly listened to the radio as well.

Things were strict in the Nurse's Home. We couldn't go to parties because of the rules, except for hospital dances, and escaped out of the lounge window when the Home Sister wasn't present.

Matron and a Home Sister managed nursing staff recruitment, rotas, welfare, and shared hospital wisdom.

In the first part of the year, I was not allowed to complete technical tasks, just to make myself useful. I helped in the kitchen, passed items to doctors, and studied simultaneously.

A senior nurse trained me how to give bed baths, do dressings, take temperatures, and make poultices. The work posed challenges, and I went to bed at ten pm nightly. There was nothing disposable in those days, aprons, syringes. We boiled everything in hot water to sanitise it. It was not joyous; it was damn arduous work, but I was required to do my time and learn my trade. I felt doubtful at times whether this was the career for me, but I persevered.

Initially, no milk kitchen was available on the children's ward. Thus, we resorted to boiling a kettle for the babies' feeds. Regrettably, I left the kettle on the stove for too long, causing it to burn and develop a large hole. So of course, the Staff Nurse sent me to the Matron's office.

"Nurse, why are you in trouble?"

I raised the kettle and peered at Matron through the hole. She must have found it amusing, but she did not let on, although I suspect she was stifling a laugh.

There was a bit of a delay before she responded, shaking her finger at me with the words, "Oh nurse, you must be more careful and watch what you are doing!"

"Yes Matron," I replied meekly, and made my escape as quickly as I could! I did not want to incur her wrath and receive a hideous punishment involving washing one hundred bed pans in the sluice, a task most student nurses hated, or nasty night shifts.

Another time, early on in my training as a student nurse, the Staff Nurse asked me to collect urine samples from each of the children in the children's ward where I was working. I suppose it was to check for protein, or any other irregularities in their urine.

At age nineteen, I decided it was quite an annoying task as the children were not cooperative or were asleep. The implications were unknown to me.

I did not plan to be insubordinate or unprofessional but used my natural practical skills and saw no harm in it. Having collected a large sample from an older child, I decanted a bit of urine into each of the bottles. Each bottle was labelled relating to each individual child. I used one sample for all the children's results.

Completing this remarkable piece of work in record time made me proud of myself. I was absolutely flabbergasted when I later discovered the potential consequences of my actions and realised that nobody had caught on. The Staff Nurse must have been surprised to find no signs of disease in the children's urine samples. The sick children appeared to be well. I was very relieved nothing harmful resulted from my ignorant stupidity. A bit of knowledge can pose a danger in such an environment.

We followed countless regulations as nurses. The nurses' uniform style varied according to one's level of experience. My nurse's uniform was a striped dress, pinafore, and a white cap with white hairgrips and special shoes. The shoes were black and designed for comfort during extended use. They cost five guineas, and we only got three pounds per month, so they were expensive to buy. However, those were the rules which we were all expected to follow, without exception.

I was stubborn, and did not wish to spend five guineas on the regulation shoes and so bought cheaper black shoes instead. Unfortunately, the Ward Sister spotted the non-regulation shoes that I wore, and she again sent me to the Matron's office.

As I sat outside, awaiting my fate, my friend Ena, also a student nurse, passed by, and I pulled her to one side saying to her, "Quick, quick Ena, take your shoes off and let me put them on."

"Nancy, Matron's never going to fall for it!" but she just shook her head in dismay and passed me her regulation shoes.

Just as I was putting on my right shoe, the Matron called me into her room. What timing! She spotted I was wearing incorrect shoes on my feet straight away. I got into trouble twice - first for not having the right shoes and then for trying to conceal it by wearing my friend's shoes. I got a good telling off.

Matron went quite red in the face and lifted her eyebrows in surprise, saying, "Nurse Flanagan, you should know better, and as for dragging your friend into this, it only adds to your disgrace!"

I muttered my apologies, and she told me she expected to see regulation shoes on my feet the next day or would suffer the consequences. I rushed out in my lunch hour and bought a new pair, to my personal disappointment at having to spend so much of my hard-earned money. Without them, I would have cleaned bed pans for days!

However, having broken many rules at the Convent School as a child, being scolded didn't really bother me.

Whilst walking through the hospital grounds one day, I received wolf whistles from builders on the scaffolding above. I got revenge on these men though, as I learned how to wolf whistle like a boy one afternoon in the nurse's living room, taught to me by a friendly nurse called Esther.

"Nancy, just put two fingers on your rolled-up tongue. Press down with your fingers and blow hard."

I tried for quite a while, and eventually after making squeaks and squawks, I let out an ear-splitting whistle. The girls were so impressed.

Winking at Esther, I said, "I can't wait to do this."

I enjoyed the camaraderie, being giggly with the girls, dancing around and acting the fool. There was a rule which banned men from the Nurse's Home. We understood it, but if we spotted a man, like a trade's person, we whistled loudly. To attract attention to the man, but also to annoy our Home Sister, whom our unladylike behaviour enraged.

Opposite the Nurse's Home were the Law Courts, where the judges walked along in a procession daily. They wore smart gowns and wigs and looked self-satisfied. We didn't miss the chance and whistled at them from below the window ledge. whenever possible Mine was the most ear-piercing whistle of all. Not being able to trace the sound's source was a large irritation to them, but it amused us greatly.

Being a student nurse, I was unsure of the ward's happenings, and the hospital cleaners mocked me. If the phone rang, initially I would try to ignore it. My heart raced hesitating to respond. The Brummie accent wasn't easy for me to understand. My Irish accent remained, although softened. People knew my accent when speaking as a Connacht Irish accent from Connemara.

We worked hard and long hours, finding our own entertainment whenever we could. As pranksters we placed buckets of water on the top of any slightly open door and watched it fall on top of the person entering the room as they opened it, drenching them. No-one ever got me though. I was cautious and I always checked before entering a room.

The student nurses were not so keen on the skeletons used in anatomy classes, and I borrowed such a skeleton, calling him 'Gerald', for a prank.

We removed the lightbulbs at the Nurse's Home, making it hard to see when going upstairs to bed and placed cotton across the stairs, causing potential tripping hazards. We spread marmalade on the bannisters and placed 'Gerald' at the top of the stairs. Whoever made it past the booby traps came face-to-face with Gerald's bony frame.

We pranked the girls by placing cereal in their beds, making it impossible for them to get their legs under the sheets. They suffered an uncomfortable night's sleep with the cereal crunching beneath their toes.

The Sister in the Nurse's Home, formerly in the army, was strict and unpopular among us. She was unimpressed to hear a nurse scream blue murder as she ran the gauntlet of our booby traps and met Gerald, the skeleton face to face, his bones clanking at the top of the stairs. She banned pranks afterwards, much to my disgust.

"Too disruptive," she said in response to my question about it. Thankfully, they never found out who had purloined Gerald from the anatomy class cupboard, or it could have been a quick end to my nursing career, although I think the Home Sister suspected it was me. The other nurses and I laughed about it long and hard though.

"Did you hear Lucy scream when she finally got to the top of the stairs and met Gerald?"

"You are a card, Nancy Flanagan," my best friend Ena said often to me.

Being a prankster, I still longed for home. Even missing my youngest brother, whom I fought with over the smallest of issues. My relationship with the other trainee nurses was that of 'class clown'. I was a show-off, reckless, just like in my childhood, yet something deep in my soul made me a professional with patient care.

As my training progressed, I collaborated with patients suffering from contagious diseases. I worked in the Sanatorium, and I placed the patients into special cubicles whilst donning a mask and gown and washing my hands before and after each patient visit.

Matron often grasped the wrists of nurses, warning them to cleanse their hands and arms. She made them scrub them again until their arms were red raw.

Each cubicle contained a patient with measles, or chickenpox, diphtheria, or tuberculosis (TB). The hospital strictly forbade nurses from transferring diseases between cubicles. The nursing profession would have looked upon this as an utter disgrace. Matron taught us a strict regime of asepsis nursing. Also known as barrier nursing. We never had cases of cross infection.

The hospital arranged the Sanatorium's cubicles on a balcony, alongside a lawn. We worked with only a roof over us and the patients. There was little protection from the elements. This was a supposed wonderful way for TB patients to recover. The belief was sunshine (heliotherapy), and fresh air gave a positive effect on the body.

On one side of the sanatorium there was a handwashing tap. On the other side, there was a lawn. It was cold in the wintertime, when scrubbing your hands and elbows. I was only young when I started, and it was tough going. However, I took great satisfaction from seeing the patients get better. I may have been in trouble for minor things with Matron when I was a student nurse, but I always took my nursing duties seriously.

When children arrived at the Sanatorium, we destroyed their clothes and toys as a precaution against infection. If they were young, they did not understand why we did it. When they got better, we offered them new clothes and toys.

One little boy cried for a time because I needed to remove his favourite teddy bear. Explaining that the teddy bear was ill and going to a toy hospital, I bandaged its head. He got a replacement teddy bear which resembled the old one, and he cheered up and recovered. He was a sweet boy, only about six years of age.

I enjoyed caring for the children, but it was disheartening if they didn't make it. I remember bringing a child to the morgue without a porter and placing them there. Those were the dark and difficult moments we as nurses dealt with.

* * *

Becoming a fever trained nurse was a special time for me as I fulfilled a dream and made my family proud. I cried on receiving my fever training nursing certificate, and thought to myself, *Nancy, you are on your way now.*

Not wishing to stop there, I sat for my finals and reached the level required to start at the Queen Elizabeth Hospital in Birmingham to train as a State Registered Nurse.

The Queen Elizabeth Hospital, built in 1938, combined a hospital and medical school. It was an exciting environment to be in, never knowing what challenges lay ahead for a junior nurse. Being registered as a student there thrilled me. I couldn't wait to get stuck into whatever was required of me.

The hallways echoed with the sounds of hurried footsteps from students, nurses, and doctors' daily business. A smell of antiseptic lingered in the corridors with the occasional beep from a patient's heart monitor. I desired to belong to that world.

The hospital was busy, with around eight hundred in-patients daily. Its reputation was as an excellent training hospital for both nurses and doctors.

Becoming an SRN was a clear upgrade from being a fever-trained nurse. My responsibilities grew, and I dealt with a variety of cases. I recall helping a young girl named Beth, who, at five, required an iron lung because of polio.

Most people who contracted polio did not always have visible symptoms, although a severe case could infect the brain and spinal cord and cause paralysis. The disease weakened Beth's breathing muscles, and she survived thanks to the iron lung, which did her breathing for her. Setting Beth up in the iron lung was stressful, as the machines were giant ventilators about seven feet long.

She lay inside with just her head resting outside; with a seal around her neck to create a vacuum. The way it worked was with bellows at the base of the device, doing the work of a human diaphragm — it created negative pressure, so Beth's lungs could fill with air. Sadly, Beth didn't survive for more than a few months. Having cared for her daily, it was difficult not to let it affect me. She was an adorable and brave little girl.

A very sick child was once in the ward suffering from salmonella poisoning. She was a beautiful baby, and I so happened to nurse her mother in the General Hospital before returning to Little Bromwich Hospital.

Upon seeing me, she stated, "As it's you, I know my baby will receive excellent care and recover under your supervision."

As the Nursing Sister, I tried everything, but her parents brought her into hospital too late, and she died. It was terrible. It broke my heart, especially as the mother showed such faith in me, but the baby was too far gone. The Mother brought Easter eggs into the hospital for the other children, hoping her baby would recover. It was interminably sad. I will remember the beautiful baby and the baby's family forever.

In addition, the grief I saw from the baby's mother reminded me of my own grief at leaving my beautiful baby behind in Ireland. This experience made me even more determined, and I promised myself one day I would return to Ireland and reclaim her.

After passing my finals and becoming an SRN, I received a letter from mammy.

'Táim an-bhródúil asat', in Gaelic means, I'm very proud of you. Our letters were in a mixture of Irish and English. I

imagined mammy telling the neighbours how yet another one of her offspring had achieved something in life. My sister Pauline became a nurse too, although based in Kent, she was nowhere near Birmingham.

I wrote to mammy about my siblings and daddy. Did she know about Maeve and her time at St. Augustine's Convent School with the nuns? She said as far as she knew Maeve was doing fine, but it never stopped me from thinking of her daily.

She wrote back every time, stating, "Nancy, we are proud of you. Keep on making us happy, love and prayers, mammy and daddy."

I realised she didn't want to address the issue but pushed it under the carpet. Maeve was seven years old by now. I longed for her happiness with all my heart.

Chapter 7

AT AGE TWENTY-FIVE, I returned to the Little Bromwich Hospital to oversee a general ward, with a Staff Nurse and eight to ten other nurses. I felt gratitude to have trained at the Queen Elizabeth Hospital and was ambitious, but to run a ward single handed was an enormous responsibility.

It was early morning on the ward, and we were completing observations on all the patients. The cheerful morning light filtered through the large glass windows designed to brighten the ward up, whilst the poorly patients were tucking into their breakfast. The Staff Nurse confirmed all the patients were being attended to and didn't require any extra medication.

Matron Wallis approached. She was getting on in years and it amazed me when she appeared. It was as if she glided on small round wheels attached to the soles of her feet, like a silent assassin. She was an imposing figure in charge of patient care, catering, and cleaning at the hospital. Matrons were all-powerful and organised the nursing staff with military style precision.

She was no exception and loved and excelled at her job. As the Ward Sister, I interacted with her often. It was fortunate that we understood each other well. I noted she was in an unusual hurry, and her glasses sat right on the end of her nose, pointing at me in a condemning fashion.

"Sister Flanagan, a new patient from the General Hospital has been transferred to your ward. He needs rest and recuperation, and we are best placed for that. There is a suspicion he is suffering from an infectious disease, and as a fever trained nurse, you are the best person for the specialist care needed."

The hospital transfer didn't surprise me, often picking up waifs and strays the General Hospital felt were in the way of their precious beds. Hearing about the patient's possible infectious disease caused worry and tension.

"Matron, is there no space in the Sanitarium here?"

"No, Sister Flanagan, they are full to the gunnels. I've checked!" Of course she had checked. Matron always worked at maximum efficiency.

I smiled at her.

"Okay, then we'll assign the new patient to the side room and monitor him appropriately. Let's see how he is now."

Matron quickly left, leaving me to head to the hospital entrance, where the ambulance arrived. They took him to the private room beside the ward. It was designed for patients who could not stand the hustle and bustle of hospital routine. Patients existed still suffering from war-induced shell shock.

Upon arrival at the main ward, I inquired about the patient's name from one of the ambulance men.

"We haven't been able to get it for you, Sister Flanagan. There was no documentation on him."

"We couldn't trace any family," the attending Staff Nurse finished explaining.

How very odd. I made eye contact with the ambulance man, arching my eyebrows in surprise.

"Who picked him up, and from where?"

"A passerby found him collapsed in the street," said the senior ambulance man, Jim.

The patient seemed lightweight and fragile when transferring him from the trolley onto the bed.

"He was very lucky, Sister. They found him half-way down a tight, dark alleyway, propped up against the wall. Fortunately, a passer-by heard moaning and investigated the noise. She called a police officer, and the police officer called the ambulance."

"Very lucky indeed, Jim."

Jim was a senior ambulance man with many years' service under his belt. The job affected him physically and emotionally due to the sights and sounds he had experienced during his service. He witnessed stabbings, a rare shooting and heartbreaking traffic incidents in the course of his career.

He banned his son from ever owning or driving a motorbike because of the awful road traffic accidents he encountered. He was lucky to have a wonderful support network of family and friends, or he may have suffered from a nervous breakdown. Jim was an unsung hero.

The ambulance men took off the new patient's jacket and laid a red, heavy-duty blanket over him because of the chilly April air. Sweat poured down his forehead, causing his dark hair to stick to it. His eyes rolled back in his head, and his complexion turned a pasty grey.

"He doesn't look good," I said to the Staff Nurse. "Let's take his temperature. He may be suffering from a fever. Getting him on a drip and administering fluids is wisest."

The tension in my voice was clear to the Staff Nurse.

"Make sure you follow infectious disease protocol until we know what's wrong with him. Masks and gowns are required whenever someone enters or exits the room and remember to scrub your arms up to your elbows. I cannot risk any cross infection with the other patients."

Staff Nurse Wilkes nodded her agreement and cascaded the information to the other ward nurses.

"I'll put on my gown and mask and examine him. When is Mr Peters due on the ward?"

Suddenly, the mystery man let out a piercing scream and shouted something unintelligible. We jumped sky high, not expecting such a heart-rending noise to emanate from deep within this man's chest and throat. He showed signs of agitation. Although semi-conscious, his arms and legs were twitching, and he moaned deeply, as though in pain.

"Jesus!"

My widened eyes and dropped jaw revealed my surprise. Patients often moaned or yelled as if in pain. This man's scream was distressing, catching even me off guard.

"That was unexpected!"

"It shocked me too," said the Staff Nurse, shaking her head.

"It's from the high fever. Please inform the other nurses that he is a top priority."

She left me alone with the new patient. Intense sunlight streamed in through the bedroom window. The room wasn't unpleasant. With a metal bed with soft pillows, an oxygen bottle and mask and resuscitation equipment, it was an oasis of calm, away from the noisiness of the general ward.

I could tell he disliked the bright sunshine, as he squinted his eyes and blinked rapidly, so I gently pulled the curtains shut, blocking the harsh rays of sunlight from flooding the room.

It was a shame the ambulance men didn't realise that he

may have been infectious and given us some warning. We could have ensured mask and gown usage when meeting him at the hospital. Determination of physical ailments, rather than diseases, was easier. They did their best.

Leaving his room, I followed the protocol of fever-trained nurses, thoroughly scrubbing my arms to the elbows to avoid carrying any germs which were transferable. I re-entered the room, now wearing a mask and gown. Studying the mystery man, his appearance didn't sit well with me. His continued piercing screams and loud shouting in an unintelligible language were unnerving.

The way he clutched the bedclothes, as if it was his lifeline, was concerning. You learn to cope as a nurse, to forget your own feelings, but somehow this patient was different. When prising the bedclothes away from his fingers, he tried grabbing at them. I got him to release his fingers slowly by using the soothing voice I employed when dealing with a child, and it seemed to work.

"Now, now, let go. There's a splendid chap. I need to change you into something more comfortable. You can't wear your suit in bed."

He looked at me with a confused expression, his face pale and drenched in sweat. His face was narrow, with a receding hairline. With short, dark eyebrows and a small moustache, he wasn't distinctive in appearance. However, despite the illness, he exuded authority while appearing ordinary. Not arrogance, but a natural confidence.

As he tried whispering, I leaned in but I could not hear him. His eyes were a light brown and looked sorrowful. Then he started coughing and hacking. His face contorted with each forceful cough, his body doubling over in discomfort.

Bringing him a bowl to cough into, I saw there were specks of blood in the phlegm coughed up from his lungs. He collapsed back onto the bed, exhausted.

I removed his clothing, which was old-fashioned. Although we were in 1953, it easily dated back to just after the war. The jacket's front buttons were polished, and it seemed as though someone had mended a hole in the trouser leg, possibly torn from catching it on something. Clearly, he took pride in his appearance and cared for his clothes.

Substituting the suit for a hospital gown, he let me move his limbs to accommodate it but was very thin with a withered left leg. This type of atrophy was known to me. He had contracted polio previously.

His high temperature, 104 degrees Fahrenheit, confirmed a fever. Beneath my fingers, his skin felt warm and clammy. A nurse, clad in a sterile gown and mask, approached the patient's bedside and inserted a saline drip into his arm.

"Good Gina. With his elevated temperature, he needs fluids. I asked Staff Nurse Wilkes earlier, but she wasn't sure. Do we know when Mr Peters is doing his rounds?"

"Should be in an hour, Sister," answered Gina. "Gosh, poor man!"

She stepped back and surveyed the broken man lying in the bed. Gina was a qualified nurse, excitable and enthusiastic, but resolute.

"Sister Flanagan, how old do you reckon the patient is?"

"Looking at his overall appearance, I'd say in his fifties, Gina, but it's difficult to determine. You can return to the ward now."

She tossed her blonde hair, nodded her head, and scurried off. Out of all the patients in the busy ward, this man was the sickest. I mulled over his symptoms and a shiver of dread went through me as I realised, he may indeed have tuberculosis.

Thank goodness we put him in the side room in the ward. I tended to many patients suffering with tuberculosis whilst training in the Sanatorium. They did not all survive, even with our best efforts.

Mr Peters was likely to confirm my assessment with a proper diagnosis. Tuberculosis caused symptoms such as a bad cough, lasting three weeks or longer, an accompanying pain in the chest, coughing up blood or phlegm from deep inside the lungs, fatigue, weight loss, lack of appetite, chills, fever, and sweating.

Working as a fever trained nurse brought me closer to despair more than at any other stage of my career. The saddest thing was seeing patients decline and die. Half the patients with pulmonary tuberculosis died. It was ridiculously hurtful indeed and I vowed then and there to keep a professional distance. I hoped the new patient was the surviving type.

Mr Peters entered the ward, his tall figure casting a commanding presence. I felt a flush of relief to see him and explained the mystery patient's symptoms. Despite his rush, I insisted he examine him, as he disliked the disturbance of dressing up.

"This is an urgent case, Mr Peters."

As nurses, we treated consultants like gods. One consultant, whom I shall not name, insisted on my bringing him a coffee daily to his office and two chocolate biscuits covered with a white linen cloth. If the coffee wasn't hot enough, he got annoyed.

That happened in my early student days, and I had learned since then that consultants are just people with more medical experience. Nowadays, I treated them like any other person. Needing to run the hospital ward properly, there was no time for inflated egos.

Consultants were called 'Mr' instead of 'doctor', which was confusing but normal.

The junior nurses said to me, "How do we speak to Mr Peters? He's so forbidding!"

I retorted, "Imagine him naked then, or going to the toilet. Even the Queen goes to the toilet!"

"Sister Flanagan!" they looked at me aghast, then giggled as they scurried off to their duties.

Now attired in a gown and mask, Mr Peters mumbled, "Hmm."

He examined the man with a voice filled with curiosity and intrigue.

"Sister Flanagan, your action was prudent to put him in this side room. I believe he has tuberculosis. I suggest we get an x-ray of his chest and lungs and put him on the Streptomycin injection treatment plan immediately."

"Yes, Mr Peters, of course, straight away," relieved he had confirmed my own suspicions.

"Tuberculosis is not hereditary, so the family history is unimportant. Just a decade ago, the patient's condition was likely to leave us helpless, but now in 1953, the odds are more favourable for a recovery. What concerns me most is this patient is not in the best physical shape."

Our support and the Streptomycin treatment would aid his recovery, but a lot depended upon his ability to fight the disease. Tuberculosis was curable if detected early. I prayed we got to him soon enough.

Mr Peters said, "Let's see what his chest x-ray says, but he should be transferred to the Sanitarium, Sister Flanagan."

"The Sanitarium here is full. We can nurse him back to full health in the ward. Once ready, we can take him outside for fresh air."

Mr Peters nodded. "The main rehabilitation focus is to lower his temperature, keep him comfortable and give him fluids and the injections."

I acknowledged Mr. Peters with a smile, knowing what to do but needed his instructions. We exited the room together, and I looked back to witness the patient's restless state.

Are you going to make it? I pondered.

Despite everything, I sensed the patient's powerful will to survive. His shouts and piercing screams upon entering the hospital ward were deeply moving, giving me a strong desire to know more. Over the years, I had developed a sixth sense as to a patient's character from encountering them at their lowest ebb. He maintained an authoritative presence but still acted like a gentleman.

He sparked a deeper level of compassion than normal, but I didn't know why then. Time was going to be my guide.

Chapter 8

THAT NIGHT THE MYSTERY patient experienced laboured breathing and a pale, wan face. He was very poorly. I didn't want to leave him until his fever lessened, so I spent much of the night checking in on him. He seemed fragile, both physically and mentally.

Despite not being conventionally handsome, the mystery patient possessed an undeniable allure. This, together with a muted display of appreciation for my caring of him when he was lucid, drew me closer than I usually allowed myself to be to a patient.

He wasn't very communicative yet, mostly unintelligible ramblings and sudden shouting, but I hoped once his fever broke, I could learn more. There were secrets yet to be uncovered.

When the fever took hold and he thrashed around in his bed, his limbs agitated and jerky, I hated it. Applying a cold compress to his head, I ensured he drank enough fluids. His illness and the war scarred him, without a doubt. Tuberculosis was such an awful and debilitating disease. He was fighting for his life.

The hospital night shift wasn't my favourite time. Night-time at the hospital lacked the usual hustle and bustle of nurses and doctors caring for patients. Instead, there were sounds of patients snoring, needing bedpans, or muttering in their sleep. The patients lay cocooned in starched sheets. The beds creaked as bodies shifted. Some slept fitfully, their dreams haunted by fevered visions, such as in the case of the mystery patient. Others stared at the cracked ceiling, tracing imaginary constellations until they finally dropped off to sleep in the early hours.

It was an eerie and spooky time, and easy to imagine seeing shadows in the dark corridors. I frequently sensed indescribable life force energies and attributed those energies to previous hospital occupants who passed away.

Tonight, I was on a night shift with one other nurse, Gina. Having qualified in nursing the previous year, she was both enthusiastic and easy to work alongside. She dealt with the patients' practical needs, so my role that night was to complete administrative work at the nurses' station, apart from occasionally seeing to the mystery patient. Gina understood he was under my personal care.

The clock above the nurses' station was an old sentinel. Its pendulum swung with measured precision, counting down the hours until dawn. Each tick was a heartbeat, each tock a sigh. I glanced at the clock often, my eyes tracing its golden hands every hour until finally our shift ended, and the day nurses arrived for the patients' handover meeting. The scent of antiseptic lingered in the air.

The workday began for many upon returning to the Nurse's Home at 8 am. It wasn't modern in style, but I was lucky. As a Ward Sister, the hospital allocated me a comfortable bedroom to myself, and I typically enjoyed a restful and peaceful sleep.

The plants I placed on the windowsill made me feel happy.

I checked if any of them needed a drink of water. The worn wooden floors which flexed when walking on them in bare feet, and my exceptionally soft bed cover, which was a patchwork quilt of many colours, were things I loved. My Aunt May made the quilt, and it was special to me. She gave it to me as a going away present when leaving Ireland and was my favourite aunt. It wasn't home, but it was homely.

Sometimes I enjoyed reading or listening to the radio, but my tired body protested, and after yawning, I quickly fell asleep. There were blackout curtains in my room, which made it seem like nighttime, although there was bright sunshine outside. Something untoward woke me up.

Was I awake or still asleep? Unsure, I whispered into the shadows, *hello?* My eyes darted back and forth in the gloom, trying to focus. All was quiet, but something was wrong. The atmosphere didn't feel right. Straining to catch the faintest of sounds, I sat bolt upright in bed, and I pulled my bedclothes tightly over me. Shivering, I felt frozen, my skin prickling with unease, and my palms were clammy with anxiety.

The bedroom was pitch black, with limited light for me to see. There was undoubtedly something there. I heard a low, guttural rasp, barely audible. My senses were on high alert, still trying to hear the muted sounds. The room was on the ground floor of the Nurse's Home, and sometimes I left the window open for fresh air.

Did a cat get into my room? A stray which slipped through the open window? I couldn't identify the sound. It was primal, ancient.

A grey mist formed everywhere, coiling around the room and surrounding me in light grey wisps. *How can a mist form inside my room?* It was bizarre.

My brain was still half asleep and not computing this vision at all. I couldn't comprehend it. *Surely it was impossible.*

The mist thickened, obscuring the room's contours. There was a loud swooshing noise, and my body flinched. It sounded like fluttering wings, but how was it possible? It seemed improbable that a bird would enter the room. *What was going on?* My mind frantically searching for answers, I hoped there was nothing trapped in the room with me. My panic surged at the thought I wasn't alone.

My nerves were on edge. A chill spread throughout my body. I hated not understanding a situation and I needed to know what was happening. My hand flew to my mouth in horror. I tried desperately to stifle the scream which was working its way up into my throat. While looking intently, the mist had cleared, revealing a large mass forming by my bed.

In the dim light, what I saw was at least seven feet tall, with hands and feet shaped like a man's, but with red blotchy skin covering its entire body. Twelve wings flapped back and forth on its spine, six on each side. The wings beat in a frenzied rhythm, and it hovered in one spot, much as a hummingbird does. But its aspect was both mesmerising and repulsive.

I knew it was the ghastliest sight I had ever seen in my life. The smell disgusted me. I cannot tell you how appalling the aroma which emanated from this beast was. Putrid, it felt like I was encountering something which had decayed long ago, with rotting flesh. I made a gagging sound in my throat, and I turned my head to one side to gasp for fresh air. Nausea rose from my stomach, and I fought hard not to wretch and be sick.

Unpleasant situations occurred daily in the hospital, but I had smelled nothing as repugnant as this before. There was saliva dripping from its large fangs onto my bed cover, onto my beautiful patchwork quilt from my aunt. That angered me.

I strained to see its whole body and caught glimpses of its barbed tail thrashing in all directions. Its yellow glowing eyes fixated on me. They were ethereal. This creature was definitely from a realm beyond this one. Since it wasn't an angel, I made the sign of the cross and I called upon God to help me. It was definitely from beyond the veil.

Growing up, I had experienced psychic dreams, and more recently, I had the vision with Frederick, the army soldier who wanted to give a message to his wife Hilda from beyond the grave. I had happily delivered the message to Hilda, but this demonic visitation in my bedroom was frightening me deeply. Demons were inherently evil, and I hadn't suffered a visitation such as this one before.

The beast made a strange hissing type of sound, and animal bones and skulls linked to its vile body clanked against each other as it moved around. Continuing to hover at the bottom of my bed, with strange noises emanating from deep within its throat, the hissing sound abated. But I preferred the hissing sound to this low growl, reminiscent of a dangerous animal waiting to pounce. The skulls hanging on its body appeared to be from small, wild animals, but I couldn't be certain.

Without a weapon to protect myself, fear paralysed my body. Unsure of my next move, with no idea of what I was dealing with, I tried to talk myself into taking positive action. My mind searched for a way forward in the inky blackness.

Come on, Nancy, you are just dreaming. Pull yourself together, I thought. But it wasn't working.

I wanted to offer up a full prayer but couldn't choose one.

Should I be pleading to God, the Virgin Mary, or to my own Guardian Angel?

If there was a distressed patient or someone in need of help, I would have acted without concern. Summoned someone, discovered a weapon, or simply yelled at the monster. But on my own, I just wasn't able to move.

"What do you want? Leave me alone!" I screamed out into the black void. The creature remained silent, leaving me uncertain if this was a nightmare or reality. Fear rooted me to the bed, and my once sturdy muscles quivered as though fragile feathers caught in a tumultuous storm. As the mist swirled around, I realised this wasn't a mere apparition; it was tangible. This was a messenger from a realm beyond ours, a dark realm of nightmares and evil, its existence stitched into the fabric of chaos, which had slipped through the curtain separating our world from theirs.

With no other choice available, I opened my mouth and let out an unearthly scream which appeared to me to last forever.

The scream ripped throughout the Nurse's Home until my bedroom door slammed wide open. In ran matron. The sound of the door opening made the horrifying creature vanish and the mist dissipate immediately. Matron wrapped her arms around me, as I continued to scream.

"I'm here, Sister Flanagan," said matron, hugging me, concerned at my conduct.

With the beast gone, matron couldn't confirm the cause of my scream or the reality in my room. Something unexpected happened. She struck my face with her right hand, and a red imprint remained on my cheek for some minutes afterwards. I stopped screaming and looked at her in astonishment.

"I'm so sorry, Sister Flanagan," said matron. She continued, "It was the only way to snap you out of screaming hysteria. I imagine it was an awful nightmare."

Bursting into tears, I leaned into her arms, and I sobbed for a time but decided not to tell her details of the awful vision. Hugging her back, I thanked her. Having her by my side was a great relief. She was practical, and full of common sense, but behind that professional facade lay a generous heart. She looked at me with concern in her eyes.

"Sister Flanagan, you are one of the most important people in this hospital. Your work is exemplary, and I will not allow you to be upset. Having worked excessively and devoted considerable time to the tuberculosis patient, it's time for you to take a break."

Nodding, I responded, "Perhaps you are right."

"Today is Wednesday. Come back into the Ward from next Monday onwards. I can arrange cover so you can rest properly."

"Thank you so much, Matron," I responded with heartfelt gratitude.

After a brief silence, I asked her, "Do you believe in evil spirits? Demons, I suppose you would call them."

My words hung in the air. Her smile towards me spoke volumes.

"Nancy was that your nightmare?" she asked. "It's difficult working in a hospital dealing with people's illnesses. Sometimes patients are lost whom we like, and it's tough."

I wasn't sure she could understand.

I replied, "Yes, it's difficult, but it's part of our job. But demons, Matron. Evil spirits, wanting to do us harm?"

She studied me closely, "Is it something you believe in Ireland, Nancy? All that Celtic history?"

67

For generations I'd heard stories that beasts walked among us, ranging from Primeval, bat-like monsters that preceded vampires, through to summoned demons. In Ireland, we called them a *deamhan*. Spiritual entities which incarnated into physical form to interact with our world directly.

"The only demons we face here are our own internal worries, Nancy."

I smiled and nodded. She was so straightforward and down to earth. Of course she didn't believe in evil spirits.

After a few minutes, her worried eyes met mine and said, "Before I leave, I just want to make sure you are okay?"

"Yes, Matron, thank you. You don't have to stay any longer."

However, there was no earthly chance of me gaining any further sleep. I was far too scared and traumatised by my experience. After she left, I felt the patchwork quilt at the bottom of my bed. It was damp from the creature's saliva. It was thick, cloying, and nasty, with a disgusting odour. I shuddered, got up, and washed my hands repeatedly.

Removing the quilt from my bed, I put it to one side for washing later, although unsure if I could remove the stench of the demon's saliva from it. The quilt meant so much to me. I felt crushed.

Getting back into bed, I sat with my back wedged against the headboard, opened my curtains, and watched the birds in the trees through my window. After working the previous night, it was now late afternoon. The sunshine pouring through my window was comforting to me, as I was still felt terrified, and I would never forget the touch of that ethereal mist and the scent of the creature.

I wondered if I'd ever sleep again without feeling the weight of the veil against my skin. Too many questions, with no answers. *What was the thing I saw? Why was it there? Where did it come from?* It was revolting. Having a daytime visit from such a beast felt far stranger than a nighttime visit.

Was the visitation a punishment for my sins? I felt guilty every day for leaving Maeve behind in Ireland. *Did I cause this?* I wondered.

It wasn't a ghost or spirit which haunted me in my nightmare, but something darker and more malevolent. Summoners bring demons to earth to commit acts of torment. What was the reason for its visit? Did my action of leaving Maeve to an unknown fate attract such a demonic visitation?

The fright I experienced left me shattered and confused. Dragging myself out of bed, my eyes were heavy, and my body sagged with fatigue. I washed and cooked something to eat, but I wasn't hungry.

I experienced the supernatural both during my childhood and as a nurse. When inexplicable things happened, I brushed them aside, putting them down to coincidence or just odd events. When I was young, I sometimes saw non-existent people in the streets. Pointing them out to mammy she took no notice, saying I suffered from an overactive imagination.

I considered my psychic experiences run of the mill because I was so accustomed to them, not really understanding them myself. A gift or a curse? When I told Hilda about Frederick's message, she interpreted it as a gift, but if my past behaviour had caused this demonic visitation then I considered it to be a curse.

The best cure was to work harder, and I got dressed, ready for the next hospital shift. I behaved as though it was just another ordinary day, but I knew the experience would continue to bother me.

No time to dwell on it. Patients needed to be seen, no time to spare. Once I fixed my nurse's hat to my head with my regulation hairgrips, I became Nancy Flanagan, the Ward Sister again.

Chapter 9

MATRON SENT ME BACK to the Nurse's Home when I appeared at the hospital for the night shift, seeing I was still exhausted. Truth be told, I didn't get to sleep that night, anyway. No more nightmares, I just listened to music all night on the radio to distract myself.

As I walked back into the hospital the next day, Matron's concerned expression met my eyes, urging me to take time off after my unsettling nightmare. The beast's stench lingered in my mind and the more I reviewed the experience, the more real it became.

I wasn't ready to take a break yet from the hospital, as I was intrigued by the mystery patient, and my curiosity persisted. It's true to say that work was a useful diversion. Dwelling on the awful nightmare in the Nurse's Home was useless. I needed to forget it.

I checked in on the mystery patient. He looked weary, like someone whose experience included trauma. More verbal communication this time, but just please and thank you. His accent was strong, although I was unsure where it came from, however he was very respectful whenever we interacted.

Walking around the main ward that morning, Julie Arnet beckoned me over to her bedside. Julie's right arm was twisted at an awkward angle from falling over her mischievous cat at home, breaking her arm in two places. She had spent the last two weeks in the hospital.

The ward contained twelve beds, with curtains separating each bed to give maximum privacy to the patient. There were large glass windows to let in light where possible. Luckily, the beds were metal framed and on castors, so we were able to move them around easily. The nurses' station was at the front of the ward where we kept valuable information and made medical decisions.

The ladies liked to chat with each other on their beds. Others preferred the curtains pulled for privacy, but it was never quiet in the ward, as there was the constant hustle and bustle of patients being observed, taking medication, or leaving or joining the ward. The ward came alive at 6 am every morning, and we needed to get round all the patients with breakfast, observations, bed baths, and medication, ensuring it was gleaming before Matron came on the ward inspection.

Julie was a plump lady, fifty years old, with a lovely smile. Her laugh was contagious, and I liked to chat to her when it was quieter on the ward. I approached Julie's bed, a cup of tea cradled in my hands, I gave it to her carefully. Her eyes held questions, curiosity abounding.

"Sister Flanagan. What's the story of the man in the side room?"

I looked up in surprise, wondering why she was asking. Her interest in the mystery man, knowing her tendency to gossip, piqued my interest.

"We don't know Julie; he didn't have any paperwork on him, so we're left to wonder about him."

She looked intrigued and leaned towards me.

"You know Sister Flanagan; I have a relative who is German?"

I wished she got to the point quickly, as I was still tired from a lack of sleep.

"No, I didn't, Julie."

"I learned German from my cousin when I was a child. In the side room, the man, he shouted out in German.

It was 1953, and the war only ended eight years prior. Many Germans had settled in Britain post-war, yet conflict echoes persisted. So many families had lost loved ones.

"What did he say?"

I smoothed out Julie's bed sheets, adjusting her pillow. She lifted her head, eyes alight.

"He cried out, 'Please, not the children!' Or at least I think so. Sometimes it was unintelligible, but that was the gist of it."

I moved back to Julie's side of the bed.

"Thank you for bringing it to my attention, Julie. He had just a bad dream then."

The cup of tea I brought her sat untouched, forgotten. I tried to give Julie a low-key answer, but the memory of that scream, the raw primal sound which clawed its way from the mystery man's depths, lingered. The sound was nightmarish and haunting.

She motioned for me to approach her, closer and closer, until her face was inches away from mine.

"Sister Flanagan, do you think he's a Nazi?"

She rolled her eyes, speaking in a stage whisper. Definitely going for the maximum dramatic effect. A loud guffaw escaped from my mouth.

"Highly unlikely, Julie," and shook my head. But, walking

away from Julie's bedside, I felt a creeping sense of unease. No paperwork, no identity. A man shrouded in mystery. Inquiries were necessary. The war was responsible for scarring families. Was he a Prisoner of War (POW), who refused to return to Germany and instead worked on farms or the roads?

I told all the nurses in the ward to call the mystery patient 'John' going forwards. It was easier for us to identify him this way rather than call him 'mystery patient.' An English name, a shield against curiosity. But if he was German, silence was crucial. Anti-German sentiment still smouldered; wounds remained unhealed in Britain.

Matron approached me. I swear the woman was on hospital wheels as she moved without making a sound.

"Sister Flanagan, I have news relating to the mystery patient. The x-ray shows a slight shadow on his lung. At this stage, Mr. Peters thinks rest and recuperation can replace the need for an operation. Catching it early is crucial for his full recovery, dependent on his care and physical fitness."

John was becoming a huge focus on my working day, and I personally felt it was down to me to save him. We experienced a busy morning in the ward with a couple of new patients. Checking on John before lunch, he was fast asleep, so I left him alone.

A yawn escaped me. The Nurse's Home was nearby, so I quickly returned for a nap. Patients shouldn't suffer due to my weakness. Suppose if critical choices must be made?

During my absence, Molly arrived to help. A volunteer who visited the hospital every week, she was quite old, but loved helping with the patients, offering them tea, and a friendly chat, especially if they didn't have a family and they felt lonely. The sterile, white walls and fluorescent lights of the hospital created an uncomfortable atmosphere for new patients.

Molly was fastidious about volunteering. She visited all the patients, particularly new ones. Molly enjoyed meeting them because it made her feel needed and useful, and as she lived alone, with no close family left to speak of, she looked forward to the interaction with them.

Tiptoeing into John's room; her purpose was unwavering. Tea and sympathy. I had banned no one from John's sanctuary, but the nurses knew he was receiving special personalised care. None thought to mention it to Molly.

Returning from my lunchtime nap feeling refreshed and raring to go, there was a scream, and the crashing sound of a teacup and saucer breaking into a thousand pieces. In the side room, I found both John and Molly. She was on her knees, looking up in amazement at John.

John, weak from tuberculosis, winced, with his hands over his ears to block out the noise. The suddenness of it was shocking, and he looked confused as I questioned Molly.

"What on earth, Molly?"

Molly's eyes widened and she pointed a shaky finger. "Sister Flanagan. Do you *know* this man?"

I helped her to a standing position. John removed his hands from his ears but remained confused about Molly's presence in his room. Staff Nurse Wilkes burst in, mop and bucket in hand, eyes wide with surprise. The spilled tea, the shattered teacup—it was chaos. Molly's arm extended, finger outstretched, directly aimed at John, her eyes fixed on him with intensity.

"This is a German man," Molly declared. John, weak but alert, met her gaze.

"I speak German."

He spoke with a heavy German accent, but clearly understood her, and spoke exceptionally good English. Leading
Molly out of the side room quickly, wanting to create as little
fuss as possible, she continued shaking her head at me in
disbelief.

"A German in the hospital."

I heard the soft footsteps of Staff Nurse Wilkes as she
returned, her shoes rubbing against the linoleum floor.

"It's okay, I will deal with this."

She attempted to speak but nodded and returned to the
main ward. I steered a shaky Molly to Matron's empty office.

"Molly, it is unacceptable to make such comments. The
War has ended, and various nationalities, Germans included,
now work and reside here."

Tension filled the air, Molly's words having caused discomfort. She shook her head.

"But, Sister Flanagan, what sort of German is he?"

"He's someone who needs hospital care, Molly, and it's our
job to give it. He's pleasant, and there are no complaints."

"Sister Flanagan, what if he's a bad un'?"

"How did you know anyway, Molly?"

"Huh?"

"How did you know he was German?"

"Julie told me Sister Flanagan. He looks it doesn't he, with
those Germanic features!"

I thought Molly knew a dark secret to share, but not at all.
She had gossiped with Julie Arnet and wanted to examine John.
I guided her with gentle precision, navigating her through
the swinging ward doors.

"Thank you, Molly, but until we know more, please don't
approach John or mention him to anyone."

She nodded, but I could almost smell the excitement radiating from her, a scent of anticipation and enthusiasm filling the air. She was excited to tell her friends about the encounter.

Nursing involved interacting with many people, which could be more challenging than treating physical ailments. People were complex, while a particular illness or injury followed a defined process.

However, Molly's strength of feeling made me stop and think. *Who was this man? Should his presence concern me?*

In his weakened state, John didn't pose a threat, but I wanted to know more. It was strange not to have found any files or documents containing the patient's information by this point. What secrets was John harbouring, and was there a price for unravelling them?

Chapter 10

I WAS IN THE hospital so often it felt like I lived there. The mystery patient was coming round now, and doing well, after having fought hard to rid himself of the disease. Despite his weakness, he managed to eat. Only gentle soups with potatoes or rice to begin with, but his strength was building.

The florescent lights in the hospital hummed, whilst other nurses in the hospital wards busied themselves, their soft soled footsteps echoing along the corridors.

His dimly lit hospital room held secrets. There was no paperwork, no background information available. Just a stranger lying in a sterile bed, clinging to life. He fascinated me and I wanted to learn more. Despite a heavy accent, he spoke good English but only made polite conversation revealing he previously lived in Vilnius, Lithuania, but that was the only information given.

After propping him up on his pillows, I gave him a cup of tea and asked questions. It was a while since arriving at the hospital, and details of his circumstances needed to be known. The refusal to provide a name on several occasions was concerning and decided I should adopt a more direct approach.

"You need to tell me more, you know that?"

Although he sat up with a cup of tea nearby to revive him, he regularly drifted in and out of consciousness. Opening his eyelids, which remained heavy, he regarded me wearily.

Julie, the nosy patient from the main ward, was relentless in her pursuit of the truth. Certain he was German, she still harboured ill-will towards Germans from the war. She badgered me to know more. I shielded him from prying eyes, but the rumours wouldn't abate.

"Let's set the record straight. Malicious gossip disrupting the hospital is unacceptable."

He focused on me, but his face remained expressionless.

No way would I give in and pressed him further for answers.

"Julie heard you shouting the other night, having a night-mare. You shouted out, 'Bitte, nicht die Kinder,' and everyone could hear it in the main ward."

Still no comment.

"Apparently, it meant, 'Please, not the children.' What is this all about?"

What horrors were witnessed by this man? He glanced at me, his apprehension showing.

"Alright, I will share what I can," he said grudgingly, realising the questions would continue if he didn't answer me.

Shuffling in the bed and fiddling with the bedclothes, he picked up his spectacles. His hands trembled as he adjusted them, the only link to the past. The blanks needed to be filled in regarding his life. Cleaning the lenses with his pyjama sleeve, he confessed, "My family contained military doctors, and I wanted to be one too, but could not afford the years of study required. World War One changed everything."

His voice cracked with emotion when revisiting the battles

of World War One, which he took part in.

"I fought in three intense battles: Flanders, the Somme, and Verdun, alongside my best friend Klaus. In particular, Verdun was a long and gruelling battle, lasting just over three hundred days, and both sides suffered huge casualties. The battle was brutal. Death everywhere. I lost close friends. Barrage after barrage of artillery fire from the French. Earth covered the fallen. It was a complete slaughter."

Absorbed in the story, I nodded. His eyes misted over at the vivid memories being relived.

"I remember, Klaus sat on the floor of the muddy trench. His eyes were widened to their fullest extent, shaking badly. Approaching the Unteroffizier, I explained Klaus was no longer effective as a soldier, suffering from shell shock, and unable to hold a rifle."

A solemn tear fell as he continued, "The Unteroffizier, accustomed to soldiers feigning illness or self-harming to avoid danger, came over to Klaus, saying, 'Medic, here, now.' After examining Klaus, the medic glanced at the Unteroffizier and nodded."

"I assured Klaus of his safety at the hospital, but his personality changed forever. At least he didn't die."

'John' sat there with me, reflecting on the past. He chose not to disclose everything to me just then. I think he liked me and was afraid I would reject him. I could see his memories were strong and I could tell he was thinking over his experiences in detail. It was difficult not to grasp his hand, to offer him comfort whilst he reviewed his past, but I was always the professional nurse.

Unlike Klaus, John knew he was not a dashing, smartly turned-out type of soldier. He wasn't an outgoing, brash kind of personality. He wore a contemplative expression, eyes focused and deep in thought as he discussed the war placement with his family. His father passed away in 1904 when he was seven years old, leaving him with his mother and older sister, Clara, with whom he enjoyed a deep connection.

With his first taste of war looming, he carried more than just a rifle; he carried his family's love and memories.

Helga, his mother's voice, trembled with sadness as she uttered the words, "I wish you didn't have to go off to war."

"I understand, mama, but there's no choice. We are fighting in Flanders, and the Imperial German Army needs our help."

His mother shook her head. Born in 1897, in 1915, he was still a young man.

"But the gas, the chlorine gas used on the British and Canadian forces at Ypres in April, was brutal."

He nodded, not liking it either.

"I know mama, but it was used on us as well."

She shuddered. Using poisonous gas was devastating for any troops which encountered it. A horrific weapon, it damaged lungs and eyes. Some suffered a slow and agonising death. The idea of that happening to her son was overwhelming.

His mother spoke to his sister, feeling frustrated and flustered. Her only son was taken away for a war which she wasn't sure they would even win.

"It's not right Clara. How much has the German army progressed? Just because they want to beat the French, and the Belgians won't let them pass."

Clara sank into the plush armchair, her fingers gently caressing the soft fabric whilst watching her brother's every move. He intended to travel to Flanders on a troop transport that day.

She attempted to hide her fear. Losing young lives in the Flanders fields was overwhelming. Her brother didn't have a malicious bone in his body, and she loved him very much.

"Just keep your head down, and please return quickly, so we can finish the card game."

He smiled then.

"In order to beat me again, Clara? Why don't you re-enact the Flanders battle with my miniature lead soldiers, trenches and artillery pieces? Remember, there are even prisoner transports and field hospitals."

"No thank you. I don't really wish to think about it. They can stay in your room."

His mother approached and brushed down his jacket with her hands as he stood up.

"I don't much like this grey colour on you. It makes you look washed out."

He laughed at his mother, a typical comment from her.

"Thank you, mama, but it's not a fashion parade. Itchy wool though."

Clara carefully examined her brother's uniform, taking in the crisp lines and polished buttons.

"The pockets add a delicate touch to the front of the jacket. The red stripes on the trousers look smart. However, if it's warm, you may feel hot in that outfit."

Her eyes travelled down his form, noting the impeccable shine on his knee-high leather jackboots. He looked older than his years.

"Overall, not bad at all."

"I prefer the Stahlhelm steel helmet to the Pickelhaube

helmet. I think it gives better protection."

Clara paused, placing her teacup down on a side table, lost in thought.

"To think we were discussing classical literature last year, and now we are discussing uniforms and helmets."

Sad and concerned for her brother, she felt it was all so unfair. His mother's eyes welled up with tears as she pleaded, "Write to us, and write often."

So many young men were already returning injured or had died in battle in Flanders. His face was stern, and he tried to look confident, to hide the anxiety and terror he himself was feeling.

"Of course, mama. I must go now," and after giving both Clara and his mother Helga big hugs, he left their modest home, intent on being precisely on time.

Walking through the streets of Darmstadt, he passed Ducal Castle, a historic fortress built in 1568. It always gave him chills when looking up at its fortifications, a mixture of baroque and renaissance architecture. A magnificent building. He wished he could see the original moat. He loved local history, and his sister Clara over time developed both a love of classical literature, but also medieval history. He knew she'd become a historian one day.

One of the army transport vehicles passed him on his way to the pickup point.

"Hey!" he heard a familiar voice shout, "You are going the wrong way."

Smiling, he walked confidently, realising he was going the right way, and knew Klaus was joking.

He graduated from Ludwig George-Gymnasium, secondary school, and Klaus and he were best buddies.

He noted during basic training in the makeshift camp in Darmstadt, whilst learning how to march and follow commands, some recruits were as young as fourteen years old. The youngsters struggled to match the swift pace of the physical fitness training, with faces flushed and brows furrowed in determination. It was obvious the army was becoming desperate for more troops, whatever their age. They also received weapons handling, marching, and formation drills training.

The training duration varied, typically ranging from weeks to months. However, soldiers needed a minimum of a year's training or experience to be considered fully effective. He didn't particularly enjoy the training.

"Klaus, this is shit," he said one day with feeling when they'd experienced a difficult physical challenge. The Unteroffizier told them the importance of using their bayonets, which they attached to their Gewehr 98 standard rifles. The bayonet came with a 17-inch blade, and he showed how they should use it to kill their opponent by sticking it in their stomach or head. Soldiers considered it a critical piece of equipment.

"I can't do it," he said, disturbed by the thought of hand-to-hand fighting.

Klaus felt differently.

"Look, our fitness and weapon skills are crucial for battlefield success."

Looking at Klaus he made a vain attempt at sticking the bayonet in the straw dummy the army gave them to practice on.

"I would rather shoot them than stab them with a knife on the end of my rifle." He doubted his ability, even then. It seemed uncivilised and Neanderthal.

Klaus was a distinct personality type and approached the training with gusto. He attacked the dummy with a flourish, and he smiled at Klaus' level of enthusiasm. Klaus was a successful sportsman at school and continued his sporting pursuits at university. He possessed an engaging personality. They were total opposites, but perhaps that's why they got on so well.

"We must confront them in the trenches or in darkness. This is important."

He nodded but feared for their vulnerability in Flanders. He worried about the safety of Klaus, himself, and the young soldiers. Despite having few friends, Klaus was like a brother to him. In close combat, Belgian or French fighters would easily defeat the youngsters. He believed Klaus would fare well but was unsure of his own response.

He decided for the moment to use his bayonet instead to toast bread on or clean his shoes with. He lacked soldierly qualities. Reports of the awful conditions in Flanders, in- cluding trenches, mud, filth, and constant exposure, reached the training soldiers. He was particularly concerned about bombardments, machine gun fire and potential gas attacks, but he knew they were in this war together, and all they could do was train hard and do their best in every circumstance.

He and Klaus weren't involved with Flanders for very long. Their platoon moved to north-central France, specifically along both sides of the upper reaches of the Somme River.

"How much longer do you think we'll be stuck on the Western Front?" complained Klaus.

"You moan too much, Klaus. We've only just arrived at the Somme. Some soldiers have been stuck here for eighteen months."

"Yeah, well, I'm sick of the bombardment, it's endless," and as if to underline Klaus' point, another salvo of artillery shells came over their position in the trenches. This certainly wasn't the glorious type of war Klaus envisaged when he received his draft notice some time before.

Klaus felt separation anxiety from his two younger brothers and his sister. He constantly wrote home. It was an interesting turnaround. His outgoing personality grew subdued and quiet, whereas his friend seemed to come into his own. He maintained a sensible mindset and a practical approach to everything, remaining calm under fire. But was growing increasingly worried that Klaus was suffering from shell shock, as he noted his hands tremored regularly.

"Yuk, here comes the hard bread to go with our delightful, canned meat and weak coffee for lunch."

"Don't worry so much, Klaus, Falkenhayn, Chief Commander will see us right."

Another bombardment suddenly came over the trenches, showering them with dust and dirt. It caused a deafening roar and constant vibrations. The bombardment was continuous for seven days.

"These British bastards are trying to destroy the trenches and weaken our defences," Klaus muttered as he wiped the fresh dirt from his uniform, hair, and eyes.

He nodded.

"Yes, they are trying, Klaus, but I don't think they are succeeding. We're still here, right? Our concrete defences are holding."

"It's 1916, and I imagined a very different life from the one I'm currently living."

"Didn't we all, Klaus? Get your head down, now!"

The next day, the salvo of artillery bombardment suddenly stopped.

They were still secure in their trenches. The concrete defences protected them well, and there was a shout from one of their comrades, "Get ready. The British soldiers are advancing across no-man's-land."

He felt amazed.

"What? They are walking into our heavy machine gun fire. This is insane?"

Still secure in their trenches, they set about adding to the fire power raging against the thousands of British soldiers advancing across no-man's-land.

Klaus said breathlessly, "Stupid fools. They thought our defences were down due to their artillery bombardment."

He continued to shoot at the advancing soldiers. With the heavy German machine gun fire, it was like shooting fish in a barrel.

He shook his head.

"They are just walking towards instant death. This is a massacre!"

Klaus was shooting wildly. On the brink of insanity, he became unrecognisable from his friend.

"Don't feel sorry for them, they would shoot us if it was us out there. Think of all the friends and fellow soldiers we've lost so far."

He surveyed the surrounding trench. It was full of smelly mud, rotting corpses and rats eating the bodies who were once comrades.

Their uniforms were alive with lice, no matter what they did. Klaus spent the previous night trying to burn the lice in his uniform with a candle. Their bodies popped from the heat. The alternative, picking lice out of their uniforms by hand, was ineffective and time-consuming.

"This is for the Fatherland," screamed Klaus. Then he shot and reloaded as quickly as he could. The sounds of bullets flying around, heavy machine gun fire, shouting, and screams of pain deafened thousands of British soldiers as they continued to advance, only to face brutal and premature ends in their lives.

He sighed, picked up his rifle and shot at the advancing soldiers. He just didn't feel the same way as Klaus did.

I watched his face closely. It was obvious the memories from these battles were obviously causing him great pain and felt a strong sense of empathy for this man.

Returning from his musings he picked at the bedclothes, saying, "I was one of the lucky ones," his voice was fragile.

"In 1917, the British Army captured me, and I was imprisoned for eighteen months in Skipton, North Yorkshire. My English improved during captivity in the camp."

His eyes shifted to the window holding distant memories and wondered what he'd witnessed behind those barbed wire fences.

"I was well treated, but contracted polio whilst in the camp, causing my left leg to wither. It is a constant source of discomfort, a reminder of what was lost."

I felt a hot flush of pity. His vulnerability tugged harder at my heart.

"It is frustrating, as I cannot do certain things, and I hate to rely on others."

"Tell me more," I urged, "Your life journey?"

He hesitated, then spoke of Darmstadt, where he was born,

July 10, 1897, and his dreams of becoming a doctor.

"So, it is true. Born in Darmstadt means you are German."

He shrugged awkwardly and continued, "I achieved a degree in Chemical Engineering, from the University there."

"World War One." His voice wavered. "Countless lives lost. Good people gone. All futile. War..."

"...is futile." I finished for him.

I longed to hug him in that instant and offer comfort beyond the sterility of the hospital surroundings, but my professionalism held me back. Still, my heart reached out, feeling drawn to this man.

His black-rimmed spectacles trembled in his hands, twisting them over and over, anxious as he spoke. He was struggling to sit upright, exhaustion pulling him down. Laying back in his bed, he was completely depleted of energy. The tuberculosis took a vast toll on his already fragile body.

Patting his arm gently, I whispered, "Rest now. I will return when you feel stronger."

He closed his eyes as his head rested on the pillow, and I departed. The information he gave didn't seem on the face of it to add up. Only mentioning World War One, which had impacted on his emotions and body too.

The quality of the suit we removed from him upon arrival didn't match his possible background as a POW from the Second World War working on roads or fields.

Despite his attire, could he still be a political prisoner? He didn't sound or look Jewish and, having changed his clothes when he first came into the hospital ward, I noted he wasn't circumcised. Did he witness or participate in more horrific events during the war?

On leaving the hospital, I carried the weight of his World

War One memories into the hallway. His mystery clung like a shadow. I waited for him to feel better, eager to learn more about this puzzling man.

Chapter 11

THAT EVENING, I SOUGHT out my old pal, Andrew Potts, for a chat regarding the mystery patient. He was always a fountain of knowledge, especially on war related matters. A fabulous friend ever since starting at Little Bromwich Hospital, he made my nursing life much easier to bear.

The first time I ever met Andrew was typical. Exiting the new supermarket one morning, I physically bumped into him carrying tinned fruit, evaporated milk, a tin of beans, Daz washing powder and a packet of crisps. Dressed in my starched white nurse's uniform, I rushed out of the shop thinking of all the things I needed to do back at the Nurse's Home. Rushing everywhere was not unusual for me.

As I steamed out of the supermarket door, I rebounded off Andrew's muscular body, ending up on the stone floor of the street, having dented the tins, spilled the Daz everywhere, and squashed the crisps. I'd ended up on the floor, surrounded by all my shopping in various states of disarray. The scene was an absolute mess.

With his hands on his hips, the man looked down at me and burst into fits of laughter.

"My dear nurse, are you alright?"

I got to my knees, then he took my hand and drew me up

into a standing position.

Responding, I said, "I'm alright, but my bits and pieces are beyond help!"

Laughing, he said, "Come on, nurse, I think I owe you a drink."

He seemed a nice enough chap, so after dusting down the powdery Daz from my nurses' uniform, I followed him to the local pub. Over a shandy, he told me his life story.

Andrew was a senior officer in the Second World War, but the Germans shot him in the shoulder early on, which meant he could not use a firearm and received an honourable discharge from the army. Despite this, he continued to follow the war's progress with interest.

Imagine a well-dressed man, with dark hair and brown eyes, with a penchant for a fedora hat, which sat on his head Frank Sinatra style. Sporting beige slacks, the latest fashion, and a casual dress shirt, he cut a romantic figure. Handsome and smelling divine, wearing the latest aftershave, I guessed he was in his early thirties.

Andrew quickly informed me, so his invite might not be misconstrued, that he was both single and gay. He was open and shared the challenges he faced as a gay man serving in the army during the war. He'd very much kept his sexuality under wraps, as it was no-one else's business but his own.

"I just wanted my life to be mine, Nancy, without judgment. Why should I live in fear?"

Believing same-gender attraction was an illness, the Catholic Church did not support gay individuals. My relationship with God was personal. A 'lapsed' Catholic, I possessed more liberal views than the Church, and all that mattered to me was that Andrew was a good person.

"People can be very judgmental, Andrew."

Of course, I had experienced plenty of judgment myself from my family and the Church in Ireland, as my child had been born out of wedlock. So, I felt an immediate affinity with him.

We clicked, and he became one of my absolute best friends. meeting at the pub weekly to vent and solve the world's problems. I reflected on the missed opportunities for the female population as he was such a good-looking man, sporting a fabulous smile.

On this day, we met at the usual spot, the Custard House Tavern, nestled on Blake Lane. A pub, old and with a vast apple orchard and garden to the rear. It was a wonderful refuge for secrets and whispered confidences. Happily, I settled into my usual seat to share information on the mysterious man at the hospital.

As I explained the situation, Andrew leaned in with sharp eyes and said, "We can't establish the facts until we know this chap's name."

My frustration simmered.

"I know Andrew, and am fully aware of that, but he has shared some fragments from his past. I know he's German and lived in Vilnius."

The unknown story gnawed at me like hunger. What was he hiding?

"No paperwork means no verifiable identity. There is something afoot, but I can't quite put my finger on it."

Andrew's gaze held mine as I tried to explain more about the mystery man. I felt he had suffered during the First World War and wondered if he was a victim in the Second World War. Whilst explaining this, an intense feeling of dread and fear washed over me. There were the nightmares. Demonic visions which danced at the edges of sleep since the mystery man's arrival. Coincidence?

I decided not to mention the nightmares to Andrew, fearing he would scoff at me and dismiss it as imagination. He was so down to earth. Plus, there was no obvious connection between my nightmare and the mystery patient. I clung to reason as my heart raced.

"The patient is polite, Andrew, but unsettling. His general demeanour is one of deep sorrow, tinged with fear. Guilt maybe?"

Andrew's hand found mine, a steadying anchor. I felt emotional telling him and didn't understand why I was overreacting.

"He doesn't sound a threat, Nancy, but my ex-army colleague works within the repatriation department. If you could find out his name, then we'll know for certain."

Determined, I vowed to pry it from the mystery man's lips. My heart overflowed with gratitude for Andrew's unwavering support.

"Don't worry Nancy, we will unravel this," a conspiratorial smile played around his mouth. "Now, drink up your shandy. Isn't curfew 10 pm?"

I looked at my watch, panic seizing me.

"Oh, my word. Only ten minutes left to get back to the Nurse's Home. Take care Andrew, you are a superstar!"

I ran from the pub and hurried back to the Nurse's Home. The back door creaked loudly on entering, but I managed to reach my room without discovery. It was 10.05 pm, and had Matron spotted me, an absolute stickler for timekeeping, I would have been for the high jump.

Chapter 12

THE NEXT DAY, THE silence of the early morning enveloped me, with only the distant chirping of the birds breaking the stillness as I walked the short distance from the Nurse's Home into the hospital. Dawn filtered through half-drawn curtains, and continued down the main corridor to my ward, where iron framed beds stood in neat rows. A strong smell of disinfectant mixed with floor polish from the cleaners' daily efforts hit me as I advanced.

Within minutes of entering through the large wooden doors, Matron approached me with her graceful glide, her eyes filled with satisfaction.

"John's eating has improved, his coughing has reduced, and it's time to encourage him to get out of bed and take a short walk."

We still continued to call the mystery patient John. I was happy about his progress but needed more information about his background before allowing him near the other patients.

"Putting my fever training nurse hat on, Matron, it is not advisable to move him into the main ward yet. He may have a lingering infection in his lungs as he continues to cough and wheeze, although without any blood present. Enjoying some fresh air is a good idea, however."

She gave me a cursory nod of agreement and sped off. The sound of her brisk footsteps echoed through the hallway as she hastened to remind a junior nurse to deal with the neglected bedpans in the sluice room. Matron was a stickler for cleanliness, and rightly so.

In the main ward, patients, propped up on pillows, traced ceiling cracks with their eyes. Others sat having breakfast, their faces etched with pain or resignation.

I put my head cheerily round John's door.

"How are you feeling? I see there is some colour back in your cheeks. Shall we go outside?"

Eyebrows furrowed, he searched my face for a hint of a smile or laughter. Was it a joke? His head tilted slightly, eyes meeting mine, "Yes, please, Nurse. I am in your hands."

"My title is Sister Flanagan, not Nurse Flanagan. Please address me as such. It helps to maintain the hospital hierarchy."

"Oh, I understand hierarchy," and gave a wry smile.

"If I'm known as Sister Flanagan, what do we call you?"

The question hung in the air, but the response was disappointing.

He hesitated, then said, "Call me John. I am aware it's what you all call me."

Fidgeting with his bedclothes, I said, "Okay, if that's what you wish."

Why wasn't he prepared to share his real name? What was he hiding?

I left and returned with a worn but functional wheelchair.

"This looks so ancient, it could be from World War One."

"As old as me then," quipped John.

Smiling, I mentioned that the equipment, though not the

latest model, should do.

"Looks fine," said John with a grin.

"Wrap your arms around my neck. I can take your weight and will slide you into the chair."

It was an awkward moment, but I managed to move him into the chair without too much difficulty. He was lightweight, now just skin and bone, although less grey than a month ago. He covered over his withered left leg with his dressing gown.

"You must begin walking soon, John. Matron's orders!" I smiled.

"I will try, Sister Flanagan. Although, it is quite difficult to walk with my left leg, plus my right leg suffered some damage whilst riding motorbikes during the war. Walking can be very tiring, and I may need a walking stick."

"One step at a time, John. Don't worry, we will go at a suitable pace."

The wheelchair's squeaking wheels echoed in the corridor. The hospital doors swung open to reveal a serene garden, with vibrant flowers and lush greenery. It was a lovely day, bright, although not warm. The birds were twittering, and the grass was freshly mown, sending out a delicious recently cut grass scent.

"We will not try walking yet, as you are still quite weak. In another month perhaps."

Whilst moving his wheelchair through the flowerbeds along the patio, he sighed, "It's lovely to be in the gardens. Thank you, Sister Flanagan."

He was so polite. Formal somehow, but pleasant and appreciative.

"Can you answer a question for me please, John?"

I moved the wheelchair next to a wooden bench opposite

the flower beds and sat down.

He pulled the blanket tighter round his body in a self-comforting motion.

"That depends. I'll share what I can."

Looking directly at him, I asked, "Why are you here, in Birmingham?"

Instead of answering straight away, he said, "Here, Sister Flanagan," leaned down in the wheelchair, plucked a beautiful pink rose from the flowerbed, and handed it to me. Smiling, I took the rose and sniffed its sweet perfume.

"I wanted to meet my Polish friend in Birmingham who was there visiting relatives."

I put the rose in my lap again. It was such an unexpected gesture of kindness from him.

He continued, "Since he was in town, I decided to visit him. Train travel is enjoyable, so I went by train to meet him. Sadly, we never met up. After leaving the train station, I suffered a coughing fit in the street, and I collapsed."

I believed his narrative and hoped he wasn't deceiving me in any way. He seemed genuine, and his explanation was credible. Time would tell.

Sniffing the beautiful rose's scent, I indicated with my hand for him to continue. His romantic gesture touched me, and I felt butterflies in my stomach.

"I caught the earliest train possible from London to Birmingham wanting to surprise my friend and spend an entire day with him. Unfortunately, I was surprised and robbed by an opportunist when they saw me in difficulties. Unable to fight back; due to weakness. You know the rest of the story, Sister Flanagan."

I nodded in agreement whilst smoothing out my pinafore,

laying the rose on top of it. The lovely scent emanated from the rose petals, distracting me.

"So, you normally live in London? Yes, I know the rest, but the best news is your recovery."

A smile lit up his face, "I'm happy to hear it."

After half an hour of sitting in silence, with John lost in his thoughts, I said, "We have spent long enough outside for today, time to return to the ward."

Wheeling him back to his room, and gently guiding him back into bed, his eyes welled up with gratitude. The scent of freshly laundered sheets arose as I positioned him.

"Nurse Flanagan, thank you."

The way he said it made me draw in my breath.

I tried to lighten the atmosphere, saying, "Remember, it's Sister Flanagan, not Nurse Flanagan," and winked at him. "There is no need for thanks. This is what I do. It is my job."

The delicate petals of the rose he gave me, slightly wilted from the hospital gardens, still held a hint of their vibrant colour. It was such a kind action to give it to me.

He continued, "I meant thank you for listening to my story the other day."

I touched his arm and admitted, "Yes, it's your story, but I don't know everything. Who are you, John?" and looked at him dead in his eyes.

Watching closely for a reaction, his eyes were friendly but gave no clues. He gazed into the distance, as if observing a scene unfold before him. His expression became dark and brooding.

"Sister Flanagan, you're right. Stay patient for the rest of the story. I need time, and it won't be easy for me to tell it."

Without warning, I felt a chill seep into my bones and

a shiver of dread ran up and down my spine. The room's positive atmosphere turned gloomy as a shadow descended upon it. *What was John going to reveal?* I wondered.

I hoped it wasn't something awful. My gut feel was that he was a good man, but this continued reluctance to tell all gave me huge goosebumps and a negative feeling I was finding hard to shake.

"No problem, John!"

I spoke a little curtly and saw the hesitation in his eyes. Nodding at him, I motioned towards the door.

"I must get on now."

His unsettling revelation about his story left me uneasy. *Was I being played?*

After finishing my work in the hospital ward, I decided I needed to catch up with Andrew again. Not only to brighten my mood, but felt I unnerved by John's comments, and I wanted to keep him updated.

I dropped round to Andrew's flat and knocked on his door. He only lived ten minutes from the hospital. He sat me down with a cup of tea in his large, airy living room. It was such a beautiful home, which came as no surprise, as Andrew loved interior design. His flat was Edwardian, but he used its best features such as the gorgeous architrave and ceiling roses by highlighting them. It was cosy indeed.

"Andrew, have you heard from your repatriation friend?"

"Not yet," replied Andrew, reaching for a large chocolate biscuit, on top of a pile of biscuits perched on his best vintage china plate.

He crunched it quickly whilst continuing, "I understand the frustration, but he told me he was overwhelmed with prior obligations. Since 1948, several Germans have stayed in England instead of returning to Germany, as well as many other immigrants. Unless this is a person of some significance, we will have to wait for an answer."

I shook my head as he offered me a biscuit from the gorgeously decorated blue and gold china plate.

"His name is vital, Nancy."

"It's so annoying. John has spoken to me, and I think I will learn his name in time, but it's awkward. He took part in World War One, fighting on behalf of the German army, and lost close friends. He was based in Vilnius, Lithuania, but was born in Germany. He desperately wanted to be a doctor but studied an engineering degree due to financial constraints."

Then a brilliant idea hit me.

"He told me the British captured and held him as a POW in World War One. Surely, they will have a record?"

Andrew slurped his tea, smiled and laughed.

"Sherlock Flanagan, patience is key."

"I suppose so, but I'm fed up with waiting."

I flicked my hair in a frustrated gesture.

Andrew leaned forward in his chair and took my hand in his.

"Nancy, I've never seen you act this way about a patient before. Almost obsessed."

I snatched my hand out of his, not wanting to admit to having unusual feelings for this man. I was a professional through and through.

"Anyway, thanks for the tea, Andrew."

A wide grin like a Cheshire Cat's slowly appeared upon his face.

"Anytime, Nancy. I can see you are itching to leave."

"There are always errands to do, Andrew."

Hugging him warmly, I left and returned to the Nurse's Home. My life was always busy, but I liked it that way. However, I found my mind repeatedly questioning who John could be. *Was he a danger to me or anyone else? What secrets was he hiding?*

Soon, matron would permit him to mingle with the other patients. Could I allow that whilst not knowing his true identity?

The question continued to circulate in my brain, and I tried my best to go to sleep that evening, not knowing the rest of the night would create even more questions needing answers.

Chapter 13

BEING A WARD SISTER is a wonderful privilege and an honour, but you risk giving your heart to your patients. It is advisable to be as professional as possible, not become too involved and remain detached, but exceedingly difficult to achieve. Heartbreaking situations arise when connections are formed with children or adults who pass away. It's awful to witness the grief their loved one's go through.

It's easy to become attached to colleagues, as you experience working together for long periods of time, managing medical emergencies and handling life and death situations. Team players, always supporting one another, always aware of each other's strengths and weaknesses.

The deadly event which happened to one of my night nurses took me by surprise, evoking deep and lasting emotions, which I never wish to experience again.

As night fell, the ward transformed into a quieter environment, a smell of liniment and candle wax lingering. Patients snored, snuffled, and muttered in their sleep.

That night, Stella called me by telephone from the hospital ward. Handling night duty alone, she was responsible for patient care. It was unusual for a night nurse to call a Ward Sister out of normal hours, and the phone call woke me up.

The telephone's distant ring echoed through my drowsy haze, pulling me from a deep sleep. Grabbing a dressing gown, I staggered into the hall to answer it. She needed to navigate the telephone exchange and operator dialling to make the call, so it must have been important.

Stella was a newly qualified nurse, and in ways still finding her feet. She possessed a profound sense of humour and was well-liked by nurses and patients alike, always ready to help.

Despite appearing fragile and skinny, she proved to be one of the strongest nurses in the hospital when lifting patients in and out of bed. We worked together, effortlessly exchanging ideas and contributing to our tasks. I liked her very much.

Bleary-eyed, I answered the call, hearing a loud click when the operator connected us on the phone. Stella's voice was tremulous and shaky.

"Sister Flanagan, I'm quite scared and don't know how to explain this."

Her fear seeped through the receiver; a chill crawled up my spine. Stella's only company in the ward were the flickering lights and shadows which danced along the walls. Some nurses avoided night duty, but most took their turn on the night shift. I frowned with concern at the fear and tension heard in Stella's voice.

"What on earth is the issue, Stella? Don't worry about disturbing me. Is it a patient? Has something happened?"

Then, without warning, my gut tightened, leaving me feeling nauseous. A tiny fear took root in my mind, with a kernel of terror building in my chest. There was no real reason for it. Taking a deep breath, I tried to remain calm, waiting for Stella's reply.

"A dark shadow followed me around near the sluice earlier

tonight and made me jump. Doors opening on their own, items crashing to the floor when I have been nowhere near them."

Stella took a deep breath.

"Something unnatural is happening, even though it sounds like madness to say it. Do you think a ghost is haunting the hospital, Sister Flanagan? My eyes are restless, darting around, unable to find a focal point which brings me peace. Whenever I sit at the nurse's station, a shadow shifts across the room, and then a terrible smell follows it. As if something is rotting."

I couldn't believe what I was hearing. The evil presence which haunted my sleep. *Was it real? What was it looking for?* A crawling dread grew in the pit of my stomach.

"Stella, listen. Can you hear wings beating? Or see glowing eyes?"

Stella's laughter was brittle.

"Wings beating or glowing eyes? No, Sister Flanagan, just what I described."

Calming the gut-wrenching waves of anxiety I felt, said, "Stella, I'm teasing you. There are no ghosts in the hospital. The passing cars are playing tricks, making shadows. As for the rotten smell. Without wishing to be indelicate, Mr Jones, who has dementia, often has accidents, and doesn't mention them."

She laughed then and said, "Yes, Sister Flanagan, I'm just being silly. The dimly lit room casts eerie shadows that play tricks on my imagination, heightening my unease. It's nothing. I'm so sorry to have bothered you."

"I quite understand, Stella, but I'll come over anyway."

My foot tapped the floor in agitation as I spoke with her.

"No, Sister Flanagan, it's fine. Having spoken with you, I feel much better now!"

Stella's fear was contagious. *What if my nightmare had followed me to the hospital? What if it desired more than my dreams? Was malevolent evil beginning to engulf my life?*

"I insist, Stella, and can't get back to sleep now, in any case."

"Thank you so much, Sister Flanagan. I'm so sorry again to have interrupted your sleep."

I put the receiver down, my mind racing. Swallowing hard, I licked my lips which were dry with nerves. Hopefully, she wasn't encountering the unimaginable thing from hell I met in my nightmare. *What on earth was going on?*

Since it was an unofficial visit to the hospital, I didn't have to wear my uniform and quickly pulled on a pair of slacks and a top. A fresh surge of dread hit me, my heart pounding in my chest. The Nurse's Home was a quick walk from the hospital, and despite the late hour, I didn't mind the chilly weather as I rushed to reach Stella. It helped to wake me up.

Bursting through the hospital doors, the hallway stretched before me, its polished floors reflecting the flickering lights as I ascended the stairs. Turning the corner into the ward, I was taken aback by what I saw.

Stella wrestled a colossal creature, part beast, part demon right in front of me. One which defied adequate description. Similar but different to the beast I encountered in the nightmare, it was still grotesque, with red, not yellow glowing eyes, arms like a bear with long talons for fingers, cloven feet resembling a goat, and a large hissing snake draped across its body. Swishing its long-barbed tail back and forth, its body was a dark black colour, and I saw why Stella thought it was a dark shadow at first. Besides its eyes, it was as dark as night. She was wrestling valiantly with it to save her life.

Screaming, "Stella!" I ran at a fast pace towards her. The gigantic snake on this beast's body writhed and hissed, and sliding along its length, wrapped a large coil around Stella's fragile neck. Its eyes glowing crimson.

John, the mystery patient, stumbled and swayed as he navigated his way through the main ward. The beast had attacked and injured him. His face bore a criss-cross of angry red scratches, while a deep crimson gash marred the back of his head.

"Sister Flanagan," he tried to speak, but his voice was hoarse. With a raised hand, he exclaimed, "Stop! Don't approach her. Don't go towards the demon, Agramon. He's unstoppable, Stella is gone."

My heart jumped in my chest as I couldn't bear the sight of Stella, defenceless against this monstrous creature. This demon. *Demon*? I thought with alarm.

In my hysteria, I shouted at John, demanding action. He hit the alarm panel on the wall and the siren went off. The situation was beyond our control. Stella suffocated as the coil tightened around her neck, silencing her desperate gasps for air. I watched as she slumped to the ground as the evil being released the coil from around her neck. It happened within seconds of my arrival with no time to react.

Hearing the alarm, the beast uttered a deep, low, guttural growl and disappeared, leaving a swirling grey mist in its wake. The disgusting smell of decay left with it. I ran to Stella. The warmth emanating from her body was abruptly extinguished as the demon, Agramon, mercilessly squeezed the life out of her. Her pulse was silent, and her eyes vacant.

Dark bruising appeared on her neck. Pressing my fingers against her wrist, I searched for any sign of a pulse but found none. She was deceased. I was in deep shock, not believing what had occurred. The demon took her life, and we were powerless to stop it.

Patients woke up to the sound of the alarm bell. How they did not hear the commotion from the beast's attack in the ward was beyond me, but Stella didn't scream or shout, she was so intent on fighting the beast. Then, when it strangled her, she couldn't breathe to speak.

John's face showed long, nasty scratches all over it. He could barely keep his eyes open, his body was aching and begging for rest. His head bled from the deep gash on the back of it.

"The police," I stammered, my mind reeling, "I must call them."

After returning to his room, I saw John's body slumped onto the soft mattress, limbs heavy with exhaustion, completely spent. Stella was dead and the hospital walls whispered secrets darker than any nightmare.

I rang 999. We were lucky in Birmingham, with the best service available in 1953. The operator answered when a red light and klaxon sounded in her office.

"Stella, my night nurse, has passed away."

Struggling to speak, tears held back, I gasped and with desperation said, "Someone attacked a patient. Please send help."

A couple of minutes later, the operator put me through to the police.

"This is Inspector Barnes from the Birmingham City Police. I will be over straight away. Please don't go anywhere."

Whilst waiting for the police to arrive, I said a small prayer and placed a blanket over Stella's body. Hesitating to disturb her, I was mindful of the delicate balance between preserving the crime scene and shielding fellow patients from the distressing sight of her lifeless form. The fire alarm was jarring and unhelpful, so I went to switch it off.

Some patients were half asleep or lacked information when asked about the incident. They only started to wake up after the fire alarm went off. Seconds later, Stella was dead. No one else saw anything, only Peter, a hospital patient.

Peter told me he witnessed the incident. The way he described the beast was as a black clothing clad man. He was old and suffered from poor vision.

"When the assailant approached John's room, Stella called out to him, following him, asking who he was and what he was doing there? Startled, John emerged from his room to see what the commotion was."

"At that moment, the assailant attacked Stella, pushing her backwards, and she fell over. John struggled with him, and the assailant scratched his face, trying to grab him."

Stella's demise had devastated Peter. He said the attacker struck John's head with a large object, which John later revealed to me was the beast's barbed tail. Peter suggested the assailant hit John with a fire extinguisher. His eyesight was poor, and his bed was far away, a broken leg preventing him from helping.

I didn't see any of this, however. John had battled the demon, receiving a scratch on his face and a blow to the back of his head from its barbed tail prior to my arrival.

Peter continued, "Stella, went back to the assailant, trying to stop him from hurting John."

She was brave, and I wasn't surprised that she did this. A resilient person, it was sad the way her life had ended.

Peter excitedly continued, "John shouted, 'Nurse, look out!' and tried to get between her and the assailant, but the assailant put his arms around her neck, strangling her, and she fell to the ground almost immediately, ending up slumped on the floor."

It was at this point Peter saw me enter the ward.

"I saw you rush in, Sister Flanagan, but it was too late. The assailant fled the hospital through the double doors into the night."

My mind was reeling, experiencing an overwhelming mixture of emotions and questions. I threw my arms up in the air with anger, not knowing where to direct my angst, and tried to keep my composure, but repeatedly thought of poor Stella, and the suffering she had endured.

There was no family to whom I could explain what happened. Her parents died when she was young in a car crash. Images of Stella over the time she worked for me flashed through my brain. Her smiling face, her approach with the patients, her frustration with hospital bureaucracy. I saw so many images of her and couldn't believe she was gone; it was just unimaginable.

Was this to do with John? Stella intercepted the assailant in the main ward, preventing him from reaching his room. The mystery was deepening, and now someone I cared for had died. This was not good enough. I needed answers.

I wanted to see John and hear his side of the story. I was glad he survived, but deep down knew there was likely a connection between John and the incident. Something to do with his past had incited the attack. He knew who or what it was. *How was that possible?*

I entered his room and observed him.

"You look terrible John," I said.

He looked beaten.

"Not surprising really, Sister Flanagan," John mumbled.

"I think we need to patch you up," I said, examining his seeping wound.

I wasn't surprised to find his blood pressure was raised. He shook his head, then looked at me with tears in his eyes.

"I'm so very sorry."

At that moment, my temper got the better of me, unable to keep control.

"John, what the hell is going on? Stella is dead," and a lump formed in my throat.

"I know, Sister Flanagan, and am very sorry."

Fuming with anger, I composed myself in order to listen to John. He picked at the bedclothes anxiously.

"I suspected a link to your past. I sensed it and felt you were trouble, John."

My rage was evident to him.

"Sit down, please."

As I sat on the chair next to his bed, his face tense, he continued, "In 1941, I was involved with HKP (Heereskraftfahrpark) 562 and stationed in Vilnius, Lithuania."

Despite my reservations, I knew it was time to face this unpleasant narrative.

"Yes, you told me you were in Vilnius, but what was HKP?"

I crossed my legs and waited to hear further.

"After the outbreak of World War Two, the German Army drafted me. I ran the Wehrmacht engineering facility, which managed vehicle repairs in Vilnius, Lithuania. Under Nazi control, it became a forced labour camp."

His words faded off into the distance as my brain tried to compute what I was being told.

With menace I said, "You were in a labour camp? I assumed you were some sort of prisoner. You mean to tell me you were not a prisoner?"

Outside of his room, one patient was calling for a nurse, and set off their bed alarm. The medical staff quickly attended to them, so I returned to John's story.

Shaking his head, he said, "I created workshops, and convinced the SS to get the most productivity out of the Jews by keeping their families together. Giving out work permits to any Jewish man. They learned to repair the vehicles, and it was their best chance of survival. It entitled them, their wives and up to two children to be safe in my care."

"I don't know if I believe you," I whispered, traumatised by what he was telling me.

"You might be a German Nazi or Nazi sympathiser who murdered Jews."

I spat the words out at him, feeling another flame of anger in the pit of my stomach.

He looked down at the floor and started coughing, hacking, in obvious discomfort. Of course, I ran over with a towel and a bowl, my nurses training taking over.

After he gathered himself, he continued, taking the occasional deep breath.

"There were Germans whose behaviour I am ashamed of. It is hard to understand their mentality, but they followed Hitler. Believing in his hype, and a pure Germany."

He stuttered, "I did my absolute best to help as many Jews as possible. I made a deal with the SS in 1943, increasing the workforce from three hundred and sixty-four Jews to one thousand. By prioritising prisoner and family safety, I improved their rations."

I didn't want to hear the rest of the story. It was fantastical to me, and overwhelming. There were many difficult moments I encountered as a Ward Sister, but this was one I had never envisaged.

"I'm sorry. I must get a breath of fresh air."

Panting from feeling emotional, I needed space to think. Eager to flee from him, my stomach twisted with anxiety. I didn't know his identity, but he stood against England and their allies. He served the German Nazi regime, reminding me of the horrifying atrocities committed in their name. In that moment, I felt intense rage and experienced a strong desire to hit him.

"I understand," he said, his face dark with emotion. "Thank you for listening to me."

He lay back in his bed, quite exhausted from his explanation and the night's occurrences.

Before I left his room, I countered, "But this doesn't explain who or what attacked you tonight, John, or whomever you are."

Despondently he said, "There are still supporters of the Third Reich, Sister Flanagan, and they will enlist whatever help is needed, from whatever source is available to them."

"But it doesn't exist anymore, John, does it?"

"Despite that, there are still Nazis who endorse its ideology. You may not see them or hear them, but they are there. Martin Weiss is a perfect example of a wicked man. He oversaw the ghettos and camps in the region, murdering Jews in those camps. He is still around today, free, and without justice, having been served."

I observed fury and pain in his eyes.

"What attacked me and Stella tonight was a demon. The demon, Agramon. These demons infested the Nazis from the satanic rituals they held and made them twice as evil. They conjured the demons up," and I could hear the pain in his tone.

At hearing those words, I turned on my heel and left his room. My legs felt numb and shaky as I walked away. *Was he telling the truth?*

His explanation was strange and unexpected, to where I felt sick to my stomach. *Why did a demon attack John and Stella?* The demon singled out John, which was obvious. *What was the connection between Nazis and demons?*

With the war ending just eight years ago, the memory of Nazi behaviour remained fresh in people's minds. The carnage they created was mind-numbingly horrific, polluting the world with their evil.

In Ireland, there was mythology and folklore on demons, monsters, and evil entities, but was John making this connection up to hide his own actions in the war? *Did he commit war crimes?* I was so frustrated. Nothing made sense and I wanted to scream!

Stella, whom I took under my wing, was dead, and I needed to understand it. Hearing further nurse and patient activity in the ward, I hastened to assist my colleagues. Anything to rid myself of the shock I was feeling.

As human beings we all have a capacity for good or bad actions, it just depends as to whether we choose the light path or the dark path. We constantly have internal struggles whilst trying to navigate the 'right' path. I was not prepared to believe the Nazis were not responsible for their own actions. I know they were. Of course they were!

However, it seemed John was suggesting that demonic interference was playing on that pendulum which we all have within us, helping the Nazis to go so far into the darkness that eventually they fell into a murky abyss of evil.

I needed time to process the horrific event. It was all too fresh and raw.

Chapter 14

INSPECTOR BARNES ARRIVED AT the hospital, and we spoke at length. Polite and helpful, but I was in a state of shock, and I found it difficult to give sensible answers. As the Ward Sister, he was required to speak with me, as well as my being a witness to Stella's death. The hushed whispers of our footsteps echoed in the otherwise silent corridor as I discreetly led the Inspector towards matron's office.

My heart sank as I realised the rest of the nursing staff would need to be told about the incident. It was going to be stressful and heart-wrenching. Matron should be told first.

There was no quick message system in case of emergency within the hospital, only the slow telephone operator link. So, I asked Inspector Barnes if he was able to send a policeman around to matron's accommodation with a private message. He agreed, and one was dispatched. Sinking into matron's voluminous armchairs, we started to discuss Stella's background.

"Yes Inspector, it's absolutely true. She has no next of kin," I answered quietly, still in distress.

"Stella lost her parents in a car accident years ago and does not have any siblings. If she needed a reference at any time for anything, I vouched for her."

Trying to keep a clear head, I answered the Inspector's questions but felt traumatised. My cheeks were stained with a steady stream of tears, blurring my vision and making it difficult to see. Stella was dead, dead, dead.

Reaching for the box of tissues which matron kept on her large wooden desk, I saw her diary was open but chose not to read it. The Inspector looked at his notebook.

"It appears Stella was the unfortunate victim of a break-in."

"But who would break into a hospital, unless searching for drugs? The hospital's security guard is elderly, and he occasionally falls asleep at night. Stella didn't disturb him precisely because he's old. Perhaps interview him, Inspector?"

The inspector licked the end of his pencil and nodded, deep in thought.

"This isn't making any sense, Sister Flanagan. The hospital drugs were safely stored behind locked cabinets, ensuring their security. There would be no easy access. Am I correct?"

"Yes, you are correct, Inspector."

Whilst dabbing my eyes with the soft, white tissue, he continued, "We are confounded, to be honest. Do you have any idea if Stella had enemies?"

I vigorously shook my head.

"Not that I am aware of. Stella split up with her boyfriend, but I understand it was amicable."

The Inspector wrote 'boyfriend,' down on his notepad.

"What is his name?"

I furrowed my brow, searching my mind's filing cabinet for the elusive name, but it remained out of reach.

"One of the nurses, Gina, is a good friend of Stella's. Was a good friend of Stella's."

Oh, how awful to have to use the past tense.

"She will know."

"After speaking with Gina, can you let me know? Our initial thoughts are that this is a random killing. Not associated with Stella at all."

"Why do you think that Inspector Barnes?"

My body felt the aftermath of the night's events, and I shook uncontrollably.

He put his hand on my arm in concern.

"Are you all right, Sister Flanagan? I think you are suffering from shock."

"It's okay Inspector, I will have a sweet cup of tea in a moment to calm my nerves."

He nodded.

"Okay, well, as far as we can tell, she disturbed someone attempting to enter one of your patient's rooms."

My heart jumped in my chest.

"Yes, John."

The Inspector turned the next page in his notepad.

"Did you witness Nurse Lewis being attacked by the assailant?"

"Yes, Inspector. I rushed into the ward but was too late. Someone strangled her. Unfortunately, I missed getting a good look at them."

Stating Stella was strangled heightened the reality of the situation. The Inspector smiled solemnly at me.

"That concurs with the testimony of the patient, Peter Wells. It looks like both the patient John, and Nurse Lewis put up a fight. The patient, John, exhibits facial scratches and signs of head trauma. We have interviewed him, of course, but he is not in a particularly good state of health."

I fiddled with the pencils on matron's desk.

"He is recovering from tuberculosis, but he is not physically strong. It is hard to believe he fought anyone."

The Inspector shuffled his bottom on the armchair opposite matron's desk, large, but not particularly comfortable for whomever sat on it.

"From the evidence we've gathered, he tried to protect Nurse Lewis. She was eliminated by the assailant as she crossed his path. When the patient John managed to smash the fire alarm, that's when the assailant decided to leave. It saved John's life. What a pity it was too late for Nurse Lewis."

"This whole situation is gutting, Inspector," wiping my eyes again.

"John also explained what happened, and it matches what the patient Peter Wells said as well. The assailant was described as wearing a black coat, black gloves, and black balaclava. A useless description, to be honest, and it still doesn't answer the question as to why someone attacked them?"

"It is concerning for all, Inspector."

He sucked the end of his pencil, deep in thought.

"By the way, you haven't given me a surname for John."

I shrugged.

"We don't have details of his surname, Inspector. He's been too poorly with the tuberculosis. We call him John for simplicity's sake. I will obtain his full name and provide it to you later if that is acceptable?"

"No problem, Sister Flanagan. He's not under suspicion. It's just for my records."

The Inspector closed his notebook with a loud snap.

"I imagine your patients have many questions, Sister Flanagan."

Not wanting to face them, I wrung my hands in despair.

"What should I say, Inspector? I don't know what to say."

He stood up now, having finished questioning me.

"It is an ongoing investigation, but Nurse Lewis passed away and John was attacked. Sister Flanagan, their own safety will be worrying them. Reassure them there will be extra security at the hospital. We have officers stationed outside until further notice."

We left matron's office, and I guided the Inspector back to the hospital's exit.

"This is a serious situation, Sister Flanagan. One murder, but there could have been two deaths. We do not know why it happened, or even if they will try again."

"I will do my best to explain, Inspector, and keep them calm."

He left the building, and I walked despondently back to the ward, consumed by guilt that I was unable to protect Stella and save her. My heart and soul were endlessly sad. Such a nice young woman. This happening to her was unthinkable.

Matron arrived at the hospital then and I was so glad she was there. There was silence as I shared with her what had occurred.

Matron's words hung in the air, her voice filled with a mix of resignation and wisdom.

"Sometimes in life, we cannot explain what happens. It makes no sense. The Lord has a better plan in heaven for Stella."

"Yes, Matron," I whispered.

My emotions were swinging wildly from anger to sadness.

"She came to such a violent end, undeserved, and one we cannot explain."

Reaching for Matron's tissue box again, I pulled out another tissue. *I need to replace those*, I thought to myself automatically.

"I'm sure the police will uncover the answer to it all, Sister Flanagan," said Matron kindly.

I said with feeling, "If they don't, I will!"

My heart was breaking, and I intended to discover what had occurred at the hospital.

The police allowed the hospital staff to remove Stella's body and take her to the hospital's mortuary. *How was I able to move on from her death? How would any of us handle it?*

Hollow and defeated, I said a quiet prayer for Stella and retired back to the Nurse's Home for what was left of the rest of the night.

Morning approached in a few short hours, and I needed to face the staff and patients. I couldn't think of any answers for the many questions they were bound to ask. At that moment, it felt completely hopeless.

Chapter 15

THE STERILE WHITE WALLS of the hospital, and the smell of disinfectant, faded from my memory when I closed my eyes. Throughout the night, lying in bed, I tossed and turned, unable to get comfortable or go to sleep.

The vivid image of John's facial scratches and Stella's lifeless body haunted my thoughts. Having to inform the nursing staff and patients of Stella's death was shocking and wasn't sure if I could keep myself together in front of them.

John and I were the only ones aware the assailant was a demon which had attacked them. There was no easy way of explaining what happened to the staff and patients. Why demonic hauntings were occurring remained a mystery to me and John's explanations seemed nonsensical.

The next morning, arriving at the hospital, I felt sick. The taste of anxiety filled my mouth as I approached the nursing staff, my mind racing with worry. Cramming them all into Matron's office meant the patients couldn't hear me speaking to the staff.

They stood where there was space, sat on chairs and perched on Matron's large desk. The group received the awful news in shocked silence. Staff Nurse Wilkes said she felt unsafe being at the hospital, and many of the other staff members said something similar. The situation had unsettled everyone.

Wearing a calm expression, I took a deep breath, and tried to appear composed so the staff didn't panic.

"I cannot be one hundred percent certain, Staff Nurse Wilkes, but I believe us to be safe. The police have officers stationed outside the hospital standing guard, just in case the assailant returns. John foiled him, and the police think it is highly unlikely he will return."

There was a murmur among the group, desperate for reassurance.

"For the moment, please go everywhere in twos and be vigilant. For the coming week, I would like two nurses on night duty together, please. No one should be left alone."

I noted how sad and downcast they all looked.

"The hospital will host Stella's memorial service shortly after the funeral. It would be good if you could all attend."

Gina raised her hand, asking a question. She struggled to hold back her tears, so I handed her a tissue.

"Stella was my friend Sister Flanagan. We went out for drinks together often and I know her ex-boyfriend, Todd Dennerly. He is okay. Should I contact him about this?"

"He should be told, but you don't need to be the one to tell him what happened. The police wish to interview him, but not as a suspect. They will contact him shortly. It was a random act, in their opinion."

Gina lowered her head, pleased she was not the one to have to break the news to Todd. It was so raw and painful. I found it difficult to hold in my own emotions. Stella was so young, with such a wonderful future ahead of her. It felt surreal, as if her absence defied logic and reason.

Staff Nurse Wilkes spoke up then.

"Why was she attacked, Sister Flanagan? Why did Stella have to die? None of us understand."

Reviewing the assembled group, their faces wore such sorrowful and confused expressions, so painful to witness. Working closely in hospital together day in and day out, it was like losing a family member.

"We just don't know. The police are investigating the situation, of course, but it seems it was a random attack. Poor Stella was just in the wrong place at the wrong time. She was very brave, indeed."

Matron squeezed into her room and took over.

"I will speak to the patients, Sister Flanagan; You should rest now."

"Thank you, Matron,"

I was relieved as the situation had tired me out. Having been through the terrible experience of seeing Stella die in that way took a huge toll on my body. Reliving it each time, explaining what happened, was horrific. John had experienced two World Wars and saw close friends die daily. No wonder he was fragile in both body and mind.

"Right nurses. It's business as usual for the patients, please, and let's have no gossip."

The tasks and demands on us as nurses would hopefully numb the reality of the situation. I didn't want to feel any more sadness. Each person in the room exchanged a solemn nod with matron, filing out of her room, one by one, back to the hospital ward. It was a miserable procession.

Staff Nurse Wilkes said, "Should I look after him today?"

She was referring to John, of course. A determined expression showed on my face, as I politely declined Staff Nurse Wilkes' help.

"It's okay, Staff Nurse Wilkes."

"I thought you might want a break, Sister Flanagan," she stated with kindness, putting her hand on top of mine.

"It's best if I continue to look after John."

Resolute, I gave her a reassuring smile. In a way, I was claiming him, but only as a professional.

The exhaustion showed in my drooping shoulders and weary eyes, making it clear I was really in no condition to be of any help to anyone. However, I was determined to soldier on.

The next day, matron suggested I definitely take a few days off and visit my cousin, Patrick. We spent time together as children and, although three years older than me, I remained close to him. Prior to his calling to the priesthood, he acquired a motorbike and took me on rides to the countryside or nearby Slane town.

Chapter 16

ONE DAY BACK IN 1944, when I was younger, I saw a poster on the wall. A psychic fayre was taking place in Dublin, 5th May. I was sixteen then and asked mammy for permission to go. She was not keen, because psychic fayres were unpopular with Catholics.

"Ah go on Mammy, let her go," said Sean.

"She won't get into any trouble; it's just a few crystals."

"Mammy, crystals!" I exclaimed in excitement.

I regularly collected shells and bits of glass off the beach. The thought of having crystals was exhilarating.

Mammy gave in, and said she didn't mind me going alone now that I had reached a certain age. She liked us to have a level of independence.

The date for the fayre arrived and I headed off to Dublin full of hope and excitement. I rushed off the bus and looked for the Town Hall. That's where the psychic fayre was to be held. The entry was free, a pleasant surprise, and I looked around the hall.

There was a buzz in the place. The fayre itself was small but with a variety of stallholders all selling pagan gifts such as dream catchers, plastic unicorns, and a myriad of crystals such as Rose Quartz, Black Obsidian, Green Aventurine, and

Tigers Eye.

I approached a large stall in the hall's corner and looked at the Rose Quartz crystal on display. It was a pretty pink crystal, and I liked it, so I asked the stallholder why it was a useful crystal?

"Oh, my dear, Rose Quartz has a long history which goes all the way back to Greek mythology. You know Aphrodite, the goddess of love?"

I said, shuffling with embarrassment, "No, I don't know."

The stallholder tinkled with laughter.

"Aphrodite was the goddess of love. She cut herself by accident when trying to save her lover, Adonis. Their blood mingled together, and it stained the quartz. A subtle pink and rose quartz were born."

I laughed, shaking my head.

"Go on now, it's such a long tale."

"I consider Rose Quartz as a stone for beauty and as a symbol of love."

"Sure, it's not for me then," I smiled at her and walked away.

Moving further away from the lady's stall, I looked around. There was every type of book imaginable on wellness, the art of Reiki, energy, healing, medium ship, and psychic phenomena, but none of it interested me. I saw a stall selling silver necklaces with sprites and angels.

There were candles and incense to buy if you wanted to meditate. It would not have suited me, of course; I was always on the go, so the idea of remaining seated for a full ten minutes seemed unfathomable to me.

For a Catholic girl who attended church, I knew the Church frowned upon paganism. If paganism was demonic, then why was the spiritual community I met on this afternoon so open, welcoming, non-judgmental, caring and inclusive? I felt it was a misconception by Catholics.

I encountered tarot card readers, mediums, psychics, psychic artists who claimed they channelled art and drew loved ones who passed away. Healers, reflexologists, head, body, and neck massagers. I met professed druids who told me they went to Stonehenge for the Summer and Winter Solstices to commune with nature. It all seemed very exotic to me and exciting.

There was a stall with a dazzling array of crystals, reflecting the light in every colour. The stallholder had fashioned the crystals into all kinds of shapes and sizes: skulls, horses, or just solid blocks. I spotted an uninteresting crystal right in the corner, which was greenish grey. It was not pretty in the slightest, but its appearance made me focus on it and drew my attention.

The stallholder introduced herself to me as Mia. She wore a long black dress with a vibrant blue scarf around the neckline. A beautiful sapphire crystal necklace was draped over the top of the scarf, glittering, and twinkling in the hall lights. The necklace was ethereal and attractive, but I kept looking back at the greenish grey tiny crystal at the back of her stall.

Seeing me examine the crystal from afar, she happily declared, "This crystal belongs to you."

A classic sales pitch, I suppose, but it fascinated me.

"It is moldavite. Do you want to hold it? Careful, though, it is powerful."

She placed the tiny greenish grey piece of crystal into the palm of my left hand, right in the centre. It made the ends of my fingers on my left-hand tingle, and I felt quite emotional.

"This is tiny, but it feels heavy as it's resting in my hand."

"I told you it is a powerful crystal and has attached itself to you now. It is yours."

"Is it a crystal or a stone? I asked enthralled, hopping up and down with a high-pitched voice.

"Moldavite is a natural glass and is unusual because meteorite hits on the earth formed it. People call it the Holy Grail stone because it has an intense frequency and high vibration. It is why it is making your hand tingle. I know it as a transformation crystal. There is only one place on earth where this crystal is to be found."

"Where's it from then?" She had me hooked.

"15 million years ago, the moldavite crystal formed itself. An asteroid broke into two pieces. The two pieces hit the earth at such a high speed they spattered across the Czech Republic, Austria, and Germany. You cannot source this crystal easily. It is from out of this world."

"So, it's not from earth?"

I was incredulous.

"No, and it's becoming rare as stocks are in short supply, obviously."

Mia moved around to the front of her stall. A small audience was gathering as she got into her stride.

"People believe the stone has healing properties and helps you to discover past lives. It also helps to remove emotions and clear your aura of attachments from a previous past life. You should keep it with you and sleep with it under your pillow."

I didn't want to let the crystal go. I found it intoxicating, and it drew me to it, as if it was calling to me.

"It can bring you good fortune, and if you wear it close to

your heart, it will help you with love and relationships."

The tiny, unassuming, and unattractive crystal did something in my hand. It vibrated with energy and radiated heat all along my arm. I saw another woman showing interest in the moldavite.

"I will buy it," I said decisively, with a stamp of my foot.

Her eyes widened, and she said, "That's grand, then."

Then she told me the price, and I nearly fell over with shock. As I paid Mia, she leaned over and whispered conspiratorially into my ear, "But you know you are one of us, don't you?"

Her comment startled me, and she grinned when she saw my surprise.

"What do you mean?" I spoke.

She handed over the moldavite to me in the little velvet pouch as I handed her the money, but didn't answer me directly.

"Enjoy your crystal and remember it will bring you good luck and protect you. Keep it with you."

With no money left, I decided I might as well go home. I mulled over what she said. Her words echoed in my mind, me being 'one of them.' *What might she have meant?* I pondered.

From then on, I kept the crystal with me at all times. It was my constant companion. Shame I didn't have it on me when I had the abusive experience at eighteen. I didn't tell mammy about the crystal, knowing she didn't approve of such things.

The crystal pulsed with energy whenever it was in my hand, and I wondered what made it behave that way, but told no one. It became a comfort to me and remained my secret. I kept it in my pocket and put my hand over the pocket to feel it pulsing underneath. It helped me feel better in times of stress.

Chapter 17

THE WEIGHT OF STELLA'S incident continued to burden my shoulders, while the hospital's walls pressed firmly against my exhausted frame as I entered the ward the following day.

Checking in on John, I saw the back of his head bore a deep, jagged gash where the demon's tail had struck him, but it was healing under the gauze placed on it earlier. The red, angry scratches on his face would eventually fade into faint pink lines. Unfortunately, the gouges were deep, but I cleaned them well to avoid any possible infection.

Pale and fragile, but after everything he had experienced, he was recovering quickly, a resilient person. However, how quickly the deep wounds inflicted upon his soul would heal was a different matter.

Pulling up the chair next to the bed, I sat down and got comfortable.

"Tell me about your family, John."

Looking up, he said brightly, "There is Clara, my sister. But I have not been in touch lately and our conversations have been sparse. I lived with my mother and Clara in the early days of my marriage, but it became a battleground with intense arguments and raised voices. Clara did not get on with Isabel, my wife. Every day, they fought like cat and dog."

I put my hands in my lap and listened intently. John was telling me more than he usually did.

"When Isabel and I got married in 1933, she was twenty-seven, whilst I was thirty-six. A perfect age for having a child, Isabel desperately wanted children, a topic which should have been discussed prior to us marrying. The First World War suffering, with dead, maimed, and orphaned children, led to my decision to not become a father. The world's turmoil made it impossible for me."

His face reflected the guilt of that decision, but with all the trauma he had experienced, one could understand how he felt.

"She carried a deep-seated resentment for the decision and never came to terms with it. Isabel never forgave me for denying her motherhood."

Since my family and the Church denied my motherhood in Ireland, I empathised with how she felt. Hearing John was married; I felt a sudden flush of jealousy. Mentally shaking myself. John was in his fifties, and likely to be married. He took his spectacles off and twisted them in an agitated fashion.

"Despite the love for my sister, the arguments with Isabel created an unmistakable divide between us. Even worse, Clara left home without a word, and because of the sudden departure, my mother never forgave Isabel. However, I felt I was to blame for it all. Clara had agreed with my hesitation to have children, and Isabel resented her for it."

He looked at me with an unresolved sadness.

"I guess I will contact Clara, but I am unsure if she'll want to see me. Although she backed me against Isabel, I backed Isabel. What a mess!"

I tried to reassure John.

"At least she'll want to know you're safe. And what about Isabel, your wife?"

He looked away with sadness, and continued, "She died, Nancy, from tuberculosis. Isn't that ironic? She only lived for six months, passing away in 1945, as the Second World War was ending. My mother passed away not long after. Her body weakened as she battled liver cancer."

Reaching over, I took John's hand in mine. What a sad situation.

"I want to learn more, John," I said, curious, searching for his true identity.

He viewed me with surprise and ignoring the question remained silent, prompting me to continue, "What is Clara like?"

"She moved to Marburg, in Western Germany, a hundred miles from Cologne. A pretty place, with a hilltop castle, timber-framed houses, and winding cobbled alleyways. Very quaint. It has one of Germany's oldest universities, and she got a job there as a lecturer in medieval history.

"Gosh, what a clever lady," I smiled at John. A warm smile spread across his face in return, crinkling the corners of his eyes.

"Clara is an expert in medieval history and very passionate about the subject."

It was clear he was proud of her. Then his face changed expression, becoming more serious.

"She studied the history of paganism of the Middle Ages, where sorcerers worshipped the devil and offered sacrifices. Fourteenth century demonologists mention these events in their writings. Some pagans moved from worshipping God to worshipping the devil. She is exceptionally clever and has a thirst for knowledge, especially regarding Satanism."

The comment irked me, and I removed my hand in irritation. He knew I saw the demon attack him and Stella, so he brought up demonology because Clara was an expert in the occult, knowing I did not wish to discuss it. Was there a link between Clara and this whole situation?

"You might like Clara, Nancy. A woman with shiny brown hair, light brown eyes, and a warm smile which lights up a room when she enters it."

"Did she ever marry?"

The need to learn everything about this man persisted. I was relieved his wife was no longer alive. Was that wrong of me?

"Clara came close to it once, Nancy, but her studies were her priority. She travels all over the world looking for information on satanic rituals, spells, potions, and witchcraft relating to medieval history. Marburg's skyline is adorned with majestic medieval churches, a testament to its rich history. It's no surprise she's settled there."

Clara sounded an intriguing woman. I craved his sister's approval, but why? I wanted her to like me because I liked John.

"I am going away for a while."

He nodded. "Of course. It's understandable, Nancy."

His eyes sparkled mischievously as he asked, a playful smile tugging at the corners of his lips.

"But where to? I'll miss your sweet voice dearly."

But I couldn't respond lightly.

"Stella's funeral is tomorrow, followed by the memorial in the afternoon. It will be a sombre and upsetting atmosphere.

The other nurses have come to the realisation that any of them could have died in the same way."

John nodded, "Yes, that's true, Nancy."

"My cousin Patrick is a priest. We were close as children. I have decided to visit him in Bath. He'll bring me immense comfort."

John nodded gravely, stating, "They organised the funeral quickly."

"Stella has no family. Matron took it upon herself to arrange and coordinate it all. She's been marvellous. Funeral attendees will include hospital staff."

"Should I attend?"

"John, please come to the memorial. Nurse Wilkes will assist you in the wheelchair. It's only right you pay your respects."

"Of course, I will. Enjoy meeting your cousin, but I will miss you," he said, touching my face with his hand.

Smiling at John, I felt uplifted, both at his affectionate gesture, but also from knowing I would see Patrick soon.

The next day, Stella's funeral loomed. It was a canvas of sorrow, with soft sobs and sniffles from weeping individuals echoing around the church. Todd, her ex-boyfriend, came to the funeral and brought beautiful flowers, making me cry even more when I saw them. At the memorial in the afternoon, I gave a eulogy for Stella, telling the group what an exceptional person she was, her humour often seeing us through busy and challenging times.

John, true to his word, attended the memorial. Arriving in a wheelchair, he was cared for by Nurse Wilkes.

The severity of what happened lingered, casting a shadow over my thoughts as I grappled with the possible connection to John or even Clara. There were so many unanswered questions. I yearned for respite from the pressure and the pain.

Chapter 18

AS THE TRAIN PULLED away from the station, the decision to go to Bath, fully supported by matron, to leave the hospital behind with its haunting memories, gnawed at me. Visiting Patrick for some well-earned relief from the trauma of Stella's demise was a wise decision. There was no doubting I needed it.

Patrick was a cousin with whom I maintained a deep bond ever since our childhood. Seminary life consumed him, the sacred teachings and ancient texts substantiating him as a man of faith. Patrick entered the Seminary at twenty, when I was seventeen, soon to be eighteen. If only he had stayed home, I wouldn't have tasted the bitterness of regret after the abusive incident with Jimmy.

He didn't yet know about my nightmarish experience with a demonic visitation but was aware of my psychic tendencies from an early age. He certainly knew I was a lover of animals and able to heal minor injuries, seeming to communicate with them easily. But the psychic abilities were always a positive for me before the demonic experience occurred.

Booking a room in a small inn near Bath's parish church was a delightful discovery. The place lived up to its description of being quaint, cosy, and welcoming.

Speaking to Patrick on the telephone, we were immediately transported back to a time of giddy teenage jinks, enjoying a carefree life. Time passed quickly, and I was now twenty-five, and he was twenty-eight.

"Any nice apple trees in your area?"

I couldn't resist teasing. His laughter danced across the telephone line.

"Nancy! I expected you, as a nurse in a serious profession with big responsibilities, would have changed."

I laughed, twisting the phone cord round my fingers in excitement.

"Don't worry, Patrick, I stay within the rules now." "Glad to hear it," he chuckled.

"I miss those crazy days, though. They were so simple." "I'm looking forward to seeing you, Nancy."

"See you tomorrow at 3 pm," and I put the receiver down back in its holder.

Settled into my cosy room at the Crescent Inn, I felt an unexpected unease. The lingering spectre of a demonic attack, a nightmare which etched scars on my psyche, made it difficult to find solace in unfamiliar surroundings. Only thoughts of Patrick, my childhood companion, offered any semblance of sanity.

Despite my restless night, I lit some scented candles, as there was no way I could sit in the dark and managed to drift into slumber. The following morning, I embarked on the short journey into Bath. The city's blackened walls stood as solemn witnesses to the bombings which ravaged the town in 1942. Yet, amidst the remnants of destruction, the Royal Crescent remained untouched—a beacon of beauty and resilience.

Walking towards St John's church, it looked majestic. The

towering spire reached high above the city, commanding attention against the backdrop of the skyline. Built with aged stone and weathered wooden beams, a standing relic of the 1800s. Patrick felt proud to belong to a historic church in a historic city.

As a new priest, acceptance by his flock was important to him. It was unusual for someone of such an early age to receive such an elevated level of responsibility within a large diocese.

Finding the way to the Parish office, gold letters on the door pronounced, 'Father Patrick Flanagan.'

As I knocked loudly, he said, "Come in," and I pushed the door wide open. The scene which confronted me was unexpected. Having assumed Patrick would rush towards me for a massive hug, instead I witnessed a shattered man, and I stopped dead in my tracks.

"Patrick," I whispered, my voice strained, "What's happened?"

From a large, battered armchair, he looked up, struggling to focus.

"Hello, Nancy," he murmured, "I'm so glad it's you."

The silence stretched for a few minutes, and I puzzled over the lack of movement.

Eventually, he said, "I can't see Nancy."

His words lingered, and time stood still. The pain of Patrick's physical state sliced through my heart.

"Since when? How?" I stuttered, my voice cracking with emotion.

Bending down, I pulled him into a desperate hug.

"I'm so sorry," the words tumbled out as Patrick sat there, and I absorbed the scene.

"How am I going to explain this to you, Nancy?" he said, shaking his head.

Patrick was as close to me as a brother, and any pretence of professional nursing behaviour vanished.

As I sat on the edge of the armchair, ruffling his blonde hair, he explained what had happened. How could such a young man be blind? His bright blue eyes stared off into the distance.

"Lock the door," Patrick requested, his voice trembling, "I don't want anyone to disturb us."

I got up and twisted the key in the lock.

"We're safe," settling back onto the edge of the armchair. Goosebumps prickled my skin, and my heart fluttered. *What was he going to tell me?*

Then, as I held Patrick's hands in mine, the reddened skin and blistered patches I saw on them were shocking.

"Patrick, your hands, are burned?"

He nodded. "They don't hurt any more, not now anyway."

Turning his hands gently over in mine, I said, "Were you in a fire? What has happened?"

Patrick's voice quivered as he spoke. "Nancy, part of the Catholic Church, deals with deliverance and exorcism. Deliverance looks at the whole person and their needs for healing of heart, soul, and body. It aims to bring freedom from all forms of demonic oppression. Exorcism is whereby God confronts demonic oppression in an individual. We address the demons, take authority over them, and force them to leave. As an ordained parish priest, the bishop asked me to help with deliverance."

He then explained that a young parishioner from his church, Robert, stopped going to church, drank too much, and was abusive towards family and friends. He was a lost soul, and his mother reached out to Patrick for help.

"Youngsters sometimes join the wrong sort of crowd, Patrick. It doesn't mean the devil has affected him?"

He emphasised with his finger, "When I visited Robert, he was out, so I asked his mother for permission to search his room. The room's dimly lit corners housed unsettling statues, while inverted crosses and occult symbols adorned the walls, confirming to me the need for deliverance or perhaps an exorcism. As priests, we closely observe an individual's physical appearance for any signs of distress or unusual behaviour. Those struggling with mental health may display unsettling demeanours, resembling a haunting presence, so we have a process to determine which situation it is."

Discovering my cousin's battle with the occult was both surprising and macabre. Did this connect to me because we were close? *Was this linked to John?* Or did the demonic attention relate to my difficult past, and being 'bad?'

"Patrick, how did you burn your hands and damage your eyes?"

"A demon harmed me spiritually, not physically, Nancy."

Concerned and confused, I looked at him, feeling flummoxed.

"How can a demon damage your eyes spiritually?"

With my nursing background, this was a puzzling concept. I turned over Patrick's hands, studying the deep burns.

"My hands may carry scars as a record of the fight with evil. I don't know if they will improve."

His eyes stared through me, the pupils not appearing to react to light as I held my hand over his eyes.

"Although my sight is impaired, I have faith that my vision will return."

He couldn't see, and looked the wrong way, believing he faced me.

"Have you received a medical opinion, Patrick?"

I was so worried.

"No need, Nancy. I understand the demon's motive and the solution for my recovery."

"Really?" I felt frustrated.

"Belief in the power of prayer will save me," said Patrick.

He explained further. On returning to Robert's house, he advised his mother should burn all the satanic objects, including books and art.

"Once her son's room was rid of all the satanic items, I needed to deliver him from the evil which was permeating his life."

As Patrick retold the story, it was unbearable. He was such a good person; he didn't deserve to be injured.

"I carefully gathered each item, arranging them neatly inside a bag. Until I located Robert, I couldn't exorcise his demons fully. Hexes and curses had attached demons to those objects. He must have taken part in demonic rituals involving sacrifices, most typically animal sacrifice. It was a stronger and more powerful evil than I first imagined."

"So, what did you do?" I asked, worrying even more now.

"I went to the forest where his mother said Robert vanished to every night. The flames danced and flickered as I tossed the items into the crackling bonfire. As I cast them in, a heart-rending ghostly scream emanated from the flames. Rather than purifying the objects and casting out the evil, the scream summoned a more malevolent spirit."

I anticipated Patrick's words before he spoke. I knew it deep in my gut.

"It attracted Azazel, a genuine force of evil, in fact said to be Satan's head demon. Whilst holding a picture of a red and black pentagram, a flame shot forwards and struck my hands, burning them."

My eyes widened in astonishment as Patrick vividly described the menacing demon, its twisted horns and fiery eyes mirroring the nightmare which haunted me. With wings on its back, red skin, and yellow glowing eyes. I shook my head, swallowing hard, remembering the grotesque creature which appeared in my room.

"The air carried a pungent scent of sulphur. The demon said in a low growl, 'I am Azazel, tremble before me.' His tail whipped round towards me, striking my face and eyes. The pain was overwhelming, and I lost my sight. Agonising pain shot through my hands while my vision blurred. The acrid scent of burning wood and smoke assaulted my nostrils, making it hard to breathe, but I managed not to fall into the flames. God saved me when I remembered the special prayer which rejects evil."

I give my will, purpose, future, my whole life to God. I take my stand with God against all sin, all evil and every kind of demon.

It agitated Patrick, recounting what happened to him, and it was terrible to see him so upset.

"I was blinded, Nancy, and then I felt a blast of stifling air as Azazel flew past me and disappeared."

My face showed how flabbergasted I was, although Patrick couldn't see it.

"I cannot believe this has happened to you and must tell you something important. But first, tell me, what happened to Robert? How long ago did this all happen?"

Patrick shrugged.

"It was only a week ago, Nancy. The day after this incident, Robert went missing. He is considered an adult at nineteen, so the police will not recognise him as a missing person, but his mother is distraught. When I'm well, I'll hunt him down and rid the world of the evil manifesting in him. I believe now he's fully under a demonic possession."

Then I told Patrick Azazel was the same demon which had appeared in my nightmare.

Now Patrick's face showed total astonishment.

"Nancy, you should have told me sooner!"

"The dream I experienced, Patrick, started off as a dark, haunting scene, but gradually transformed into a vivid, ethereal visitation. It was terrifying."

I explained further to Patrick that John was attacked, and Stella sadly died at the hospital. He felt horrified and was unsure how to respond.

"Nancy, you've faced hardships as well. I never realised."

Nodding in agreement, I said, "We have just held the funeral and memorial for Stella. Not only have I been sad and needing a break, but I also looked forward to seeing you, but this?"

I was so disheartened by his condition.

"Do you think it's interconnected? These happenings have only occurred since John first appeared at the hospital."

Patrick tried to convince me he was going to be fine, but I was dubious. He gained strength from his faith, and I admired him for it. Particularly as my faith in the Church was wavering. I still believed in God, a higher power, a divine creator, just not religion itself.

"Turning back to the subject of John. What is the link between us, Patrick? Why are demons going after us? I just can't fathom a reason why."

He felt intrigued and said he wanted to meet John.

"Maybe I can work it out, Nancy. The connection?"

I nodded, saying, "There must be one. You know I've always experienced psychic visions. We talked about them when I was a teenager. You never told me it was my imagination, unlike mammy."

He gesticulated with his hands, saying, "Look at your abilities with animals, loving them and caring for them, Nancy. You have something special."

I told him then of my desire to care for him and help with his healing.

"No, Nancy. I am a priest, so you cannot stay with me."

"I am a nurse, Patrick, and I will care for you. I will arrange lodgings for both of us at the Inn. It is picturesque, but more than that, it's comfortable."

He smiled, knowing I wouldn't budge.

"Okay, Nancy. We will see. I have spoken with the bishop. He advised me to take time off, pray daily and promised to add me to the Catholic Prayer Line."

"What's the Catholic Prayer Line?" I said, bemused. Even having been brought up a Catholic, I hadn't heard of this.

"It helps Catholics to pray for anyone who needs help. You don't need to know someone to pray for them. The power of prayer is immense, Nancy, I promise!"

He was a kind soul and this situation happening to him of all people was completely unfair. I was overwhelmed and needed time to process it all.

Chapter 19

LOST IN THOUGHT, I WAS STARING out of my bedroom sash window at the Crescent Inn in Bath, contemplating life's rapid changes. Each day was a whirlwind of activity. As the Ward Sister, chaos brought me solace until recent inexplicable events disrupted my world.

A demon murdered an innocent junior nurse at the hospital, and I would never forget the chilling sight of her lifeless body. The weight of grief and disbelief suffocated us all after Stella's death, in a place normally filled with care and love. It was an open, festering wound, which refused to heal.

Trusting my instincts, I believed John held the key to events, and I was determined to uncover the truth, even if it meant pushing him harder for information.

Patrick needed peace and quiet. So that evening we went to my lodgings. The landlady welcomed us, eyes curious but discrete. I investigated Patrick's room. It was fine, bigger than my own room. The door closed behind me, sealing us in from the outside world. Making sure he was comfortable, I bid him goodnight.

He lay on the sofa, falling asleep almost immediately, although restless. Returning to my room, I endured an emotional, sleepless night, suffering a maelstrom of sadness and anger. He was my primary concern. Vivid images of us running through fields, smiles wide and carefree, played on my mind. There was never any interest shown by Patrick beyond friendship, but also, I believed he received the calling to the priesthood from a very young age.

Looking back, I remember seeing the excitement in mammy's eyes as she spoke of Patrick's acceptance of the seminary, her voice filled with pride. Patrick was an altar server and sang in the choir at weddings and funerals. With an angelic voice and face, it foretold his path as a priest.

Losing a best friend was difficult, but I was happy for him. I remember going round to my aunt's house, where he sat in the lounge on his own, curled up, reading a book.

I bounced over to him, "Hey, you, I've heard the news!" He looked up, put his book down, and smiled at me.

"Hello Nancy. Yep! I am going to be a priest."

I gave a mischievous smile.

"But all the local girls in Navan will be heartbroken, Patrick."

He laughed, "I do not think so, Nancy. Anyway, I got the call to follow the priesthood, and it's what I want."

I settled onto the comfy sofa, sinking into its soft cushions beside him.

"When are you going?"

Sadness flowed through me, and I felt downcast.

"I am off to the Seminary in Dublin next week. No time to waste."

He seemed happy and excited.

"I will miss you, Patrick."

He ruffled my hair, and there was genuine concern in his eyes.

"Nancy, I won't be a million miles away!"

I was seventeen when he left Navan. If only he stayed longer, but at least our bond survived the chasm between friendship and faith.

My thoughts returned to the present moment. It was now the next day in the afternoon, and I returned to Patrick's room to check in on him. His health concerned me. Without a medical opinion on his eyes, I'd push for assistance if there was no improvement. Patrick, once vibrant, now fragile, stirred from his slumber on the sofa.

"Hello sleepyhead!" I whispered.

"Hello, Nancy. What time is it?"

Stretching his arms over his head, a yawn echoed through the room.

"4 pm, Patrick."

"Is that the time? I have slept so long," he said, shaking his head.

Leaning towards him, I whispered, "Any change in your eyes, Patrick?"

He squinted. "I am not too sure. The blurriness seems slightly reduced, but honestly, it's still hard to tell."

"We will take things easy. However, we need to speak to John. The reason may become clear after a discussion on why demon Azazel is stalking us."

Fully awake now, he sat upright.

"I understand, Nancy. So, you know, Azazel is the leader of the Grigori, fallen angels who married mortal women and produced a line of monstrous children called Nephilim. Nephilim, some claim, are giant beings. They are warriors. It's claimed they exist, living in underground caves."

"Yippee", I said, "More monsters to worry about!"

He smiled at me.

"John's sister, Clara, is a well-versed scholar in paganism and demonology. Do you think she could be the catalyst? Has she provoked the underworld? John mentioned the demon which pursued him was Agramon."

"Agramon is the demon responsible for fears and phobias. These attacks are meant to frighten us."

"John knew the name of the demon. We must unravel the secrets he's hiding."

Patrick scratched his head. He was calm.

"Nancy, I know it sounds incredible, but God will protect us. He beat Satan before. We will banish the Grigori, the Nephilim or any other entities."

My skin crawled at the mere thought of it all. Once Patrick was dressed, we left the cosy bed-and-breakfast, the land-lady's confusion trailing behind us. He leaned on my arm, his hand light on my shoulder. Despite eye troubles, he didn't appear blind to others. Taking a taxi, it skilfully navigated us through the busy traffic.

I put my hand on Patrick's arm.

"It will take time, Patrick, to get back to Birmingham."

He seemed resigned to the journey.

"No matter, Nancy, I am still tired, and will sleep on the train,"

Sleep like a baby he did, whilst my thoughts and worries and concerns kept me wide awake the entire way. The rhythmic sound of the train's wheels on the track was soporific, but my mind raced ahead, and I wasn't able to nod off.

Pulling into the train station at Birmingham after the journey from Bath, my body felt shattered. Patrick had enjoyed a dream free and refreshing sleep, making me envious.

Scrambling to obtain another taxi, I left Patrick hanging onto a lamppost. After several minutes, a black cab stopped and scooping him up, we got in. A small hotel near the Nurse's Home seemed the best choice for Patrick's overnight stay.

"Sorry, Patrick, no men allowed in the Nurse's Home, even for a priest."

He laughed aloud.

"It is fine, Nancy. I will try and remember my church exorcism guide. It is important for me to focus my thoughts on the details."

On arrival, making sure he felt safe and comfortable, I guided him to the bedroom.

"Nancy, please stop fussing, will you?"

He gestured a little impatiently.

I hugged him briefly, saying, "No worries. Let's meet tomorrow after breakfast at nine o'clock."

He waved me off, saying, "Go on, Nancy, the taxi's waiting."

I shouted back as I left, "Sleep well!"

"You too Nancy, goodnight," responding mechanically, his mind preoccupied with the demons.

Hurrying from the hotel to the black cab which remained outside, I thanked the cabbie for waiting.

"Where shall we go next, Miss?" the driver said, a little impatiently.

"Just the Nurse's Home please," and gave the address.

He tutted, "It's just round the corner, Miss, within walking distance."

"Walking alone at midnight doesn't appeal to me."

He nodded, "That's true Miss, I get your point."

The imposing brick building of the Nurse's Home loomed

before me as the cab pulled up to the entrance. After paying the cabbie, I entered stealthily through the heavy metal back door, aiming for silence. The door closed loudly, but the noise was minimal.

Hesitant to bump into anyone and answer awkward questions, I hurried to my bedroom. As soon as I entered, I left the light on, just in case, collapsed onto the bed, and pulled the cover over me. I was still wearing my clothes.

Within seconds, I lay motionless, limbs sprawled, eyes closed, sleeping the sleep of the dead.

Chapter 20

THE FOLLOWING MORNING, I returned to the quaint hotel, its walls adorned with faded floral wallpaper which whispered secrets of bygone days. With the air smelling of freshly brewed coffee, my stomach rumbled. The breakfast room, bathed in soft morning light, held an air of anticipation.

Patrick sat near the window; his silhouette etched against the pale curtains, eyes, once haunted by the recent encounter with Azazel, now held a quiet resolve.

Taking the seat opposite, the wooden chair creaked in protest. Patrick's gaze met mine, resilience etched into lines around his eyes. Those eyes once saw the otherworldly, divine, and malevolent, but now they were blind to the physical.

"Patrick, you got to the breakfast room alone?"

His lips curved into a half-smile. "Yes, Nancy. This situation won't get me down. God is with me."

Patrick's faith was impressive and unwavering, despite the darkness which clawed at his soul.

Leaning forward, doubts swirling, "This terrible experience with Azazel. Has it affected your faith in God?"

Patrick's gaze shifted to the window, where raindrops danced on the glass. "No, Nancy. It has deepened further. God called me—sometimes out of life's worst tragedies comes something better, silver linings."

My teacup beckoned, its warmth promising solace. I filled it to the brim; the liquid scalding my throat as I drank it down, hot and stimulating.

"The blindness is temporary, Nancy. At least I hope so. The Lord has kept me safe overall and I am not frightened."

The hot, sweet tea gave me instant relief.

"Thank goodness we're back in Birmingham. The hospital ward will be awake now. We have questions that need answering."

My voice lowered.

"I'll take you to meet John once I feel completely safe in his company. I don't want to encourage any further demonic interference if it's connected to him, as you're vulnerable whilst your eyes heal."

Patrick's frustration showed, "I understand, Nancy, but think we should meet soon."

As if on cue, the toast arrived—two cold slices, their edges brittle. I devoured them, the crunch of echoing urgency. The tea fuelled my determination, and I pushed back my chair.

"We'll find answers," I promised.

Advising Patrick I would return as soon as possible; I rushed out of the door. When I arrived at the hospital, the scent of antiseptic lingered, mixed with a faint hint of disinfectant and fresh laundry. I saw some of the nursing staff and mentioned my holiday. Then I checked in on John.

Surprised, John set aside his book as I peeked through the door.

"Nancy, no nurse's uniform today?"

"I'm on holiday, but wanted to see how you were?"

"Staff Nurse Wilkes has been kind, but it's very nice to see you."

Was I blushing? Surely not. It was because I wasn't in my uniform and felt exposed somehow. My uniform was my professional armour.

As we chatted, John expressed a desire to go out for a drive. Feeling happy he was doing well; I was uncertain if he should leave the hospital yet. Although beating his illness, he still seemed fragile.

He wanted to meet up with his Polish friend, Father Novak, in a neutral setting. Perhaps he could shed some light on John's background? John couldn't go alone because of his poor health.

Although not there in an official capacity, I moved around the room, tidying up various hospital items, unable to stop myself. Once a nurse, always a nurse.

"Matron is the person I need to ask, John. There is a hospital minibus which goes into town. No doubt you can manage the drive into town and back, but with support. You are recovering from tuberculosis, and you are supposed to have complete rest."

"No," he said, locking eyes with me, "You need not come."

John would not discourage me from going with him, figuring his friend might answer some of the many questions which John seemed reluctant to answer, such as his real name. Remaining steadfast, I confirmed this was his only option.

"You've been in the hospital for two months, mostly resting in bed. We've only been able to take you into the garden. After what happened at the hospital with Stella's murder, and your near demise, it's important to have someone by your side for support and reassurance."

I saw his expression.

"I repeat, it's not negotiable, John."

John's voice was intense as he spoke, pointing his finger, leaving me in no doubt.

"If I need you to leave, you must do so immediately. Is that clear, Nancy?"

I laughed, shaking my head, and said, "That's very dark, John, and ridiculous!"

The atmosphere grew tense, as if a heavy weight had settled upon his shoulders. He was obviously concerned for his safety, and by the sounds of it, mine as well.

My voice was soft and measured, as I spoke with a deliberate tone to prevent any escalation.

"Okay, but your behaviour seems out of character. Is this related to the demonic attack?"

He looked flustered.

"I will explain to you in more detail later, Nancy."

I wouldn't leave him if something serious happened. Of course not. John lay back in his bed.

"I know you do not understand the demonic situation, Nancy. I need to keep you safe. Remember, we are dealing with dark forces, and they are unpredictable."

It was nice to know he cared. My own feelings of care were growing beyond what was required as a nurse. Subconsciously, I knew I was taking a deeper, more personal interest in him. Leaving John's room, I eagerly approached Staff Nurse Wilkes to let her know I was willing and able to take John into town.

"I don't mind since you are busy on the ward."

She smiled and mentioned we should check with matron first but thought it would be fine.

Chapter 21

HAVING OBTAINED MATRON'S PERMISSION, I helped John into a wheelchair from his hospital bed and wheeled him out to the hospital minibus. The hospital had equipped the minibus with sturdy ramps and secure seating, ensuring the comfort and safety of the patients. Helping John onto the ramp, I seated him at the back, freeing him from the wheelchair, as he was still so lightweight and fragile.

The scent of fresh air and distant fields wafted through the open windows as we picked up speed in the old minibus. After fifteen minutes, the vibrations from the engine reverberated through the seats, heralding our imminent arrival at the centre of the town, as Harry, the driver, worked his way down through the gears.

I glanced at John. He occupied the rear seat of the minibus. "Are you quite secure there, John? It looks awkward?"

John's face lit up with a wide smile, mirroring my own. The sudden jolt of the minibus caused John to reach out, clutching the seat in front of him for stability.

Harry the driver shouted, "Sorry all, I was trying to avoid a gigantic pothole in the road!"

"No worries, Harry," I said, laughing, "Just try to keep us in our seats, please!"

Glancing back at John, I said, "I'm so sorry. Harry here likes to think he's a racing driver."

"I'm hanging on," he said, and smiled at me whilst shifting his leg.

We reached the centre of town, and the Minibus dropped us both off at the Italian cafe in Denbigh Road, Bordesley Green.

John stood up as upright as he could, taking his first steps without relying on the wheelchair. His head was healing, and the scar from the demon attack was improving. His hair covered the scar.

I had brought a wooden walking stick with me from the hospital. In John's hand, it appeared an elegant addition. Despite a hunched stature, he maintained the dignified air of a true gentleman.

We approached the coffee shop, with John taking small steps. His friend was outlined, sitting in the window. The coffee shop was an excellent choice by Father Novak. It was interesting that John agreed to meeting with Father Novak without checking if he could leave the hospital, such was his determination.

Father Novak dressed himself in a dark black suit and a clergy collar, which was bright white against his ecclesiastical suit, a more practical choice than a cassock. Older than John, he possessed the brightest shock of white hair I have ever seen. Sitting with a confident demeanour, I could imagine him in front of a large congregation giving an engaging sermon.

It took me aback when John first told me his friend was a Polish priest. I grew up around nuns and priests during my childhood, but it surprised me a soldier and a priest would be such good friends. Even more so when you realised that Father Novak was Polish, and of course, during the Second

157

World War, the Germans invaded Poland.

On entering the coffee shop, there was the gentle chatter of customers and a hiss of the espresso machine filling the air. It was Italian in style, with a lovely ornamental gold and red décor, and looked to be offering the most delicious coffee and pastries.

I guess Father Novak chose this Italian coffee shop because there were individual booths for us to sit in, and we wouldn't need to worry about being overheard. The owners had covered the seats in a bright red satin, and in front of us were two round wooden tables. The wall at the back displayed vibrant paintings depicting rolling hills, vineyards, and charming villages of the Italian countryside. I wished we were in a faraway place now, away from the recent traumas. We missed the sunshine on the dull and overcast day.

A strong whiff of brewed coffee greeted me as I sat down opposite both. I introduced myself as John's health worker, and Father Novak said, "Oh, I hear you are much more, Sister Flanagan. John tells me you have worked miracles to get him back to such good health."

I leaned over and shook Father Novak's hand, smiling at him whilst saying, "He's still got a way to go, but I do my best, Father."

"Are you a Catholic?" Father Novak enquired in a direct manner.

He fixed his gaze upon my face, awaiting my answer.

"I was brought up a Catholic, Father, but wonder why you ask?"

The forthright question from the priest surprised me. Just then, the server approached us, asking if we were ready to order. We told her, and the server brought the drinks quickly over to us. I watched as John savoured the dark richness of his black coffee with two sugars. Father Novak chose tea with lemon, and I wanted breakfast tea. Being Irish, a tea drinking habit was ingrained.

"Father Novak collaborates with Pope Pius XII and wants to check on your level and depth of commitment to God."

I went red as I used to be a practising Catholic, all thanks to my mammy, but the exhausting nursing shifts left me too tired to attend church on my only day off, Sundays. I felt guilty, but I was powerless to change the situation. Since being outcast from Ireland because of my illegitimate baby, I didn't feel in step with the Church and became a lapsed Catholic, with no desire to return to its teachings.

Father Novak leaned forwards and patted me on my knee, which I found to be a little patronising. His wrinkled face softened with a reassuring smile, his eyes filled with warmth and compassion.

"It's alright, Sister Flanagan, I can see you do not have time to attend the Lord's house. If the Lord is in your heart, you pray and try to follow his teachings, then it is appropriate enough for the Catholic Church."

"Thank you, Father," I whispered, a little overwhelmed at this benevolent, but intimidating, priest.

Patting my knee and telling me I was a good Catholic, although I did not attend church, was irritating. I didn't want his approval or that of the Church and maintained a private relationship with God. After that, it was difficult to feel at ease.

Why was it so important to Father Novak whether I was a Catholic or not? Was John a Catholic? It seemed like some sort of test. Father Novak continued throughout to call him

John. Getting frustrated, I decided it was time to delve deeper into John's identity and background. Exasperated, I looked at both Father Novak and John.

"It's time for the truth. Don't you think?"

There was tension in John's eyes as he shifted in his seat. The sound of my heavy sigh revealed to John my dwindling patience. I hoped my determination for the truth wasn't damaging the friendship which grew between us.

Father Novak, feeling my annoyance, looked at John.

He said, "I trust Nancy, Father Novak. Unaware of the complete story, she only knows segments of my life, such as my presence at the camp in Vilnius, but not my role."

"Alright. I think, Bruno, I think you had better explain the situation to Sister Flanagan. It is crucial she comprehends it and understands the risks we face from the demonic interference involving the Nazis."

I turned to Father Novak, "Please call me Nancy."

I did not want him to feel he needed to be formal. Father Novak nodded. He looked at John, urging him to respond.

At last, I knew his real name, Bruno. I waited for further explanation, feeling a wave of anticipation. Particularly regarding the demonic interference.

"I was in the labour camp in Vilnius, Lithuania, but as the Camp Commandant. My name is Major Bruno Siebert."

His voice resonated with authority as he stated his full name. I was at a loss for words and recoiled in horror. Recalling the haunting stories of atrocities committed in the camps, the taste of bile rose in my throat. How could I reconcile the friend I treated in hospital with the evillest of individuals who oversaw so many deaths? Father Novak comforted me with a touch, recognising my expression of disgust.

"Nancy, hear him out, please. He is a decent man."

I nodded, although when I swallowed, there was a lump in my throat. Hearing this was disturbing, and I couldn't bear looking at him.

Bruno's voice continued, heavy with emotion.

"Nancy, let me clarify, I wasn't a Nazi, but served in the German Army. Amid challenging circumstances, I directed my efforts towards safeguarding workers and ensuring they remained outside the Ghettos. I ran the camp, and I exaggerated the skills of the Jews and their expertise in the automotive industry to save them. Each worker possessed a yellow work permit. The SS issued the certificate."

He looked up at me, and he could see my concern.

"The permits covered them, their wives, and up to two children. Families who didn't receive a certificate sometimes handed over a child to a one child family asking them to add them to their certificate pretending they were a family member, to save their life."

I nodded but felt overcome. Crossing my arms, I viewed him with suspicion. Was he different from the person in the hospital, the polite gentleman? Was I deluded all this time, thinking he was a respectable person? I gritted my teeth to hear more but first needed the answer to my question.

"Was this a concentration camp, Major Siebert?"

My voice was accusatory, unsure of my feelings, as I sat across from a German soldier who fought in bloody battles for his country.

"Nancy, it was such a dreadful period. I feel a tremendous level of guilt. Hitler's war machine was irrepressible, and very cruel. The camp in Vilnius was not a concentration camp, but a forced labour camp. The Nazis were still brutal. When

I recount these stories in peacetime, they seem even more repulsive, and to think I was part of it."

He shook his head in shame. My stomach was nauseous in revolt and my skin felt like something was crawling along it. I underwent a sense of fear, too. My movements became still. I took a deep breath.

Bruno sat next to Father Novak on the satin cushion of the booth, but when he explained in depth, leaned forward towards me with his head resting on his hands.

"I listened to the fervent speeches and chants but distanced myself from the Nazi party because of my disagreement with their racist ideology. The Jews were people, not animals. What was the reason for the Nazis mistreating them? I was in the German army, not the SS. I needed to act, yet it required careful handling from within."

As Bruno recounted his experience, I moved as far away from him as possible in the booth. It was a natural, physical reaction to what he was telling us. Father Novak studied my responses to Bruno's explanation and looked concerned, but also thoughtful.

"With clinical and thought-out precision, the SS dehumanised the Jews. The Nazis used them for general labour and removed the community leaders and younger males. They thought through how to transport, kill, and dispose of the bodies."

I noted how sad and downhearted Bruno looked whilst telling his story. Despite his association with the German army, it was clear Bruno was troubled and slowly, bit by bit, I began to feel less antagonistic towards him.

"There was a strong antisemitic feeling among the local Lithuanians. I was aware from the time the Soviets occupied Lithuania; the locals felt Jewish society had supported the Soviets during those two years. Nazi Officers called upon Lithuanian volunteers to conduct killings within death squads."

My eyes widened in shock and disbelief as I heard this, my head shaking in utter horror. Unbelievable and tragic; the locals joining in the killing spree. Sounds of laughter drifted over from a table nearby where two women sat drinking coffee and eating pastries. Their behaviour was jarring and incongruous, juxtaposed to the tragic tales I was hearing. They say ignorance is bliss, and in this case, they were right. I wished I could join them in blessed ignorance.

"In 1943, the Jews tried to build a resistance group to upset the German apple cart. None of my workers were involved, but we heard about it. The Jews faced quick and severe retribution, unable to resist for long, lacking military experience. They followed academia or scientific pursuits or were religious. The Jews lacked resistance against the Nazis."

Drawing in a large breath, absorbing what Major Siebert told me, the enormity was difficult to comprehend. Tears welled up in my eyes. Taking a handkerchief from my pocket, I dabbed at them.

"Workers escaped into the forest. The SS threw the remaining work detail members into a shed. The Nazis burned them alive as a punishment for the other prisoners escaping. I was not involved in this crime."

"There were one thousand prisoners, including families, in my camp. I weighed the Jewish workers to guarantee they got enough nutrition and built bathhouses for them to have baths twice per week. The SS were intent on starving them, so we bought rations from non-Jewish co-workers. I turned a blind eye to the illegal food market."

Was he telling the truth? It seemed unlikely, but here he was, sitting with a Catholic Priest, who Major Siebert said supported the Pope within the Vatican. He must be telling the truth. Major Siebert took a deep breath and a sip of his drink. The recounting of this history was wearing him out.

"Do you need a break? You look pale."

I placed my hand on his forehead, checking his temperature. He felt clammy to the touch.

"No, the burden on my mind feels like a heavy weight, dragging me down. I want to tell you the entire story."

"I think he's alright, Nancy. He needs to explain everything to you," said Father Novak.

He touched my arm reassuringly.

"I travelled to Kaunas and Riga to secure workers for the camp, visiting the Wehrmacht headquarters and SS administrative offices. Sympathy or empathy was of no use, only hard financial facts. The Wehrmacht needed the Jews to work on their vehicles. There were spies and informers everywhere. Somehow, I kept the peace."

He looked sad as he stated, "There were terrible Nazis. In 1944, Martin Weiss from the Gestapo supervised the removal of children from the camp. I was not there that day. The Nazis took the children to their deaths. He was such an evil man. The pain and suffering of the families in the camps will forever remain lodged in my memory."

Bruno's face as he recounted his experience was haggard and withdrawn. It cost him emotionally to go through it with me.

"The Gestapo and Lithuanian Police dragged any child up to the age of sixteen to the departing trucks. They seized the children by their feet and swung them into the back of the trucks, where they smashed their heads and bodies."

"Mothers refused to leave their children on their own and went with them to the trucks. Parents blocked from passing through police lines screamed for their children. The terrified children screamed back at their mothers and fathers. The situation was hideous. Only a dozen children escaped this terrible event."

Clamping my hand over my mouth, I cried out. The story the Major told was pure evil. I couldn't imagine what those poor parents went through losing their children. Certainly, I knew what it was like to lose one, although under different circumstances. I felt a combination of distress, anger, and sorrowful emotions.

"They must face consequences for their actions, Major Siebert. Whatever the circumstances, there is no excuse for their heinous behaviour. If you were involved, you should face retribution, as well."

Maybe I was blunt, but the subject called for it. I felt too awkward to call him Bruno, but in the light of his confessing to being a Camp Commandant, I couldn't think of him as my John anymore.

"The families mourned the loss of the abducted children, leading to unrest in the camp. The devastated parents of the murdered children were jealous of those children who escaped and their families. Parents whose children did not survive often asked, why should your child live and my child die?"

"Martin Weiss, the evil man who orchestrated and participated in the atrocities, remains possessed by demons. One prisoner told me as the Nazis took her child away; the child's mother screamed at Weiss that he was a murderer. He removed his pistol from his holster, eyes black. Looking her in the eyes, shot her in cold blood."

I looked at him, astounded.

"You are claiming demonic possession?"

"He is telling you the truth. Demons are real," said Father Novak with some volume.

I looked around me, not wanting anyone else to hear our unusual conversation.

"Father Novak, I am aware demons are real. I saw one in a nightmare, but it's difficult to accept the link to the Nazis. There is no excuse for the Nazis' appalling behaviour."

He shook his head, saying, "No-one is suggesting forgiveness, Nancy, not at all. God will judge them, and they will go to hell. We just want to remove their demons and free this earth from their continuing evil. They must not be allowed to further harm others."

Bruno said, "Free will is a God given right for every human. They make choices which determine their fate. We are here to safeguard the freedom of choice from demonic interference."

He appeared unwell, with a visible grey pallor on his face.

"Do you need a drink of water?"

He said, "Thank you, Nancy, but I want to get to the end of this."

I heard the soft footsteps of the server. She asked if we desired more to eat or drink. We said not now. It was clear she wanted to clear the table and get us to leave. It was past 5 pm.

Realising Major Siebert needed to finish telling his life story, I went back to her, requesting more tea. She looked unimpressed but scurried away to organise it.

Despite prior knowledge of the Holocaust and its atrocities, hearing first-hand accounts from a participant was both astounding and gruesome. Major Siebert reluctantly took part in the Nazi war machine, striving to assist workers, but I was unsure of my feelings. John's character was hard to reconcile with my newfound knowledge.

Were he and Father Novak making excuses for the actions of the Nazis, which was inconceivable. Was he trying to cover up his own shortcomings? Were they saying demons infested all the Nazis, the whole sorry lot of them? Their actions undoubtedly required consequences.

The murky depths of depravity humans could reach were unbelievable. Inwardly, I prayed for it never to happen anywhere in the world again but in no way could the Nazis be forgiven for their actions, whether or not they were drawn further into the darkness by evil temptation.

Chapter 22

THE SERVER BROUGHT THE TEA with an angry expression. I thanked her, confirming we would not be too much longer. The cafe was empty, only we remained now. She cleared away the other tables and cleaned around us instead.

Bruno tapped his fingers on his empty coffee cup, lost deep in thought. The cosy atmosphere of the coffee shop continued to be a soothing refuge from the jarring descriptions of pain and suffering.

"In 1944, we heard the Russian Army was to liberate Vilnius. The Nazi High Command forced me to tell the workers they were no longer under my protection and were moving to the West. SS Oberscharfuehrer Richter stood there as I gave the speech. The workers understood the veiled threat, and the tension in the room was palpable. Having heard stories of the Nazis' mass killings of Jews in other Lithuanian camps, they became frightened."

"That was a risk insinuating the prisoners were unsafe with the Nazis in your speech, Major Siebert. It was courageous," I said.

He bounced his good leg under the table nervously.

"The SS guards caught those who did not hide under portable toilets or in roof spaces. Unfortunately, five hundred workers turned up at roll call the next morning. The Nazis took them to Ponary, North Poland, and slaughtered them. We could only save a dozen children out of the entire camp, and continued to hide them until liberation came."

The stories were depressing and painful, so I stroked my hair in a comforting motion.

"I worked so hard to keep the workers and their families safe, and they were so close to the Russians liberating them. All my accomplishments were in vain, merely postponing the inevitable. That guilt and shame will stay with me forever."

He sat with a slumped posture; head hung low, and I used the handkerchief from my pocket to wipe away yet another tear. Unable to fully catch my breath, I found it difficult not to burst into body wracking sobs. Many horror stories emerged after the war, but he vividly conveyed the devastation of those times. A feeling of sadness tinged with anger rose from within me, and I wondered if Major Siebert did enough to help the poor prisoners in their time of need?

In the cafe's corner, I saw the server staring, and wiped my eyes quickly, not wanting her to overhear the private conversation.

"The Gestapo tore through the camp looking for the remaining hidden prisoners. They hunted down family members, including women and children, and were indiscriminate, wanting to exterminate everyone. Those they discovered were immediately executed in the camp courtyard situated behind building two. Their remains are still there today."

In the dimly lit cafe, Major Siebert's frustration and sorrow hung heavy in the air. My gaze shifted to Father Novak, who had bowed his head in prayer. As Major Siebert poured out his heart, I handed him a fresh handkerchief, its fabric crisp

169

against his trembling fingers. The tears fell silently, and I felt the weight of his pain, wanting to wipe them away, but the gesture seemed too intimate.

Major Siebert's voice cracked as he recounted the story, raw emotion etched across his face. The room closed in, suffocating us all. That moment made me realise the experience was a deep wound in Major Siebert's soul. He was resilient, but the painful memories threatened to consume him.

"Two hundred and fifty prisoners remained hidden in the camp until the Russians came. The Nazis had to leave. Following the Nazis' departure, Poles came to loot valuable items at the camp. The Russians bombed the area, and the prisoners ended up in Polish bomb shelters, but at least they were free."

He sat back again, looking weary.

"I left with the retreating German army but surrendered to the American Army in the West. The British and Americans put me on trial in 1947. As you said, Nancy, the court should punish me for my part in the camp. However, many prisoners testified positively that I was humane. The court exonerated me from blame, but I won't ever get over what happened."

My heart warmed as he truly was the John I knew at the hospital, but suffering from major stress. Thank God, as I didn't want to admit it to myself, but I had developed feelings for him at hospital.

Exhausted in every way, he declared, "I have morals and empathy for all, regardless of their religion," and collapsed back onto the satin cushion in the booth.

The double life he led daily caused a moral dilemma. The person on the inside knowing that what the Germans were doing to people was evil, and insufferable, but the person on the outside having to portray himself as a senior officer of the Wehrmacht, ready and willing to obey Hitler's rules. This internal conflict broke Bruno's spirit and mind. What he said next took me by surprise.

"This story continues to haunt me, Nancy, and may affect you as well. When I said the demonic infestation of Martin Weiss was real, I meant it. The demon residing within him was part of a legion of demons. I saw their demonic ways; I came face to face with such evil manifesting itself in the Nazis daily."

His impassioned statement took me aback and hit me like a gut punch.

"Do you think perhaps you are just saying this because it's so hard to believe human beings can be so degenerate in their behaviour? The demons are not an excuse for the Nazis' actions."

"No," he said vehemently.

"Nancy, you do not understand. I saw demonic symbols scratched on the walls and floors of the camp by the camp guards, such as pentagrams. The Nazis committed horrific, ritualistic killings of prisoners without boundaries. They sacrificed men to the devil whilst speaking incantations, wearing dark cloaks, and getting together for meetings late at night. The Nazis, driven by their sinister ideology, willingly welcomed the presence of the devil into their midst."

Father Novak stared, watching my reaction to Major Siebert's background story.

"My sole purpose in life is tracking down these demons. On my way to meet Father Novak, a demon-infested man attacked me, wanting to kill me. There was murderous intent in his eyes. Thankfully, a woman alerted a police officer about the man, who promptly pursued and summoned medical aid. My mission and beliefs have endangered me for a while, but I am determined to succeed."

Gripped by his explanation, I craved further knowledge, yet a part of me sensed an ominous future for myself.

"Father Novak is someone I knew before the war and he is a long-time friend. The outbreak of war came between us, when Germany invaded Poland, but after the war I realised Father Novak was the ideal person, as a demonologist, to join forces with. Our aim being to cleanse the Nazis and to rid the earth of evil."

Father Novak patted me on the arm as if to confirm it. "I have experience with exorcisms and can eliminate evil from the earth."

Was it true the Nazis were incarnate demons who followed the devil's guidance? It added another layer to the sorry story. Patrick and I encountered our own demonic incidents, so I was at the very least willing to listen.

"Bruno and I have united to eliminate the Nazis' demons, offering redemption but not forgiveness. Our incentive has been the evil perpetrated by them on the Jewish populous. If you meet our very dear friends whose families were part of the Holocaust, you will understand our motivations to do this."

Their upright intentions impressed me, but I believed only those who experienced the Holocaust should comment. I fidgeted, shifting in my seat, avoiding eye contact. The conversation was taking an uncomfortable turn.

"Neither Bruno nor I are Jewish, but we empathise with their suffering, and by removing evil from these demonic souls, we aim to eliminate the future potential for pain and suffering from this earth forever."

* * *

I continued to struggle with fathoming the idea of demons infiltrating the Nazis, but a childhood memory flashed before my eyes. My mind drifted back to my childhood when I sat in the kitchen in our home in Ireland, my legs dangling from the wooden kitchen chair, the scent of freshly baked bread filling my nostrils, listening to the soft lilt of mammy's voice.

"Father McKenzie believes in spirits, Nancy."

"No way, Mammy."

She sat by the fire recounting the story to me, whilst I was eating a piece of her delicious soda bread. I was fifteen years old.

"Yes, child. According to Father McKenzie, there are things in heaven and earth which remain unknown to us. He saw spirits, both good and evil. The devil is everywhere, and so is his army. It's important to say your prayers every night, like a good Catholic girl. The Lord keeps us safe."

"But why does he believe in them?"

She sighed loudly.

"Because he suffered an attack, Nancy. Returning from a parish visit one night, an assailant hit him on the head."

"Just a possible robber, Mammy."

"Ah no, it wasn't. The devil possessed the attacker, Nancy, and told Father McKenzie the very same."

Pondering mammy's story in bed that night, I said my prayers, asking God to keep me safe, and deliver me from evil. My thoughts wandered back to the present day and Bruno's story.

I queried with him, "But there were executions of war criminals, and others sought refuge in countries in South

America. There are no remaining Nazis, are there?"

"They are not Nazis anymore, Nancy, but both demons and Nazis. We will not rest until we remove every demonic influence from the world. My German nation became infused with evil, and all Germans will rightly live with the guilt of the Holocaust for generations. The suffering intensified by these demons motivates me to seek justice for their victims."

His eagerness was clear, but I struggled to grasp his message. My brows furrowed in confusion.

I countered, "It might be a case of mental illness? Ending up brainwashed and crazed by Hitler's power trip, finding enjoyment in killing rather than being infested by demonic influence?"

Bruno sighed. He realised he wasn't convincing me entirely.

"Nancy, I can only advise you from personal experience. Dark shadows in my room, voices whispering to me, telling me about my forthcoming downfall and, of course, the man in the street attacking me, and then later at the hospital as well."

Feeling angry, but unsure why, I asked, "What makes me interesting to them? Can you answer me that?"

His eyebrows raised in query.

"Perhaps because you are associated with us, Nancy. We represent the light to challenge the darkness, and they wish to frighten us to stop us."

Then he shrugged his shoulders, confused by my opposition.

"You experienced a demonic attack and saw the demon murder Stella. I know you did. Why deny their existence?"

The faint sound of porcelain rattling filled the air as my grip tightened on the teacup I was holding. We were both becoming annoyed.

"I'm not denying their existence, Major Siebert. It's diffi-cult for any normal person to accept demons are everywhere and had infested the Nazis. Yes, I know the Nazis believed in psychic powers, astrology and the supernatural, thinking it was going to help them win the war, but the practical, scientific side of my brain questions it."

Major Siebert shook his head. His spectacles steamed up with condensation from hot breath and frustration.

"It is not my imagination, or the tuberculosis, although physical weakness has made me an easier target. A spiritual war between angels and demons is currently raging on earth and in heaven, believe me, and you are becoming a part of that battle, Nancy."

Chapter 23

FATHER NOVAK FELT IT was time to intervene, to convince me of their mission. I looked at the walls of the coffee shop behind him, wishing I was visiting one of the iconic landmarks such as the Colosseum, or the Leaning Tower of Pisa. Soft, warm lighting cast a cosy glow, reflecting off the gold accents and created an intimate atmosphere.

The sound of a classic Italian song played softly in the background, adding to the ambiance. The server was dressed in a crisp white shirt and black apron. I could hear the soft shuffling of her feet as she lingered nearby, waiting for our departure. Earlier patrons sat at small, round tables, engaged in lively conversation, or quietly reading the day's newspaper. The coffee shop, once bustling, now contained only us.

I tried to focus on Father Novak's words.

"Nancy, Bruno has called me in to help, as I am experienced in dealing with satanism and all it involves. If you have read the Bible Scriptures, then you will know there was a war in heaven, and Lucifer, the most brilliant and beautiful of God's angels, became horrified at God's plan for human beings to exist. Lucifer felt God was lowering himself to our human nature and refused to serve him. He annoyed God, and God banished Lucifer from heaven with his minions down to earth."

"I am aware of this, Father Novak."

I rattled my teacup, still irritated, although not knowing why.

"These fallen angels became the demons who roam the earth and do whatever they can to drag us down to hell through temptation. We believe demons infested Hitler and members of the SS. Hitler worked on the hearts and minds of the army, showing what total power could do. He encouraged atrocities and acts of pure evil. Hitler persuaded the soldiers to give consent to the devil to inhabit their souls."

Glancing at both of them, I said, "I need to tell you about something you don't know. I dreamt of a demonic visitation and witnessed Stella's murder by a demon. However, there is a third demonic situation which you are unaware of."

"Go on," said Major Siebert, gesturing with his hand.

"My cousin, Patrick, is a young priest, and he recently became involved with deliverances and exorcisms. Whilst trying to burn satanic objects which belonged to a possessed parishioner, a demon appeared and blinded him. Priests often receive visitations, but the demon which attacked him was from my nightmare, suggesting a connection between us."

Father Novak nodded at Major Siebert, who looked pensive.

"The demon blinded Patrick with its barbed tail, and I'm unsure whether the injury is temporary or permanent but am upset and angry about it."

Major Siebert put his hand on mine when he realised Patrick was especially important to me. Leaving his hand there for a while felt nice, but equally distracting. I shifted my gaze towards Father Novak.

"How much experience of the occult do you have, Father

Novak?"

His face showed a strong confidence, but a passivity, no arrogance as he declared, "I have performed over seventy thousand exorcisms, Nancy. I must have moral servitude to confirm the devil's presence in a person. Witnessing levitation, speaking in unknown languages like Greek or Aramaic or has supernatural knowledge, or indeed displays superhuman strength, are indications of possession by the devil."

Major Siebert looked at me again to see if I found Father Novak's account credible. I looked back at him and nodded. I was okay.

"Do not worry, Nancy. We don't expect you to join the mission against these monsters. I just asked Father Novak to explain as a courtesy, wanting you to understand. The Nazis' actions were unforgivable as they succumbed to temptation and transformed into vessels of evil. We can now grasp the source of the intensified cruelty suffered by their victims."

I still wasn't sure but understood their motives to be good. My friend a nurse, Jan, travelled to the Auschwitz-Birkenau Concentration Camp for the ceremonial opening of the Museum in 1947. Her cousins were from Slovakia. Of the nine hundred and seventy-three Jews from Slovakia admitted to Auschwitz in 1942, only eighty-eight remained alive. After witnessing the torment and torture inflicted by the Nazis on her relatives, she was forever changed.

"Have you spoken to the authorities? They could help in your quest, surely?"

"I tried just after the war. During the denazification trial, but they mocked me when I mentioned the devil. There is no help available."

Father Novak looked at me and my stomach gave a lurch. He still intimidated me.

"We need to know if you believe, Nancy. There appears to be a connection, and although I'm not certain as to why you are involved, it seems you are, and your safety is paramount."

Wanting to be conciliatory in my response but truthful as well, I said, "I believe in God and respect your beliefs, but it is just a fascinating theory, although I am aware demons do exist."

Father Novak's face darkened, registering disappointment and with a terse response said, "Just a theory, Nancy? It is not. Hell creates demons, soulless and godless."

Major Siebert interjected.

"Look, we are all getting tired. Father Novak has travelled all the way from Rome, Nancy."

"Directly from the Vatican," said Father Novak.

I nodded but wished to end the conversation.

"Forgive me, but reconciling this information is difficult for me."

I looked at my watch and stood up.

"In ten minutes, the minibus will come to collect us from the market square."

The server felt relieved, realising we were finally about to leave, and came over quickly to clear away our tea plates.

Father Novak also stood, and I shook his hand warmly.

"Please forgive my questions, Father. How long are you staying for?"

He held onto my hand longer than was normal, wanting to make a point.

"Reluctance is understandable, but I must entreat you to be careful, as it is possible the demons are watching. Could we meet your cousin, Patrick, especially as he's a priest involved in exorcisms; he may be interested in our mission?"

"Yes, of course, I will introduce you both to Patrick, but I don't imagine demons could have any further interest in me, Father?"

He smiled then, letting go of my hand.

"Perhaps because of the special light I perceive in your soul. Remember, these demonic beings thrive in chaos and disrupt lives. Please be careful."

Major Siebert shuffled to his feet, leaned on the walking stick, and we bid farewell to the priest before heading back to the minibus.

"It all sounds rather extraordinary," I said, as I helped him onto the minibus.

"You're not a complete believer yet, but you'll see. Reflect on what you've heard, Nancy, please."

Once we got back to the hospital, I left Major Siebert in his room, and checked on Patrick at the small hotel, telling him of Major Siebert's revelations, including Father Novak's comments.

He sat in his usual comfy chair.

"Nancy, you know I have been involved in deliverances and exorcisms for the Church. I must say that if Father Novak, such an esteemed priest, is telling you that demons have possessed the Nazis, you should consider it seriously."

Feeling unsettled, I paced around the comfy room.

"But does their mission have any connection to us? Why were we targeted by demons?"

He could tell I was frustrated but kept his calm.

"Somehow, we have become interconnected. The answer will become clearer, but it is important I meet with both Major

Siebert and Father Novak as soon as possible."

I left Patrick, and returned to the Nurse's Home, needing to rest. It was a stressful day, an unbelievable day, which included meeting Pope Pius XII's Exorcist. Something completely unexpected. There was no denying Bruno and Father Novak's sincerity in their mission, but I grappled with conflicting emotions and unanswered questions.

I was meeting Andrew the next day for lunch and I felt grateful. Laughter with him was necessary after the difficult subject matter covered with Major Siebert, or should I say Bruno?

As I lay on my bed and I closed my eyes, allowing my mind to wander and envision the memories and experiences of the past few weeks, I really couldn't decide whatever was likely to happen next?

Chapter 24

I GUILTILY LEFT PATRICK in the small hotel but needed to meet Andrew for lunch. Patrick didn't know Andrew, and I didn't want to complicate matters. He stayed back and considered the demon situation, ready to pray and find solace in rest.

Making my way to the usual meeting place, laughter and lively conversation spilled out onto the street as I opened the modern glass doors of the pub and went inside. Andrew's positive outlook on life and down-to-earth attitude were grounding. Ordering a lemonade, I settled down in my favourite chair in front of the fire to have a long and interesting chat with him.

The supernatural side of Major Siebert would surprise Andrew for certain, but in the past, he had told unusual and spooky stories from when he served in the army. A soldier declared he saw and heard ghosts of fallen comrades in battle. Despite Andrew's attempt to laugh it off, the soldier, William, frequently mentioned the ghosts. Although Andrew had suspicions of shell shock, William surprised everyone with his revelation of prophetic knowledge of battles. He claimed to be guided by deceased soldiers who warned him of danger and provided advice on self-defence.

When a sniper injured him and caused him to leave the army, Andrew jokingly wished William had warned him in advance. William's visions were so accurate that, to this day, he couldn't explain them. Based on this, I felt confident he would be open to hearing what was happening with Major Siebert.

Andrew entered, looking as dashing as always. Excited, he grabbed a beer from the pub's long wooden bar, he gave me an enormous hug, and he sat down in the chair next to me.

"Good Lord, Nancy," said Andrew, expelling a massive breath of air whilst digesting the news.

Describing the chaotic scene at the hospital, with Nurse Lewis rushing through the corridors to stop the attack and Major Siebert in a state of distress, I gave a vivid picture of Stella trying to help him but subsequently being murdered by the attacker. He mulled this over, whilst cradling his beer. It was such an awful story.

"We are aware of the strange and inexplicable supernatural occurrences in our world, aren't we, Nancy?"

Seeing telling the story upset me, he squeezed my arm in a gesture of sympathy. Mentioning Stella always brought a lump to my throat. Then his more practical side kicked in.

"What's the name of the Catholic priest?" he said, taking notes.

"Father Novak."

"No way!" exclaimed Andrew.

"He is famous for being the Pope's demonologist. Since the Pope ordained him as a priest in 1939, he's been Pope Pius XII's Chief Exorcist. I know about this, because as an army officer, I had to analyse the war's progress and study current affairs.

Andrew was such a fountain of knowledge. He continued, "The Vatican is powerful, but they did their absolute best to remain neutral and be considered as a separate sovereignty during the war. Whilst studying information on the Pope, Father Novak's name came up. The supernatural appears heavily related to the history which surrounds the Vatican's archives."

His eyes sparkled with curiosity, and he leaned forward in his chair in excitement.

"It is an interesting fact that he is a friend of Major Siebert. People considered Rome to be pro-Nazi rather than pro-Jewish."

My hands trembled, fidgeting with the pencil in my coat pocket.

"Major Siebert claims he wasn't a Nazi, just a German soldier. Plus, that's quite a comment to make against Rome?"

Andrew's statement was confusing, and I was surprised that he knew of Father Novak.

"Pope Pius XII never spoke out against deporting Jews from Rome to Auschwitz in 1943. The silence of the Pope during the Holocaust created bitter discussions. The Roman Catholic Church and their relationship with the Jews is far from healthy."

"What a shocking story," shaking my head in disbelief.

"Did the Pope fear Hitler and therefore remain silent about the Jews?"

It was my first time hearing a negative comment regarding the Pope and the Catholic Church. My parents brought me up as a Catholic, and I believed everyone else was Catholic as well as a little girl.

"Before the army discharged me, I helped to locate displaced refugees, Jewish orphans, or families after the war. Didn't you hear the story of the nun in France who kidnapped two young Jewish boys, whose parents died in a Nazi concentration camp? Surviving Jewish relatives attempted to have the children returned to their families, but the Catholic Church refused because they had already been baptised as Catholics."

"Are you serious, Andrew? They can't deny the families their children?"

As a lapsed Catholic, I knew the rigidity of the faith's rules, although what Andrew told me seemed absurd.

"Thousands of Jewish orphans hid in convents, monasteries, and churches, including those with Catholic families. Separating orphaned children from their families led to fear, bitterness, and complete distrust of the Catholic Church among Jews in Europe and America."

"My God, how horrific!"

Standing up, I walked up and down the pub for a minute, taking measured steps to calm my anxiety.

"It's hard to believe, but I witnessed this myself. Do you believe in this demon occult stuff, Nancy?"

I sat back down.

"Father Novak is a demonologist and famous, as you said, so who knows? I've had inexplicable experiences with dying patients, feeling their life force flow through me as they passed away. Yes, I believe in the supernatural, Andrew."

It was time to tell Andrew about my nightmare, the horrifying image of the menacing evil entity causing Stella's tragic death and the evil beast, the same one which visited me, inflicting damage to Patrick's eyes.

Andrew was quiet for a while as he absorbed the information. As a forthright individual, he always took a practical approach.

"Nancy, I will carry out further investigation into both Major Siebert and Father Novak. The occult stories worry me, as I don't want you in danger, especially after the hospital incident. Let's meet soon, for a debrief, please."

Appreciating Andrew's concern, I said, "Andrew, in the meantime, please be careful as well. Each person connected to Major Siebert, including myself, Stella, Clara, his sister, Father Novak, and Patrick, have all experienced disturbing encounters with evil entities."

Andrew's eyes crinkled with amusement, his laughter echoing around the room.

"Don't worry, Nancy. I will eat garlic and watch myself after midnight."

Exasperated, I said, "Andrew, garlic wards off vampires, not demons."

He smiled. "I know, Nancy. I'm just teasing you, to lighten the mood."

He stood up, hugged me, and he promised to contact me about discussing this matter at the hospital. Blowing me a kiss, he was gone.

Leaving the pub, I felt happy I'd told Andrew everything, and returned to the hospital to talk with Major Siebert. Entering his room, the low hum of the medical equipment was familiar, and I heard the gentle voices of the nurses and patients in the ward. The chitter chatter in the background was comforting.

The harsh light in Major Siebert's room illuminated his tired face, and I felt sad. Checking his vital statistics and deciding all was well, I sat in the chair next to his bed. He was almost asleep, but rubbing his eyes, he sat up and smiled.

We chatted, and the subject of his sister arose again. He said he hoped Clara had settled into her job at the university and enjoyed the surroundings Marburg offered. As he spoke about her, his eyes filled with a bittersweet sadness, and I realised he was regretting they were no longer as close as they once were.

Observing his worried expression and fidgeting hands, I made up my mind to offer guidance on Bruno's wellbeing to her. Oh, there it was. My first thought of him as Bruno, not Major Siebert. Would I be able to say his name to his face? I wasn't sure.

I argued in my head whether I should contact Clara without asking Bruno's permission first, but she was his closest living relative, and I felt it was my duty to mention the tuberculosis and his subsequent recovery to her.

Leaving his room, I made my way to matron's office. The dimly lit room with antique furniture created an atmosphere of timeless elegance as I sat at her desk composing a short telegram to send to the University. It was a palaver, but because the hospital possessed a decent telephone, I could dial 190 for the Central Post Office and speak my message to the telegraphist.

Clara received my telegram that very same day, and I received one back the next morning, stating she was coming to England. Telegrams were so short, she said little, but I hoped she would explain further. She was worried because I had mentioned his illness.

I felt a joyful anticipation of seeing Clara, described by Bruno as having a bright smile and warm eyes. His family was becoming important to me, and I was enjoying getting to know him. Learning more about him, particularly his motivations, was intriguing. I felt his family could fill in the gaps about his life, although I did not expect to meet Clara quite so soon.

Chapter 25

POOR PATRICK, HIS EYES were still blurry, and his well-being caused anxiety, but at least the cosy little hotel room where Patrick was staying was comfortable, with low-level lighting. All day Thursday, I looked after him and we listened to the radio together.

Having organised his favourite meal, but feeling twitchy said, "I'm so sorry Patrick, but I need to return to the hospital tomorrow."

He tutted, then smiled, his mischievous eyes twinkling with amusement, playfully taunting me. It hurt that he couldn't see through them.

"I understand, Nancy, but am curious about Major Siebert's well-being, with numerous unanswered questions. Please organise a meeting soon."

"Patrick, I promise to set it up, but you need to see a specialist."

He shook his head decisively, "Don't worry, Nancy, the Lord will make my eyes better."

Then impatiently, he said, "Go, Nancy; I am quite happy listening to the news on the radio."

His voice lingered in my ears as I dashed off. Rushing to the Nurse's Home, I bumped into matron upon arrival.

"Sister Flanagan! Aren't you on holiday? God knows you need the rest!"

She wagged her finger at me.

I ignored her concern.

"How is John doing? I might pop in and see him."

Her eyebrows knitted together, and a shadow of worry crossed her face.

"That's not possible, Sister Flanagan. He felt fit enough to discharge himself, and didn't say where he was going. A charming man, but a stubborn one."

I was irritated Bruno had left the hospital without telling me, and my expression conveyed my annoyance to the matron.

"Sister Flanagan, come to my room briefly."

I followed, wondering why. On her desk sat a white envelope.

"He left you a note, Sister Flanagan, and I'm sure it will tell you more."

"What if the bump on his head from the attack caused permanent damage, Matron?"

But it was more than that. With the demonic activity taking place, I was worried Bruno could be in real danger.

Matron handed the sealed envelope to me. Focusing on the note, I removed it carefully, the words in the letter leaping off the page.

I couldn't wait for your return, Nancy, as we must act now. Both Father Novak and I can feel it. The devil is gathering a legion of evil entities and will bring them forth from the depths of hell soon.

His note didn't make me feel better. It seemed that if anything, demonic activity was likely to increase and I felt even more concerned, especially after Stella's murder, and the attempted murder of Bruno.

Matron wittered on, "To be honest, Sister Flanagan, he seemed fine, and a collective sigh of relief echoed through the ward on his departure. The patients felt unsafe with him in residence, worried about future assailant attacks. Anyway, Father Novak came to collect him, he is a nice man."

I continued to read the note. The handwriting was elegant, though the ink smudged the words in places.

We have heard of strange acts of terrorism and sadism growing throughout the world. Father Novak and I know these wicked acts are demons at play. Their influence spreads like dark tendrils, reaching into every corner. Our group will meet shortly to discuss a course of action, and I would be happy to introduce you to everyone.

The meeting is at St Barnabas' Church, Little Bromwich, at eleven o'clock on the fifth of May, hoping you can make it, Bruno.

The meeting was today, and soon about to happen. I set the note back down on matron's desk. Feeling a sense of urgency, I wanted to make sure he was safe, but I was also interested in meeting the others involved.

I turned and asked, "Where is St Barnabas' Church, Matron?"

She smiled and shook her head in stark surprise.

"Just round the corner from here, Sister Flanagan, but I am astonished you don't know it. The church narrowly escaped destruction by fire during the war bombings, due to a fortunate change in wind direction. Some believe it was divine intervention, and it remains a source of inspiration."

It made sense to me that Bruno and Father Novak were meeting at a place of worship considered to be sacrosanct.

"Thank you, Matron, I appreciate the help. How is morale in the hospital?"

With a soft smile, she inclined her head, "Fine, Sister Flanagan, thank you. Together, we can stand tall and face whatever comes our way. Sadness prevails among the rest of the nursing staff, but I keep them busy."

Putting my hand on her arm, I nodded, "That's best."

As I left her office, a woman appeared, asking for Bruno at the nurse's station. Looking tired and dishevelled, I overheard her say she had travelled to Birmingham from Germany and was staying at the Grand Hotel. Excited, I realised this must be Bruno's sister. What timing!

Matron ushered the woman into her room furnished with the large, but uncomfortable armchairs and the solid wooden desk, and signalled for me to join them. As we sat down, Clara introduced herself and Matron looked at me, confused. I responded.

"Sorry for any confusion, Miss Siebert. We didn't know Major Bruno Siebert's name for some time, so we gave him a temporary name whilst in the hospital, calling him John."

I looked over at matron. Being a professional, she refrained from making the situation awkward and simply raised her eyebrows in agreement.

"It is lovely to meet you, Miss Siebert. Would you like some tea? It's no trouble to fetch some for you."

"No thank you, Matron, I'm fine."

I smiled warmly at Clara, my eyes crinkling with genuine joy, and I introduced myself as Sister Flanagan.

"I've been caring for your brother in the hospital. It's nice to meet you as well. I am stunned you have travelled all the way to Birmingham from Germany?"

"Yes, I have," she smiled in return. "After receiving your telegram, I decided to come."

I nodded.

"The message may have been a surprise, but I wanted to inform you about Bruno's illness, although he has been making a significant recovery."

Matron then advised her Major Siebert had discharged himself from hospital and was visiting Father Novak, who was still in Birmingham. The news immediately horrified Clara, as she was concerned about his safety.

"Despite feeling tired, I am eager to see Bruno. This is disappointing news."

Clara's accent influenced her voice, sounding educated and friendly.

"I've been anxious, not just about the tuberculosis, but because I kept seeing Bruno in my nightmares."

My eyes widened and I quickly focused on her when she mentioned nightmares. My stomach lurched, and I pondered if the demonic activity we had encountered might link to her nightmare as well. I hoped not. I leaned forward intently towards her.

"Could you tell me about your nightmare, Miss Siebert?"

She shifted uncomfortably in the large armchair.

"I would prefer to discuss it with Bruno directly, Sister Flanagan."

Disappointed, I made a mental note to ask Bruno about it later.

"Referring to Bruno, please don't worry, Miss Siebert. I know where he will be. He and Father Novak, his friend, were going to a meeting at St Barnabas' Church in Little Bromwich at 11.00 am today."

A sigh of relief escaped Clara's lips, the tension melting away.

193

She posed the question, "Are you going to the meeting, Sister Flanagan?"

"Definitely, Miss Siebert. I will be there."

Clara looked at her watch and, tapping it, said, "It is getting late, and I had better get a move on. How far is Little Bromwich from the centre of town, Sister Flanagan? I want to return to the hotel to freshen up before attending."

"It's six miles from here, just a quick taxi or tram ride, Miss Siebert."

Clara politely bid farewell, shaking hands with us both before departing. After Clara left, I explained about Bruno's situation to matron. She expressed complete surprise, but agreed he was a decent man. Nothing was mentioned about demons or evil entities, knowing that would be too difficult a pill for her to swallow!

On returning to the small hotel to join Patrick and discuss a course of action, I found him relaxing in a typical Patrick way. Being blind, he prayed while listening to the radio news. Sharing the news of the meeting at St. Barnabas' Church, he was excited for the opportunity to meet both Major Siebert and Father Novak, to both satisfy his curiosity and find answers to our unanswered questions.

Chapter 26

I DISCOVERED THE NOTE from Andrew regarding Bruno in my pigeonhole at the Nurse's Home. I found it just as I was just getting organised to meet everyone at St. Barnabas' Church.

The note confirmed the information received from his friend Eric in the foreign office. Andrew's summary, which established Bruno's trustworthiness, thrilled me indeed. I planned to thank Andrew with a hug and a pint for comforting me.

I went to meet Patrick, and then we made our way to St Barnabas' Church. On arrival, he pushed open the creaking, weathered wooden doors of the church, revealing its hallowed interior, with me trailing behind him, guiding him to the nearest pew. A faint scent of old books and polished wood lingered in the air of the old church, adding a comforting feel.

It was not just a place of worship but a vibrant community hub and was revered by the local community. The church's architecture was beautiful and although old, many of its stained-glass windows depicting biblical scenes remained.

"Patrick, there's a light in the church's back. Sit on the pew and wait for me."

Feeling for the wooden seat part of the pew with his hands,

he sat down and started praying. As I walked to the back of the church, the dimly lit church hall revealed Bruno and Father Novak sitting side by side, their expressions solemn and contemplative.

"Nancy!" Bruno exclaimed as he spotted me.

I ran over and gave him an affectionate hug, to my surprise. Our eyes met, a sudden connection, unaware of my need to see him before. I felt butterflies in my stomach.

Father Novak greeted me with a warm smile, his eyes crinkling at the corners.

Then I asked Bruno, with some trepidation, "What's your estimate on the number of mission supporters showing up?"

"Nancy, I'm unsure, but hopefully some will come."

Father Novak saw me watching him.

"I'm just a little tense. This meeting is especially important. How many will attend? We just don't know."

Bruno, too, was nervous, and the atmosphere in the church felt heavy. He felt this way since the group knew about him. Would the group accept him? This nervous, twitchy, restless Bruno didn't fit with the calm and composed character I was used to. Though the meeting was being held in a house of God, the increasing evidence of demonic activity made him question our safety.

The thought of lurking demons was frightening for everyone. It was becoming more important than ever that we banded together. Strength in unity! The demons were sweeping us deeper into the unknown. The dimly lit church contained flickering candlelight, casting dancing shadows on the walls.

"I would like to introduce my cousin, Father Patrick Flanagan, to both of you."

Father Novak nodded approvingly.

"That would be a wonderful idea, Nancy. A fellow priest would be welcome."

"He's been wanting to meet both of you. As I told you previously, an evil entity blinded him, so he's currently sitting on a pew for safety reasons. I will go and fetch him."

On approaching the pew where I left Patrick, I found he was no longer there. Instead, he was standing in the middle of St Barnabas' church, opposite the altar, with his arms outstretched, head angled up towards the ceiling, with his gaze fixed on something I couldn't see.

He was praying, and a bright white shaft of light shone down upon his head. But where was it emanating from? It was so brilliant I needed to shield my eyes. The rest of his body appeared bathed in a golden light.

"Patrick," I yelled, "What's going on?"

Patrick stood stock still, answering, "Don't be afraid, Nancy, don't worry, God is with me."

He continued to pray, and Father Novak entered the church from the church hall, followed closely by Bruno.

"Don't approach him, Nancy," Father Novak shouted over to me.

"Let him be. Let the Lord do his work."

I remained motionless, my gaze fixed on Patrick as he fervently clasped his hands and bowed his head in prayer. Father Novak was also praying, and I realised they were chanting the same phrases. Bruno came and stood next to me.

I asked him, "What on earth is happening, Bruno? I do not understand. Also, I meant to tell you it was Azazel I saw in my nightmare."

197

He was surprised, and said, "How do you know the demon was called Azazel, Nancy?"

"Patrick told me Azazel was the demon which blinded him with its barbed tail. The description was identical to the entity which visited me."

He put his hand on my arm to comfort me.

"Nancy, Father Novak is performing a ritual to cast out the demonic attachment, which is causing Patrick's blindness."

I watched as Patrick continued to look up to the ceiling, holding out his arms in supplication, stretching up tall, whilst Father Novak stood next to him. A radiant aura surrounded Patrick, as though in the presence of a divine being.

"But Bruno," I shook my head decisively, "A demon didn't possess Patrick."

"No, I know, Nancy, but he received the demonic attachment from Azazel's tail."

I give my will, purpose, future, my whole life to God. With God, I oppose all sin and every kind of demon. Begone!

I give my will, purpose, future, my whole life to God. With God, I oppose all sin and every kind of demon. Begone!

Patrick and Father Novak kept chanting this.

I give my will, purpose, future, my whole life to God. With God, I oppose all sin and every kind of demon. Begone!

All of a sudden, I realised the church was full of people who had quietly entered, standing amongst the pews. The atmosphere shifted, evoking simultaneous feelings of fear and exhilaration.

The people encircled Patrick and Father Novak, and I heard the quiet murmur of their voices, which grew until realising, they, too, chanted the same incantation. The power of the group chanting the prayer together was overwhelming.

I give my will, purpose, future, my whole life to God. With God, I oppose all sin and every kind of demon. Begone!

The chant rose to a shout. I felt a further shift in the atmosphere. The air crackled with electricity, almost lifting me off my feet. I felt peculiar. My moldavite crystal in my pocket pulsated wildly, punctuating the change in the atmosphere. The chanting grew to a deafening crescendo, and the bright white light directed at Patrick's head flashed even more brightly than before. Then it disappeared, and Patrick fell hard to the floor with a bang.

I ran to him, terrified he might be hurt.

"Patrick, are you alright, Patrick?"

He slowly sat up. Patrick's bleary eyes blinked open, adjusting to the brightness of the room.

"I can see Nancy, I can see. The attachment is gone."

Tears streamed down my face, and I hugged Patrick, having witnessed something special, a miracle. Patrick's and others' unwavering faith in the Lord saved him from evil.

What a joyous moment. He focused his bright blue eyes on me, and my heart leapt with gladness. It was unbelievable and took my breath away. I would remember this moment forever.

I gestured towards his hands, "Look at them, Patrick, your hands look normal. The burns, the scarring, it has all gone."

Although no longer attending church, I prayed to God privately, and this miracle had renewed my faith in God. The situation of having to leave Maeve, my daughter, in Ireland, rocked my world and led me to question my faith. This time, God had answered my prayers and given me fresh hope. I did not believe in following religion as I believe it causes division, but I have always believed in God.

"I was not expecting it to happen. I hoped to get my sight back, but this is a bonus."

Patrick stood up, feeling much stronger than before. There was an enormous difference in his confidence.

He said happily, "I am restored," and reached out his now recovered hand to Father Novak. Father Novak shook it with gusto and said, "I'm Father Julius Novak. So pleased to meet you."

It was a lovely, touching moment.

"Thank you, Father, so much!"

Father Novak just shook his head and said, "Don't thank me. I'm just the channel for the Lord, as you know."

Patrick just smiled and nodded. "I do Father Novak, I do."

Bruno equally stretched out his hand to Patrick and said, "It's an absolute pleasure, Father Flanagan. Let's sit down. We need a discussion."

A hush descended across the group as I then stood up and addressed them from the front of the church.

"Thank you all for coming and for helping with my cousin, Father Flanagan. We are forever grateful."

The group responded with smiles and nods. Father Novak took over.

"Thank you for attending and witnessing the Lord's power first-hand. Much work is needed to free these men from evil entities. May I introduce you all to Major Bruno Siebert? You know his story, but it's vital to hear the evidence against these men from a first-hand witness."

Bruno stood up to address the group. Fiddling with his spectacles, I saw he was nervous. The group knew all about his being the Camp Commandant in Vilnius. Some were sceptical and wanted to hear his side of the story. He ran a forced labour camp, but on the plus side, he was in the German army, not a Nazi.

"The power the Nazis received under Hitler's command put them on the path to temptation. They enjoyed dominance and supremacy over ordinary people in the belief they were the preferred Aryan race. There was greed, and the gluttony of enjoying the riches the senior officers received, the stealing of gold, silver, money, clothing, and art from the Jews and all the other races they persecuted."

The group murmured agreement, warming to Bruno, and believing him. I stood close by, wanting him to feel my presence. Bruno's voice grew louder and more fervent as he denounced those who embraced Hitler's ideology.

"They aimed to eliminate their opponents from the face of the earth, subjecting them to a hellish existence."

His voice built to a crescendo.

"Our mission aims to bring justice to innocent victims who have suffered greatly. I did my best, but it wasn't enough. I am here, now, ready to avenge those victims and rid the earth of the evil which harmed them."

There was silence as Bruno's words sank in. There were a few hand claps, which escalated into thunderous applause. Bruno sat down. He was smiling, realising he was being accepted by the group. After a few minutes, I turned to Father Novak.

"But how do we determine a 'bad person' from a 'demonic person'?"

"I understand it seems confusing. Detaching themselves from their family unit, the person becomes distracted, with no interest in the happiness of family members. They commit more sins until it becomes clear they are under the power of the devil. A person labelled as 'bad' may be on the path of temptation and sin."

To comprehend further, I inquired, "Does a demon possess anyone who commits wrongdoing?"

"No, of course not, Nancy. Sadly, there are people who commit crimes and atrocities who are suffering from severe mental illness. An exorcist conducts a psychological evaluation to distinguish possession from mental illness."

Bruno spoke out then.

"But we are discussing Nazis and the SS, Nancy. They were way beyond being 'bad.' It is obvious they were the epitome of evil."

"How do we erase the demons? What must we do?"

Asked Luca, Dimitri's brother. They were identical Greek twins with relatives in the war who had suffered at the Nazis' hands.

"The worst perpetrators of all, Hitler, and Goebbels, killed themselves. The Court charged twenty-two of the highest-ranking Nazis with war crimes against peace, conspiracy, and humanity at the trials in Nuremberg, but there are evil Nazis remaining for us to deal with."

Patrick spoke with confidence, but like everyone, was feeling the pressure of the situation.

"This is the fundamental question. We track the remaining individuals down, and one by one, restore them to baptismal grace, freeing them from original sin. Confession achieves this but in freeing them from the demon within, it is necessary for them to confess."

"I estimate we need to tackle fifty of the most serious Nazi's left," said Bruno with flushed cheeks.

"We are not seeking retribution. The mission is to remove

the demons and banish them from this earth, sending them back to hell from whence they came."

I questioned our position further.

"Father, wouldn't it be risky to cleanse the Nazis in groups? Holding down fifty Nazis in groups of two hundred and fifty people would be difficult and dangerous. Plus, there are not two hundred and fifty of us here?"

The room fell silent whilst contemplating the problem. Perfection was imperative, with no margin for mistakes or errors. Evil incarnate could cause irreparable damage if we failed.

Chapter 27

BRUNO TURNED TOWARDS THE church hall, startled by the unexpected sound of a woman's voice echoing through the space. Clara bowled into the meeting at St. Barnabas' Church, just as I thought she might. Her eyes widened as she took in the intricate details and grandeur of the surrounding architecture.

We were in a small Norman church nestled in a tranquil, leafy setting but one which exhibited the Romanesque style with rounded arches, especially over the windows and doors. Her eyes sparkled with delight and a wide smile spread across her face.

With determination, she announced to the assembled group, "I have a solution, folks."

A prolonged silence engulfed the room. Clara stepped forward with purpose, her body language commanding attention. She raised her voice, reiterating that she knew how to do it.

"I was lucky enough to witness this morning's events from the back of the church hall."

She gestured towards Patrick and Father Novak.

"Seeing Patrick's sight restored was an incredible experience, and I want to help you all."

When Bruno heard her voice, he shrieked, "Clara," his eyes

opened wide in astonishment.

Her head tilted in a quiet nod. "Bruno, let us speak later, after the meeting."

She had travelled from Germany to see her brother, but didn't want him to interrupt her while speaking to the group. She simply added, "I'm glad to see you're well, Bruno."

He nodded and looked at me with eyebrows raised. He was astonished by her presence. Glancing back, I shifted my gaze.

"Miss Siebert, I'm so pleased to see you here."

She smiled, "Sister Flanagan, I meant to tell you earlier at the hospital how much I appreciated you looking after my brother."

Expecting a handshake, her arms enveloped me in a warm embrace. Bruno raised his eyebrows even higher, realising that I had previously met Clara at the hospital. I hoped he wasn't angry about my contacting her without telling him first.

"Is the group open to hearing my thoughts?"

She faced everyone, smiling and nodding at every single person in the room. Standing tall and proud, Clara introduced herself.

"I am the sister of Major Bruno Siebert, and I witnessed the haunting images of the atrocities committed by the Nazis when he worked in the labour camp. Nazis desired Bruno's assimilation, but he resisted and he never killed anyone. Instead, his battle became an internal one."

Murmurs circulated among the group, but the group felt positive about Bruno, as he had rejected Nazi racism and appeared to be a decent man.

"Bruno experienced a challenging time running the camp. Despite appearing to be a nationalist, he fought daily for the struggling Jewish community. Bruno's mission was to make their existence tolerable, but in the end, he couldn't protect them all. He saved two hundred and fifty lives, and those families will be forever grateful."

She looked around the room, smiling at everyone, confirming his brave act. The room erupted into cheers and shouts of bravo. My hand gently rested on his shoulder, offering support and a comforting touch. Bruno felt happiness at the response from the group. From the very beginning, he feared the group may despise him.

"Thank you everyone," he said, continuing, "I am fully committed to our cause to stop future suffering. Witnessing Nazi atrocities, I vow never again will such evil take hold."

The group clapped and cheered. Bruno was forming a strong bond with the group members. Clara continued with her summary.

"I am a historian, with a deep and enduring curiosity relating to pagan rites and the occult. Not because I am anti-religious. Quite the contrary, as I possess a Lutheran Church background, just like Bruno, and regularly engage in prayer and attend church."

She nodded at Father Novak.

"We are similar, Father, but I believe in the Protestant reformation of the Catholic Church. However, we are not too far apart in our beliefs."

Father Novak smiled at Clara and dipped his head in polite acknowledgment. She said the bible was the ultimate authority on matters concerning faith and she held a firm belief in the scriptures.

"There are historical documents and photographs which show the Nazis taking part in occult rituals and gatherings.

Nazism represents the epitome of evil in the present era, a massive regression to paganism within the Christian community of Europe. The Antichrist is not one individual person, but a force of destruction. The Hitler war machine destroyed not only buildings through their bombing raids, but also humanity through their unswerving cruelty."

She continued, "The Thule Society was a group focused on Aryan mythology, which played a role in the early formation of the Nazi Party. It's known some prominent Nazis, like Rudolf Hess, were associated with this society."

There was a murmur of appreciation among the group. Clara was articulate, interesting, and spellbinding to listen to.

"The chilling blueprints and meticulous records reveal the calculated and methodical planning behind the Holocaust. The Nazis picked beliefs based on pseudoscience to support their world-view. This strange magical world enchanted and drew in high-ranking officials of Nazi Germany, enticing them into the hands of the devil until he inhabited them all. An arch manipulator, as are all demonic forces, Hitler twisted the teachings of Christianity to further his cause."

Her confident voice resonated with authority as she shared her extensive knowledge of the occult and the Nazis. She was going to be a definite asset to the group.

She continued, "Your discussion has revolved around how to cast out demons from these human beings through confession. Remaining calm and thinking instead of reacting is crucial in all situations because they are unpredictable and will attempt to scare and enrage us. Be watchful when facing demons of various shapes and forms."

Father Novak nodded at Clara, saying, "Thank you Clara for

the explanation."

He continued addressing the group in a gentle yet commanding tone.

"The entities will seek your sympathies, as they follow the devil's orders to avoid harsh consequences, but dare to suggest they should turn to Jesus, and an insolent answer will be given back to you. A fallen angel has no remorse. A demon knows what will 'tempt' you, and though cannot read your mind, they can plant visions. They will try to drag you down and offer temptation, step by step, until you pass the point of no return."

A voice, unfamiliar, spoke up from the rear. She said she was Saskia, and she seemed to be in her early thirties, with short brown wavy hair. Worried, her brows furrowed, and her eyes darted around.

"Sorry to interrupt you, but I experienced a dream last night. A nightmare. It was paralysing and scared me witless. Based on your words, it seems a demon was attempting to tempt me.

Clara encouraged her to speak.

"Please tell us what happened?"

Saskia, speaking nervously, continued, "I was alone in my hotel room."

Clara's outstretched arm beckoned Saskia to step closer, her hand gracefully guiding the way.

"We all need to hear this."

Saskia gracefully moved her way through the group to the front, wearing a white top with small embroidered blue flowers, blue jeans, and white trainers. I didn't know Saskia yet but recognised her face.

Her hands were shaking, and Clara put an arm round her

shoulders.

"Take your time, Saskia."

"I fell asleep. The room appeared hazy and surreal, with distorted shapes and shifting colours. It was difficult to tell if I was asleep or awake. There was a whitish grey mist which wrapped itself around me like a blanket."

My ears pricked up as she described what happened.

"Don't tell me, Saskia, was there a disgusting smell, too?" I asked her.

"Yes! I thought I was going to be sick from the foul smell. It made my stomach churn, and I felt wretched. Lingering in the air, it was fetid and overwhelming. The air was thick with it."

"Go on, Saskia," encouraged Bruno. We were on tenter-hooks to hear what happened next.

"This thing appeared next to my bed. Huge, with red skin and red eyes, it changed into a tiny, wizened old man. I thought it was a hallucination, but the smell made me realise I was awake. I'm ashamed to tell you the next part."

Bowing her head, we could see her distress from the body movements and trembling hands.

"Saskia don't worry. We are all friends here."

I opened my arms in a welcoming gesture.

"Throughout my life, my family has been short of money, possessions, and a decent home." a single tear rolled down her face. She wiped it away with the edge of her sleeve in a jagged movement.

"The creature spoke to me."

Wow, that's new, I thought, the demons hadn't said anything in any other incident so far.

As Bruno listened to Saskia's testimony, his expression

showed an unwavering intensity and focus.

"The beast said it could give me things beyond my wildest dreams, an expensive car, an ostentatious house, endless money. If I gave my soul to the devil, whatever I wanted was mine."

This was an innovative approach by the demons, and my mouth fell open in alarm. Obviously, they offered Saskia direct temptation to inhabit her.

Clara, with a thoughtful expression, told Saskia, "I believe the devil dislikes the plan to purify the Nazis and eliminate the demons."

Nodding in agreement, I said, "But Saskia, what did you do?

"I didn't want to commune with the devil. So, I prayed and tried to drown its words out. Picking up my crucifix from the side of the bed, I repeated the Lord's Prayer over and over again. The thing screamed and ranted. So, I hid under my blankets. I wasn't brave, but didn't know how to handle it, so I kept praying.

"Did it speak to you again, Saskia?"

Her experience was intriguing, but horrifying.

"No, but my bed levitated inches into the air. It rose off the ground, and I stayed under the covers. My skin had goosebumps, but that doesn't capture the terror I felt."

Father Novak nodded.

"Demons occasionally levitate people, things, and themselves. We may experience this when we start the cleansing process."

Saskia continued, her voice shaky, "The fear overwhelmed me, but concealed it from the beast, shouting out, telling it to go, that I loved Jesus, and kept praying hard. The smell went and the visions too. The smell took an hour to dissipate. It was extremely strong. Eventually it stopped bothering me, and my body was drained, but I'm so glad it went."

She sat down on the nearest pew with a thud, exhausted from telling us all the story.

Father Novak spoke up.

"Saskia, you did the right thing. Well done! This demon was Mammon. He tempts a man with money and material things, but you didn't give in. The demon went after your weaknesses, but you stayed strong."

"We are proud of you, Saskia," I shouted, and the group clapped. She smiled a shy smile, but it was a warning to us all.

Bruno said, "We are being targeted by evil entities, and must be on our guard at all times. Just do as Saskia did. Don't give in. Don't get angry either, as the entities feed off negative feelings. Stay calm, pray, and it will stop."

Father Novak stood up and, facing everyone, said, "We know what the quest is. I am certain we will succeed, as we have God on our side."

Chapter 28

HAVING EATEN SOME SNACKS and drunk gallons of tea and coffee to keep us awake in the church, and to recover from Saskia's revelations, Clara stepped forward and took a small square box out of her bag. It seemed unassuming, white, but with a strange aspect to it. A smooth, almost translucent material which resembled human skin covered the box.

The room fell silent except for a loud, sharp intake of breath from Father Novak.

"It cannot be. How is this possible, Clara? For centuries, the Vatican searched for this and was the holy weapon I hoped to source."

Clara held in her hand something vitally important, which Father Novak believed to be mythical, a legend mentioned by Pope Pius XII to Father Novak years ago in the Vatican. The Pope wanted Father Novak to find it. He couldn't, and Clara held it now in front of him. His eyes widened and jaw dropped in disbelief.

"Yes, Father Novak, it exists, and I have studied pagan beliefs in relation to biblical teachings and gained a knowledge of the occult, satanic rituals, and pagan practices for many years. Through research, I uncovered ancient texts which revealed the methods necessary to break the devil's grip on humanity. "

"From druids, Clara?" I knew about druids from Ireland. What an incredible story she told, her German accent adding to the mystery.

"Yes. The druids are high-ranking priests within the ancient Celtic cultures. Being Irish, Nancy, you must know the history surrounding druids? Dating back to at least the 4th Century BC."

I nodded, "Yes, but Clara, my understanding is that some were bad."

"There are misconceptions, Nancy, because they choose not to document their religious beliefs and were secretive, holding ceremonies in sacred groves and natural shrines and building temples."

Clara suggested she received help from druids, but in Ireland, I learned at an early age from mammy not to trust them.

"The Gaul's sacrificed criminals by burning them in a wicker man, but the Celtic people sacrificed animals, like livestock or working animals, and worshipped the forces of nature."

Pushing back against Clara's explanation, I said, "They believe in tribal gods and goddesses, not God the Father, and Saint Michael the Archangel."

Clara wouldn't be dissuaded.

"The druids I encountered may not fit the definition of 'good,' but they possess intriguing knowledge. They value the earth, nature, and the forces of good over evil. I was introduced to Angelina by them. A Seer, born of druid ancestry. God chose her as a prophet. At ten years old, she is just a child, but she revealed this unsurpassed spiritual, holy relic to me."

Clara explained she had previously received an invitation to meet with Angelina.

"Although I was dreaming, I was also awake. This is the medium Angelina communicates through. It was an incredible experience and I realised I must go to South America to secure the holy relic without knowing why."

My curiosity piqued, I asked, "What is Angelina like?"

"Incredible! When I met her, she appeared at our meeting place with her mother, with long, dark hair, and sunglasses. As they approached, her mother whispered something to her, and she looked towards her mother's voice. I quickly realised Angelina was blind."

I responded, "Wow, so the sunglasses were dark glasses, intended to hide her disability from others and protect her from invasive questions?"

Clara nodded.

"She's sensitive to people and environments, instinctively recognising negative people or situations. Powerful visions occurring at the age of ten. Imagine what her powers will be like when she reaches adulthood?"

Bruno's eyes drew away from our conversation, and fixed on the object Clara held in her hand.

"But what is it? It looks like skin?"

With a luminescent sheen, a glow, it fascinated him.

"Yes, Bruno, the skin from Saint Michael the Archangel covers this box."

We saw the smooth, pale skin draped over the box, appearing ethereal and divine but Patrick shook his head.

"This is impossible, Clara? Archangel Michael is the chief of all angels. Angels are separate creations from humans. How is angelic skin possible?"

He became agitated, saying, "Angels possess intellect and will, enabling them to exercise knowledge and love. However, they lack physical bodies and live a non-embodied existence. Angelic consciousness differs from human consciousness. Unlike Father Novak, I've never heard of this holy relic before."

I looked at Patrick and I gestured he should allow her to continue. It was unlike him to become so perturbed. Clara remained unconcerned.

"It is not like human skin or akin to any animal or human skin on earth, but I assure you, Father Flanagan, this is Archangel Michael's skin covering this box, and you must believe me. Have faith and maintain a firm belief. The box isn't the best part, either."

Feeling tense, I looked over at Father Novak. He was still shaking his head in disbelief as we witnessed a mythical holy relic coming to life. Standing stock still, we held our breath as Clara opened this wondrous box, where the skin covering shone, though it was no longer light in the room but quite dark.

Bruno reached over, intertwining his fingers with mine, creating a comforting and intimate connection. I shook like a leaf in the church's tense atmosphere, and he had observed it. He made me feel safe.

Clara then took out a very white, bright, and shimmering feather. It bore no resemblance to a bird's feather. With separate tiny feathers which almost looked like individual crystals, they shone and glimmered, knitted together to make one long feather.

She held the delicate feather between her fingers, marvelling at its softness and intricate details.

"But it looks like just a feather, Clara."

"No, Nancy, it is not an ordinary feather. This comes from the wing of the Archangel Michael himself. Believe!"

The room fell silent as we processed this incredible information. Father Novak then did something unexpected. I watched him in amazement as he positioned himself in front of Clara and got on his knees, and lay flat on the ground before her, with his arms outstretched in supplication.

"Father Flanagan, you need to pay homage to Archangel Michael. The Pope in the Vatican noted this holy relic. Our search has lasted for years. It is the real thing. Show humility towards the feather and believe Clara, please."

"You all need to pay homage now!"

He addressed the group. Bruno nodded his head at me, and we got on our knees. Patrick got down onto his knees and, with his hands clasped, prayed. Clara smiled from ear to ear. Her hands trembled as she unwrapped the ancient artefact. Unsure of the reaction it would evoke, she was relieved that Father Novak believed her. Through her research and interaction, she understood the sinister forces they were battling. Now they owned a holy weapon sent by the divine creator to use against those forces.

"Forgive me, but can you explain to us how the feather of Saint Michael the Archangel's wing can help us battle evil entities?"

"Nancy, watch please," said Clara as she recited a prayer which both priests knew well.

Saint Michael the Archangel, defend us in battle; be our protection against the wickedness and snares of the devil. May God rebuke him, we pray and do thou, O Prince of the heavenly host, by the power of God, thrust into hell Satan and all the evil spirits who prowl the world seeking the ruin of souls. Amen.

The feather glowed brighter; it rose high into the air and emitted a pink glow which covered all of us, its iridescent hues catching the light.

Clara said with authority, "This is our protection against the evil demonic forces. Saint Michael the Archangel is protecting us through this feather taken from his wing. A demon cannot inhabit, tempt, or demonise us whilst under his protection."

The feather ascended to the top of the church hall, glowing pink, and rotating in circles.

"It's checking our hearts, seeking out evil, making sure we are pure of heart and soul," said Clara.

"What occurs when the feather encounters someone impure?" a group member asked with trepidation.

"Don't be concerned, we're all on the right side, and the feather will recognise it."

The feather finished rotating, the pink glow faded, and it floated back into Clara's hand. Placing it back in the ornate box, she cradled the gift with reverence, her eyes gleaming with awe.

"This is our most precious gift from God. We must keep the feather safe. If a demon gets hold of it, or anyone takes it who is not of pure heart, it will go black, wither, and disintegrate."

"Clara, I'm still unsure how you got this," Bruno said, touching her arm.

"More easily than you may think, Bruno. I travelled to Buenos Aires to see Angelina, the child prophet. She lived in a villa miseria, a sort of shanty town. Angelina's family welcomed me and assured me I was safe."

"I realised she was someone with supernatural insight and visions of the future, seeing beyond the present into other realms. When receiving spiritual revelation, what she sees appears as real as what we see."

Clara's eyes sparkled with a glint of urgency as she explained the importance of the holy relic for the quest.

"I heard there was a Seer. A Prophet. The Vatican wanted to contact her, but you got there first, Clara," said Father Novak, smiling at her but also irritated.

Clara then explained to the group that the Lord had decided the spiritual battle between good, and evil was gathering pace, and we, as God's children, needed support during this difficult time.

"God said, 'Michael, I want you to remove a feather from your right wing. It will reach the rightful keeper. Let it go down to earth.' Saint Michael placed the feather from heaven into the box I'm holding, then let it fall to earth."

Angelina then told Clara, should she wish to receive the box, to recite the following prayer on reaching her home in Germany. In the softly lit bedroom, shadows danced on the walls as she knelt before her bed, her hands clasped in prayer.

"My beloved Archangel Saint Michael, wanting to be numbered among your devoted servants, I offer and consecrate myself to you, and place myself, my family and all I have under your most powerful protection."

Clara was so animated at telling the story of the feather, she held everyone's full interest.

"I waited, but nothing happened, so I said it a second time. I went to bed, fearing false hope. The next morning, the box was by my bedside. It shimmered, and I touched it, feeling shocked as to how smooth the covering was. Then I remember it was from Saint Michael at God's behest, and prayed for a time, thanking the Lord and Saint Michael for sending it."

"What an amazing story," I said, my eyes wide with awe, giving her a warm and genuine smile.

"How do we bring together all the Nazis in one location?"

Bruno spoke up. "I have a plan, Nancy; do not worry. It demands dedication and hard work, but we can do it."

I smiled at Bruno, noticing how tired and pale he looked.

"Is it time to take a break?"

I looked round the room. The weariness in the group's voices and the occasional yawn betrayed the long hours we had spent talking and debating.

"Please keep it somewhere safe, Clara. It is the most holy relic I have ever seen."

Clara patted the box, saying, "I will guard it with my life, Father Novak. Don't worry." Bruno's voice carried a confident tone, laced with anticipation, as he shared his words, "I have a plan, but it's not ready to be revealed yet."

"I'll pray for everyone today. Let us rest, recover, and recuperate. Once we're prepared, we'll notify everyone," said Father Novak.

We made our way out of the church hall, feeling blessed. I walked along with Bruno and Father Novak, with Patrick and Clara walking just behind us.

"What's next?" I said to Bruno.

"I am working on the plan, Nancy, but it needs careful thought. It is a crucial step for us to take. Consider it a work in progress. It involves us all travelling to South America, to Argentina, to locate, cleanse, and hold to justice the most senior Nazis. Father Novak has a fund from the Vatican which we can access to pay for it."

It might be both exciting and frightening, but I was up for it. Bruno was taking charge of matters now and I loved it.

"Clara, where are you staying?"

Bruno looked at her with concern.

"I am okay, Bruno; I am staying at the hotel in the centre of Birmingham. The Grand Hotel. It is a lovely old building and I am looking forward to my bed as I have not stopped since I got here," and she smiled at him.

He smiled back.

"We need to talk, Clara."

"I understand, Bruno, but let's prioritise the more pressing matters," she stated.

"OK, I guess we have time to catch up."

Bruno's gaze shifted towards me.

"I'm going to find a hotel and lodge with Patrick."

He nodded.

"Father Novak, where will you stay?" I asked.

"Oh, I am with Bruno in the small hotel."

"Ah yes, I remember," I replied.

I moved, so I was walking next to her.

"Are you sure you will be okay, Clara?"

"I feel protected, and will call you, Bruno or Father Novak if I have any problems."

"We all have somewhere to lay our heads tonight. The experience was remarkable."

Clara said, "Shh, let us not discuss our spiritual weapon. One never knows where something demonic was lurking."

"Clara, you're spot on," Father Novak affirmed.

We parted company and went to our respective hotels, on our knees, with tiredness.

Patrick and I found a suitable bed-and-breakfast, different from the previous one. The soft cushions and plush blankets provided well needed comfort as we nestled into our room.

I shielded Patrick from the landlord's scrutiny, wanting no questions asked.

I let Patrick in, but he stayed silent for a few minutes, then his excitement burst forth.

"Nancy, what an incredible experience. A demon attacked me, then I saw a holy spiritual artefact sent by God, but most of all, having my sight restored. A direct miracle received from God. I don't think I'll ever have a greater experience than this."

I gave Patrick a nod of agreement, my eyebrows raised. Moving from a comfortable sofa, I slumped onto my bed with exhaustion. My body was telling me it needed to rest but the thought of going to Argentina was pulsating in my brain.

"I'm going to see Andrew tomorrow for a pub lunch, Patrick, whilst Bruno and Father Novak iron out the details of the trip. Can you manage here alone?"

"Yes, of course, Nancy. I'm thrilled to see again and excited by Clara's holy relic. I will contemplate our next steps tomorrow. You enjoy your lunch with Andrew."

After Patrick said protective prayers, we crawled under the covers of our respective beds and were snoring before our heads even hit the pillows.

Chapter 29

WAKING UP EXCITED FROM the previous day's events, I wanted to share what had happened with my best pal, Andrew. Leaving Patrick snoring in bed; looking so sweet with his white, blonde hair tousled on the pillow. I crept out of the B&B, not wanting to disturb him.

No doubt, everyone from the meeting was exhausted. Excited and fearful at the same time about the possible trip to South America. I noted Bruno's natural authority was showing through in the group. He was now a solid part of our community.

As I entered the pub, and sat in my favourite chair by the fire, its flames cast a warm glow. Super excited to see Andrew, i waited for him to arrive.

From the moment I had bumped into Andrew as a student nurse in 1947, he became my best friend, and I felt a genuine affection towards him. Knowing he was gay cut any possibility of romance, which made me feel comfortable in his presence. Not only that, but he also utterly understood and accepted me, flaws and all. Never judgmental, always fun!

The minutes on the pub's enormous clock face on the wall opposite ticked by. As the time passed, my initial delight turned into a growing unease, until eventually, my anxiety reached a peak. Over an hour later, I was overly concerned. This was unprecedented. Andrew was never late. Having been in the military, and super organised, he was a stickler for punctuality. He was someone I relied upon; solid, stoic and a loyal friend, with a calm personality. Something untoward must have happened to him.

The pub was quite empty, and I felt sorry for Pete the Landlord. He took on the pub years ago and spent money refurbishing the old Victorian building, with a charming blend of vintage and modern style. Regrettably, the old-fashioned look was preferred by his customers, and the refurbishment was unappreciated. People are fickle.

"Pete, any chance Andrew was in here tonight?"

Pete wiped the long modernised wooden bar down with a white cloth. Eyebrows furrowing as he glanced at me.

"No, Nancy. He was here yesterday with his friend Eric, drinking beer. After a few hours, they left in good spirits, pardon the pun, and I haven't seen him since. Why?"

"No worries. I'll pop over to his flat instead and catch him there instead."

Andrew lived fifteen minutes from the pub, and I imagined various scenarios as to why he hadn't left his home. There was no-one there to help him if he was in trouble. Andrew lived in an Edwardian style flat conversion on the first floor, and Andrea, his neighbour, lived on the ground floor.

It was a stylish home, and the first time I visited it, I fell in love with the spacious sized rooms, lofty ceilings, ornate detail, and absolute elegance, which of course suited Andrew down to the ground.

This was a home rich in features. Dating back to 1910, it possessed a carved porch, timber railings, beautiful cornicing in the living room, and the key feature of stained-glass windowed doors. The flat was his pride and joy. One of Andrew's pastimes was painting watercolours, so the natural light the voluminous glass windows afforded him was perfect.

On reaching his flat, I rapped on Andrew's door, listened but heard nothing, now worried. I ran over to Andrea, who was in the front garden.

"Good afternoon, Andrea. Have you seen Andrew today?"

She turned, stopped watering her plants, smiled, and said, "No, sorry Nancy, not today. Is everything okay?"

"He's not answering his front door, and we were supposed to meet at the pub. It's so strange."

Realising I was worried, she paused before revealing, "I have a spare key to the flat, Nancy, for emergencies. Does this qualify as an emergency?"

My gut was doing back flips, and my senses were tingling.

"Yes, I think so, Andrea. Can you get the key now?"

She dropped the watering hose, ran inside, and grabbed the spare key. The creak of the hinges echoed through the hallway as she opened Andrew's door, breaking the silence.

As we entered the flat together, I sensed something was very wrong indeed, but nothing could have prepared me for the sight in his living room. My eyes widened in shock, reflecting the horror which gripped me. The room was in disarray. Andrew sat on the floor with his back against the sofa, a bluish-purple colour in the face, sobbing, tears streaming down his face, with a ligature wound tightly around his neck.

"Andrew!" I screamed.

There was no time to waste. He'd tied the cord from his dressing gown round his neck, and it was strangling him. Remembering the meticulous training at the hospital, where

I learned how to handle ligatures with careful precision, we created a small gap between the tight cord encircling his neck and my trembling hand, allowing him to gasp for air. I carefully unravelled the tangled cord, freeing it from its knots. It was touch and go.

On releasing him from the dressing gown cord, he flopped sideways onto the floor, crying. Andrea and I sat back on our heels in utter dismay. My mouth hung open, but no words escaped as I struggled to find my voice. My heart raced, trying to recover my composure. Although my nursing instincts took over, Andrew was my friend, and I was in a complete state of shock.

Andrew was muttering. I leaned in towards him and heard the word demons. *Did he say demons?* Of course he did. This was no surprise anymore. Demonic interference was everywhere.

"What do we do, Nancy? Take him to the hospital? He tried to commit suicide," Andrea said breathless from the shock.

"Yes, but Andrew has never been suicidal?"

The demon forced him, I thought.

Our breaths hitched, and we could hear the pounding of our own hearts in our ears. Being a nurse, I recognised the importance of evaluating his mental state at the hospital, but the mention of 'demons' was alarming.

Andrea said, "We need tea, Nancy, for shock. You decide what to do."

My heart overflowed with gratitude towards Andrea for giving me the authority to make the decision regarding Andrew's wellbeing. I struggled to lift Andrew onto the plush sofa, his body sinking into the cushions, his face showing signs of exhaustion, his breathing laboured from the ordeal.

"What on earth, Andrew?"

Hearing about what happened was necessary, although I didn't want to upset him further.

"I saw it, Nancy. The only man to see hell."

His voice quivered as he spoke, his words saturated with fear and desperation.

"Nancy, I didn't want to go to hell. I wanted to go to heaven."

I took Andrew's hand and stroked it, whilst his body shook violently, unable to stop.

"Andrew, no one is condemning you to hell. I will not allow it. Patrick, Bruno, and Father Novak will not allow it either. Taking your own life will not help you."

He explained he met Eric for drinks the day before and they had laughed and joked around. After leaving the pub, they went home in different directions. Walking along, Andrew felt uneasy and on edge, as if someone was following him. It was early evening and still light, but he felt unsettled. Looking back, he found nothing and saw no one.

Cutting through a dark alleyway to get to the flat, because it reduced his journey time home by a couple of minutes, he darted down the dimly lit alleyway as normal. As he hurried down the path, shadows shifted on walls, dark shadows loomed larger in the passageway, and he smelled a vile odour, akin to sulphur. Then he heard low, menacing growls. The smell grew stronger as he walked along, and he increased the speed of his footsteps.

"Something smelled dead, rotting in that alleyway, Nancy."

My heart skipped a beat.

"I heard low, guttural sounds, animal noises, yet not an animal. It was so confusing. Dark shadows appeared all around. Initially they moved but now remained static. I shouted out for help, but none came, so I yelled at the black outlines, demanding to be left alone by them."

How many more friends and family members would encounter a demonic experience? I thought.

His voice shaky and faltering said, "I stopped walking as the shadows made the alleyway pitch black and were disorientating. The biggest shadow of all formed into a large, dark mass, and a huge shape of a beast appeared. It was horrid."

His fingers tightened around my arm, leaving faint impressions on my skin, as he animatedly shared his story. This was the first time I had seen Andrew in such a poor state. Normally a powerful individual with an air of authority, this person was a quivering wreck.

As he spoke, a vivid image of the monstrous creature formed in my mind, causing a shiver to run down my spine. I swear from the description given it was the same demon from my nightmare. It was Azazel. I was certain. With the yellow glowing eyes, reddish skin, a barbed tail, and bones of animals hanging off its vile body.

Azazel had targeted Andrew. Now it was obvious. The demons wanted to frighten those closest to Bruno and me. *When was this going to end?*

"It flapped its wings, Nancy, countless wings, forcing me to move further down the alleyway, intimidating me with its body. Calling out, I hoped someone would enter the alleyway and help me, yet no-one did."

He shuddered, saying, "Then something odd happened. A doorway appeared in the wall. There was light, but not a bright light. It was just a bit lighter than the alleyway. The beast pushed me through the doorway. I suppose you could call it a portal. What I saw next was unspeakable."

Andrew took a deep breath, and I shivered, as though someone had walked over my future grave.

"Rooted to the spot for five minutes, I scanned the surroundings. It was a dark realm, a black, unyielding darkness, and I couldn't see much. But amid a blazing fire, evil entities hurled people into a burning furnace, leaving me terrified. The lost souls were screaming, Nancy! Bone-chilling screams. I felt their pain as the demons threw them in, they were tormented by the demons beyond belief."

I shook uncontrollably at Andrew's description.

"Other souls stood around, weeping, moaning. It was horrifying. God was absent in this place, Nancy. No forgiveness, no light, no love, worse than death itself, with no hope for redemption."

My family brought me up as a Catholic, believing in heaven and hell. To me, such a place existed.

"Did you see the devil, Andrew?"

"It all happened so fast, Nancy. I have no idea."

Andrew started crying again, so I stroked his hair. There was a black mark imprinted on his scalp. I rubbed it, as I thought it was dirt, but it remained. A weird sound emitted from Andrew as I rubbed the mark. Almost like a growl. I imagined it, surely.

"It's okay, Andrew," I said, trying to reassure him.

Andrea reappeared with the tea. She glanced at me, as if to ask was he alright?

"He will be okay, Andrea, he just experienced a terrible nightmare and is reacting to it."

I pulled Andrea to one side, so Andrew wasn't likely to hear our conversation. Her face softened with a mixture of concern and hesitation as she looked at Andrew.

"Going to the hospital won't help him. He just needs company. I'm going abroad and I can't change it."

Andrea said she didn't mind looking after Andrew. She was such a good person. I told her it was likely he would mention demons and hell, but said not to worry, and to avoid discussing it. Then I explained to Andrew what would happen. Andrea would look after him and I vowed to visit him at my earliest opportunity.

"Andrew, please promise me you won't try this again. Andrea will stay with you until my return from South America."

"I won't, Nancy, but I wish you were staying here. It was hell, Nancy, and I saw unimaginable sights. Things no human should ever see."

I drew him in close to me for a hug.

"I'll be back as soon as possible, and we will defeat these evil entities with God's help. Please rest and recuperate. I will send you a telegram with contact details so you can keep in touch. Andrea will take good care of you."

My mind was still buzzing. The image of a monstrous creature forcefully shoving Andrew through a swirling, fiery portal flashed in my mind. *Did anyone visit and return from hell ever?* Poor Andrew, it must have been horrific, whatever it was.

"How did you get back home, Andrew?"

"I only spent a few minutes in hell, Nancy. It was full of burning fires, with a strong smell of sulphur. People's suffering and torment there is beyond description."

He turned away from me, coughing, trying not to be sick. I tried to comfort him, holding his hand.

"The beast pushed me hard, and I tumbled through the portal, catching glimpses of swirling colours and distorted shapes before crashing onto the grimy pavement of the alleyway. I rose, then sprinted until my heart felt like bursting, and arrived here. It was so awful. Lying awake all night; beside myself with fear."

"Andrew, it's not interested in you. It is trying to frighten me, Bruno, Patrick, and Father Novak. It's part of its game plan."

I hugged him again.

"I am deeply sorry for what has happened."

Andrew was still distraught.

"Nancy, I just wanted to reach heaven."

"This is not the way, Andrew. I promise you; Patrick and Father Novak will send you protective prayers. The demon sent a message through you, but it was only a warning shot. Azazel opposes our going to South America to cleanse and confront the evil entities contained within the Nazis."

"Please be careful, Nancy."

"Don't worry about me, Andrew. Good people are taking care of me."

Andrea allowed us to speak privately. Now she reappeared and I explained Andrew just needed to recover and that I didn't believe he would try to commit suicide again. If she was worried, she should call an ambulance.

I hugged Andrew one last time, then left to see Bruno urgently. Patrick and Father Novak needed to pray for him. I felt angry and guilty for involving Andrew in this.

The situation strengthened my resolve to stop this monstrous interference in people's lives forever. Meeting Bruno opened a doorway to a hell I wasn't sure existed. Now I knew it did, and we needed to slam it shut forever.

Chapter 30

A WEEK PASSED, AND it was time to travel to Argentina. Arrangements were swift, and ever since I had seen Andrew, it was a whirlwind. I kept in touch with Andrea but time was lacking for a further visit, as there was too much to arrange. She kept a watchful eye on him though, promising me updates on any issues.

I made my way to Bruno's hotel near the airport and spoke to him. Knowing Andrew's situation was shocking and how upset I was, he wrapped his arms around me, providing me with comfort and reassurance. The demons were giving us a stark warning not to travel there.

"We will proceed, Nancy, whatever the cost."

I nodded, feeling the weight of our purpose.

He was so resolute, so determined, that I felt a wave of desire flood my body. It took me unawares, and he seemed oblivious to the beating of my heart. It was so loud in my ears, I was certain he would hear it. But at that moment his focus was elsewhere.

We went to see Patrick and Father Novak, and they said protective prayers for Andrew. I was so nervous about leaving Andrew in England whilst in South America, but knew Andrea was taking proper care of him. I pictured Andrew enjoying

Andrea's home-made treats and meals, knowing he was in safe hands, but it was still difficult.

The sound of matron's kind voice resonated in my ears as she granted me the extra time off, unaware of my hidden intentions. On the journey to South America, we enjoyed endless food, sometimes the meals lasting for three hours, but I hated the smoke in the plane's cabin as I didn't like cigarettes at all. After hours of travel with overnight stops, we reached Argentina. It was thrilling since I had only travelled to Ireland and England previously.

Once we checked in at our hotels and took naps, we visited the important destination for the mission straight away. The grandeur of the Buenos Aires Metropolitan Cathedral made it the perfect setting, with towering spires and intricate architectural details. An old Catholic Cathedral, consecrated in 1791, it was in the city centre, overlooking the Plaza de Mayo in the San Nicolas neighbourhood. The spot appeared perfect for the exorcisms.

It was a huge cathedral with an impressive nave sporting Venetian style tiles on the floor. The towering cathedral boasted intricate stained-glass windows, casting a kalei-doscope of colours onto the polished floors. A significant cathedral for Catholics, it contained the fourteen stations of the cross. Each station depicting the events from when Pontius Pilate condemned Jesus to death through to Jesus's final entombment. Sadly, we were unaware at this time that this cathedral lacked the sanctity and safety expected.

The ex-Nazis who escaped to South America often gathered here for satanic rituals, confirmed by the locals we spoke to later, after the exorcisms, who said they heard noises and saw strange lights emanating from the cathedral late at night.

Whispers of eerie chants and unsettling incantations echoed through the air, fuelling suspicions of occult practices.

The Nazis brazenly gathered within the sacred walls of a revered place, mocking divinity. If it was true, then we had found the worst spot possible to carry out the exorcisms, completely unaware of the danger facing us.

"What time are they due to arrive, Bruno?"

He was sitting on one of the long pews, and didn't answer straight away, seeming anxious, his deep brown eyes boring into mine, and I smiled.

He anticipated a crowd of ex-Nazis, eyes filled with curiosity gathering at the reunion venue, celebrating achievements of the Third Reich. Unaware of the true purpose of the meeting, the Nazis believed that although Hitler was gone, someone senior could take his place. This idea appealed to the senior officers in Hitler's ex-army, owing to their arrogance and ego.

"Shortly, Nancy, shortly."

I could tell he was nervous, and I was frightened we were inviting Nazis to gather there. The weight of our actions lay heavy on our shoulders, but it was necessary to bring them together to offer redemption. Redemption but **never** forgiveness.

Out of the fifty Nazis Bruno invited, the majority, a staggering ninety percent, agreed to attend the meeting. With forty-five Nazis attending, the reunion spanned three days. We expected to deal with fifteen Nazis at a time and needed seventy-five helpers minimum in attendance on each day. The group grew closer with our mission, and it was heartwarming to experience that.

Father Novak's stern gaze swept across the room, emphasising to the group the importance of understanding the intricacies of the exorcism. Demons were deceitful and manipulative and would create divisions if we allowed it. He exuded confidence, and although sixty-five years old, possessed an unbelievable level of energy to combat the devil. I found his personality to be comforting, making us feel safe around him.

"The devil's spirit is horrendous. The person owned will blaspheme and may speak different languages as we cast out the demons. They may appear to transform into some kind of beast or animal, as demons manipulate the light, creating an illusion, and you will feel the person's body convulsing under our hands."

He mentioned the possibility of vomiting nails, metal, glass shards, or similar objects, and let the group know they were not to pay attention or touch items the possessed men vomited, as a demon might have cursed it.

I listened to Father Novak explaining the different things a possessed man did. The timbre of his voice carried a sense of authority and experience, as if it held the echoes of past exorcisms. The person owned by the demon could have superhuman strength, as he'd seen people climb walls and ceilings before. Maintaining enough individuals was essential to manage the menacing demons. I shivered with apprehension. There was a challenging battle ahead.

"Keep in mind that the majority of possessions originated from the dark incantations woven during the last world war."

A shiver ran down my spine.

"We will break those spells; and deliver and exorcise these demons. Our guide is the scriptures, and tools are prayers and faith."

In the room, I studied everyone's faces as we chanted, "Don't be scared. Stand in your faith. We will overcome. Our group is powerful," and I finally felt at home.

Chapter 31

A SMELL OF INCENSE pervaded the cathedral. It was ostentatious indeed. We spent hours discussing with Clara how to defeat the evil entities. She informed us that demons gather in clusters within a hierarchical system, but by strategically removing the weakest demons, we could effectively manage the group exorcisms.

"The aim of every demon is deception, division, diversion, and discouragement. These are the four areas they concentrate on. They will be divisive and pit us against one another. We must guard against it at all costs."

I looked around the group. They responded well, nodding in agreement, united towards a common goal.

After speaking to the group, Clara requested Bruno's presence in a side chapel. She clearly wanted to share her nightmare's details, which led to her visiting England. Ever since arriving, it had been a whirlwind of activity, so she had waited until we reached Argentina to explain in full.

Bruno said, "Clara, Nancy is a loyal friend, and I would like her to hear about the nightmare, as she suffered from something similar recently. It may apply to her own experience."

Clara's eyebrows raised when she heard Bruno call us staunch friends. He was a moralistic man, and there was a large age gap between us. I feared she'd assume something inappropriate had happened. Bruno's wife, Isabel, died from tuberculosis, so technically Bruno was free to have a romantic relationship if he wanted to, but it wasn't something I had thought about until recently. I wasn't sure if a relationship with Bruno had crossed his mind at all.

"Of course, Bruno. Would Father Novak and Father Flanagan like to hear the details as well?"

We gathered and Clara explained how she had dreamed of the German Nazi Swastika on a flag, fluttering in the breeze. The Jewish symbol, the yellow Star of David, then came into view, which the Nazis forced the Jews to stitch onto their clothing during the war to mark them out as being Jewish.

"It was unsurprising to see both symbols, as I had encountered them before. However, there is a web of connections between the war, the persecution of Jews, and sinister satanic rituals. The nightmare left me sweating and fearful of the potential consequences if we were to neglect this situation."

I let out a large breath. Clara had hit the nail on the head and corroborated what Bruno had told me.

"There were two men and a woman, standing in a chalk circle. A fire blazed in front of them, but there was no smoke, just a crackling, intense bright yellow flame dancing around them. The older man held up his hand, fingers trembling, chanting an incantation. The woman, younger, but no less resolute, stood at his side. I could see that Bruno was one of these people, but I couldn't see the features of the other two."

She frowned as she tried hard to remember the details.

"Flames engulfed the three of them, then a windstorm, followed by sheets of rain, and holes appeared on the floor, like a mini earthquake. Bruno looked up, his gaze shifting from the flames up to the heavens. Then the dream vanished, and I woke up feeling fearful. It was an advanced warning of doom."

Clara's description of her nightmare was vivid and visceral. I saw she was sweating profusely as she recounted the story.

"My heart rapidly thumped in my chest, echoing in my ears as I gasped for breath. The fire I saw in the dream surprised me, as fire is often a symbol of purification, but in this nightmare, it appeared uncontrolled and filled with negative energy."

As we stood there, listening to Clara's experience, the pieces of the jigsaw clicked into place for me. She had described the elementals attacking Bruno, Father Novak, and me. The realisation scared me half to death. She looked at us in turn.

"I needed to tell you about it, Bruno. Thankfully, Sister Flanagan contacted me, so I knew how to reach you."

Bruno's hand found Clara's shoulder, a silent reassurance of his support.

"You're a part of this now," he softly murmured. Then he exclaimed loudly, "Fate has woven our paths together and we're a unique assembly. A fellowship of specialists, each with our own gifts."

Moving to the larger part of the cathedral to rejoin our group, we could see their faces displaying a mixture of determination and fear. Everyone felt tense.

Bruno addressed the group.

"Father Novak must oversee the Exorcisms, as he has the broadest experience. Remember, he is in control and in charge. Egos are not a factor here. Jesus holds the utmost importance in the room."

We all murmured, "Amen".

Father Novak continued, "Be one hundred percent certain of the Lord. Our hearts are true. Whichever religion you belong to, please say whatever prayers you need to reach a state of grace. For the Catholics present here, Father Flanagan and I will take confession, followed by mass, and present the Holy Eucharist. Our faith is the strongest defence of all, and it is likely these evil entities will test your faith to breaking point."

Clara added, "People, please note. The demons feed off human energy and function at a low vibrational frequency. We must keep control of our fear, anxiety, and resentment. There must be no violence. We are their energetic source, and must project love, peace, joy, and happiness as they cannot absorb those higher vibrational frequencies. Let us make sure we band together in love and strength!"

The group shared nods and hugs. I believed the group to be making friends with each other for life. It was very comforting.

Patrick spoke up, "Remember, the person we assist must desire the exorcism. Therefore, seek out the trace of humanity which remains within them. Facing the evil entities head-on is crucial. God defeated Satan. We will channel God; and we will defeat Satan."

I asked Patrick how to achieve this. It sounded almost impossible to succeed.

"The Nazis enjoyed the power and the money inviting the devil in. How are we going to discover any humanity when they have none?"

"Nancy, possession can occur if you sin, as original sin separates man from God, but there is such a thing as Satanic Ritual Abuse. The Nazis engaged in this. Through blood rituals, the participants offered their bodies as vessels for the devil's presence, but not everyone wanted to invite the devil in."

Patrick's eyes shimmered with hope and sincerity as he spoke these words to me, "There is a spark of humanity in every single person, Nancy. We will find it. Do not doubt it!"

Chapter 32

THE HUSHED WHISPERS OF anticipation echoed throughout the cathedral, mingling with the distant sounds of footsteps, as we waited for the first Nazi to arrive. He was our first exorcism test case.

I watched as Martin Weiss strode with purpose into the cathedral, looking around him as he entered. He saw me, nodded, and I directed him to one of the three chapel annexes attached to the nave. In synchronicity with the sombre mood of the day, the stained-glass windows were dark, allowing only a faint glimmer of daylight to show through. It contributed to a heavy atmosphere.

A disdainful smirk played upon his lips, his eyes darting around the room until they fixated on Bruno at the far end. Bruno told me later that Martin Weiss was little changed from when he saw him last in Vilnius. He still wore glasses with a pinched and angry expression on his face.

He shouted, "Where is it? Where's the reunion? His head swivelled, "And everyone?"

No doubt he expected to see Nazi memorabilia gracing the walls, such as the Swastika with an eagle atop it, or even a military tribute.

He said to Bruno with relish, "I am not surprised the

meeting is being held here. It shields our glorious Third Reich from prying eyes and uninvited attention. Of course, I know this place from the ratline setup."

I looked over at Bruno in horror. We knew about the secret passage, 'the ratline', but had no clue that the grand cathedral was connected to the Nazis. The room fell silent as shock and disbelief etched across everyone's faces. The ratline was where the Catholic Church helped Nazis to escape and come to South America after the war.

Somehow, the demons had duped us. Once a sanctuary, now tainted by evil. I needed to understand how we came to choose the location. Then I remembered it was Clara's suggestion. We thought we were controlling events, but we may have unexpectedly walked into a trap.

Martin Weiss continued, "It pleased me to receive the message; I have been wanting us to get together. We must rise from the ashes like a Phoenix to be born again."

I shrank back into the shadows. Bruno's face twisted into a grimace as he uttered, "Nice speech, Martin. You need to take a seat."

Bruno showed Martin where to sit down right in the middle of the annex. He sat down with a confused expression on his face. Then he nodded, believing he was the honoured guest, there to receive praise and adulation from all. The next event would be shocking.

I observed his annoyance as he witnessed the two priests exiting the cathedral's nave. Patrick glanced at me as he rushed past Martin Weiss, and saw from the way Father Novak was moving, he was in a serious state of mind.

Martin Weiss roared at Bruno and stood up. He was furious. "What is going on here? Priests?"

Bruno shouted back, "Shut up, Martin, and sit back down!"

"How dare you? Where are the others? I refuse to stay for this ridiculous charade."

Grunts and breaths filled the room as Bruno and Patrick wrestled Weiss back down into the chair.

Bruno commanded, "Sit here and listen. Let us uncover the humanity within you."

Martin's eyes widened, a flicker of fear and recognition dancing within them as the dormant demon inside him stirred. His face contorted with rage and a dark, evil expression spread across it.

Father Novak shouted over to Patrick, "Spray him with holy water, Father Flanagan, we need to check which demon he is harbouring!"

Patrick threw holy water over Martin Weiss, and he screamed. Venomous words flowed like a toxic river out of him directed at both Patrick and Father Novak. Father Novak approached Weiss with a solid gold crucifix, his robes swaying with each step.

Saying the Lord's prayer under my breath, I felt worried for both Father Novak and Patrick's safety. I saw group members who were standing in the nave, enter the small chapel annex. They wanted first-hand experience of the exorcism.

Father Novak shouted over to Patrick, "Join me, Father Flanagan now. Come, say the Lord's prayers with me."

As the exorcism proceeded, my mouth went dry, a bitter taste of dread filling my senses as I dropped to my knees. The memory of the horrifying demon beside my bed rose in my mind, and I fought the urge to escape the cathedral annex and focused instead on helping Patrick, Bruno, and Father Novak. Hot and cold sensations overwhelmed me, accompanied by a deep nausea.

The demon inside of Martin Weiss raged and roared, shouting out in unknown languages, which I later found out to be Aramaic. Bruno shouted back at the evil entity. The demon brought forth horrifying images of *Kinderaktion*, the event when the Nazis separated children under sixteen from their families. It wanted to taunt Bruno.

The demon knew Bruno had suffered major stress because of his role as Camp Commandant. Bruno blamed himself as he was not present during the *Kinderaktion* and could not stop it. The demon wanted to play on Bruno's vulnerability, knowing it would make him uncomfortable and insecure. Bruno was the weakest link within our group due to his war history. Its eyes gleamed with hate.

"Stop it, demon," shouted Bruno.

The vivid images of the terrorised children flashed through his mind like a vibrant slide show. My heart ached for Bruno, as he was having a terrible time. The evil being inside Martin Weiss' body enjoyed Bruno's discomfort and laughed maniacally..

"Feel their pain, Commandant. Look at their mothers screaming for their children in the trucks. You didn't save them. Why weren't you there?" he taunted him mercilessly.

The demon wanted to destroy Bruno's sanity and sent further visions of the terrified families. His words echoing around the room, dripping with accusation. Bruno's eyes remained haunted, finding it difficult to shake off the vivid images which consumed his mind. Father Novak saw what was happening to Bruno.

"Stand firm in your faith, Bruno. Remember, he is trying to discourage you. Do not let him."

I ran to Bruno's side, feeling the weight of his suffering, like a heavy burden pressing down on my own shoulders. Taking his hand, I clasped it to my chest.

"Don't surrender to it, Bruno."

I tried to convey the compassion I felt for his situation. *Did I love him at that moment?*

Bruno yelled, telling me to let go and stay away whilst calling out to Father Novak, "He's too strong, Father. I can't do this."

Bruno's eyes brimmed with tears from the visions the demon was sending him.

"Yes, you can Bruno," Father Novak shouted back.

Bruno's situation was terrifying. He fought against the visions, desperately trying to focus on anything else he could.

"Tell me your name, demon, tell me it now, dark being from hell," shouted Father Novak, demanding a response.

The tension in the room was overwhelming. The group members had tied Martin Weiss to a chair earlier, but the chair was clearly levitating.

Patrick yelled, "Keep him restrained! Hold him down!"

I wanted to help, but knew I was no physical match for the evil entity's power. The demon inside Martin Weiss continued to provoke Bruno.

"Where is your faith, Commandant? I am stronger than you. Your faith will not save you. You have been a failure all your life!" screamed the demon.

Five further members of the group rushed towards the chair to help, their hands clutching its edges, desperate to prevent the demon from ascending higher into the air. It was already inches off the ground.

Martin Weiss began choking and vomited up a repulsive

large piece of metal. The metal was mixed with white phlegm.

"Disgusting," a member of the group said. Despite retching, he steadfastly held onto the chair.

"Don't let go!" shouted Father Novak.

The piece of metal fell to the floor with a sharp clang as it exploded out of Martin Weiss's throat. It was a small gun barrel. We identified the small barrel as being German, and everyone made the sign of the cross. They clung stubbornly to the chair which Martin Weiss was in. It was shaking extensively and trying to rise further off the floor. I closed my eyes and prayed harder. I stood in front of Bruno, trying to think how to help. His eyes filled with tears and his face twisted in anguish. He pushed me away again, struggling to bear the demon's relentless torment.

Bruno held his head in his hands, trying to block out the vile visions as the demon screamed and laughed in delight. A wild wind swirled in the room. The wind was an elemental summoned by the demon contained within Weiss' body. It was a chaotic and confusing scene.

Bruno maintained a strong faith in the Lord, doing his best to ignore the demon through prayer, but it was hard going. His insecurities and doubts were affecting his mental strength. How much longer could he endure this torment? He was petrified the demon's wicket behaviour would send him into a state of total madness from which he would never recover.

Clara calmly entered the room. She saw that although Father Novak and Father Flanagan were praying hard, trying to manage the demon, Bruno was having an intense internal struggle.

She soon realised, although not a precise replica of her nightmare, Bruno was in serious danger. Watching from the sidelines, I saw her open the special box and take out Saint Michael, the Archangel's feather. Her voice rang out with determination, echoing throughout the room.

"Now we will know the truth."

I shouted out to Clara, "Please help him, Clara."

It was agony watching Bruno suffer from the demon's taunts and jibes.

"Don't worry, Nancy, it will all be okay," she responded calmly.

The feather fluttered up high in the room, and the name Mammon appeared in blazing letters, floating high above us.

"Ah, the demon, Mammon? We know who you are now! You love money, material wealth and the greedy pursuit of gain," shouted Father Novak as he saw the burning letters rise up to the ceiling.

The demon screeched; it was a chilling, ethereal sound. Then it pronounced in a dark, gravelly voice, which was not Martin Weiss's, "So you know my name, priest, so fucking what?"

"You have a wife and three children, but you don't deserve them," shouted Clara. "Watch this, Mammon."

The feather twirled in the air, painting vivid scenes that engulfed us in a mesmerising show. A panoramic view unfolded before us, stretching out in every direction. I couldn't believe my eyes as Martin Weiss's own three children's fearful faces replaced the anguished expressions of the camp children displayed in the vision.

He saw his wife, terrified and screaming, reaching her hands out for the children, his children. He never experienced such direct emotional pain before.

He took deep jagged breaths as he saw his own hand reach

down to his gun holster, lift the pistol and aim it at his wife. This happened in slow motion, adding to his fear and pain.

Bruno shouted, "You shot a mother in cold blood who screamed 'Murderer' because you took her child's life. Witness your wife, about to be shot in the same manner."

"No, oh no," he moaned.

He felt his wife's pain, fear, and his own horror at the unfolding vision. Tears shone in Martin Weiss' eyes.

The demon Mammon emitted a guttural scream from deep within him. He shouted out in his own voice, "No, this cannot be happening. I do not want this. Stop it, stop it now!"

O glorious Archangel St. Michael, Prince of the heavenly host, defends us in battle, and in the struggle, which is ours against the principalities and powers, against the rulers of this world of darkness, against spirits of evil in high places.

Father Novak's lips moved, his eyes closed in deep concentration, as he recited the exorcism prayer, and cast out Mammon's lower minions. Weiss's body contained six demonic minions. We witnessed the black shadows and every time one left Martin Weiss' body, he screeched aloud. It was an excruciating and deafening sound.

Patrick joined Father Novak and recited the same prayer with him. They were having a positive effect on the demon.

Father Novak shouted to the group, "Hold tight, hold tight now! We are close!"

The group secured the chair to the floor, ensuring it didn't budge. It had stopped trying to levitate further and fell to the floor with a thud.

Bruno was recovering, as the demon no longer taunted him. It was concentrating instead on clinging on to the soul of Martin Weiss. I returned to his side, clasping his hand in

249

mine. This time he didn't push me away but gripped it hard. At that moment. we were an indomitable team, undefeated when together.

Weiss steeled himself to confess and renounce the devil, his trembling voice quivering with exhaustion. We were winning the spiritual battle.

"My children, my wife," he chanted.

Father Novak shouted to him, "Renounce the devil!"

His voice trembled with urgency as he commanded, "Mammon, leave this man! Confess, Martin Weiss! Show us the humanity you have left. Confess and repent! Be a penitent man," continued Father Novak.

He spoke the exorcism prayer, *O, Saint Michael the Archangel, come to our aid and break the last grasps of Lucifer on this man's soul.*

Martin Weiss had little strength remaining. We had found his vulnerable spot, his family. Hard to believe, but he felt a powerful love for his three children and his wife.

The priest, with a stern expression, pointed a finger towards Martin Weiss, demanding his renunciation of the devil.

"Renounce the devil Martin Weiss, renounce him now!"

Patrick and Father Novak continued with their prayer, *O, pray to the God of peace. He may put Satan under our feet, so far conquered he may no longer hold men in captivity. Carry our prayers up to God's throne, so the mercy of the Lord may come and lay hold of the beast, the serpent of old, Satan and his demons, casting him in chains into the abyss, so he can no longer seduce the nations. Amen.*

The prayer's words echoed, growing louder and more forceful. The exorcism prayer possessed an immense and unstoppable force. A sharp ear-splitting scream emitted from

Martin Weiss's throat.

"Yes, yes, I renounce the devil. My heart aches with regret. I am sorry! I confess to *Kinderaktion*. I confess to the murders in Ponary, but please save my children and my wife."

Father Novak shouted, "Begone Mammon, you are no longer wanted by this vessel. You can no longer have his soul."

And with a final loud shriek, Martin Weiss' eyes rolled back in his head, and he collapsed on the floor in front of us. There was a thunderous clap as he fell. The rose-coloured glow which shone over all of us from the feather turned black as it absorbed the darkness from Weiss's soul. Then it vanished in an instant.

The feather floated down from the ceiling. Clara's nimble hands snatched the feather, her fingertips cradling its softness before placing it back in the box.

"Oh, my Lord," I gasped, my voice filled with awe, as I collapsed into the seat next to me. It was unlike any other experience I'd had.

Bruno was on his knees; feeling shattered, Father Novak was on his knees, as well. Clara stood holding the feather next to them, feeling victorious. Martin Weiss lay motionless on the cold, hard ground. He was unconscious.

"Saint Michael, the Archangel, would be proud of us," said Patrick, breathless and exhausted. He, too, knelt on the floor.

"I am proud of all of us," said Bruno, relieved but weary.

"I am proud of you, Bruno. You held on and didn't let the evil thing win."

He smiled into my eyes. Then he shouted to the assembled group, "Fabulous work, everyone! What a fantastic effort from you all. We did it!"

Although we felt drained, we also felt elated and clapped

and cheered.

"Are you okay, Father Novak?" said Patrick, concerned at the effort required during the exorcism.

"Yes, Father Flanagan, I am," he said, wiping the sweat from his brow.

"We did it, Father Novak," said Clara.

She was feeling animated and so happy because the holy relic had a significant impact on the demon.

"It was useful to see how we worked together on Martin Weiss, one of the evillest of the infested Nazis," Clara said.

"He was an excellent test case," said Bruno.

"Yes, we did it, but he is just one person. How will we tackle so many? Forty-five replied to your message, Bruno, and we are supposed to exorcise fifteen per day," said Father Novak.

He continued, "I am unsure if we can defeat so many demons in one day, let alone for three days."

Clara said, "I wanted to see the power of Saint Michael, the Archangel's feather, and it is indeed incredible, but I believe if we want to work on a group of possessed Nazis, we need more help. We need a lightworker."

"What is a lightworker?" I asked, confused, going back to Clara's earlier comment. I'd heard the term ages ago but never grasped its meaning.

Clara nodded and answered, "Lightworkers are high vibrational spirits who drive themselves and others around them forward. They serve humanity and individuals. They can be protectors and guard us against negative entities."

I sat, my mouth agape. Her description ringing in my ears. She was triggering something deep from my childhood.

"They guided ancient civilisations, and they are still here, guiding all of us forwards. Through their presence, lightworkers radiate a vibrant energy that uplifts and illuminates those around them. They provide light in a world which is often filled with darkness and evil, as candles against the dark. I believe they can amplify the feather's effect and heal and exercise the demons on a mass scale. Their biggest fears are failing their divine purpose and not being able to fulfil what is needed."

Clara sat down at this point. The adrenaline surge of the experience was draining.

"But do they operate within the Church? Are they a kind of priest?" I asked. My brain was buzzing, and I wanted to understand their role properly.

"No," said Father Novak. They are more spiritual than religious. We do not recognise or acknowledge them in the Catholic faith."

Clara responded, "Yes, but Father Novak, the group we have gathered here represents multiple religions. The Catholic Church doesn't collaborate with new age spiritualists, but they still believe in a divine power, like God. We need all the help we can get to battle this evil."

Chapter 33

CLARA'S VOICE FADED AS I was drawn to recall an interesting experience from my teenage years. The term lightworker scared me, so I had pushed it to the back of my memory. Clara's description and explanation brought my childhood memories streaming back.

Once at a fairground with my sister, Ursula, I spotted a fortune teller dressed in a huge cloak with stars emblazoned upon it and felt drawn to enter her tiny tent. The old lady, for she was quite wrinkled, nodded and smiled at me, indicating I should sit down.

As I sat down on a small chair opposite a table where a large crystal ball was displayed, she said, "Pay me first, dear," and held out her wizened old hand.

I slapped my head in surprise and staring at her said, "I did not realise I needed to pay you. Didn't you indicate for me approach and enter the tent?"

The old lady cackled.

"You looked at the crystal ball, seeking a reading. But you must pay, dear, this is how I earn my living. I'm a Roma and come from an extensive line of Roma."

Digging into my pocket, I pulled out a note in an exasperated manner. "Is this enough?"

Really, my attitude was quite rude. Paying no attention to my blunt approach, she took a moment to examine the note, and responded, "It's usually double, dear, but I will make an exception for you."

Then she took my right hand in hers, and I felt hazy and disassociated with my surroundings.

"What's happening? I don't feel right."

"Do not worry, dear, it is your energy field, a potent energy indeed. When I spotted you looking at the crystal ball, I saw your purple aura."

"What does that mean?" I asked, still feeling quite odd.

"You are a natural healer and have a gift."

"A gift?"

I was feeling strange and shuffled my bottom on the hard wooden seat. I didn't understand anything the old woman was telling me.

"Yes, my dear, you are a lightworker."

"A what? What is a lightworker?"

She smiled at me.

"A person here to help everyone. Bringing light to darkness, goodness to evil. Look at the brightness, my dear."

Her tent shone as if a firework was set off with a brilliant white light.

I felt confused responding, "But my sister, Ursula, is the good person in the family. Not me!"

"The white light is emanating from you, dear, not from the crystal ball, or the tent. It comes directly from your soul!"

The old lady was vehement in what she told me, so definite in her storytelling, and I was feeling so odd, I suddenly became afraid.

"This is a trick," I exclaimed, almost shouting at her. This elderly lady must be a fraud.

"You made the light appear. You are just a fake. This is a load of rubbish. You just wanted money from me. I am going. Old hag!"

She shook her head dismayed at my response.

"No, no dear, please do not deny your gift. It is a gift from God, and someone will need your help someday. It is your destiny."

I ran out of the tent as fast as my legs would carry me, terrified. The responsibility of helping others frightened me, as I wanted only to look after myself. I preferred the company of animals; I couldn't imagine helping humanity. Ursula stood nearby, looking concerned.

"You were longer than expected Nancy?"

"Yeah," I said, trying to stand up tall and look grown up. Then I said with bluster, "She was rubbish, a complete waste of money, Ursula. What an old hag!"

"Nancy!" Ursula admonished me.

I ignored her scolding, but my heart raced, and I couldn't understand what had happened with the old woman. The tent was tiny, so where did she hide a spotlight? It was a complete mystery. What did she mean I would bring light to others? I tried to put her out of my mind. A lightworker. What rubbish indeed...

Chapter 34

EVERY ACTION, LIKE A stone thrown into a pond, creates ripples that touch others in life. The actions of the Nazis with the Holocaust created a huge ripple, affecting humanity forever. It was a stark lesson to us all. There may be times of injustice, which we are unable to prevent, but we must always stand up against it.

I stood opposite Clara in the ornate and ostentatious Buenos Aires Cathedral, and experienced an epiphany, a spiritual awakening. My life's puzzle pieces aligned, igniting purpose within me. My destiny was to help humanity. To rid the earth of the demonic forces and evil entities which permeated every part of our troubled world, starting with the Nazis.

This realisation explained the way I felt as a child growing up. Although in a loving family, I never quite fitted in, not at home, or at school, and differed from everyone else. So many unusual experiences happened when completing my nursing training. Sometimes I was not standing next to a patient, but floating high above them, watching from above. This usually happened during their dying phase.

Certainly, my closest friend and trainee nurse Ena said how strange it was, because I seemed to expect when they were going to pass away, often identifying the exact day, hour, and minute of their passing.

My close cousin Patrick had an unwavering commitment to the Church that surpassed my own. In my soul, I sensed a greater purpose. There was a powerful pull towards helping others, a definite calling, but not towards the Church.

Nursing was a worthwhile role in helping those who were sick or suffering. With little financial reward, long hours, and arduous work. It was vocational and I experienced a deep sense of contentment from doing the role and helping others. Clara explained further to the group.

"A lightworker's motivation is to improve the world. Enhance people's lives and elevate individuals to a higher level of consciousness. Lightworkers vibrate at a higher energy level, enabling them to be a positive support for others in their daily struggles."

This recognition that I may be a lightworker, was registering on a meaningful and deep level. I remembered my experience with the moldavite crystal, which was carried on my person.

The stall holder at the psychic fayre said I was 'one of them.' As a teenager, I was selfish but felt an immense amount of compassion for animals, which, as I became older, grew to include people. I had to rein in this compassion as a nurse, or it could have destroyed me.

Sensing others' emotions, even when insincere, convinced me I was an empath. Moving towards Clara, I gestured with my arms excitedly.

"Clara, in my youth, a fayre fortune teller labelled me a lightworker. Feeling young and scared, I pushed the news aside."

All turned towards me, curious and surprised at my outburst.

"I have only just figured it out. I have hoped to be useful, to bring light to the dark."

The realisation of being 'good' was overwhelming. Societal expectation and family shame made me always think I was 'bad.' Accepting my gift brought an end to feeling being different and not belonging, allowing my soul's purpose in this world to become clear. This development astonished everyone, and there were murmurs among the group. Patrick, my cousin, looked at me.

"Nancy, I felt from the very beginning you were someone special, and possessed a healing gift, especially with animals, but realise now your healing gift goes much deeper."

Through excitement, the energy grew inside me, soaring through my body, from my toes, and out through the top of my head. It was exhilarating! I found what I was supposed to be doing, my destiny, my life's purpose, and it felt incredible.

Bruno glanced at me and said, "I always thought you were special, Nancy, from the very first moment we met."

I felt a warm glow at his comment. Father Novak smiled and nodded. Clara expressed surprise when I told her about my moldavite crystal and how it was important and special to me. She asked me if I understood its full powers.

"Are you aware when it pulses and seems to radiate energy, it is reflecting your own energy back to you and amplifying it? This is wonderful news, Sister Flanagan."

"Oh, for goodness' sake, please call me Nancy, Clara!"

I danced around on my tiptoes in the middle of this impressive nave in excitement. Sometimes the cathedral felt cold, but right now it felt very warm.

Clara replied with enthusiasm and happiness, "Yes, of

course I will. Nancy, now you can use your crystal to amplify the feather's powers. We can work within small groups and cover more exorcisms at once."

She turned towards Bruno and Father Novak, nodding to them. Clara then walked over to me and put her hand on my arm.

"Nancy, you are meant to be here doing this work. It is your calling. Angelina told me I was to receive additional help from someone she wasn't able to identify but would make themselves known. She said they were important for our success. I believe the someone is you, Nancy!"

She continued excitedly, "You are our secret weapon, a beacon of hope. You are the Irish Mystic, Nancy!"

I smiled at Clara with unrestrained happiness, having carried so much guilt for so long. God chose me to guide people from darkness to light. Patrick, Father Novak, and Bruno all hurried over from where they sat in the pews, and gave me huge, impassioned hugs.

"I know you will make a positive difference to the quest, Nancy," said Father Novak.

A rushing noise filled my ears, and I held back tears, but of happiness.

"Little cousin, Nancy. Who knew it?"

A mischievous grin spread across my face, and answered him, "You knew it Patrick, you knew all along."

Bruno placed his hand on my shoulder and said, "We need you, Nancy. We were supposed to meet in the hospital, don't you think?"

Quivering at his touch, it amazed me how emotional I felt. An electric shock passed through my body. As the days went on, I respected him more and sought his approval. I was always drawn to Bruno's side. Neither of us ever said anything, but did he notice me constantly near to him? I longed for him to come forward and tell me how he felt and hoped he felt the same as I did.

I sat down, exhausted but I felt my nerves firing off in all directions. What a revelation, what joy, thank God!

Chapter 35

WE WERE STILL GATHERED in the outstandingly beautiful, but oppressive cathedral having gone through the experience of the cleansing of one of the evillest Nazi perpetrators from the Second World War. Now there was the pressing matter of what to do next with Martin Weiss having completed the first exorcism.

William Adami, the Hungarian born supporter, pointed directly towards Martin Weiss.

"He is currently unconscious, so there may not be any trouble, but we are unsure of his state after waking. This is the first exorcism where we have combined both the feather and Father Novak's power together."

Father Novak felt caution was an important consideration.

"I think, take him and secure him in our room as a precaution. We'll ensure this man faces justice and won't be set free."

There was also the desire to keep him hidden from the other Nazis until the next meeting.

"Let me help carry Martin Weiss to your lodgings, Father Novak," said Patrick.

Father Novak, no longer young, felt the pace of events. Bruno was okay, but not yet fully recovered from the tuberculosis, plus the onslaught of his mental health by the demon, Mammon, had worn him out.

"No way, Father Flanagan. We can do it. It is the least we can do after the outstanding exorcism conducted here today," said William Adami.

Five strong individuals carefully lifted Martin Weiss, their arms supporting him, whilst Bruno and Father Novak followed on. Clara departed for her hotel, while Patrick and I went to our humble lodgings. The revelation that I was a lightworker still resonated in my head and heart.

Patrick's voice carried a mix of conviction and apprehension as he uttered, "There's no going back now, Nancy."

"I know, Patrick. Don't worry, I feel like good things are just beginning."

Once we reached our lodgings, we headed to bed and crashed out, both shattered. Morning arrived quickly, birds chirping, light peeking through the curtain. I went to bed feeling fantastic but woke up with a terrible headache and a sense of unease.

"Patrick," I whispered as I came to.

He muttered before rolling over and going back to sleep, blankets covering his head.

I said, "Patrick," a little louder this time, and he opened his eyes saying, "Nancy? It is early, isn't it?"

"Yes, Patrick, but can you feel it? There is something very wrong."

Patrick sat up bolt upright in his bed.

"Oh no, Nancy, I can feel it as well. We need to locate Father Novak."

I dressed and sat biting my nails, whilst Patrick dialled the hotel room where Father Novak and Bruno were staying.

263

There was no answer.

"Let's go to them, Nancy," said Patrick, making moves to dress himself.

"Yes, but what do you think has happened?"

They were staying at the Alvear Palace Hotel. A hotel dating back to 1932, palatial in design. Like an 18th century French Chateau with crystal chandeliers and gold leaf wall décor. Patrick and I had stayed in a small hotel. It was humble. but we preferred it. Just then, the phone rang. The operator put me through, and I answered it, but it was not Father Novak or Bruno; it was Clara.

"Nancy, I am worried as I cannot get hold of either Father Novak or Bruno this morning. We agreed last night to meet at 6 am at their hotel. It is 7 am now and both men are nowhere to be seen. Bruno is such a precise person, and if he says to meet at 6 am, he means 6 am."

We agreed to meet up with Clara as soon as we could at their hotel.

Patrick was ahead of me, waiting by the door.

"Let's go," he said.

Since his eyesight was returned to him, he was full of energy. As we were near to the hotel, we walked there as quickly as possible, both of us feeling a sense of dread.

Chapter 36

ON REACHING THE HOTEL, we found Clara standing outside reception, looking concerned. She had managed to locate Bruno and Father Novak, and they appeared fatigued and downcast. I could see scratches on Bruno's face, and Father Novak held an injured arm. Moving over to the seated area in front of the gardens, opposite the hotel reception, we sat down quickly to discuss past events.

"What on earth's happened here?"

Looking at the despondent scene made me worried. The scratches on Bruno's face were superficial, but Bruno shook his head.

"We've lost Martin Weiss, Nancy."

I ran to Bruno's side, saying, "What? How did you lose him? What do you mean?"

"We carried Martin Weiss back to the hotel, not expecting him to wake up so soon. We were securing him to the bed when he came round."

Father Novak continued, "Yes, he spoke to us. Of course, the situation confused him initially. He said he had lived a normal and happy life until the war came along. The government drafted him into the army and prior to the war, he worked as a plumber with his father. In 1941, he joined the SS and became a Technical Sergeant. Despite being at a low-level rank, the Nazis gave him the responsibility of overseeing the Vilnius Ghetto."

"Imagine that," I said, amazed. "He went from being a plumbing engineer to the evil man of the Ghettos."

Bruno's expression was dark.

"He couldn't recall much beyond being assigned by the Nazis to the Vilnius Ghetto. Nothing of the appalling things he did, the murders he committed. Jews in the Ghetto knew him for his merciless cruelty and frequent beatings. The story recounts his shooting of a man smuggling food through the Ghetto gates."

I looked again at Bruno's face. It was mottled with despair at the situation, and my heart hurt for him.

"We messed up, Nancy. As this was our first Nazi exorcism, we didn't know what to expect."

Father Novak said, "We untied him, Nancy, but then an elemental appeared."

"An elemental?"

Clara nodded, as she knew what they were.

"Whilst not all elementals are dangerous or evil, the malevolent ones possess strength, which can pose serious problems. Nasty entities causing harm if provoked, called upon, or challenged. They are shapeshifters and can appear human like or as waves, butterflies, or lizards. Any kind of animal."

"You have to be kidding!" I was unhappy at hearing this.

"In paranormal history, those who are knowledgeable advise to stay away from entities with greater power and potency than normal spirits or demons."

I couldn't believe there were other evil entities, similar to demons in existence. The underworld was repulsive and demonstrated we were ignorant of what we were facing.

Bruno paced around, saying, "We just didn't expect it, Nancy, demons, and elementals working together. Last night, the demon, Mammon, conjured up an elemental to aid him, if you remember?

I nodded, indeed remembering.

"Unfortunately, a person we thought was a group member was actually a shapeshifter, an elemental."

Father Novak said, "Mammon was furious with us for casting him out from Martin Weiss's body, and his minions as well. He lost his powerful status within the dark realm and wanted revenge, not through re-inhabiting Martin Weiss, but instead recited a spell calling upon an elemental."

I saw that Bruno looked pale and wan.

"Bruno, you need to rest properly."

I wanted to touch his face and hair, and bring him relief, but it was too public.

"I do, Nancy. You are right, but cannot rest, especially now. We are facing a bigger evil than we ever expected."

"Should we move away from the hotel reception? We are standing in a group here and may attract attention?"

He nodded, and we all moved towards a seated area just in the small gardens in front of the hotel.

As we sat down, he resumed the story.

"I called out to Peter as I thought it was Peter Stout, the Slovakian. He stood there, not leaving like the others who brought Martin Weiss in. He shape-shifted from human form into a huge black rabid doglike creature, a spine- chilling beast."

I shook my head in fright exclaiming, "Oh God, this is horrifying!"

Bruno gave a horrible description of the black doglike beast.

"The elemental appeared with large fangs, black eyes, huge paws with sharp claws. Long, low, deep growls emanated from its throat. It was eight feet tall, and covered in black fur, resembling a bear, but more like a dog. Glowing eyes showed venomous hate. I took a large step back. It was a heart-stopping sight. But Father Novak yelled at me to stay away."

He leaned over and patted Father Novak on the back.

"Father Novak moved in front of Martin Weiss, who was sitting on the bed, to protect him. He was so brave; I will never forget it."

"There was no time to react. It was going to hurt Martin Weiss. The elemental leapt forward, and he shouted, 'No, you don't!' and I recited the Lord's Prayer in Latin. When the elemental lunged at Weiss, I knocked the elemental away but injured my arm. It was such a gigantic creature; it took all my strength."

Bruno said, "Fear had immobilised me. Without Father Novak's protection, I may not be alive today. The sight of the frightening beast terrified Martin Weiss and he fled. We don't know where he went. As a loose cannon, we need to find him. He's in danger, but is also a danger to us if he meets up with any other Nazis and tells them about what's happening."

I said, "He won't do it as he's reformed, and returned to God, Bruno."

"I hope so, Nancy, but we can't take the chance. Martin Weiss ran out the door and the elemental and its mist disappeared along with him."

Taking Bruno's hand without thinking, it was icy, and I squeezed it, saying, "Bruno, you must go somewhere warmer to recover. Combining hot days and chilly nights is unhealthy, and it's still early, so it's not warm yet."

Clara smiled at me, and said, "Nancy, ever the nurse!"

I smiled and released his hand. A hot flush moved from my neck up to my face. Clara saw I was blushing. *What must she be thinking?*

"Father Novak, can I see your arm?"

He acquiesced, and we both stood up. I slid up the sleeve of Father Novak's cassock. His elbow displayed extensive bruising in yellow and purple shades. The elemental had not broken his arm, thankfully.

"Although your arm has been bruised by the elemental, and looks awful, I do not believe you have broken it. However, it's best to get an X-ray at the hospital for certainty."

He shrugged, "Nancy, I cannot currently go to the hospital. Your word for it will do."

We decided to walk back to their hotel. As we reached the reception area, we noted the Receptionist, Pilar, was sounding flustered and on a walkie-talkie speaking to someone.

"Some guests saw a large black creature, a slavering dog, roaming the grounds of the hotel, so I'm getting hotel security to look around."

"Gosh, Pilar, I hope you find it." I said, trying to be supportive in tone but felt worried at this news.

Bruno guided us to the side of the reception area, reminding us to stay alert as the elemental might still be present.

He said, "What is it searching for? Or is it searching for the Archangel feather?"

I shrugged.

"God knows. Do you think it is looking for Martin Weiss? Unfinished business?"

Clara, said furiously, "It better not be seeking the Archangel feather. It's our holy weapon against the evil entities we are encountering. We need it!"

Chapter 37

A BLOOD CURDLING, DISTRESSING SCREAM which pierced our ears, came from the garden area. My heart nearly stopped. What was happening? We ran towards the source of the scream. As we reached the sunken pond and seated area, we saw Martin Weiss, with his throat caught in the huge fangs of the elemental.

"My God," I screamed in horror at the disturbing sight.

Bruno gripped my hand tightly as we all watched the elemental intent on its task. It was immense, with huge teeth and was as dark as night. It took the form of a rabid dog, a grotesque fusion of beast and shadow.

Martin Weiss flailed around with his hands and feet in a desperate dance of agony as the elemental sank its fangs further into his neck, locking its jaw. Martin Weiss's lifeblood dripped down its body.

He screamed and screamed, a chilling sound which echoed into the distance. Blood sprayed across the sunken stones as the elemental ripped his throat out with an untamed fury. The sound faded as he passed away. There was blood everywhere, pooling around the lifeless form. Martin Weiss was gone, dead, and I will never forget the sound of his screaming and the sight of the terror on his face as the elemental tore him to pieces.

Bile crept up into my throat and I clung onto Bruno's arm for dear life. Patrick stood next to me, as I managed to hang onto my stomach's contents, but only just. Bruno steadied me, as my legs felt like jelly threatening to give way. Clara, poor Clara, emptied her stomach into the nearby bushes, her horror mirrored in tear-filled eyes.

Patrick started saying a prayer for Martin Weiss and bowed his head. He made a desperate plea for Martin Weiss's soul. It was all over in seconds. The elemental hunted Martin Weiss and had found him. Mammon's decision was clear-if it was denied taking Martin Weiss to hell, it ensured we couldn't have him either.

The elemental transformed into a grey mist and disappeared into the ground. It achieved its goal for its summoner, its task complete, and went back to whence it came.

Hearing the commotion, the security team arrived, but too late. The Argentinian police were called by the hotel to investigate the death. Meanwhile, the security team recovered Martin Weiss' body and took it to a separate area away from everyone. It was a huge setback.

"What do we do, Bruno? Do we postpone the cleansing until later?"

"No, Nancy. It's a complication, but the forces of evil are gathering, aware of our plans. They will do their utmost to stop it, so it's imperative we move forwards as soon as possible."

The sun was high up in the sky, and it was getting very warm, as two police cars approached, with blue lights flashing and sirens sounding. They pulled up at the hotel and four officers emerged. A tall man with dark hair and a beard walked towards us from the first car.

"I am Inspector Larios from the local police station. Can someone explain what has happened here?"

We had witnessed something supernatural, and it shook us all. Martin Weiss would not be taken to hell, but neither would he find peace among the living. Clara, ever sensible, took the Inspector by the arm.

"I think I can explain Inspector, please come with me," and she took him inside the hotel reception area and they sat down together.

"Thank God for your sister, Bruno. We're unsure how the Argentinian police will react to this whole situation. We don't want to be thrown in prison and left to rot."

Clara did an outstanding job of deflecting suspicion away from us, but we were instructed us to stay in Buenos Aires by the Inspector until the coroner conducted a postmortem on Martin Weiss' body.

Father Novak was horrified at Martin Weiss' demise, remaining quiet and introspective. Upon hearing the Inspector's order to stay in Buenos Aires, voiced his protest. He stated he must hurry back to the Vatican to see the Pope. The Inspector was adamant we were required to stay in the Buenos Aires area. He didn't believe any of us killed Martin Weiss, but the case wasn't straightforward, and we were the only witnesses to his demise.

Martin Weiss suffered unusual and inexplicable injuries, fortunately ruling out our involvement. Clara didn't mention the supernatural aspect to the death because she knew Inspector Larios wouldn't comprehend it. Explaining Martin Weiss' war history, Clara said it was more likely by someone who wanted revenge.

Inspector Larios remained unconvinced by Clara's explanation of the murder. Lacking alternative theories, he reassured her the postmortem results would shed light on the incident, and suggested they rest in the meantime. He was aware German Nazis were living in South America, so her suggestion it was because of a grievance against Martin Weiss was not absurd but the injuries to Martin Weiss were so extensive and violent, he didn't think they were inflicted by a human being either. A total mystery.

We went to sit in the gardens, away from the police activity.

I said, "Father Novak, don't go to Rome, you are needed here."

"I don't think he meant to go just yet, Nancy," said Patrick.

"Fear not, I will send a message to Monsignor Vitale explaining my position here," said Father Novak airily.

I said, "What matters most is we are all okay, and we found the hidden humanity within Martin Weiss. Whilst I acknowledge the value of every life, I won't mourn his passing."

"Nancy, we are fighting a huge spiritual battle here, and everyone we can save through the Lord is a success," said Bruno.

I felt scolded but continued, "It's been an extremely long day. You can't stay in this hotel now, Bruno. It is just not safe and holds a nasty memory."

Clara said, "My room at the Palacio Duhau Hotel is immense. It has a separate spare bed and another sofa bed. You are welcome to stay with me."

Bruno looked at Clara. He was so happy they had been reunited as brother and sister again. Before they left for her hotel, I matched her stride for stride, just out of Father

Novak's earshot.

"Do you think Father Novak is acting differently from normal today, Clara? Out of character?"

"I noted he seemed anxious, which is unusual for him, granted. He's been through a tough time though, Nancy."

Clara walked very quickly. I barely kept up with her.

"I know, Clara, but something is niggling at me."

I quickened my pace, needing to walk off my anxiety.

"Oh, do not worry, Nancy. I am sure we are all jaded after today's proceedings. Rest as much as possible before the big event."

"Yes, right, as ever, Clara? Okay then, Patrick and I are off to our digs. See you all at the cathedral," and I scooped Patrick up with my arm through his arm, keen to have some rest. Thank goodness we hadn't scheduled an exorcism for that very day.

Chapter 38

WE CONTINUED TO WALK to our less prestigious and tiny local hotel. It was in a less salubrious area than Clara's hotel, with local children playing in the plaza mayor. They were always there until late, every day.

Music spilled out from the lively salsa bar nearby, and I wished we could enjoy the pleasures Buenos Aires held instead of us all being caught up in a spiritual battle. *Would life ever return to normal again?* I wondered. Gosh, I felt tired. Thank goodness we could have a decent rest before tomorrow and the first of our group exorcisms.

I refocused on our situation. The police had interviewed us for hours and it was starting to move into early evening.

"Patrick, something feels odd about Father Novak's attitude."

He shook his head and smiled at me.

"Your imagination works overtime, Nancy, although he has been a little prickly of late, an he did disappear for a while earlier. When I asked him about it, he deflected the question."

"When Patrick? How? The group took Martin Weiss to the hotel, and Bruno and Father Novak went with them."

"No, Nancy. Father Novak peeled away from the group," said Patrick.

"Okay, we can ask Bruno about it tomorrow, but how strange?"

"Besides the Archangel feather, Father Novak is the major player in these exorcisms, and now you too, as a lightworker, Nancy. It will all work out."

Smiling at Patrick, I was unsure of my worth, but I would find out soon. *Was the gift given by God a gift or a curse? Could I manipulate that power?* So many unanswered questions.

Having reached the tiny hotel, I checked there was no one nearby as I turned the key in the bedroom lock. Ever since the demonic happenings, I was more cautious, even though Patrick was nearby. Reflecting on the day's events, I questioned Father Novak's character. What was going on in the background? What wasn't he telling us?

You are being ridiculous, Nancy Flanagan, I thought as I lay down to rest. The next moment, being near Patrick, I forgot my troubles and was soon fast asleep.

We had a long sleep, and the next morning, we made our way to Bruno, Clara, and Father Novak's far more ostentatious hotel. My knuckles tapped lightly against the wooden door of their bedroom, creating a gentle rapping sound. Patrick and I waited briefly by the door. We could've met them downstairs for coffee but couldn't wait to see them.

Hearing movement inside the room, it was obvious Bruno was now wide awake and keen to get things moving. He was out of bed and getting dressed when Clara opened the door.

"Come in," she smiled.

"We can wait for you downstairs, Clara, if preferred?"

Bruno said, "No, it's fine. We need to make a new plan. Martin Weiss was our trial run, and it went sadly wrong yesterday."

Father Novak was also awake and dressed. Clara rubbed her sleepy eyes, signalling to Bruno she needed a moment to wake up.

I smiled at Clara, then asked, "How are you feeling, Father Novak?"

"Okay, Nancy. My arm feels stiff, and I have limited movement, but you're saying the demon didn't break it, so I'm relieved."

Bruno said, "Nancy, you are an absolute treasure. What would we do without you?"

Clara stared at me, recording the joy in which Bruno said it. I felt Clara noticing the intimate looks which had taken place between Bruno and me over the previous days, but it didn't seem to worry her.

There was a plush sitting area with two armchairs and a beautiful rug on the floor in the voluminous sized bedroom, so Patrick and I sat down to relax whilst they finished getting up.

Clara continued, "Indeed, she is a gem, Bruno, but now it appears Nancy has become an alchemist, capable of magic."

I shook my head at this statement. Father Novak shook his head also, but for a different reason.

"Don't call Nancy an alchemist, Clara. In the Catholic Church, we associate alchemy with satanic rituals."

Clara smiled. "We don't agree on too much, do we, Father Novak?"

Bruno looked fixedly at Clara, a note of tension in the air. He always wanted unity.

"Clara, stop discussing Nancy's light-working powers. We don't know the extent of them, and they may come to nothing. We must be fully prepared for the three days of cleansing, starting today."

She smiled at him. "We will be fine, Bruno, and Nancy. Don't fret so much."

Father Novak walked towards Clara's bed and approached the cabinet.

"Is this where you keep Saint Michael, the Archangel's feather, Clara?"

He intrusively inspected the top of the side cabinet. She nodded, wondering why Father Novak was inquiring in such a precise and demanding manner.

"Can I see it, please?"

I said to Bruno, "We wanted to join you for a coffee downstairs," trying to deflect the tension which suddenly arose in the room.

Father Novak continued hovering next to Clara's bedroom cabinet.

"Can I look at it please, Clara?"

He was insistent. Clara wasn't too happy about it, but she acquiesced.

"Of course, Father Novak, but please be careful. Angelina told me it is very delicate, and you know its power. We need it today with the group exorcism dawning. It is in the drawer."

Clara's hesitant tone and slight tremor in her voice betrayed her unease. We watched as the priest reached down, his fingers trembling. The skin covered box emerged from the drawer. A relic which had eluded the Vatican's grasp for centuries.

He took a sharp intake of breath and picked the box up, looked at it, examined it, and said, "I cannot fathom how you are able to possess this."

Clara's laughter in response held an edge.

279

"It's not mine, Father Novak. Angelina was clear. God bestowed upon me this gift to cleanse the damned. The feather shall first return to the Seer and then to God."

I backed Clara up, my irritation matching hers.

"She's told you this already, Father. Destiny guides this feather."

But his frustration flared up and he couldn't control his reply.

"I am ordained! I serve God daily. You are but a transient vessel."

Patrick's confusion mirrored mine. Father Novak's demeanour was uncharacteristic, unsettling, and he frowned as he watched the scene unfold. Clara snatched the box away from Father Novak. I couldn't believe that they were fighting over it.

"I am sorry you feel this way. It's religious to you, but spiritual to me. I am responsible for its safekeeping, and I will guard it with my life!"

Father Novak looked angry and snorted with derision at Clara.

"This is a gift from God. It's divine and should be with the Pope. He's the closest to God on earth.

He looked over at Patrick for support, but Patrick said nothing. Bruno stepped forward; anger etched in his features. He gestured with his hands, remonstrating, saying "Enough!"

He continued, "You surprise me, Father Novak. Clara's the caretaker of the feather, and it's how it must be."

There was an uncomfortable silence. Father Novak quickly apologised to Clara and left the room. Bruno and Clara looked at one other askance, whilst Patrick and I exchanged worried glances. She clenched the box to her chest.

"What on earth? What is wrong with him?"

Clara was still annoyed and bothered by his behaviour.

Bruno said, "I have known him for years and have never witnessed him behave like this before."

"Look," I said, taking on a more practical attitude.

"We shouldn't worry too much. He's tired from yesterday, and his arm is sore."

Clara nodded and said, "Let's join him for a coffee downstairs. It is just a storm in a teacup, nothing more."

But as we made our way downstairs, I was left with a discontented feeling. We relied on Father Novak so much it was difficult to reconcile his actions with his character. *What darkness was touching his soul?* Indeed, we were about to find out.

Chapter 39

THE HEAT WAS SUFFOCATING in Buenos Aires. The sun was beating down hard. A strenuous time lay ahead of us. There was a nervous, tense feeling deep in my stomach. The grand cathedral stood tall, its intricate stained-glass windows casting colourful patterns on the stone floor. At 11 am, the group reconvened at the front of the cathedral's large wooden door to review the schedule before the cleansing. The terrible news was circulating among the group, and they hoped Bruno would explain what had happened to Martin Weiss.

"Phew, I said to Patrick as we walked to the cathedral. It is so damn hot! Sorry Patrick, I did not mean to say damn. I know you are not keen on me blaspheming. At least the cathedral is nice and cool inside."

He laughed at me and said, "Nancy, some things never change."

I clapped him on the back, enjoying the laughter, as it relieved the tension of the day. We were tired and knew there was a massive spiritual battle coming up. I felt apprehensive as I didn't know what part I was going to play during the exorcism. My energy as a lightworker should amplify the feather's power, but I didn't know how yet.

On approaching the cathedral, we hugged each other. I was

ecstatic to see different nations and religions joining together for the same cause. It was a critical moment in our journey. Father Novak was the last to arrive.

"Father Novak, we were worried. We missed you for coffee at breakfast."

He looked worn and harassed and distracted, but we put it down to the overall exhaustion we were all feeling. I sensed he was in a conflicted state of mind and in quite a depressed state.

We were unaware of the reason for his frustration. He told Monsignor Vitale on the phone that he searched Clara's bedroom high and low for the box, whilst we were all having a coffee but emerged from her room empty-handed. Clara, being smart, took the box, leaving him to only guess its whereabouts.

"I had something to eat and drink, then I needed to get fresh air. Do not worry."

Clara's eyes met Father Novak's, her smile warm and genuine. Patrick pulled him aside in a chapel near the main nave.

"Father Novak, I hope you don't mind me asking, but where were you just before the elemental shape shifted into that awful beast?"

Father Novak looked shifty. He wasn't happy Patrick noticed his disappearance, but he knew he better explain it.

"I was required to speak to Monsignor Vitale. In fact, I've been speaking to him just now as well. The Pope had an important message for me."

"Really?"

"You don't need to know, Father Flanagan. Only those who need to know are informed."

The rudeness he was encountering from Father Novak bemused Patrick. As Father Novak spoke, his face twisted with anger, his eyebrows furrowed, and his lips pressed together. It was odd.

"Was it difficult to call the Vatican from here?" Patrick pondered out loud.

"The Vatican's influence is significant, as you know. So, I managed. Anyway, there is talk of me becoming a cardinal, but I must fulfil a certain obligation first."

"Congratulations, Father Novak. That's exciting news!

"It's uncertain as yet," he snapped.

He walked away from Patrick; his steps purposeful as he made his way towards the main group in the nave. Patrick couldn't understand; Father Novak seemed like a different person.

Father Novak addressed the group.

"The Catholics among us, we need to pray. I will take your confession with Father Flanagan and say mass. I hope each of you has performed your religious rituals, ensuring purification in the eyes of God. We need to be in a state of baptismal grace to beat the demons."

The non-Catholics exchanged nods of understanding, while the Catholics obediently trailed behind Father Novak into the area of the confessional.

Every Catholic took the Eucharist during the mass held after confession. These were important sacraments which Father Novak or Father Flanagan needed to perform to give everyone the maximum protection under God's holy favour.

The sacraments now completed; Clara addressed the assembled group.

"Hello people," she said, and grinned at them all.

"This is a momentous occasion." There were nods and murmurs.

"We have never tried a group exorcism on this scale. I am confident with the support of the Archangel Saint Michael's feather we can exorcise a small group."

Father Novak nodded at Clara.

"Nancy, as a lightworker, ensures our victory."

Everyone cheered and clapped. The atmosphere, although tense, was positive. I addressed the group. The cathedral was huge and laid out in the style of a huge crucifix. We settled in the cathedral's largest side chapel.

"We only have a brief time left. The Nazis will arrive in the next few hours. Does everyone know what they are doing?"

Everyone busied themselves with their tasks. Patrick informed Father Novak of the struggle against hatred for Nazis by the group. They confirmed their feelings during their confessions.

"They repented, and I absolved them from their sins, but there is a strong feeling among them. I thought you should know."

"Do not worry, Father Flanagan. It is all under control. They are in a state of grace now, as we have absolved them. It will be fine."

Chapter 40

I TURNED MY ATTENTION to our special visitors due to arrive at the cathedral. Not the Nazis, but first a group from the local Jewish community. Argentina's Jewish community is the largest in Latin America. Europeans settled there after the Holocaust in and around Buenos Aires.

I wanted them to speak to us before starting the cleansing process and reached out to seek their approval. The primary motivation behind our actions related to what happened to their families. Various supporters in the group were Jewish, with connections to lost family members, but Bruno, Father Novak, Clara, Patrick, and I were not Jewish. Given the sensitivity of their history, we aimed to avoid offence. Although it's true to say the Nazis also discriminated on a mass scale against political groups, the travelling community, the disabled, and many more.

The esteemed guests were punctual and arrived at the hour, just ten in the group. Meeting them filled me with joy but also tremendous sorrow for their lost relatives. I sat them down with something to drink and they told us of the shocking suffering their families had endured.

Herman Levin, a Polish Jew who moved to Argentina, spoke first. He lost family members during the Holocaust and told of his personal experience. We gathered round the chapel, sitting on chairs where possible, and listened to Herman's testimony.

"I still suffer from survivor's guilt. The soldiers tried to pull me from my father's arms at the concentration camp. My father pleaded to take him instead of me, but they didn't listen, of course, and ripped me from his arms."

Herman was a tall man with a black beard and deep brown eyes. He kept his head low down as he recounted his sad story.

"I was lucky, being hardy and strong, I avoided the gas ovens at Auschwitz by working in 'Canada,' the area where we collected the clothes and personal items from the camp prisoners. The memory of the belongings taken from murdered prisoners will haunt me forever. Those items were a grim reminder of their deaths."

Herman sadly shared the worst part of the story – never seeing his father again. The mystery of his father's demise was a constant source of frustration and interminable sadness.

His story added to the sorrow in my heart. I felt lucky to not have experienced such a terrible hardship. Living with my family in Ireland I experienced difficulties, but I loved each one of my family members, and the thought of losing any of them made me feel ill. In addition, I felt great empathy for these families who had lost each other, as I also experienced separation from my daughter.

One by one, in turn, each survivor told of their own harrowing, heartbreaking story.

My heart beat faster as they told of families being pulled apart by the Nazis. One such famous Nazi being Joseph Mengele, whereby he selected those prisoners he wished to save, and those who would go to the gas chambers. Mothers and babies in particular faced horrifying fates in gas chambers and mass graves. Fathers and sons succumbed to typhus or diphtheria, which raged in the unhygienic and overcrowded camps.

One person told of people throwing themselves onto the barbed wire or electrified fences, wanting the guards to shoot them because they were overwrought at the cruelty they saw and experienced.

Others told of fierce German Shepherd dogs menacing the prisoners, especially if someone tried to run and the guards sending the trained dog to rip the person into pieces.

It was mind numbing to hear story after story of unbearable pain and suffering. It was unbelievable what these poor people had endured. How did the Nazis reach such levels of depravity? For some, it would remain a mystery. We felt we knew part of the answer to it. The Nazis became power mad, but inviting in Satan into their souls amplified that evil behaviour. They built an unholy bond with the devil. However, that did not excuse their actions, and those actions could never be forgiven.

Chapter 41

I SAT IN THE SAME CHAIR, listening to their testimonies for a couple of hours, unable to move, my heart feeling their anxieties as they recounted the horrors of the time.

Mina, another Polish Jew, told how they took Jews from the Lodz ghetto into a camp at Chelmno. This was early in the war, before the gas chambers of Auschwitz Birkenau. Instead, they used gas vans where the Nazis pumped carbon monoxide gas directly into the van, condemning the prisoners to a slow and painful death.

The SS found the method too slow, so they accelerated the murder process by employing gas chambers at the extermination camps. The Germans strove for maximum efficiency, even when murdering innocent people.

Mina tracked down her sister and niece through word of mouth and minimal documentation. The Germans attempted to destroy all evidence of these camps after the war. After the Nazis poisoned the victims in the vans, they dumped them in the forest. She managed to locate their last resting place in Poland and held a heartbreaking service for them.

A Polish woman with wavy red hair and a gaunt look about her face and body stood up and said, "I need to avenge my husband's family. He survived Auschwitz. The Nazis sent him there as a child of fourteen. Because he was strong and looked older than his years, they put him to work. But his whole family perished there, thereby losing two brothers, a sister, his parents, and various aunts, uncles, and cousins."

She trembled with emotion as she continued, "I promised him on his deathbed I would avenge these deaths. He died quite young of pancreatic cancer, but the Nazis hastened his death from the food shortages at the camp and stress from the loss of his family."

I said, "On behalf of all of us, we are so sorry for you. Look around and see the shared stories of family loss. We are all from different countries but have come together as one. We are all followers of God, which is important in this situation. Despite diverse backgrounds, we all share the common goal: eliminating evil to alleviate pain and suffering."

My words felt vacuous, unable to adequately describe the pain these people had endured. Being a nurse, I aimed to safeguard, care for, and heal people. As a lightworker, I wanted to remove the darkness from their lives and bring light into their hearts.

Devorah was a Holocaust survivor. The lines on her face spoke of the hardships she too had endured. She and her sister Alona were Jewish, and they came from a small town near Krakow in Poland.

Their father owned a shop and when the Germans invaded Poland, Nazis banned Jewish shop owners from owning and running businesses anymore, so their father bartered for food with the items from the shop. It was the sole means of obtaining food for the family.

The families which gathered shared tragic tales, each one more difficult than the last. The Nazis stripped the families of their rights and imprisoned and murdered them, dying from starvation or ill health because of the conditions in the extermination camps. Devorah wanted to tell her story, wanting us to understand the level of fear her family lived under daily.

"We never considered leaving Poland as a family during the German invasion, assuming the war would not last for six years."

She wrung her hands in despair. "My older brother escaped by running to the Russian border, although we never heard from him again. We lived in constant fear of what the Gestapo might do to us, as they were indiscriminate in their cruelty."

The families nodded their heads and murmured their sympathies to Devorah's story. They knew directly how it felt when the Nazis targeted, tortured, and abused them,

"In March 1942, the Gestapo arrived on mass in our town centre. They herded us out of our homes and made us stand in rows for hours whilst they checked there was no-one left in any of the houses. Then frog marched us to a hanger where the Germans kept aeroplanes, near a forest, just outside of town."

She wiped a tear from her face as she remembered the horror of it all.

"If anyone tripped or fell, the Nazis shot them on the spot. It was terrifying. We sat on the bare concrete floor of the hangar building, with no food or water. The Germans separated us from one other and placed us into distinct groups daily, and we heard shots coming from the woods. They kept us this way for five days."

I took hold of Bruno's hand, needing to feel a tenderness and be comforted by his touch. Their stories were harrowing.

Devorah continued, "The Nazis moved us to another small town by horse and cart and we were forced to share a tiny room with other families. My father had maintained useful connections and managed to get forged documents for my sister Alona and I, stating we were not Jewish. It meant we were able to travel back to a town nearby and live with an aunt. Two weeks later, Alona and I heard about our family. The Nazis had deported them, and I never saw my parents and the rest of my siblings ever again."

She sorrowfully wiped further tears from her eyes. I handed her a tissue from my pocket with tears in my own eyes.

"This is so sad, Devorah. I am so sorry for all of you who have lost loved ones."

William Adami spoke up.

"To prevent a repeat of these crimes, Nancy, we must tell the stories of these families."

Devorah nodded and said, "Thank you William."

She then said, "But I wish to finish my story."

"Yes, of course, go ahead, Devorah," I said, smiling at her.

"In 1942, the Germans instigated the 'Final Solution'. They wanted to cleanse the world of all Jews. My sister and I left the town we were in and reached the Ghetto in Krakow. We found work in a shoe workshop, but then, of course, the German war machine continued its indomitable path, and the Germans liquidated Krakow Ghetto and removed it from this earth."

Many of the group shook their heads. This was a tough story to listen to.

"Alona and I were not able to escape the Germans. They marched us to Plaszow. This was a Jewish Cemetery, which became a labour camp. It was a horrendous place. As we arrived in the cramped wagons, our sight was met by three men the Nazis hung from the ramparts. It was shocking and filled our hearts with fear."

"There were no huts to stay in. We built them, using the headstones from the cemetery to make a pathway. It was a grim and depressing scene, carrying bricks and timber from the cemetery to make the huts. People arrived every day, which meant we had to constantly make room for them."

She looked over at Bruno.

"The Camp Commandant was not like you, Major Siebert."

Bruno looked embarrassed and said, "I know Devorah. I wish I were there to help."

"The Commandant of our camp was an animal, a swine," she continued.

"He owned two Great Dane dogs, and if a prisoner irritated him, he incited the dogs to tear the person to pieces. One day, a group of fifty men left the camp for work. They returned with little bits of food for the rest of the camp. This gesture angered the Commandant, and he punished all fifty men by shooting them and throwing them into a hillside trench."

More murmurs arose, this time with anger attached. William muttered under his breath. I knew he was struggling not to shout out forceful words against the Nazis.

"When the prisoners failed to meet the Commandant's expectations, provoking his anger, he had them tied them down to tables, and another prisoner whipped them twenty-five times as a punishment."

She swallowed hard, finding it difficult to continue.

"In the heat of the full sun, the Nazis loaded us into cattle trucks on the railway line like sardines. Without sanitation or water, people either passed out or died immediately. When we arrived in Auschwitz, more dead than alive, we were moved by

293

the Nazis to the barracks. There were one thousand women to a barracks, with eight people allocated to one wooden bunk."

Devorah painted a stark picture of the suffering she and her sister endured.

"The latrines were unimaginable, and we did everything at set times. If we wanted to wash, it depended on being able to obtain water. There were no towels or soap. Certainly, nothing like a toothbrush."

The families present in the cathedral were sobbing now, as they recalled related stories of their own families' distress.

"The Nazis transported us from Auschwitz to Belsen, three thousand women of all different nationalities, squeezed into the cattle wagons. Alona and I arrived at Belsen early in the morning. The camp was isolated. No food, no water. We contracted Typhus and were past caring what happened to us."

She sighed and wiped her eyes.

"In April 1945, we were liberated, but my sister Alona passed away eight days after liberation. I will never forget it. I survived. Now I believe it's because of your mission: to avenge our families and rid the world of this evil."

There was silence for a few minutes, then Bruno spoke up.

"Yes, Devorah, you are right. Thank you for your support and for giving us the will to complete our quest. It is especially important you are here, and it is God's will. Our goal is to bring light to the darkness and peace to the world."

Devorah made us emotional but reminded us of the validity of our mission. Bruno squeed my hand and I squeezed it back.

"Alona is proud of you, Devorah," said William.

She nodded and wiped a tear. William strode over to her and gave her the biggest bear hug possible. After a while, the visitors finished telling their life stories. Feeling drained, I couldn't fathom their enduring resilience. The aim of their visit was not to escalate anger and desperation for harming the Nazis, but to highlight the value attached to our deeds.

They wanted to share their experiences, and we grew closer as a group. They knew we were putting ourselves at risk fighting the demons on their behalf, but it was a quest worth fighting for.

We thanked our guests for making the trip, and there were hugs and tears exchanged.

After the guests left, Bruno said, "Let's revisit the moral question later, Nancy. Let's focus on our task right now."

I nodded and sighed. We knew we had a huge task ahead of us, but after hearing these testimonies, they only served to strengthen our resolve and our belief.

Chapter 42

THE COOLNESS OF THE stone walls and the smoothness of the wooden pews in the cathedral invited us to run our fingers along their surfaces, grounding us in the historic space. But I didn't want to contemplate the evil rituals the Nazis had held here. Despite the warmth outside, a chill permeated every corner of the cathedral, and my body gave an involuntary shiver.

Juan Peron was still in power in Argentina in 1954, although his wife Eva Peron had died the year before. He brought in reforms for the people which were positive, but we were aware of some brewing unrest within Argentina amongst the army and the church, who were against Juan Peron's ideals.

We heard of fighting in the streets, and riots, but Argentina's political situation was difficult, and we couldn't engage in local politics. Focusing on our mission was paramount.

I noted how the cathedral smelled of incense and old books. There was a thin layer of dust on the pews, and it was musty.

The storytelling from our special guests left us all feeling even more committed to pursuing evil and ridding it from the earth. The group gathered in the nave to discuss the elemental situation. Since an elemental disposed of Martin Weiss, we needed to know more about elementals and were discussing our strategy.

"How do we fight an elemental if one appears?" William gesticulated with a shrug.

The rest of the group exchanged knowing glances; their eyes filled with a mix of concern. Martin Weiss suffered a horrific ending. No-one wanted the same fate.

Father Novak replied, "The evil entities summon them through spells cast to do their bidding. Each elemental is powerful, although not too intelligent. Possessing night vision, they have a built-in resistance to physical damage from non-magical weapons and don't tire."

There was a low hubbub of discontentment among the group. Guidance was needed from Father Novak on how to defeat them.

"The grim incident which took place yesterday resulting in Martin Weiss's murder suggests we may be in over our heads," said Bruno.

Father Novak went further, not realising he was creating grave concern among the group.

"Air elementals are fast, dexterous, and have a combat style of attack," he gestured in the air with his hands.

He continued, "The water elemental is strong indeed. Unlike a fire elemental which cannot stand water or cold, so you can freeze a fire elemental, water elementals do not care."

I felt the general annoyance of the group.

"Father Novak, how do we defeat them? Frankly, that aspect hasn't been explained fully by you at all."

He looked at me askance, "You cannot defeat an elemental, Nancy, whilst the demon is still present. You can slow it down, but until we remove the demon, the spellcaster, the elemental will just continue its mission."

There was a stunned silence from the group, and a couple of women whimpered. This was a shocking revelation. Prayer was not a powerful form of defence against elementals and their dark forces. Simply put, the elemental would not relent until the demon was exorcised by a priest.

I felt dispirited and was aware my face looked like thunder.

"Father Novak, this changes the entire situation."

He was slightly taken aback by my comment.

"I am sorry if I didn't explain the challenges and consequences of the exorcisms we are undertaking fully. I battle evil through exorcism daily in the Vatican and forget the external world. Exorcisms have been our practice for two millennia. Please do not worry, we will defeat the evil entities, especially when working together."

William shouted out to the group. He was effectively our general.

"Make sure you get into your preassigned group before the Nazis arrive. Advance organisation is necessary, everyone."

He turned to Father Novak, saying, "We have assigned five people to each Nazi to assist you, Father Novak."

Clenching my jaw, I looked at Bruno and Clara for back up.

"This is a spiritual battleground, Father Novak, and I speak for everyone here when I say the demons will throw every available evil resource at us, and we need every holy reserve at our disposal to fight back."

"We need a battle plan. This new development puts us in a precarious situation," said Bruno.

Father Novak didn't seem to have a reply to this thorny problem. Frustrated, I walked over to Clara for advice. She was always sensible and grounded in her approach to everything.

"Clara, there are women who are terrified now, because they don't feel they can fight elementals. These women should not be involved."

Clara was deep in thought but nodded at me.

"Yes, Nancy."

"Clara, are you listening to me?"

She waved me away.

"Give me a minute."

I huffed, puffed, and walked over to Bruno.

"I know she's your sister, Bruno, but what's up? She's not listening to me."

He looked at me with a wry expression.

"Leave her be, Nancy. It means she is working on something to help us."

Then Bruno urgently placed his hand on my arm and exclaimed, "Nancy, listen, time is moving forward quickly. The Nazis are coming in less than an hour. I agree with you though, fighting elementals is not a task for the women. Maybe they can provide a medical and recovery area in the cathedral's rear hall, in case of injury."

Anxiety was affecting my nerves.

"Bruno, this is becoming more like an actual physical war rather than a spiritual one."

Patrick stood up at that point. He was also troubled at the news about the elementals.

"Nancy, I don't want you getting involved in any sort of physical fighting."

I exhaled and smiled over at Patrick.

"Don't worry, Patrick," I reassured him, placing a comforting hand on his shoulder.

Patrick's face was serious. He was fully aware of my stubborn streak.

"The Lord will protect us but keep out of the fighting. Do you hear me?"

"I agree with Father Flanagan, Nancy."

Bruno was quite definite and looked overly concerned as he said it. Although I believed he would have said the same to anyone in the group, it gave me a warm feeling deep inside. I smiled at him with a full heart.

"The women and I will set-up a makeshift hospital. We brought medical supplies from England, but didn't anticipate needing them."

Bruno smiled and said, "I knew you would come fully prepared, Nancy."

The room filled with clattering chairs and shuffling supplies as I gathered some of the women together and we prepared for the worst.

Chapter 43

AS WE CONTINUED MAKING final arrangements for the spiritual battle to come and I had overseen the building of the hospital style recovery area at the back of the cathedral hall, Clara said, "Bruno, Father Novak, Father Flanagan, and Nancy, I need you all here for a moment, please," and beckoned us over to her.

"I've been in communication with Angelina. She told me that the elementals are emerging from a hellish gateway within the cathedral crypt."

I was incredulous. The elementals were coming up from beneath the cathedral itself, right underneath us.

"The cathedral's walls were built by its patron facing inwards to try and keep the elementals trapped in the lower levels of the pit itself, but remember, this is a portal, and it cannot imprison demons or elementals. We must trap the elementals somehow or block the portal altogether."

"But how?" I said, shuffling my feet with anxiety. This seemed impossible.

Clara pointed to her carpetbag, positioned nearby to deceive Father Novak as to where she was keeping the holy relic. She had concealed the box upon her person, and she wouldn't let it leave her side. Father Novak's earlier behaviour had put her on her guard.

She whispered to me, "It is a weird sensation, Nancy. The small box in my pocket feels as heavy as a stone."

I knew what she meant. My moldavite crystal always felt heavy in my hand, or in my pocket as well. I watched as Clara bent down, picked up the carpetbag, and placed it on the ornate gilt wood altarpiece in front of her.

The Neo-Baroque decor of the cathedral, with its ornate statues and intricate paintings, appealed to Clara's love of historic buildings and their architecture. Although she knew it was an evil place, giving her the shivers.

Clara briefly admired the altarpiece before addressing the group directly.

"Hitler coveted the artefact I will share. When he was younger, he met an expert on the Holy Grail."

My eyes widened in astonishment and my mouth was agape in surprise.

"Clara, you haven't got the Holy Grail, have you?"

Nothing would surprise me less. An unusual woman with endless tricks up her sleeve, anything was possible. She laughed and shook her head.

"No, Nancy, not this time, but I have secured something equally important. Hitler met Walter Stein, a historical researcher of the Holy Grail, who said Hitler would wield unmatched power one day, later stating he radiated pure evil. Then Hitler saw an exhibit in the Hapsburg Museum which ignited a passion in him."

I was curious, as was everyone else, to know what this second holy relic was.

"In 1938, under Hitler's orders, the Germans put this holy relic on a special train to Nuremberg. The SS guarded it, as Hitler believed in its absolute power. Interestingly, the Americans took possession of this religious artefact two hours before Hitler committed suicide on 30 April 1945."

Clara was such a fountain of knowledge, and I loved listening to her explaining things. Then she dropped a bombshell.

"This artefact will help us close the portal to hell, trapping the elementals and demons. This has become an urgent matter which requires our immediate attention."

"But Clara, we commence the mass exorcism today. This action will be too late to help us."

"I know the timing is off, Nancy, but it is our best hope. Hopefully, we can fend off these evil elementals in the meantime, until we can stop them from coming through the portal."

Father Novak was the most desperate of all to learn more about the holy relic. I watched him closely. His eyes carried a strange and brooding look, whilst he sweated profusely.

"What is this item, Clara? I can't imagine you received a second holy relic?"

"Ah, apologies, Father Novak, didn't I say?"

She announced with a flourish, "The Spear of Destiny! It's the holy lance, the one which the Roman Soldier, Longinus, plunged into Jesus's side to check he was dead after being crucified on the cross by the Romans."

I looked over at Patrick and Father Novak in amazement. They had fallen to their knees and were lying on the Venetian style mosaics of the cathedral floor, praying, and crying out to the Lord.

Clara took the lance from her bag. There was a simple, white cotton cloth wrapped around it, and she removed the cloth. Only the head from the spear remained, showing signs of age and pitted metal.

Glancing over at Bruno, I saw his mouth was open. Then he gave me a definite nod, meaning he believed Clara. My chest tightened, and I felt my heart hammering within it. Was this true? Bruno believed Clara, and so far, Clara was correct.

"Who will close the portal to hell?"

"Your cousin, Father Flanagan, should be the one to do it. The lance gives its holder invincibility and safety whilst in their possession. Plus, he is a priest and holds the power and authority of God through faith. It must be Father Novak or Father Flanagan, and Father Novak has his hands full here."

Father Novak interrupted our conversation.

"This is one of the most holy and legendary relics in the Church Clara. With immense powers and is as important as the Holy Grail. Where did you get it?"

"I bet it was through, Angelina," I said.

"Nancy, Angelina the Seer, confirmed to me it was the spear, which wasn't to be found in the four believed locations."

She continued, "It was not in St Peter's Basilica in the Vatican in Rome, nor the Imperial Treasury at the Hofburg Palace in Vienna, Austria. It was not located in Vagharshapat, the religious capital of Armenia, nor was it in the Church of St Peter in Antioch, either. It is here, with us, right now."

We were in awe of Clara. This was incredible. Clara possessed the actual Spear of Destiny, while everyone else claimed to have it. Clara's eyes lit up as she explained further.

"It is the key to world power, a magic wand of war, and it can give the person who possesses it the ability to command and conquer unopposed."

"But then, if it's the case, Clara, isn't it more useful for us to use it to beat the demons?" I asked.

"Ah no, Nancy," Clara said, shaking her head.

"Angelina explained to me we are supposed to cleanse the Nazis the usual way, through God, via the channel of Father Novak and with the Archangel feather."

I nodded, riveted to her explanation.

"The Spear of Destiny will help Father Flanagan to close the portal and stop any elementals from escaping. Angelina told me Father Flanagan must throw the head of the lance into the pit as it contains a nail. One of the actual nails hammered into Christ's body by a Roman Soldier whilst he was on the cross. The sacred nail attached to the lance is what will seal up the pit."

"You are full of surprises, Clara," I smiled at her.

"I protest," said Father Novak loudly.

"We cannot rid the world of this incredible religious artefact. It relates directly to Jesus Christ. The Vatican will not be pleased to hear this," gesturing dismissively towards Clara.

Rising from the pew where he was sitting, Bruno stood up.

"Father Novak, I hear what you are saying, but we are in the middle of a spiritual war of good versus evil. We need help, and if Father Flanagan can eliminate the elementals, our chances of success will improve tenfold."

I looked at Patrick.

"But how do you feel about this?"

He was both exhilarated and worried. He stood up and faced the group.

"Bruno, Father Novak, Clara, Nancy, everyone. I'm eager to fulfil this task as I believe God has chosen me and I won't disappoint him. God is with us all."

I was so proud of my cousin, willing to face the elementals solo. He turned to speak to Father Novak.

"Father Novak," he said, addressing him directly.

"I remain humble before you, as I recognise you as the senior priest. It is obvious the group needs you here with them one hundred percent. The Catholic Church calls it the Spear of Destiny, and I believe Father Novak, that this is the Spear's destiny now."

Father Novak quickly realised we were not giving in on this point.

"Father Flanagan, I believe you will succeed as you are with God. Before engaging with the enemy, please come to me and confess your sins."

Patrick's head nodded in agreement. He trailed behind Father Novak, their steps echoing in the grand cathedral as they went to the confessional box. There was a murmur among the group. This was such an unexpected development.

Patrick returned, having given his confession to Father Novak. But in all the excitement, he forgot to take Father Novak's confession, and Father Novak didn't request it. He felt he was fully protected; such was his arrogance. Patrick pulled me to one side.

"I will be fine, Nancy. Such a worrier!" I gave him a fierce hug.

"Please be careful Patrick, I know Clara said you are safe as the power of the lance will protect you, but I'm going to worry every second you are away."

I punched his arm with playful intent.

"I will be back before you know it, Nancy. Look after everyone and please take care."

I returned to the group and informed Bruno that Patrick was descending the cathedral steps towards the crypt chamber below the nave.

"Fingers crossed, he's successful."

Clara said, "He will be Nancy, do not worry."

I squeezed the moldavite crystal in my pocket.

It's up to me now, I thought. The crystal pulsed back in response. The group took a break before the Nazis arrived. Father Novak rushed off to the presbytery to arrange another difficult and expensive phone call to Monsignor Vitale in the Vatican. He told me he wouldn't be long, but I was concerned. When he returned, he recounted his conversation with the Monsignor.

"I told Monsignor Vitale that you need Saint Michael, the Archangel's feather, to cleanse the Nazis, and that as I am conducting mass exorcisms, you also need me at this moment."

I looked at Clara. Her face was like thunder.

"I thought you understood the situation, Father Novak, but thank you for making it more clear to the Vatican."

Father Novak's facial expression changed from benevolent to malevolent. He spoke to Clara in a very clipped, irritated style.

"The Vatican is in trouble. Bishops have broken their celibacy vows, cardinals who are accused of financial miscon-duct, priests who have turned out to be predatory. Someone murdered three people in the Vatican. Shot for no apparent reason. Evil is everywhere and growing daily. The Vatican needs the feather to cleanse it of the evil entities. Why can't you understand that? If I give the Pope the feather, he will make me a cardinal."

I was utterly shocked. Father Novak was a man of principles. Material gains never interested him previously, nor status. There it was. We finally understood his underlying motivation.

He wanted to be made a cardinal by the Pope. I couldn't believe it.

Clara tried to hold her temper, but struggled, so Bruno stepped in.

"Father Novak. I will say this to you in simple terms. I've never seen you like this before, and it worries me."

He looked at the priest dead in his eyes, to make his point.

"The feather stays with Clara, goes back to Angelina, and returns to God. If God desires the Vatican to possess the feather, he will surely provide it. Currently, the answer is a definite no."

"Sometimes God's calling can be very difficult," said Father Novak, and left Bruno, Clara, and me standing there with our mouths open.

Bruno said, "We don't have time to worry about this now. Let's get ready to receive our guests!"

We spent the next two days cleansing the Nazis. There were frightening moments, unexpected situations and we were utterly exhausted, but gradually succeeding in our quest. Fortunately, Father Novak appeared calmer and more like his usual self with regards to the Archangel feather over those two days.

I sensed something was off, but with just one more cleansing day left, I remained hopeful, despite ongoing concerns and fear caused by the elementals.

Chapter 44

THE MISSION to cleanse forty-five Nazis in the cathedral was concluding. My heart sang as we had made substantial progress, pro-actively removing the evil entities from the Nazis. However, there was no doubt it took a large toll on our hearts, minds, and bodies.

William Adami approached us in the medical area at the back of the cathedral with a worried expression, his eyes darting everywhere. Bruno was standing with me, discussing the various injuries our people were suffering from the ongoing battle.

"Bruno, we must stop the elementals soon somehow. They distract us from the key exorcisms, and the fire elemental burned my hands. In the cathedral's nave, I threw a Fire Blanket over it to douse the flames but injured my hands further."

Pained groans escaped William's lips as I bandaged his burned and bleeding hands.

"With these red blistering marks and bubbled flesh, I'm sure you have third-degree burns, William, and you need them examining at a hospital. This is only a temporary fix."

"Thank you, Nancy," his voice filled with gratitude and sincerity.

"No time for this now. The elementals are overwhelming us."

"Whom did Father Novak exorcise last?" I asked.

"Walter Rauff," said Bruno in an irritated manner.

"He was the man responsible for the early gas trucks which killed prisoners. With a terrible reputation for killing anyone who went up against him."

"Oh God, Mina's cousins, a sister and niece, died in some of those trucks and Walter Rauff caused their death and burial in a mass grave," I said, acknowledging Mina's pain.

"I sent her into one of the small side chapels, away from his exorcism. Her eyes had filled with tears and her face flushed upon seeing Rauff. This whole situation is very painful for her," said William with compassion.

Bruno's confirmation of who Walter Rauff was and the sadness Mina was undoubtedly suffering caused me to shiver involuntarily.

"At least we are exorcising the more senior Gestapo officers," my voice filled with conviction and defiance.

Bruno gestured furiously with his hands, his agitation clear, saying, "Nancy, it's good that we're purging the demons from these men, but their presence is still uncomfortable to witness. Representing such evil and so much harm, it takes all my strength to not want to strangle them."

His pained expression reminded me he had suffered harrowing experiences in two world wars and endured Nazi atrocities first-hand. Despite despising the SS's mistreatment, he pretended to align with them to improve the Jews' camp life. Hiding such emotions for so long must have harmed his mental health. I squeezed his hand to reassure and comfort him.

"Bruno, we are all feeling the same and doing our best in this situation."

He nodded in agreement, acknowledging I was right, but admitted to feeling sick when encountering these men.

Suddenly, a commotion began at the back of the cathedral's hall. Screaming and shouting, with a man's raised voice exclaiming, "I don't know what you're talking about."

Bruno looked at William. "What's going on?"

We rushed into the cathedral's hall and saw Mina, tears streaming down her face, advancing towards Walter Rauff, who sat on a wooden chair, tied up tightly. She held a large piece of wood in her right hand.

She screamed, "It's your fault that my cousins, niece, even my sister died in those trucks."

Walter Rauff looked terrified. He was awake and cleansed of his demons and subsequently, couldn't remember all the terrible actions and atrocities he had committed as a Nazi. I shouted over to Mina.

"We will get justice for your family, Mina. He will be tried in court and sent to prison. Don't do it, he's defenceless."

She failed to hear me. Screaming loudly, "I will kill you," she lunged at Walter Rauff, holding the large piece of wood over her head with two hands. He covered his face, waiting for the inevitable blow, but it never came.

William leaped forwards and grabbed the end of the piece of wood before Mina could bring it down onto Walter Rauff's head. As he made the move, and whipped the wood out of her hands, she fell to the floor, crying uncontrollably.

William whispered to her, "We feel the same way, Mina, but it's just not worth it. You will never forgive yourself and it won't bring your family back."

I ran over to Mina and cradled her head as she continued sobbing.

Walter Rauff looked up.

"What did I do?"

Bruno confidently stated, "You'll have the answer to that question soon enough."

Just then, Anna shouted over to me, "Nancy, Clara is calling for you in the nave. She needs you to help Father Novak. Your light energy is required to help Father Novak to exorcise a large group of ten Nazis."

"Coming Anna; I will be straight there."

Turning to William and Bruno, I declared, "I must go. Bruno, can you watch over William?"

The weight of the workload was pressing down upon William's shoulders, and he needed a well-deserved break.

"Yes, of course Nancy," Bruno smiled into my eyes. We were growing closer all the time.

Calm, Nancy, and concentrate on the task at hand. I mentally shook myself.

I went to look for Father Novak and Clara. Despite my growing affection for Bruno, I needed to remain focused.

Entering the cathedral's nave, I spotted Father Novak standing by the altar. He was reciting Saint Michael, the Archangel's Exorcism Prayer, and Clara stood by his side. An odd scene unfolded: ten Nazis, each one tied up and held down by two or three people, whilst sitting upright in old wooden chairs. It was a dis-concerting sight.

With a nod from Father Novak, Clara ascended the pulpit, clutching its worn edges. I stood with Father Novak, gripping my moldavite crystal. It glowed and pulsed in response. Once the crystal was warm, I signalled Clara to proceed.

She opened the box which contained Saint Michael the Archangel's feather. The feather touched the cathedral's arched roof. The energy passed through my body to the crystal. Light beamed onto the feather from the crystal. The feather sent out a protective pink glow, and the Nazis struggled as the feather identified each one of them as being evil, seeking to extract the darkness from their souls.

Father Novak increased his volume and said the Exorcism Prayer louder and louder. With a determined stride, he moved around the room, throwing holy water over each of the tormented souls, their faces contorted in anguish. He then laid the crucifix on each of their foreheads.

Rooted to the spot with curiosity, I watched as the Nazis spat, coughed, and choked, bringing up disgusting items such as metal, glass, and flies. They blasphemed, and spoke in foreign languages, all the while trying to escape their tight bonds.

"Watch out everyone, for these evil entities will try to play on fears and weaknesses. Ignore them where possible," shouted Father Novak.

I felt the energy of the crystal and my energy combining with the power of Saint Michael the Archangel's feather. My mind was blank, but I trusted my instincts and let them guide me. A huge wind blew into the cathedral. *Oh no*, I thought, *it is an elemental.*

Father Novak shouted out, "Be careful now! The demons are summoning elementals!"

Among the group of ten Nazis, Father Novak was having the most trouble with Franz Stangl. He sent clear visions to Father Novak of him drowning, something Father Novak feared most of all, having nearly drowned as a child. Franz

Stangl uttered a low and menacing growl.

"I will drown you and kill you, priest. You will die!"

Father Novak's voice was unwavering.

"I know which demon you are now, trying to prey on my fears, Agramon."

He continued, "I command you to leave this man, Agramon, in the name of the Son of God."

The crystal pulsed and got hotter. Placing it on a nearby table, I walked away from Father Novak.

Franz Stangl said, "I will whip you to death, priest. We are everywhere and will defeat you!"

I watched the scene unfold as the energy from the crystal merged with my energy and raced through my body. The group's desperate faces strained as they struggled to restrain the ten Nazis while the elemental conjured up powerful gusts of wind.

Dimitri shouted out, "Father Novak, we are having trouble here! What do we do?"

Clara shouted, "He's engaged in the battle, Dimitri! Hang on."

The whole situation was horrendous. Dimitri's knuckles turned white as he hung onto the chair where Stangl was writhing. Father Novak threw more holy water over Stangl, and he began coughing up pieces of leather.

I wondered why he did so, but Bruno told me later Stangl carried a leather whip and used it on prisoners. A vile man, he set up the Nazi program where the Nazis murdered mentally ill people or individuals with physical disabilities.

"Begone, Agramon, I will not fall for your sickening visions. God protects us all. Begone."

The feather rotated, and it surrounded us with visions of

Stangl's father. His father was a night guard, and he feared him, especially when in the guard's uniform. The visions of his father brought him round, suppressing the demon, and he cried out in fear.

The vision said, "Franz, how did you let me die? I starved. Why did you allow it to happen to me?"

Stangl uttered cries of "Father, I am sorry. You scared me and hurt me."

His father responded, "I always loved you, Franz."

The visions continued to surround us. The feather picked out the best moments from Franz's early childhood through to his becoming a man. None of which showed the obvious fear and distress Franz felt from his father's unkindness.

Witnessing the breakthrough, Stangl's words echoed through the room, filled with raw emotion and longing.

"Father, I loved you too."

It was an incredible moment.

Recognising the opportunity, Father Novak prepared to banish the demon from Stangl. The demon had latched onto Stangl through his childhood fear of his father, which turned him into a cruel man. Stangl now received his father's declaration of love, and it was all he had ever wanted. This was his humanity.

I was so proud of Father Novak as he shouted, "Renounce the devil, Stangl, renounce your sins! Your father loved you, Franz. Renounce them now."

Then the demon was back, its voice chilling, "Nobody wants you here, priest. Invite me in. Let me inhabit you!"

The demon uttered a low growl. Stangl's face contorted in an evil grin, but it was the demon, not Stangl. Then the demon within him laughed hysterically.

"The devil has doomed you, Priest, and you don't even know it yet."

Father Novak continued to pray, and when the holy water thrown over the demon distracted it temporarily, Stangl screamed out, "Father, I love you and I renounce the devil! Yes, I am sorry for my sins."

With force, Father Novak pressed the crucifix onto Stangl's head, resulting in a deafening scream as the crucifix burned an outline of itself onto his forehead. My crystal went white hot, and he fainted, and the crystal immediately dulled. Together, we witnessed the demon's twisted form writhe and contort as Father Novak expelled it from Stangl's soul.

Father Novak shouted, "Dimitri, take this one to the hall. We have finally released him from his evil."

Dimitri and another member carried an unconscious Stangl to the cathedral's back hall. We continued with the rest of the exorcisms, but Clara saw they were depleting my energy. She shouted over, "Nancy, there is enough power available with the feather. Take a rest now, please."

Overwhelmed by gratitude, and with a sigh of relief, that Clara had freed me from the spiritual battle, I collapsed to my knees, broken, and drained of energy.

Father Novak and Clara continued to work on the remaining Nazis. One by one, they cleansed them. By controlling exorcisms and maintaining separation, we ensured the demons couldn't transfer themselves between people. We were winning!

Chapter 45

RELEASED BY CLARA FROM helping with the remaining exorcisms, I decided to go to Patrick in the chamber under the nave, where the crypt was. Knowing Bruno's probable reaction to endangering myself, I kept it from him.

Getting up onto my feet, I shouted to Clara, "I'm just going to check in on Patrick!"

She nodded and smiled.

"Shall I tell Bruno?"

"No, Clara, let me do this myself."

She nodded again, distracted, as her focus was on the final exorcisms with Father Novak. Clara's addition to the team was terrific, and Bruno was excited to have her. He had missed her presence terribly.

As I walked past a giant hanging mirror which reflected the light from one of the large stained-glass windows in the cathedral, my reflection scared me. *Silly woman*, I thought to myself, but in truth, I was feeling extremely uncomfortable and very scared. I had found the large wooden door, the entrance down into the crypt. Making my way slowly down the ancient stone steps, darkness surrounded me, making me question my judgment.

Time passed, and Patrick and I faced enormous challenges

with the elementals whilst in the crypt. We emerged victorious but emotionally and physically drained. Our clothes were dishevelled from the fight, and there were white streaks throughout Patrick's hair, underlining the stress of the battle in which we had just engaged.

On approaching Bruno as we reached the cathedral's nave, I could feel Bruno's anger emanating from him, but I tried hard to brush his concerns aside.

Spreading my arms in a confident gesture said, "We are back, Bruno, having survived, and the Spear of Destiny was incredible."

He nodded agreeably, but his face told a different story.

"Why did you do this, Nancy? Tell me what happened? Thank God you are both safe."

Patrick said calmly, "Let's sit down before we begin the story. Didn't you hear the battle raging down below, Bruno?"

Bruno rounded on Patrick indignantly.

"Patrick, if I had known Nancy was with you..."

I put my hand on Bruno's arm, restraining his anger.

"I just couldn't let Patrick do this on his own, Bruno."

We sat down on the steps of the altar. The pews' length and width made storytelling difficult.

"The crypt is the stone chamber beneath the floor of the cathedral and contains coffins and religious relics. This one sits beneath the massive stone edifice nave of the cathedral and is large."

Bruno nodded, "Yes, Nancy, I am aware."

"Clara said Angelina mentioned an entrance to hell in the cathedral's crypt. She also said, years ago, the villagers lowered a young parishioner into the deep pit to investigate it. Once down into the pit, he couldn't stop screaming. When they retrieved him, he had aged forty years."

Bruno commented, "No explanation for what happened then, just a wild story."

Patrick continued explaining, "It was an eerie place, and I'm not surprised at the story Angelina told Clara. Descending into the basement where the crypt was, a dark mood engulfed me. Carrying the special lance in my bag, I felt it pulsating like a beacon of hope. It was such an honour to carry the precious religious relic. God called upon me and I wanted to serve him the best way possible. Everyone relied on me to defeat the elementals."

"At what point did Nancy find you, Patrick?" asked Bruno. I answered him.

"Stepping through the old wooden door, I descended into a pitch-black darkness without any light. Not wanting to shout and alert the elementals to my presence, I sought Patrick out in the dark. The room beneath the nave had a peculiar roof and side walls. Walls bricked up, hiding behind windowless frames. Who has windows in a basement? Metal fencing enclosed the crypt, as if the room might contain something."

Bruno asked, "Patrick, were you aware of the Nazi's interest in the occult and in the crypt? Heinrich Himmler was obsessed with the occult, collecting books and manuscripts regarding witchcraft and the supernatural. He may have stored the collection somewhere within the cathedral. Those items alone radiate evil throughout the place."

Patrick shuffled his bottom on the altar step.

"I didn't see any in the basement, Bruno. But who knows?"

"True, but I believe the dark forces-maintained power here in the cathedral because of their history of satanic rituals, killings, and worship of Satan," said Bruno.

Patrick continued, "When I moved the lance into my backpack, it was humming and buzzing. Anticipating the event made my mouth fill with saliva. It wasn't pleasant."

I stood up at this point and walked around in front of the altar steps. The tension arising from Patrick's retelling of the experience made me feel jumpy and on edge.

"My body shuddered, wondering how you'd manage the pit, Patrick, and if I'd made the right decision in joining you. After all, we didn't have the Archangel feather to protect us."

Patrick reached up and squeezed my hand.

"We used the Spear of Destiny, Nancy, and now we're here, and it is all good."

He turned again to Bruno.

"Nancy watched as I quietly entered the basement. Near the crypt, a large pentacle drawing adorned the stone floor. A sign from the previous occupants' satanic rituals no doubt. A shiver of dread sent jolts of electricity up and down my spine. This was the cathedral's heart and the source of its evil."

Bruno said, "I've just realised something. Whilst you were both down there, the sky clouded over and darkened. It looked like there might be a thunderstorm."

"Nancy called out, 'Patrick?' and I heard her."

I looked at Bruno. Despite his disapproval, he knew I had displayed courage in joining Patrick. Gesturing with my hands animatedly continued, "I joined Patrick, and watched his hands shake as he set down the backpack, took out the lance and unwrapped it. It was glowing a bright white and felt its power coursing through it. The crystal in my pocket pulsed and I felt a moment of realisation. I should have helped him from the very start."

"As we recited the Lord's Prayer together, there was a

terrible cawing from a massive black winged beast which appeared out of nowhere. It flew up from the pit in the crypt and approached us. Closing our eyes, we recited the Lord's Prayer together even harder."

Patrick got up and walked around. The tension was affecting him as well.

"It was a frightening moment."

William asked, "What did you do next? I would have run away, I'm sure of it."

"The beast's cries were intimidating, and we felt the wind from the beating of its wings as it hovered just above our heads, William."

Patrick said, "It scared me. I won't lie. My throat knotted with fear, and my heart was banging in my chest, but I got to work and ignored the terrible beast just fluttering above us. I tried to block it out of my sight and out of my mind. I knew it was there to distract me from the mission."

"How did it look?" William asked curiously.

"It had large yellow glinting eyes with huge round orbs, spiky looking teeth, and wet looking Black skin covering its entire body, and long talons as fingers on its hands. Unlike any creature I've seen before, but I knew it lived in hell."

I trembled at Patrick's description. It brought me straight back to the memory of the demon from my own nightmare.

"Unsure of the next steps, I heard God's voice urging me to trust my heart. Holding up the lance's head, it unleashed a blinding bolt of light which went straight into the heart of the beast. There was an agonising cry as its wings folded up and it fell straight back down into the pit. The screams echoing as it descended, but its return to hell was silent."

I grabbed Bruno's hand and squeezed it. It was unnerving

to recount the story.

"The lance's power startled me yet boosted my confidence in our well-being. Multiple winged beasts emerged from the hellhole, hovering, and screaming above the pit in the crypt."

"We heard nothing of this attack, Patrick. It's unnerving to think of this going on below us."

Bruno wanted Patrick to know.

"We repeated the Lord's Prayer and knelt by the pit, but the ordeal continued. The elementals were stirring, and a huge wind blasted around our knees. It tried to knock us over, but we kept our balance. Freezing water poured over our heads and body. Holding hands, we prayed louder as the ground trembled and gigantic holes opened around us, as if in an earthquake. The elementals attacked us in full force."

"It was truly horrendous, Bruno."

Bruno patted Patrick on the shoulder and smiled, "You are both very brave."

"I asked, 'God, if ever we needed help, it's now.' A sheet of flame shot out of the pit. It was scary, especially with my fear of fire, ever since burning my hands fighting Azazel, the demon."

I sat down next to Bruno.

"In a dreadful moment, Patrick leaned over the pit's edge. He couldn't resist peering into the dark hole, a mistake which nearly cost him his life. The elementals swirled around us. Ten-winged beasts were above, flapping closer to him all the time, willing him to fall into the pit."

Patrick nodded. "It was extremely difficult to keep my balance."

"I shouted at him to be careful, then screamed because he got dizzy, faltered, and toppled into the pit. Just as it was almost too late, I grabbed his arm and held onto Patrick with all my might. As he hung there, the winged beasts above screamed with delight, willing him to fall, but an ethereal voice said, 'Be calm. I'm by your side, you know what to do.'"

"My life flashed before me, and I thought it might be the end, but thanks to Nancy, I recovered."

William's mouth was open. He sat down hard on the step next to Bruno. This was quite a story.

"My heart was beating fast, but knowing we heard God's voice brought great comfort to us. Holding onto Nancy's arm with both hands, I swung my leg up and hooked it onto the ground over the side of the pit. It was touch and go. Then, with an almighty grunt, I levered myself out of the pit and up onto the stony ground. Fortunately, the lance had remained where I dropped it."

"Your fall, Patrick. It could have brought Nancy down as well. It would have been such a tragedy."

It was something Bruno didn't want to consider, and neither did I.

"Holding onto Patrick had been tiring, but I refused to let go, no matter what. Once he was on his back, he gathered his strength and shouted, 'God is with us so you can't harm us!' then threw the lance into the pit. There was a bright flash, a loud thunderclap, and a chorus of screams. The impact was immediate. The elementals disappeared, returning to the planes whence they came. Water went back to the sea; earth returned to the ground; the elemental fire ceased burning, and the wind dropped. It was a phenomenal moment."

Patrick continued breathlessly, "The ten-winged beasts hovering above let out alarming sounds of pain and death and shrivelled up in front of our eyes and disappeared."

William said, "It's a miracle."

"Yes, William," said Patrick. "The holy lance is beyond special. We didn't continue our gaze into the pit. The nail head from the lance swelled up to cover the entire pit entrance. Having stood up, I sank back onto my knees and gave praise to God."

Bruno stood up and gave us both massive hugs. I held onto him for as long as possible.

"God helped you, but it was brave of both of you indeed."

"The fight drained us of energy, but Patrick was triumphant and relieved, knowing we had stopped more elementals from attacking our friends."

I turned to Patrick, saying, "Your once blonde hair has little streaks of white and grey in it now, Patrick."

"It was a tumultuous event; I don't mind having them. They celebrate our victory."

"Upon your return from the crypt, the sun emerged, and birds flocked back to the trees. You delivered the cathedral from evil," said William.

Bruno said, "Well, for now, anyway."

Patrick sighed, "Yes, hopefully."

He understood it was just a temporary reprieve. Dark winged beasts and demons were regathering underneath the sealed pit at the cathedral at that very moment.

As a priest, he imagined hell to contain souls in torment, picturing darkness, fire, and pain, endless pain. Since no human had ventured into hell and returned to tell the story, the devil cherished this vision to instil fear in humans.

We knew the spiritual battle was not yet over. There was more to come.

Chapter 46

THE STONE ARCHES OF the cathedral were breathtaking, and, combined with the opulent ceiling, the cathedral revelled in an abundance of architectural grandeur. The attraction for the Nazis gathering here, was the eclectic mix of architectural styles and magnificence, which suited their overblown egos.

Bruno, William, and I went back to the cathedral's main area, the nave. Then I assisted with lifting Stangl's body through into the hall at the back. I ensured his head did not hit the intricate door frame carvings. Dimitri placed him on a blanket on the floor. On entering the hall and having glanced at Dimitri, his pained expression was one of shock.

"Dimitri, what on earth is the matter?"

"Nancy. I recognise this man. As commandant at Sobibor and Treblinka, he tortured and killed people."

A brief hesitation occurred, and I was unsure how to respond.

"The devil possessed this man, Dimitri."

"Yes, but by inviting the devil in means he is also to blame, Nancy."

This was a test. It was important not to give into hate and feed the evil entities further.

As I stood there with Dimitri, an icy shiver ran up and

down my spine. I felt a foreboding, but why? Just then, a blood-curdling scream echoed from the cathedral's main altar throughout the cathedral.

Hearing the scream, I said to Dimitri, "What the hell?"

Running, I entered the cathedral first, closely followed by Bruno and William. What I saw was a chilling scene which will never leave my memory. Clara lay lifeless on the hard, cold stone floor. It was an emergency, and I rushed over to her. Following my training as a nurse; I felt for a pulse in her wrist and neck, but there was no sign of life.

"Clara is...Clara's dead," I said aloud to no one in particular, focusing hard on my breathing until the fainting sensation which overwhelmed me passed.

On examining her further, her head felt sticky, and I gasped. It was obvious she had hit her head on the stone floor of the sepulchre below, by falling from the cathedral's pulpit in front of the altar. The stickiness all over her head was bright red from blood oozing out of a large wound.

As Bruno ran over, he reacted, realising; she was gone forever. "Clara," the word formed on his lips but as a whisper, then after thirty seconds there was wailing and a heart-rending howl from deep within Bruno's soul.

"Clara!"

He got down on his knees and cradled her head deep in his arms. Clara's death had left Bruno stunned and beaten.

"There is nothing further I could have done, Bruno. I am so sorry."

Whilst he held her, I couldn't reach out to Bruno and ease his pain. Justin Le Blanc, the person responsible for directing the Nazis' removal to the third chapel at the back of the cathedral, stood, leaning against a pillar in a state of shock.

I walked over to him and touching his arm, I said, "Justin, did you see how this happened?"

It devastated Justin seeing Clara's lifeless body lying on the cold floor and he couldn't take his eyes from her whilst sobbing and stuttering.

"Nancy, Father Novak took Saint Michael, the Archangel's feather, from Clara. I saw him do it when returning from the chapel. They were alone, but as it was Father Novak, he was beyond criticism."

Justin's words left me confused and in disbelief at the priest's actions. Taking the feather left Clara defenceless, at the mercy of demons and elementals. It seemed he would stop at nothing to obtain the feather.

Justin continued, "Clara resisted giving him the feather, but I misread the situation."

He was so traumatised by the experience, William needed to hold him up whilst he told us what happened.

"A dark black, vile demon targeted her because she no longer had the feather for protection. Thousands of disgusting flies appeared in a vast, seething mass from its gaping mouth. A wind elemental also appeared at the same time, creating a whirling tornado of flies blowing and buzzing around her, until Clara found it impossible to see."

Justin's eyes were full of tears, and he struggled to explain further, sobbing through his words.

"I watched and despite her efforts to fend off the flies, they overwhelmed her face and eyes. With the wind elemental's strength growing, and unable to see, she stumbled from the pulpit and fell hard onto the stone floor."

He turned to me, saying, "It all happened so fast, I couldn't move."

"I don't think you could have stopped it, Justin," I said, as a tear rolled down my own face.

"Poor Clara. She guarded the feather with her life and gave her life in the end. Beelzebub, the Lord of the Flies, was responsible, I am guessing?"

"Beelzebub was the demon released from Adolf Eichmann, so it is possible it was him," said William.

Patrick said, "He's rumoured to be Satan himself, in demon form."

"It was a hell of a battle," said William.

"I remember I needed to ask Dimitri for more help. Five people holding him down were not enough to secure him. He regurgitated all kinds of disgusting items, including flies, large bluebottles."

He shuddered at the recollection. Bruno shook his head in annoyance.

"I wanted to kill Eichmann stone dead, but we agreed to release the demons from these men. If only I had known," he trailed off, leaving the rest unsaid.

"But why did you want him dead, Bruno? They were all horrific men, and the demons owned them."

I felt unsettled by Bruno's level of anger.

"I hated Eichmann the same as Hitler, Nancy. He orchestrated the extermination of European Jews, including in Vilnius. His plan meant six million Jews died overall in the Holocaust."

William shook his head.

"Father Novak and Father Flanagan said we cannot kill. God is the judge and jury; we are just channels for good."

"Eichmann set up the death camps. Please keep him out of my sight, as I cannot be responsible for my actions right now," Bruno said.

"It is understandable, Bruno. We will notify Dimitri to take care of it. But where is Father Novak?"

I looked at William.

"Gone, Nancy," said William despondently.

"Father Novak wouldn't have left us, William? He is a priest, for God's sake."

He nodded with a miserable expression, confirming it was true. Father Novak had taken the feather from Clara and left us all to an unknown fate.

"I'm so sorry for your loss, Bruno. I know how much Clara meant to you."

Bruno's shoulders were heaving from the sorrow and pain engulfing him. He buried his face in Clara's thick brown wavy hair.

"We never reconciled," he said with tears in his eyes, looking up at me.

"Clara left after an intense argument with Isabel. Then my wife passed away. But we never got round to it, and I never said sorry," he murmured, burying his head in her hair once more.

"No, Bruno," my own tears cascading down my face.

"She understood your desire to resolve things, but believed we should carry out this quest first."

My face contorted in anger, as I said, "I cannot believe Father Novak left us to fend for ourselves.

"By taking the feather, he caused Clara's death. I thought he was my friend," Bruno said sadly.

William came over and whispered, "Nancy, we must leave this area, or the remaining demons and elementals could catch us off guard."

William truly supported our goals, a solid rock. Recognising the need to leave the site of Clara's death, a group of us lifted Clara's body into the back of the cathedral. We should have called the police to report an accidental death, although we believed it was murder, but we didn't.

William knew and contacted a local doctor whom he persuaded to view Clara's body at the cathedral before we buried her. He wrote the death certificate, confirming the cause of death was a brain aneurysm. We wanted to avoid police disruption and questioning. Despite knowing the truth, we wished for Clara's body to rest without a post-mortem. The supernatural element of the tragedy was impossible to explain outside of the group.

Leaving the cathedral to eat some food, Justin wouldn't stop crying. We didn't want to eat or drink but needed to stay strong. Hours passed, and we sat in silence, mourning Clara's passing. It had shocked everyone to their core.

Returning to the cathedral, we were unsure of what to do next. My light energy only amplified the power of the feather. Would the light energy, together with the moldavite crystal, be sufficient on its own? A negative mood descended upon the group.

Patrick was an exorcism priest but lacked the level of experience of Father Novak. We had cleansed most of the Nazis, but a few remained to be exorcised. He entered the main part of the cathedral with the supplies he'd gone to buy. He'd also stopped to pray at another church nearby, to thank God for his help with the elementals.

We stood by the precious statues of the cathedral which dated back to the 18th century. The interior of the cathedral was beautiful, but the vibrant interior hid the darkness lurking beneath.

I said, "Where on earth have you been, Patrick?"

Noticing Bruno's demeanour and the sadness on everyone's faces, it prompted him to ask, "Where's Clara?"

Seeing my sorrowful expression, Patrick breathed a long drawn out "No," and clenching his jaw, sat down on the chair next to me. I told him what happened as carefully as possible, not wanting Bruno to suffer further, but it was impossible to deliver the news of a friend's death without emotion.

Bowing our heads, Patrick said a lovely prayer for Clara.

"God rest her soul. She will be at peace now."

Bruno said, "We moved her into a quiet area at the back of the cathedral, shrouding her body in the altar cloth. The doctor visited first and signed the death certificate, then we buried her in the cathedral cemetery here. If you could say a prayer over her grave..."

He found it difficult to finish the sentence.

The cathedral's immense wooden roof was being repaired by local builders, rendering it unusable and causing the Minister's absence for several weeks. It suited us, avoiding the need to explain about her passing and the nature of it.

"Of course, Bruno," and squeezed Bruno's shoulder in sympathy.

Chapter 47

WHAT AN EMOTIONALLY EXHAUSTING day, and I didn't expect what happened next. Whilst rising from the pew in the cathedral for water, one of the possessed men abruptly stormed through into the main part of the cathedral, arms outstretched. He roared, cursing, and tried to hurt me. I screamed and I ducked out of the way, but he still caught a glancing blow across my cheek, scraping it with his nails.

William exclaimed, "How did he escape from the chapel behind the cathedral? We tied them all up?"

"I do not know."

Bruno spat out his words, his face contorted with anger.

"But you had better check on the remaining Nazis, as we can't have them creating merry hell. It only takes one wrong move, William!"

William rushed to the chapel's rear and found a sharp-edged cross on the altar. The possessed man had freed himself by fraying the rope against the metal edge of the spare altar cross until it broke. William took the cross and ensured the other Nazis were secure. They were a frightening spectre, growling and spitting at William, but he took no notice.

Patrick, seeing what was happening, raised up his crucifix to the possessed man. His voice resonated with conviction as

332

he recited the powerful exorcism prayer, each word carrying weight and authority.

The demons possessing the man screeched, and he leaped around with his arms and legs flailing, as if dancing an Irish jig, but in fact was feeling the pain of the lower-level demons leaving his body, one by one.

"Dimitri," I bellowed.

"Where are you?"

Dimitri came running in, breathless and bloody from previous battles.

"I'm here, Nancy. How can I help?"

Patrick continued reciting prayers and incantations, and a shiver of dread ran down my spine.

"Please help Father Flanagan, Dimitri. Instruct your men to restrain this possessed man. Dimitri called out to the helpers, who joined him in subduing the man. Patrick poured more holy water on top of the man, and he started choking and coughing, all the time blaspheming. He spat out long shards of glass amongst phlegm between swear words.

"Look out everyone, don't let the glass shards touch you!" I screamed out.

His face distorted with anger as he hurled insults at Patrick, his words dripping with venom, trying to disrupt the priest's calm attitude. The demon made revolting, guttural noises from deep within its chest and throat.

Patrick took no notice and continued chanting prayers. Then he raised the crucifix up in the air and brought it down hard onto the man's forehead. Terrible grunts and groans erupted from the man's mouth, covered in foam.

"Out now, demon, begone!" said Patrick.

"Never!" screamed the demon back.

It stuck its face in Patrick's and spat large globules of spit. Seeing this happen, I screamed, "Patrick, be careful!"

He wiped the spittle off his face with his cassock, and continued, intent on dealing with the demon.

"You are the demon, Agramon. Agramon, begone!"

"Yes, I am Agramon," growled the demon at Patrick, while writhing in the old oak chair where the followers managed to tie him down. Patrick bravely took a step forward, closing the distance between himself and the menacing demon.

"We do not fear you, Agramon. You are nothing. Return to whence you came. I command you in the name of Jesus Christ."

The demon screamed, "No, I will not, priest. Fuck you, priest."

"He's breaking free!" shouted Luca, in a state of panic.

With a roar, the demon launched the chair into the air, crashing it down. It broke into many wooden pieces. The possessed man effortlessly climbed the towering cathedral wall, his movements resembling those of a nimble spider.

Patrick's widened eyes were filled with fear at the sight of the rampant demon, and his face twisted with worry, urgently calling out my name.

"Nancy, I need your extra energy. Hold my hand whilst I ask for Saint Michael's help."

I could tell Patrick felt Agramon was a powerful demon, and he was incapable of removing him alone. Patrick's hand slipped through my trembling fingers as the man sprinted down the side of the towering cathedral and tackled Luca to the ground. Luca couldn't maintain his balance, and there was a loud thud as his body slammed downwards onto the stone floor, where his head split open. Bright red blood gushed out of a large wound.

"Luca!" I screamed.

I heard the urgency in Patrick's voice as he pleaded for my help once more.

"No, Nancy, Dimitri will help Luca. I still need you."

Dimitri rushed to Luca's side, pulled his shirt off his body, and pressed the large piece of cloth against Luca's wound. The blood turned his shirt red. Dimitri and Luca were brothers from Greece, Luca being the younger brother. They were part of a family who had suffered at the Nazi's hands. We were lucky to have such a wonderful supportive group of helpers.

"You bastard," shouted Dimitri at the demon.

The demon, no longer on top of Luca, danced around, laughing.

He hissed, "How is your weak brother? I hope he dies!"

My gut twisted with anxiety.

"Don't feed him any hate Dimitri, it only makes the demon stronger."

The demon hissed at Patrick, "You can hate me."

The words left a bitter taste in the air, leaving a lingering feeling of negativity. Meanwhile, Bruno gathered a group together, in one of the three side chapels, and they concocted a makeshift net out of ropes. His hands moved swiftly, weaving the intricate knot of ropes together. They trapped the demon in the smallest chapel attached to the nave, which spat and swore at them, like a cornered rat.

Bruno shouted, "Come on," and threw the net over the top of the demon's body.

As Patrick and I stood over the net holding hands, my energy pulsed through me and joined with Patrick's energy. Stretching my head back, I screamed as the light power surged forth, I shook from head to toe. A bright white light which emanated from both of us simultaneously filled the cathedral.

"Be gone, Agramon now. Saint Michael, the Archangel demands it, and God commands it," shouted Patrick with authority.

A white, searing bolt of light came from us both and hit the man squarely on his forehead under the makeshift net. There was a chilling scream, then silence. It happened so quickly. The demon was gone. Together, with God's help, we had cleansed the man. The men holding the net relaxed their grip and sat back down on the cold stone floor in relief. It was an exhausting experience.

Luca was taken to the first aid station, alive but weak from blood loss. Mina set to giving Luca a makeshift blood transfusion and dressed his wound. She told me to check on him later. William clapped Patrick hard on the back.

"Father Flanagan, you were incredible."

"Not just me, William, Nancy, too!"

Patrick looked relieved and pleased, but the experience of fighting the demon ha depleted us both of energy.

Bruno came over to me now. He cradled my face, inspecting for any damage caused by the demon, Agramon. His touch was gentle and concerned. My heart skipped a beat when he touched my face. My heart grasped it before my mind did. I was falling for him. His respectful manner towards me confirmed to me he was a good man.

"I'm glad you are okay, Nancy. These attacks are relentless, and so dangerous."

I gave him a hug, and he responded, "Poor Luca. Thank God he is going to be okay. Let's check on him later. I know Dimitri is worried."

Bruno continued, "We must make a new plan, as Father Novak appears to have deserted us. William, place this cleansed man with the others in the cathedral's rear hall."

William nodded and assisted in removing the man. Patrick was worried.

"Bruno, we saved thirty-one possessed men with Father Novak's help, plus that one just now, but there are still thirteen men left, and I can't do it alone."

"Especially as we don't have the holy feather anymore," I spoke up.

Patrick shook his head in despair.

"I still cannot believe Father Novak ran off with the feather. I understand he wanted to cleanse the Vatican City, but he knew what it meant for the rest of us."

"I'm not sure he knew what might happen to Clara," I said.

Bruno said with anger, "He endangered Clara's life, and ours as well. Look at what has happened."

His heart was hurting from Clara's death. It was plain for everyone to see. William whispered in my ear. He came to me rather than Bruno, as he was still hurting from Clara's sudden death.

"What should we do now, Nancy? We are unsure what to do with the remaining thirteen possessed individuals without Father Novak."

My stomach sank. William was correct. If we couldn't save the final thirteen Nazis, then we would be forced to abandon the exorcisms.

Dimitri approached Bruno from the back of the cathedral chapel. He was witnessing strange behaviour from the cleansed men and it was baffling him.

"Something weird is happening, and I need some advice,

please."

We turned round to look at Dimitri.

"The Nazis we saved, the thirty-two we exorcised from their demons. They are all waking up in the cathedral chapel."

"No way!"

I realised we forgot to plan for them after their cleansing.

"Having only experienced the one exorcism of Martin Weiss to begin with, we didn't know what would happen. He never woke up before the elemental murdered him."

We stopped to listen intently to the murmur of voices emanating from the chapel.

"Yes," said Bruno, "I can hear them. What is occurring?"

I grabbed Bruno's hand, and he clasped it tightly.

"The Nazis we saved are talking to each other. They remember some of the war and their part in it, although not everything. They are full of remorse and are penitent, recognising right from wrong. Their conversation revolves around pre-war life, with all evil intent gone."

We were glad the demons were cast out, but our bodies were showing signs of exhaustion from fighting the elementals. The delay Patrick and I took in sealing the pit resulted in injuries to some of our group.

"The mass deliverance and exorcism seem to have worked!" I exclaimed.

"Yes, but we only achieved it by utilising the holy feather," said Patrick, "Or I can only save them one by one."

He frowned at the thought of this near impossible task.

"Bruno, what should we do with the healed Nazis? While their souls are now free from demonic influence, the echoes of their war crimes cannot be ignored. We'll keep hunting evil monsters; Nazi hunters will take a special interest in them."

Patrick nodded his agreement.

"These Nazis' crimes were so heinous, they deserve to be punished for them."

I said, "Our mission here is to restore the moral order. Retribution is not what we seek."

Bruno said, "I have heard from various sources the Americans recruited the Nazis living in South America to spy for them. The Russians and the rise in communism concerns them."

He continued looking at everyone.

"There was an Austrian bishop, bishop Hudal, who hid the Nazis in monasteries and helped them to get to South America, and the Red Cross gave them passports. Can you believe that? Outrageous!"

"The Pope acted in a duplicitous manner during the war with the Nazis. He ignored both the Ratline, which helped Nazi fugitives to escape, and the Rome Escape Line, which rescued allied soldiers and Jews. Although the Nazis occupied Italy, they never invaded the Vatican. It just shows the power the Pope, and the Vatican wield."

There was a general hubbub. We knew nothing of this, and Bruno's revelations were eye opening.

"But of course," continued Bruno, "turning back to the Nazis we have cleansed. They no longer have valuable information for the Americans. I agree we should turn them over to the appropriate authorities, especially the evillest perpetrators, such as Adolf Eichmann, Albert Speer, and Erich Raeder. The Americans and British never held them accountable for their actions."

William Adami spoke up.

"There is no extradition treaty in South America. I researched it whilst looking for Nazis. But I do have connections with Simon Wiesenthal."

"Who is he?" I asked William.

"He is a well-known Austrian Holocaust survivor, and he works to locate Nazis around the world, Nancy. He is a good man."

This seemed a sensible approach.

"Bruno, I suggest we hand these Nazis over to him."

What does everyone here think? We numbered seventy-eight supporters in our group. There was a general murmur and nodding of heads.

Bruno said, "Please raise your hands if you agree with this proposal. Do we hand them over to the Nazi Hunter, Simon Wiesenthal?"

"Trust him, if he's a Jew!" shouted someone at the back.

"Motion carried. Can you set it up, William?"

A wide smile spread across William's face as he confirmed his eagerness. The group made the decision which I felt led us down the right path. It was up to the judge and jury to decide their fate on earth, and God's decision as to their fate when they shrugged off their mortal coils.

The question remained. How would we locate Father Novak and the feather? Bruno said one word to me when I queried this with him.

"Angelina."

Once we made the relevant arrangements, we passed the cleansed Nazis to the Simon Wiesenthal organisation, as we had all agreed. Simon struggled to believe our story, and was unsure how to interpret it, but after interviewing the Nazis, he noticed a substantial change in them. The Nazis were displeased at this outcome, but they had no choice in the matter.

He brought the main evildoers to trial, and we believed such punishment was justified. The Nazis needed to be held accountable for the pain and suffering they had caused to the prisoners through their actions.

We asked Simon Wiesenthal to keep our role in capturing and cleansing the Nazis a secret. We wanted to keep our group discreet, hidden from prying eyes and judgment.

After we handed them all over to Simon Wiesenthal's group for trial, we contacted Angelina's family. They were based in a local shanty town near to Buenos Aires, but I invited them to visit us at the hotel. I couldn't wait to meet Angelina finally, in person.

Chapter 48

ANGELINA POSSESSED THE GIFT of foresight. At just ten years old, she displayed a maturity well beyond her years. Angelina's family was delightful. Protective, but once we explained our situation to them over the telephone, they were more than happy to help us.

Her family agreed Angelina could visit the hotel, and I arranged to meet her face to face. Her mother dropped her off and confirmed she would return for her in an hour.

She was just as I imagined, she was a sweet girl. Unable to see, Angelina was blind, but beings blind from birth, she moved around her home easily, knowing where things were situated. Unfamiliar with the hotel's layout, I settled her on the plush sofa nestled in the living room section of Clara's bedroom.

Bruno was sorting through Clara's possessions and packing them up in the other room whilst I spoke to Angelina. We felt it was a peaceful place to meet up.

Of course, Clara being Clara, had booked a suite in the hotel, and it was a beautiful room containing paintings of Patagonia, with views of the lakes and mountains.

I called Bruno over to meet Angelina briefly before she and I focused on finding Father Novak. He was keen to meet her, as she had developed a strong bond with Clara prior to her death.

"I am so sorry for your loss, Bruno. Clara was a wonderful person."

He nodded.

"Thank you, Angelina, and I think you are a remarkable young lady."

Angelina told us she knew Clara might be in danger but did not foresee Father Novak stealing the feather and leaving her to the mercy of the demons. She could predict future events but concentrated her efforts to achieve positive outcomes. Her end goal was to promote peace and harmony where she could. Her visions painted vivid pictures of potential conclusions, but never a finite ending.

"Is it because life offers us different paths, Angelina?"

"Correct, Nancy. I never know for certain what will happen, just flashes of situations and likelihoods appear to me. However, I can tell you this. Just before Clara died, I connected to her through the feather. When she fell from the pulpit, in the last moments before death, a vivid image of her mother's face materialised in front of her, infused with love."

What Angelina said was unbelievable.

"You mean to say you were in touch with her as she died, Angelina?"

"Sadly, yes."

Angelina looked in Bruno's direction.

"Your mother was in the afterlife, and as Clara passed away, your mother came to collect her, and I heard your mother's soft voice calling her to her."

This information stunned us. I grasped Bruno's hand and squeezed it hard. I knew how much his mother had meant to him.

"Your visions are incredible, Angelina."

She flicked her long brown hair behind her in a moment of frustration.

"You may both think that, but it was a sorrowful experience for me. I realised Clara was dying, and your mother was there to claim her, but so sad I couldn't offer any help, although I do remember that I could smell a powerful scent of roses at the moment of Clara's death."

This piece of information sealed it for Bruno. He believed Angelina because Bruno's mother's most favourite pastime was to tend to her rose garden. When his mother died from liver cancer, he covered her casket in roses at the funeral. What Angelina told us was a real comfort for Bruno. He wiped a tear from his eye. I felt his pain, and I also wiped a tear from my eye.

"Thank you, Angelina. I really appreciate what you have shared and will leave you and Nancy to speak further. I need to finish packing up Clara's possessions."

He returned to the other room, and I faced Angelina on the sofa. She smiled at me.

"Nancy, I think Bruno has a soft spot for you, and you have one for Bruno."

I shook my head and laughed, feeling shy.

"You are so intuitive. I do care about him, Angelina. A bond is growing between us, but he is still married in his head. I guess time will tell if anything comes of it. Now let's turn to the matter in hand."

She smiled, and I wondered at this little girl, who although was so young, seemed so mature.

"Nancy, thanks to the Archangel feather, I can indeed locate

Father Novak for you. He has the feather on his person. Father Novak kept the feather, but Clara would have returned it to me, and I would have returned it to God. He has committed a sin, and sins have consequences."

"Can you locate him now please, Angelina?"

Angelina took my hand and became still. She wore dark glasses because of her blindness, but had been seeing visions, according to her mother, since the age of three.

She suddenly said in surprise, "Why, Nancy, you are a lightworker. Why didn't you tell me before?"

A smile curved across my lips.

"Yes, but it's very new news to me, Angelina."

"But you didn't mention it, Nancy."

"Is it relevant?"

I squirmed in my chair, and I was embarrassed. I was still learning about my gift.

"Yes, Nancy, of course it is. You amplify the light; you bring light to the dark, and it means you can strengthen my powers. I am a type of lightworker. Someone who can see future visions and occasionally connect telepathically with others."

It was a light bulb moment for me.

"Now I understand when you took my hand, it tingled."

"Yes, Nancy," she smiled.

"Now, let me concentrate. You will feel tired at the end of this process, but I will pinpoint Father Novak much more easily with your help, as you give me the additional energy to do so."

"Wait Angelina, I have my moldavite crystal here too."

"What is it?" said Angelina.

I took it out of my pocket.

"I go everywhere with the crystal, Angelina. It makes me feel protected and has an energy of its own."

It sat in the middle of the palm of my right hand. Angelina didn't see it, but I placed it in her palm, and she felt its energy.

"Nancy, it's an unimpressive size, but can sense its power."

"I've kept it ever since I got it at a psychic fayre, Angelina. It increases my personal lightworker energy. I can't imagine being without it now."

Putting the crystal back in my hand, Angelina said, "Let's begin."

I found it fascinating that she was blind yet had a sensitivity to her surroundings and people nearby. It was as if she kept her eyes. As we sat there, a powerful force surged through my body. Not an unpleasant sensation, but a peculiar one. Angelina put her head down. I closed my eyes. Angelina's brows knitted together in concentration, her mind scanning for the slightest hint of Father Novak's presence.

She said, "Yes! I know where he is, Nancy. There is no time to waste. The Pope diverted Father Novak from going directly to the Vatican. He required Father Novak to call in on a bishop in Argentina first before leaving for Rome. His flight is due in two hours at Ezeiza Airport, Buenos Aires. You can just make it in time."

I hugged her.

"Thank God, Angelina, and thank you so much!"

"You are welcome, Nancy. There is no time to waste, you must go. My mother will be here shortly, don't worry."

Thanking her again, I went to look for Bruno. He was sitting outside the room, in a small relaxation area near the lobby. Bruno had collected Clara's belongings, placing them inside her worn carpet bag. It made me sad to see it, as it reminded me so much of Clara's personality.

"I discovered something surprising."

"What, Bruno?"

He did not look happy, but not upset, either.

"Clara had an admirer, someone named Arnold," he stated matter-of-factly, his tone neutral.

"They were at the start of a deep friendship. I will contact Arnold and let him know what has happened. Judging by the letter he sent; they were close friends for certain."

"How interesting! It's nice to know there was someone special in her life."

Bruno nodded, then said, "It was good to meet with Angelina. She's quite a girl," his eyes twinkled with admiration.

"Yes, and that is the thing, Bruno. Dealing with her was like interacting with an adult. It was an amazing experience. Her mother is coming to collect her now, and we must dash to the airport! There is no time to lose!"

Chapter 49

WE STOOD OUTSIDE THE HOTEL. Patrick's footsteps echoed on the pavement as he made his way towards us, his enthusiastic greeting filling the air. I remembered that it was only a brief time ago since a demonic attack temporarily blinded him. I was just so relieved and happy that through divine help he had fully recovered.

I explained Angelina's vision to him in full, and we hopped into Bruno's hire car with him. We needed to race to the airport as fast as possible. Unsure of what we might do when we arrived, but knowing we needed to warn Father Novak that he was no longer under divine protection.

"We must intercept Father Novak, not just because he has the Archangel feather, but because he is in grave danger if he tries to engage with the demons in the Vatican," Bruno said, filling Patrick in on the situation.

"He's fallen from grace," Patrick said.

"But as a priest of many years standing, won't he realise it?"

"I do not think so, Nancy. The Vatican's arrogance has made him assume God is on his side. He believes he is invincible."

Bruno raced through the city, narrowly avoiding an accident

with his wild weaving in and out of traffic. The blaring horns and irritated shouts from other drivers filled the air, adding to his frustration. The tyres on Bruno's Peugeot hire car squealed as we came to an abrupt halt in front of the airport terminal building.

"You go in! I will follow on. I just need to dump this thing."

We ran through the airport, trying to locate the flight to Rome. We moved through the vast crowds. I apologised for bumping into people while navigating through the throng, saying sorry at least a thousand times.

"Where is the gate number for the flight, Nancy?" Patrick was panicking.

"I can't see it," I said, scanning the terminal's information boards.

"There!" I yelled. "And there's Father Novak!"

I called out to him, "Father Novak, Father Novak," but he either did not hear me, or chose not to respond. We watched him with dismay as he made his way through the doors which led to the aircraft.

"Oh no, we've lost him."

I was downcast.

"Angelina helped us find him at the airport, but we have arrived too late to prevent him from boarding the plane. What a disaster."

Disappointed that we had failed, Bruno, Patrick, and I went to get food as a consolation. There were bustling food stalls, colourful restaurants, and cafes nearby with sizzling aroma filled dishes on display. We were starving. I ordered steak with fries, whilst we sat in a cute but small Argentinian cafe. What a shame we were in turmoil over Father Novak's disappearance, as the ambience of the cafe was delightful, with soft lighting and a cosy decor.

"What now?" I said to Bruno.

The server placed our plates on the table. Each dish was beautifully presented, and my stomach rumbled looking at it.

"Muchas gracias," I said, keen on practising my Spanish.

The server smiled, "De nada."

The food looked wonderful, but Bruno teased his piece of meat around the plate with his fork.

"What now indeed?" said Bruno.

Then he reached into his pocket and threw a packet of Woodbine cigarettes on the table. He shook one out and lit it.

"Bruno, how can you smoke those? I've never wanted to smoke cigarettes."

He smiled.

"I find them relaxing, Nancy."

Patrick found it impossible to sit still. I saw the determination in his eyes.

"I have to do something."

After uttering, "I'll be right back," he went to phone the Vatican.

He returned later, his eyebrows raised in astonishment as he muttered, "Unbelievable. Monsignor Vitale will not take my call, and trying to make an international call takes forever. The operator tried to connect me four times!"

I finished my meal and was drinking a cool glass of lemonade.

"What?" I gasped.

"You have got to be kidding! Why wouldn't he take your call?"

"No," said Patrick. He sat down opposite me at the table.

"Apparently, the Pope was keeping Monsignor Vitale busy.

He was unavailable to take calls for the next couple of days. I said it was an emergency, and I needed to speak with the Monsignor, or even better, the Pope himself."

Patrick wanted to bang the table; he was so annoyed.

"So frustrating! The priest laughed at me. He didn't think it important enough for me to speak with the Pope. And did I know the number of requests they received daily to meet with him? He offered to leave a message for Monsignor Vitale, which was all he was willing to do."

"I said, please advise Father Novak not to use the religious relic, as he will be in mortal danger."

I put my hand on Patrick's arm to calm him down. He was clearly distraught.

"Patrick, it is the best we can do under the circumstances. Let's hope he realises his situation."

We finished our meal, and soon, we were back in the hire car, making our way back to the cathedral. Bruno was huffing and puffing as the traffic was busy and slow. We were completely unaware of what would happen next.

Chapter 50

AS I ENTERED THE cathedral through its huge wooden doors, with Patrick and Bruno following closely behind, we all glimpsed Father Novak at the front of the nave by the altar-piece, completely unaware of our presence. We stood there, stunned, and speechless, certain he had boarded the plane to Rome. So, now, a chance remained to retrieve the Archangel feather from him.

I watched him with disappointment, as he took the precious box containing the Archangel feather out of the right pocket of his cassock. In awe, he opened the box to gaze again at the feather. It was translucent, shiny, and lay flat in the box.

He hadn't boarded the plane as we now knew, but he had stolen Clara's feather. I felt gutted and sick to my stomach. Patrick was equally disgusted and frustrated. Frantically, he shouted over to Father Novak.

"Father Novak, it is imperative you don't use the holy relic."

Startled at hearing Patrick's voice, and spotting Bruno and me, he moved towards the first side chapel.

"I have no time for discussion. I am returning this relic to the Vatican, to its rightful place."

Trying to keep Bruno's anger in check, I took his hand and squeezed it, but his annoyance got the better of him. As Father

Novak edged away from us, he stuttered, "My sister Clara's death. It's all your fault!"

Struggling with his feelings, Bruno's voice got louder, his anger boiling over.

"You insidious man, it is your fault she's gone."

I tried to reason with Bruno.

"There's no point getting angry. We'll reach out and get the feather."

Father Novak shouted back, "I'm sorry, but the Pope needs me, and the Vatican needs the feather."

Then, after a brief silence, he shouted again.

"What did you say? Clara's dead? I know nothing about this?"

He looked confused. Father Novak continued backing away, shouting, "Sorry, I must bring the feather to the Vatican. I have no other option."

Patrick began praying and realised he was asking God for help. This was a tricky situation. He stopped praying for a moment and said, "Nancy, I think he's got a demonic attachment."

"What?"

"Yes, a demonic attachment. I can read all the signs. I'm wondering if it happened when he struck the elemental earlier?"

"Patrick, this situation is deteriorating by the minute. What can we do?"

"Nancy don't worry. I can rid him of the attachment; I just need to get closer to him."

Father Novak hurried into the cathedral's largest chapel. What happened next was shocking. As we reached the third chapel, Bruno, Patrick, and I discovered Father Novak standing stock still, in a state of terror, confronted by the monstrous demon Leviathan.

This demon, in the form of a dragon, drained energy from others with delight. I screamed at the horrendous sight, a petrifying spectre, and it brought with it the smell of death. A grotesque fusion of serpent and dragon, its seven necks snaked upwards with seven menacing heads attached. Father Novak began praying, but the Leviathan laughed and reared up before him. The beast was horrific, breathing fire and smoke from its heads.

"I am impervious to any human weapon. Do your worst mortals," it boomed.

Fire flared from its different heads' nostrils, making the cathedral hot, which was incredible amongst such cold stone walls. It unravelled its body, bringing itself up to its full height, towering above us all.

Its rasping voice continued, "Your God is full of lies, and will not help you, priest. My master, Azazel, has instructed me to take you down to hell."

I looked at Bruno and Patrick.

"Azazel has been targeting all of us, and now it is Father Novak's turn to suffer. What do we do?"

Patrick shouted.

"Father Novak, be careful, please. You cannot fight this demon with the holy relic."

His voice echoed his worry and fear for Father Novak's life. A stench of sulphur and decay filled the cathedral, causing us all to feel nauseous.

Unfortunately, Father Novak couldn't hear our frantic shouts above the mammoth serpent's deafening roars, which echoed in the nave's lofty ceiling. Watching the chilling scene unfold in front of our eyes rooted us to the spot in terror.

The priest, knowing the full power of Saint Michael, the Archangel's feather, felt he would have no issues in ridding the world of the Leviathan, but he made a near fatal mistake. He had neglected to partake in the holy sacraments, including the rites of confession, and mass with the holy Eucharist.

The grandeur of the cathedral, with its towering spires and intricate stained-glass windows, ignited a burning rage within the Leviathan, fuelling his desire to dismantle God's purpose. He hated followers of Jesus and was the natural enemy of Father Novak, a priest who followed the Lord's teachings.

As the Leviathan moved around the cathedral's giant nave above the crypt, it taunted Father Novak yet further. I watched in horror as he shouted back at the demon.

"Leave, Leviathan. You do not belong here; go back to hell."

The Leviathan laughed a horrible, deep, resonant laugh which echoed throughout the cathedral, contorting its vile tail into an attacking pose.

"You believe you have authority over me, priest? I am one thousand times more powerful than you will ever be."

Father Novak sprinkled holy water on the beast's tail, and it recoiled, then said, "Is this all you have?" laughing and provoking Father Novak.

The priest, confident in his divine protection, brandished his crucifix like a weapon and moved towards the demon with purpose.

"I know you are the demon, Leviathan. Begone. Go back to hell where you belong. I command you in the name of Jesus Christ, our Lord and Saviour."

I watched on as Bruno shouted to Patrick to help Father

Novak. Patrick tried to run over to him, but the Venetian style mosaic tiles set within the cathedral floor caused Patrick to slip. They looked beautiful, but were lethal to the moccasin style shoes Patrick wore.

He fell over, hitting the floor hard, and Bruno and I raced to help him. Blood came out of his nose, and a large bump formed on his head. He was dizzy and couldn't stand up on his own.

He rasped, "Do whatever you can. Father Novak is in mortal danger."

His voice carried an air of desperation. This was serious. The creature roared at Father Novak, and he felt the breeze from the moving serpent's tail as it whipped this way and that, just missing him by inches. He was not a young man but jumped backwards high in the air as the demon's attacks were getting too close for comfort.

"You think you can get rid of me?" roared the Leviathan.

This was the lethal moment Father Novak tried to employ Saint Michael, the Archangel's feather. Reaching into his cassock pocket, he removed the special box but noticed the skin on the box was no longer smooth but now wrinkled in its appearance.

Although he kept moving away from us, I saw Father Novak's face cloud over with confusion. He believed that he squashed the box when it was in his cassock pocket, but we knew the truth of the feather.

The seven heads on Leviathan's elongated neck spat out bright red fireballs. Father Novak jumped to the side to avoid each fireball the demon was aiming at him. The demon was getting closer to hitting Father Novak each time it tried.

"What can we do, Bruno, we are powerless. We are not

priests like Patrick or Father Novak. How can we help?"

The Leviathan sneered, "You are wasting your time and mine, priest. I told you; your God will not save you now," and its yellow eyes gleamed and glittered with hate and malice.

"You will die, priest, because you turned from your so-called God. You are full of pride and have a desire for power."

The Leviathan reared up high and made to lunge hard at Father Novak with its long-barbed tail. It lashed out with deadly precision, just missing the priest. Bruno brushed past me and ran towards the Leviathan, flailing his arms around trying to distract it. I was terrified, in case the demon hurt Bruno.

Father Novak jumped to the side again, only just evading the Leviathan's huge tail. He took the feather from the box, and said, "Lord God, I call upon you now to rid this world of this evil," and he waited for the Archangel feather to float up to the ceiling to cover him in its protective pink glow.

The Leviathan laughed and sneered as to our horror, once a symbol of divine protection, the feather curled up in the box, went black and disintegrated in front of Father Novak's eyes. We had warned him!

Father Novak had a blinding moment of realisation that he was indeed facing a life-threatening situation. His face registered genuine fear as he got on his knees and began praying to the Lord. We heard him pleading for forgiveness.

"I'm so sorry, God. My hubris led me astray. Please don't abandon me, my Lord."

I was beside myself with worry, not knowing what to do. Bruno's attempt to get the Leviathan's attention failed, and its eyes glinted and focused on Father Novak. It hated priests and possessed a deep resentment for what they stood for. It would not let him go. It would take the priest all the way to hell, and there was nothing we could do about it.

Chapter 51

AS I CONTEMPLATED FATHER NOVAK'S fate, in my mind's eye, I saw a vivid scene unfold before me, like a movie playing out in full colour. Standing stock still in the chapel, I felt Bruno reach out for my hand. He saw I was in a trance like state. I could see Angelina sat bolt upright on her bed, having one of her visions. It was so strange. She spoke directly to me.

"Father Novak is in terrible trouble. I feel fear and shame emanating from him."

She shook her head in frustration. Not knowing what to do. I stood there, continuing to watch her in my vision, and felt her concern for the safety of Father Novak, Bruno, Patrick, and myself.

Angelina lay down in her bed, as it aided her concentration, trying to send me a further message. Her ethereal figure strained, fading in and out of focus as she struggled to maintain the connection to me in the dream like state.

I gripped Bruno's hand hard.

"What's wrong, Nancy?"

Her transmission was fading. I heard an incredible roaring sound. Something was wrong.

"Bruno, I'm in touch with Angelina, but she's screaming. Oh no, Angelina," I shouted out, watching an unseen force pushing her back onto the bed. It was terrifying. *Was Azazel also targeting her?*

"She's being attacked by an elemental, Bruno."

I had closed my eyes, but Bruno could see my eyeballs moving beneath my eyelids, as though watching a scene spread out before me.

The howling winds of the elemental whistled and roared as it pinned Angelina's left arm down, followed by her right arm. It pushed her feet and legs together, restraining them as well. Seeing this happen to her, a child, made me furious. Poor Angelina saw nothing, of course, as she was blind, but she could smell the beast. That disgusting, sulphur, nausea inducing aroma that we all encountered when under a demonic attack.

"I can see it and smell it, Bruno. I don't know what to do. How can I help Angelina?"

Bruno, with furrowed brows and a concerned expression, said, "You can't at a distance, Nancy. We need help for Father Novak. He's still avoiding the Leviathan, but it's getting closer all the time."

I fixated on my vision, hearing Angelina's moans, and watched as her body twisted and strained, whilst the elemental pinned her down, contorting her body into a crucifix shape on the bed. It inverted her body, placing her head at the bed's base and her legs at the top, mimicking the upside-down cross which was used as a provocative symbol in satanic rituals, mocking the Christian usage as a symbol of the apostle Peter's martyrdom.

Unsure of how I could communicate with Angelina, I still wanted to try. It was new and made me dizzy, then warm. My senses felt connected to Angelina, although I did not know if she could hear me.

"Angelina, fight the elemental. Call your parents. It's your only option."

She screamed at the top of her lungs for her parents. There wasn't much time. This elemental was trying to distract her from continuing to contact me. I stayed watching as her mother and father rushed into her bedroom to see her levitate off the bed in the upside-down crucifix position.

They knelt in solemn reverence, bowing their heads in prayer, trying not to panic. As druids they were close to nature. Amid Angelina's torment, they beseeched Archangel Ariel, the guardian angel of nature, to help them, and fortunately she heard their prayers.

If a demon raises an elemental and uses earth, wind, fire, or water for evil, the Archangel Ariel punishes them for corrupting the earth's elements. She intervened and cast the elemental out, sending it back whence it came. The sound of the rushing wind abated, and Angelina's body fell back onto the bed. With tears of relief streaming down their faces, her parents embraced their daughter, grateful for Archangel Ariel's intervention.

When Angelina's body fell back onto the bed, we lost our connection. I felt relieved because I knew Angelina was now in the care of her parents and that Archangel Ariel had saved her. I felt my crystal in my pocket pulsing.

No feather, there is no feather.

Talking to my crystal? Ridiculous, but I was in the moment.

Why are you pulsing? Without the feather, I can do nothing, I thought.

Bruno's efforts to distract the Leviathan were having no effect, so he returned to the pew where Patrick sat. I also returned to the pew to see how he was doing. Relief washed over me as he was okay.

"Bruno, the crystal is pulsing."

"Nancy, is Angelina using the crystal to contact you?"

His comment left me wide-eyed and speechless, my brows furrowing in confusion. The experience with the elemental would have tired Angelina out. The crystal became her sole means of communication with me at this moment.

Patrick spoke to me with excitement, saying, "Nancy, I think you should close your eyes and concentrate hard. Maybe you can get through to her?"

I tried not to let panic overshadow my mind as I heard the Leviathan taunting Father Novak. It was important to focus my light energy through the crystal. The Leviathan, thinking it was winning, as Father Novak couldn't defend himself, started laughing and taunting him.

"I told you, priest; your time is up, you mindless fool."

He enjoyed the pain and discomfort Father Novak was suffering. The demon told him his own pride and self-righteousness caused his downfall and God had deserted him. Father Novak shut his eyes, bowing his head in fervent prayer, seeking solace and guidance. Remembering demons try to discourage faith in God, he said, "Lord God, I made a mistake, and want your forgiveness, please forgive me."

In all his years of exorcisms, Father Novak had never made a mistake of this magnitude. He knew it and felt desolate. He knew he had irrevocably sinned.

Bruno said, "Nancy, we have nothing to lose. Patrick cannot perform alone. With Angelina's help and your energy combined with the crystal, you could be effective. Otherwise, we are powerless against the demon."

I nodded and sat with my back to Father Novak, and the demon, needing to concentrate without any form of distraction. This would not be easy. The crystal boiled in my pocket, so I removed it and placed it on the front of the pew before kneeling. Closing my eyes, I focused every part of my being on the pulsating crystal and straight away, I heard Angelina's faint voice in the distance.

"Nancy, it's me, Angelina." I strained to hear her. The crystal hummed and glowed on the pew in front of me.

"I'm okay, Nancy. But you need to pray now to Saint Michael, the Archangel. He will hear you; and is willing to help. The crystal amplifies your prayers. Pray Nancy, Pray."

Father Novak, meanwhile, fell to his knees and prayed harder than he ever prayed before in his existence. He knew life was at risk, and wept, acknowledging his sins in full. I prayed to Saint Michael the Archangel, and Angelina prayed in the background as well. My crystal spat, hummed, and glowed. As Angelina foretold, Saint Michael, the Archangel, heard our prayers and intensified my light energy further.

"Patrick, help me now. Saint Michael, the Archangel, is strengthening my power. We have no feather, but he's sending me his energy."

Patrick stood up and, taking my hand, said, "I'm here with you, Nancy."

He too began praying to Saint Michael, the Archangel. My moldavite crystal buzzed, spat, and hummed. It sent out a radiant light. The light connected to me, and I screamed as I felt the power of Saint Michael surging through me. It was unlike any other sensation I have ever felt.

Putting my head back, an unworldly sound emanated from my throat. So high pitched and so powerful that every single window in the cathedral shattered. The glass didn't fall out of the windows but formed patterns where it splintered into shards. Saint Michael, the Archangel's power was incredibly potent, beyond any previous experience I'd had.

Bruno watched in awe as a beam of light shot out from me, hitting the Leviathan directly on its forehead. It roared in anger, frustration, and pain, understanding the angel's superior power flowing both through me, and Patrick. The Leviathan was incandescent with rage, wanting to tear Patrick and me apart, but the angels restrained it from hurting us.

With God's power, we forced it with the light beam to leave the cathedral. It was a battle royal, but with effort and our hearts beating fast, we pushed it out of the door. I can only imagine that it found its way back into hell from whence it came.

The moment the Leviathan disappeared, my crystal lost its shine and power, and both Patrick and I sank to our knees, exhausted and trembling. Angelina's voice faded away.

Patrick panted, "That was incredible, Nancy."

I didn't say much either, just nodded, overwhelmed by the experience.

The crystal felt warm as I placed it back in my pocket. Although Angelina's voice had vanished, her visionary ability assured me she had witnessed the Leviathan's defeat. What a victory, and what a special gift Angelina possessed.

Bruno pulled me close and hugged me. The experience drained me, but I also felt elated. My head was spinning with a thousand questions, but it was true. Saint Michael, the Archangel, heard my prayer boosted by Angelina and the crystal, and between us all we defeated the Leviathan. It was wondrous, a miracle, and I felt ecstatic.

I yearned to kiss Bruno, but the timing wasn't suitable. Clinging to him as he gave me a warm hug, I was certain he felt my heart beating out of my chest.

Hoping he felt the same as me, I whispered to him, "I'm so glad you are here, Bruno." He brushed my hair with his lips as we parted.

We gathered ourselves together but realised something shocking. There was one unfortunate side effect of this tumultuous event. Father Novak had indeed suffered a demonic attachment, causing his personality to change. It made him greedy and power hungry. However, once the Leviathan departed, because of Father Novak's lack of grace, God punished him, instead of cleansing his sinner's soul. We were not to be judge nor jury over Father Novak's actions, nor of God's punishment of him.

Father Novak found himself in one piece, but his memory was gone. There was no recognition of us or awareness of his whereabouts. Suffering from ninety percent memory loss, he knew nothing of the feather, or the Leviathan. Father Novak was alive, but also, in a way, very dead.

We contacted the Vatican, who collected him and returned him to Rome. Patrick later heard from a priest in Rome that Father Novak had left the Vatican to live in an isolated monastery in Italy, suffering from early onset dementia. Patrick felt sorry for him and visited him at the monastery.

Father Novak's situation troubled Bruno, as he wanted to forgive him, but as he was the indirect cause of his sister, Clara's death, it was impossible for him. It was best that Patrick went to visit him alone.

Patrick arrived and saw a centuries-old, imposing monastery. The monks took a vow of silence, so they said nothing when he arrived, but let him in, nodding as he explained that he was visiting Father Novak. As he entered Father Novak's living area, Father Novak looked up and smiled briefly, despite not recognising him.

"Who are you? Why are you here?" he asked, but lifeless behind his eyes.

Disinterested in speaking to Patrick, he waved his arm at him, trying to dismiss him.

"I don't know you. Please leave."

Patrick told me all he could do was hug him.

"I expressed happiness upon seeing him, Nancy, and that he was being well cared for by the monks."

He was off somewhere in his mind. Father Novak's memory was gone. A sad ending for this man, the Chief Exorcist of the Vatican. He had abandoned the group and caused Clara Siebert's death, but God's punishment was severe.

Patrick gave him a last, brief hug, to which he received no response. Patrick left to return to his parish in Bath, eager to see his parishioners, but still felt that his exorcism days were not over, especially as Father Novak was no longer available for the group. How right he was.

Chapter 52

TODAY WAS THE DAY we said goodbye to Clara at her memorial service. We were still all in Argentina, not yet having returned to the UK. Dreading it, I needed to prepare myself for the emotional day ahead. Hovering around Bruno's hotel room, I saw Arnold's handwritten letter, folded and sealed, neatly laying on Bruno's desk. I chose not to read it, knowing it was private and personal to both Arnold and Bruno. Bruno had invited him to the memorial, and the letter was in response to the invite.

We went to a small local church for the memorial service, not wanting to spend any further time in the ostentatious and evil cathedral as it held dark and dismal memories. The service was poignant. Hushed whispers and soft sobbing filled the air as people said many prayers. Beautiful music played while we decorated the small church with flowers and Clara's special items. This included her carpetbag, and whenever I saw the bag, it brought a lump to my throat.

Though our time together was short, Clara left a positive mark on everyone she met. Bruno gave the eulogy. And although only reunited in recent days, everyone realised how he had loved her.

There was a large turnout for the memorial service, reflecting the strong relationships Clara had formed during her life, and a closeness further developed among our group. Bruno received huge floral tributes in her memory, including an especially large one from the University in Marburg, where she was a lecturer.

Arnold gave him a beautiful bouquet of white roses with a loving message attached to them which read, "Always and forever, love Arnold."

Bruno and Arnold exchanged a firm handshake after the service. From Arnold's obvious pain and suffering, it was clear he loved Clara very much.

Standing there, feeling uncomfortable, Bruno said, "Clara and I didn't see each other in months."

He nodded. "I know you and Clara became distanced from one another, Bruno, but she hoped for a reconciliation."

I studied Bruno's face, but he just looked sad.

"Just so you know, I had already separated from my wife before I met Clara. She was an exceptional woman and didn't agree to becoming involved with me until I divorced my wife. Clara was such a special person. Thank you for allowing me to attend here today and say goodbye."

Bruno put his hand on Arnold's shoulder.

"It's a very long way for you to travel to pay your respects, Arnold, and it's appreciated."

He bowed and left the church.

Complimenting Bruno on his warmth towards Arnold, I knew he felt sorry for him. As together, they shared the grief of losing someone special. It was a tragic day.

"Losing Clara has made me realise the importance of seizing the day, Nancy. *Carpe diem*, isn't that what they say?"

Nodding, I held Bruno's hand tightly. This was such a

difficult day, and I vowed never to leave his side again.

I stored the order of service and Clara's precious photo, which Bruno valued, in my drawer at the hotel. Later, I would frame Clara's photo as a forever special and a loving memento. Her absence would be widely felt by everyone, as she was a knowledgeable powerhouse, and a strong woman.

Thoughts of the group's past adventures came to mind. We succeeded in the mission and cleansed the Nazis, including senior officers, but in doing so, we lost Clara, Stella, and almost Luca. We also didn't know the whereabouts of Andrew. *Was it all worth it?* Those deaths would haunt me for the rest of my life. The only upside was finding my purpose in life as a lightworker.

My main issue now was Maeve. That night, drifting off to sleep, thoughts of her filled my dreams. With a wistful smile, I promised, *Someday, daughter, we will be together.*

The next day, Patrick rang and said Father Novak was spiralling into full dementia, no longer recognising anyone. Anger, but also sadness, consumed Bruno over Father Novak. A long-term friend and integral group member he had faced divine retribution for his actions and, according to Patrick, wasn't doing well.

Twisting the phone cord with anxiety, I listened as Patrick said, "Monsignor Vitale has informed me, Nancy, that the Pope didn't take Father Novak's fall from grace at all well. Additionally, he expressed anger that Father Novak didn't deliver the feather to the Vatican."

"That's rich for him to say that, Patrick. He should comment on Clara's death and how sad it was, rather than the loss of the feather."

This was too much. I no longer felt connected to the Catholic

Church anymore, even with my upbringing. I believed a thousand percent in God, but religion no longer interested me.

"I know, Nancy. It's disappointing, even saying Father Novak was an affront to the Catholic faith."

"It's unfortunate, Patrick, but don't ask me to feel sorry for Father Novak, I just can't."

As we were ending the call, I felt Patrick's smile coming through the phone wire when he explained he was returning to Bath to reconnect with his parishioners. He assured me that he would be available whenever we might him. At thirty years old, he was becoming an impressive young man indeed.

Chapter 53

GOING FORWARD IN LIFE, Bruno didn't want our relationship to be based on the difficulties we had experienced, which made our emotions run high. Instead, he wanted to honour Isabel's memory and build up feelings for each other slowly. He kept a tight rein on his emotions, but we made it a priority to be together whenever possible.

The age gap separating us was insignificant in the grand scheme of things. He was a true gentleman, his integrity evident in his actions, his generosity warming my heart, and his abundant love constantly occupying my thoughts. I needed to stand or sit near him whenever I could.

We were in Argentina, handing over the Nazis to the Simon Wiesenthal organisation. The tense expressions of those present mirrored the gravity of the moment, and there was a lot of paperwork involved, but we knew it was the correct thing to do.

The first time we ever slept together was in Argentina. We were staying in separate bedrooms at the Monte Cristo Hotel, Buenos Aires, with lavishly decorated rooms and suites, adorned with crystal chandeliers, antiques and plush fabrics. I loved the classic European style and pushed the boat out financially to stay there. One night, Bruno came to stay with me. I happily saw him; I'd wondered whether we'd get together.

He was such a gentleman in all ways. Opening doors for me, carrying my bags, pulling out my chair when sitting down to a meal. He poured me a glass of my favourite Argentinian wine and presented me with flowers. Not a rose this time, as he gave me the rose in the hospital garden not long after we met, but sweet-smelling freesias.

Bruno wasn't particularly muscular, but he was slim, and upright. He was completely passionate about his mission, and that made him attractive to me, and very sexy. There was an age gap between us, but that didn't matter to me. It was irrelevant.

"No pressure, Nancy. I just want to be near you," he said, stroking my face and hair as we cuddled throughout that night, and at one point, said, "It is so difficult, I'm fighting against the memory of Isabel."

"I know Bruno, there is no rush," I said, but my heart raced with desire for him. I yearned to possess this courageous soldier who rescued one hundred and fifty Jews from annihilation.

Our bodies lay close together, and I could feel tingles working up and down my spine. I wanted him so badly, but I just wasn't sure of his feelings for me. I knew that the sad demise of Isabel's life from cancer was holding him back. I was no longer a virgin. Jimmy Dawson's abuse ended that. Nursing school had brought me a few dates, yet none felt significant at the time.

His hand brushed against my leg, and he rolled over so that his face was next to mine. His lips, brushing my neck, sent shivers up and down my body. His outline was barely visible in the dim hotel room, but he was close.

The soft sighs escaped my lips, harmonising with the tender caresses of his lips. It was all I could do not to jump on him. I didn't want to upset him. Isabel's memory strongly influenced his behaviour.

My body ached from his small fluttering kisses, and he heard my moans. It sent him over the edge. Suddenly Bruno's passion spilled over, a tangible force now.

We were both naked in the bed together, but he hadn't tried to touch me more than holding my hand or stroking my face and hair. This was different. It was as if he had been wrestling with something internal and lost. His usual calm demeanour disappeared, and he squeezed me, to the point of me being breathless.

"It's no good," he exclaimed loudly. "I can't fight my feelings any longer. My heart belongs to you, Nancy. I love you."

His declaration of love was so intense, so emotional, that I could hardly answer him back. So I just nodded, and he kissed me; a movie moment, exactly as I dreamt. He gently applied his lips to mine, softly and with a passionate but restrained intent. We both felt the softness of each other's lips, slightly moist, and there was tentative exploration with our tongues. The perfect kiss: slow, intense, then enthusiastic.

He was as sexy as hell to me, and I responded back to his kiss with a ferocity I didn't know resided within me. His touch was masterful, each caress, kiss, and stroke igniting a wildfire deep within.

Our bodies intertwined in a moment of madness. With God as my witness, I knew then that I would forever remain by his side after experiencing a memorable climax together.

We lay there panting, sweating, but deliriously happy. From that moment on, we stayed together in Argentina, exploring each other's bodies, laughing, and finally living our lives to the full.

Chapter 54

THE CROWDED STREETS OF Birmingham greeted us upon our return from Argentina in the summer of 1955. It had taken us years to sort out the cleansed Nazi trials with Simon Wiesenthal. We fell in love with the vibrant, eclectic mixture of people and food in Argentina, and my Spanish improved. It wasn't really a hardship to stay there.

However, there was a terrible political event in June 1955, where the main square in Buenos Aires was bombed by the Argentine Air Force, near to the very cathedral where we cleansed the Nazis, killing over three hundred civilians. Supporters of Péron burned churches that night.

Bruno told me it was time to leave Argentina, as the mission was complete, and the country was becoming politically volatile and dangerous. I was sad to leave this extraordinary country, but it was the right thing to do in light of the civil unrest.

Once back in the UK, Bruno and I tried to build a normal life together, doing ordinary things daily, such as cooking meals and taking countryside walks.

I had stepped away from the sterile hospital walls, seeking solace from the haunting memories of lives lost and wounds endured. Matron understood and gave me the time off from the hospital for as long as I needed, keeping the door open for my return one day. She understood the heavy burden Stella's death and Clara's passing had placed on my mental well-being. For the moment, I was able to stay in the Nurse's Home, and initially Bruno lodged in a small hotel nearby, although we were seeking a place to live in together.

Drained of energy, my crystal stayed dormant and dull. Bruno grieved the loss of his sister, continually wishing for the power of foresight and being able to save Clara. If only they had reunited sooner. He felt life was filled with what ifs.

My suspicions grew that I was in the initial stages of discovering the full potential of the light energy which God had blessed me with. Angelina's expertise was pivotal in helping me master it in time. Certainly, no further visions occurred, such as the one where the elemental attacked her. But it didn't mean to say there weren't more experiences laying ahead of me.

Having shed the label of being 'bad,' I embraced a positive self-image. The burden of guilt from my Catholic background and societal expectation lifted, and I no longer saw myself as evil because of what had happened at eighteen, when I gave birth to Maeve out of wedlock. I was even wearing brighter coloured clothes, no longer feeling the need to hide myself away.

There was one blot on the horizon. A sense of frustration lingered. On returning from Argentina, I attempted to see Andrew but found his flat locked up and no one present. The furrowed brows and tense expression on my face betrayed my deep concern. Instead, I knocked on Andrea's door, and when she answered, I felt shocked. She appeared exhausted, as if she had suffered from a great ordeal. Trying not to show surprise at her appearance, I gave her a tight hug. Questions tumbled out of me like a mixed-up pile of clothes pulled from the laundry basket.

"Andrea, how are you? Andrew isn't home. What's been happening?"

She sighed and ran her hand through her hair in a nervous gesture.

"Hello Nancy, it is good to see you. No, Andrew isn't here any more."

"What's happened? You look like you have seen a ghost."

She gestured for me to enter her flat, which was painted in pastel colours. Quite different in style from Andrew's place. It was gentle and cosy.

"I'll make us tea and explain, Nancy. It's not a cheerful story, though."

Her down-turned eyes and pursed lips hinted at the sad news she held back. Andrea made the tea, causing a loud whistle to emanate from the kettle, and a clinking of cups and saucers. The flat seemed in disarray. Andrew had given me the impression that Andrea was normally a tidy, organised kind of person.

The steam rose from the teacups, swirling in delicate wisps, as we settled into our seats on the sofa. Handing me a vintage cup and saucer, I took a sip of the warm tea and steadied my nerves. Andrea's furrowed brows and tense posture hinted at the gravity of the situation.

"I took care of Andrew after you left, Nancy, as you asked me to. However, he changed completely from the person I knew. Refusing to eat and sleep, he developed sunken eyes and hollow cheeks."

I felt sad at Andrea's description of Andrew's decline.

"He muttered incomprehensible words, his voice trembling, filled with a mix of anguish and uncertainty confessing an inner turmoil. He claimed he would go to hell but refused to go. The thought of him attempting suicide again filled me with terror every single day."

Hearing this news from Andrea disheartened me. I left England, thinking he would recover. I realised my naivety and felt embarrassed I had left Andrea to handle the situation alone. She wasn't even Andrew's relative.

"I should have got him professional help. I am so sorry. What did you do?"

"I watched him like a hawk, day and night. Despite my efforts to provide food, he ate tiny amounts, barely enough to sustain himself. It was exhausting, Nancy, but I persevered, dedicating myself to Andrew's care. It was like caring for a toddler."

A wave of sadness washed over me, leaving me feeling empty. I stood up, and walked over to Andrea, giving her another massive hug.

"This is a total nightmare, Andrea. But what eventually happened? Where is Andrew now?"

She inhaled and exhaled with a sigh.

"I have a deep sense of dread, Nancy, and don't know where he's gone. After weeks of this type of behaviour, paranoia, incomprehensible mumbling, fear of going to hell, he packed a bag, and said he needed to leave."

She struggled to tell the story.

"I asked where he was going. He uttered, 'Somewhere they cannot discover me.' The next thing I knew, he was gone. That was a week ago, and I've been worried ever since."

Andrea's face fell, her eyes welling up with tears.

"Oh Andrea, I'm so sorry. Did you call the police?"

"I did, but he's a grown man and they don't consider him a danger because we didn't admit him to a hospital under mental health concerns previously. I should have secured proper help for him, but I was fixated on making sure he was eating, sleeping, and not self-harming, Nancy."

I stroked her arm in sympathy.

"You did your absolute best. We will search for Andrew. Please stop worrying. You need a proper rest, Andrea."

She nodded with a grimace on her face.

"I am worn out."

Saying goodbye to Andrea, I thanked her for taking such diligent care of Andrew and wondered what to do next.

Going back to the Nurse's Home, I prepared a picnic and hurried to meet Bruno at the park. He was reclining on the grass, surrounded by lush green trees and vibrant flowers. It was full of ducks, squirrels, birds and was very peaceful. The park was in full bloom, and a plethora of gardeners kept it looking wonderful.

Couples walked hand in hand on winding paths. Both young and old sat on benches reading books or newspapers. There were young mums from the local parent craft class comparing parenting notes whilst rocking tiny babies to sleep in expensive prams.

The manicured lawns and colourful gardens painted a picture of idyllic suburban life. The day was bright and warm. I sat down on the grass opposite the duck pond.

"Bruno, I've heard some worrying news, and I don't know what to do?"

His eyebrows furrowed and his eyes softened with genuine concern as he asked, "Tell me, Nancy, what's wrong?"

I sighed, running my fingers through my hair, feeling stressed.

"To be honest, Bruno, I have lots of news to share, and none of it is good."

He told me to start at the beginning. Of course, he knew of the suicide attempt. I explained it whilst we were away in Argentina. Poor Andrea dealt with Andrew's psychosis alone. I felt so guilty leaving her in that position. Looking at Bruno, he saw I was worried.

"Bruno, we don't know where he is or have any way of contacting him, but he needs professional help."

I felt I had deserted Andrew in his time of need. If something happened to him... He was my closest friend, and I swore to Bruno I wouldn't rest until we found him and made sure he was okay.

Stroking my face, he said, "Don't worry, Nancy. We will track him down."

Then I told him how I had met the two interesting twin ladies with their platinum blonde hair on the train back in 1947, eight years prior.

"They were bouncy and lively, and we swapped addresses. I gave them my address at the hospital, and they gave me their aunt and uncle's address with a view to meeting in the future. They showed me a photo of their uncle when I was on the train with them. It was black and white, and grainy, but I saw the man's face. He wore the unmistakable black SS uniform, complete with the distinctive double lightning bolts on the collar, which Sylvia admired with immense pride. She wrote to me last week."

Bruno frowned. "I feel this is leading up to something concerning Nancy."

"I reviewed the details of the Nazis we sent to Simon Wiesenthal for trial and the various outcomes. Whose photo did I stumble upon? The twins' photo from the train. This time, I recognised him. It was Heinrich Himmler."

Bruno's hand clenched into a tight fist.

"But Nancy, he committed suicide back in 1945. The British documented his death. He couldn't be alive and be their uncle."

I shook my head.

"He is alive and well. They've asked to meet me because they are having a challenging time, whatever that means? Then I approached Milo."

"Milo Muller, the infantry soldier? But the Nazis we saved only remember parts of their past, Nancy."

"I know, Bruno, but a former Nazi sent Milo a message confirming that Himmler was alive. He said his hands trembled when he unfolded the note."

Taking Bruno's hands, I gripped them hard, so he knew I was being serious.

"A Nazi gave me this information on good authority. Someone we rescued from the demon infestation, and someone we should believe, Bruno."

He stroked his chin, brooding.

"Milo mentioned that there's more to tell. The note explained Himmler had tried to slip out of Germany by masquerading as an ordinary soldier, but that the British army had captured him."

"How did Himmler escape, Nancy? It doesn't sound very plausible."

Bruno frowned, worried at my statement. I had brought duck food with me and I threw the food into the lake opposite us. It was such a serene scene, an odd counterpoint to the serious conversation we were having.

"Milo doesn't understand much since we cleansed him, but he said somehow someone made an ordinary German soldier resemble Himmler."

Bruno span round to face me.

"Of course, Nancy, demons can alter the light to change a person's appearance, sometimes resembling animals, such as pigs or dogs. Imagine Azazel performing a face swap between Himmler and an unsuspecting German soldier."

I nodded. Bruno's mind was working overtime.

"Milo said the British Army had allowed Himmler to go free. The Allies were only interested in finding the main offenders of evil, Hitler's high-ranking officers."

Bruno was unimpressed at the British Army. The frustration in his voice was evident.

"I can't believe they let him go."

Putting his head in his hands, his face turned pale. I ruffled Bruno's hair and caressed his face.

"I know it's horrifying. Milo was told the man resembling Himmler took a cyanide pill, leading the British to believe it was a suicide. The British tried to resuscitate the man, but he expired within fifteen minutes. They photographed his body, took a copy of the death mask, and removed the body, burying him in an unmarked grave near Luneburg. Because the grave's location remains unknown, no-one can prove it wasn't Himmler who took the capsule and died."

Bruno's hands twisted and squeezed together, his face contorting with worry and disbelief.

"I cannot believe this, Nancy. Is there no marker or headstone? It's insane. Himmler believed he was more important than Hitler. He was just as evil as Hitler. The 'final solution' of exterminating people in Eastern Europe was his operation. With no morals and no conscience, he is a massive threat to society."

The ducks fought over the food, so I tossed more into the lake to ensure they all got some. The Mallards exhibited aggressive behaviour, intimidating the female ducks. I turned to face Bruno.

"According to the information I received from Milo, which he received from a serving Nazi fanatic, Himmler is trying to raise a new army. The faction is no longer the Third Reich. It is called 'The Heresy' and his title is 'Chief Heretic.' He is challenging religious faiths, and calling upon non-believers to rise and join him in a fresh wave of death and destruction."

Bruno approached me and encircled my body with his arms. I felt the steady rhythm of his heartbeat beating in his chest.

"He can't use any of the Nazis we cleansed, Nancy. They're in jail or working in the community."

He squeezed me.

"I still have some doubts and concerns we haven't gone far enough, Bruno. Himmler is reaching out to former Nazis, according to Milo's information."

"Yeah, but 'The Heresy' sounds far-fetched. I can't imagine anyone wanting to join up."

Nestling against Bruno's shoulder, I found comfort in his presence. He stroked my hair with slow, languid movements, and was so gentle. I wore a contented smile. Powerful feelings were developing for this man. It was such a beautiful day. However, despite my bright mood, the Himmler question weighed heavily on my mind.

"It's unclear if he's going for an anti-religion angle, or a right- wing political bias. I suppose we will discover which, but it sounds dark and satanic, right back to the demon question. We must not allow him to resurrect the horrors of the past."

I raised my head off his shoulder.

"How do we manage this, Bruno? It's unbelievable he's still alive after all this time. We cannot prove it, and don't have the Archangel feather any more. The lance's placement sealed the pit in the cathedral's crypt, but there are no other holy religious relics available to help us."

He studied my face, his gaze powerful and strong.

I continued, "Our purpose is to unite with our determined group of friends and eradicate evil from the world. With divine intervention, we rescue individuals from the clutches of darkness and guide them towards the light. We should call our group 'The Deliverers.' It's more than a mere group. We are a movement, a society."

Bruno nodded. "Yes, I like that, Nancy. But it must be a secret society."

"The evil entities targeted us because we connected with each other through the desire to rid the world of evil. I didn't know it at the beginning, but Satan foresaw how we would join forces to fight his demonic army. You with your past, Father Novak as an exorcist, Patrick as a priest, Angelina as a Seer, Clara as a demonologist, and me as a lightworker, plus the friends and supporters we have gathered along the way."

"Ah, Nancy, I guess that's true."

I smiled serenely at him.

"God works in mysterious ways, Bruno."

He pondered this for a moment, stroking his chin with his hand.

"I do like the name 'The Deliverers.' As I said, it is important to maintain secrecy for the group. We combat evil wherever we can, offering hope and salvation to those in need, but it's safer not to reveal our identities. Let us paint a vivid picture of our purpose, a creed that guides our actions and unites us."

He continued, his voice confident and strong.

"As for the holy relics, we have you, Patrick, Angelina, and the Deliverers. We will be fine, whatever the situation. Angelina sourced the holy relics for my sister. Maybe she can repeat it. Who knows?"

"Yes, Bruno, but don't forget God's part in this. We channel his love for humanity and need his support."

"True, Nancy, but Patrick will make sure we are following God's path. Don't worry."

I smiled at his positivity, and I always felt safe when I was with him.

"It's bizarre that he's the uncle of those two women, Sylvia and Linda I met on the train. Quite a coincidence. They are happy to meet in Birmingham. Do you think I should go?"

Bruno put his arm around me. We always faced trouble head on together.

"Yes, Nancy, but be cautious. Let's research them more beforehand."

As we cuddled, I watched the passers-by in the distance, enjoying the beauty and tranquillity of the park.

"I am going to be honest, Nancy. Isabel, was my future, and when she passed away, I never believed I'd find happiness again."

I turned my gaze away from Bruno.

"Isabel was a lovely woman."

He sighed a long sigh.

"We never built a family together. It was the one thing she desired most of all. Bringing children into the world seemed wrong to me after my war years."

I understood how he must have felt.

"But, Nancy, we're here, together now, and I'm thrilled to be with you."

He looked into my eyes and spoke in a soft and affectionate tone.

"We understand each other, and I hope can have a future together. A big age gap exists though...," he shrugged.

I put my finger on his lips and gave him a loving glance. My home was with him.

"The memories we created, like snapshots in my mind, flash before me, Bruno. It has been an awe-inspiring, mind-blowing, and extraordinary path which has exceeded my wildest dreams and expectations. The age gap is of no consequence to me."

Looking into Bruno's eyes; my fingers intertwined with his.

"I'm a lightworker and we can do this as one. I believe it, Bruno."

It was a lovely, romantic moment, but then Bruno's mood changed. We moved to sit on the bench, but he fidgeted, shifting his weight back and forth on the bench seat. He couldn't stay seated.

"I don't know what awaits us, Nancy. We are in a bittersweet situation, but let's gather our formidable friends together. We must locate Himmler and those who share his ideology and put an end to this growing movement."

Our eyes locked, and I leaned in, pressing my lips against Bruno's.

"We won't fail, Bruno. I believe in us."

"Yes," he said, his eyes filled with determination as he gazed into the distance.

"I hope Isabel is watching and feels happy we have found each other."

Patting his arm in response, I nodded, "I think she would be, Bruno."

This was such a positive moment. I looked forward to a bright future with Bruno, wanting to spend my life with him and build a family together. The Deliverers were a family we had built with people who became close knit friends, working together towards the same goal. But I wanted more. I wanted to meet Maeve and incorporate her into mine and Bruno's relationship.

Cleansing demons from wicked individuals revitalised me and sparked a lasting desire to do good. Saving the Nazis from their evil deeds and ensuring those who deserved trials faced justice, and avenging those families which the Nazis brutalised was satisfying.

Our connection, and the world around us felt perfect to us at that moment. We were the Deliverers. Monster hunters, willing and able to rid the world of evil. The ducks quacked and preened, and I felt calm. They looked asleep whilst floating on the water, both peaceful and idyllic.

A surprising shiver ran down my spine. I wanted the best for Maeve. To offer her a warm and comforting home, but my gut feeling said there was something wrong. I didn't tell Bruno, but I had recently experienced dreams with a child in them. The dreams were short, but a curly-haired child with black hair and blue eyes reached out her arms, asking me for help.

My focus going forwards was to bring forth God's light, nip 'the Heresy' movement in the bud, but also to reunite with my daughter, Maeve, and build a brighter future with Bruno. It was all going to be fine. For the moment, I was at peace.

Chapter 55

MY BODY TWISTED AND TURNED, tangled in the sheets, as beads of sweat dripped down my forehead. I was having one of the worst nightmares I had ever experienced and I felt my body stiffen as if in self-defence, taking shallow and rapid breaths.

Bruno was not around. He was visiting long-lost friends in town and out until late. Oh, how I wished he was here now. My eyes fluttered open, adjusting to the weakly lit room as I lay in bed. *Was this a vision or a nightmare?* The blood was beating in my cheeks.

In my mind's eye, I descended a narrow stone staircase, smelling of ancient incense and damp earth. As I stood behind a cold, stone pillar, I saw a man dressed from top to toe in a dark robe with a black hood. He licked his lips in grim satisfaction, watching his guards drag an old man to the middle of the Sigil of Baphomet hewn into the thick flagstone floor in the centre of a crypt.

Despite my intense gaze, the scene looked nothing like the dimly lit, ancient crypt of the cathedral in Argentina, where we cleansed the Nazis. These surroundings were unfamiliar to me. Torches flickered, casting elongated shadows on the roughly hewn walls. The vaulted ceiling loomed overhead, adorned with intricate inscriptions and symbols etched into the ancient stone pillar which shielded me.

The air was icy. I watched, horrified, as the flickering flames of the pillar candles encircled the Sigil and cast a shadow over the man's face. His weathered face and tired eyes, showing his age, I presumed, taken from a village nearby. The old man was familiar. I furrowed my brow, searching the depths of my memory, but the answer as to who he was had remained just out of my mind's reach.

Goosebumps rose on my skin, my body tensing with a mixture of fear and disbelief. The villagers whispered about happenings at that wicked place, as if from afar. Their tales persisted with loud screams, sounds of torture, strange lights, and dark shapes being heard and seen.

Instead of a traditional place of worship, I found myself admiring this majestic castle, its towering spires reaching towards the sky. Isolated, the castle stood amidst an ancient forest, as if seen through another's eyes.

My perspective changed, and I was no longer overlooking the castle in the vision. Again, I witnessed the elderly man on the ground, pleading for his life with a terrified expression. He was sweating, moaning, and asking something, but the language was hard to name. The pitiful cries spoke for themselves. His suffering was obvious.

The man in the long, black robes ignored the man's pleas for mercy, and he signalled the guards to restrain him with hooks attached to the marked floor. As he turned, his cloak swished and I saw a gold pentagram emblazoned on the back of it, labelled 'Oberster Ketzer,' 'Chief Heretic.'

Taking in a huge breath, I recoiled in fear. Tears sprang to my eyes. I knew who this awful person was. This was Himmler, infested by Azazel, my arch enemy, and the Deliverers' enemy as well.

The scene unfolded, and I knew it was real. This was happening. Although it was 1955, I felt I was seeing something ancient, with satanic clothing and ritualistic behaviour, although this was a recent event.

The old man's trousers darkened with a noticeable stain, wetting himself in fear and horror as he noticed a large twelve-inch knife clasped in the hooded man's hand. My mouth opened in a silent gasp, my head in my hands. I foresaw a terrible outcome for the elderly man. As I saw the solemn, ceremonial act of a ritualistic killing, an execution, the air became thick with tension, and a taste of bile rose in my throat. The hooded man declared the following in English.

Dark Lord, Lucifer, we have gathered here as your loyal legion and follow your orders as you command. We make this ancient ritual in your honour today and offer this human sacrifice as confirmation of our fealty to you.

The weight of his words settled on me as if a heavy cloak hung over my shoulders. The followers bowed their heads, eyes fixed on the man pinned to the floor. He was terrified out of his wits, his face pale, and contorted with fear. His face grimaced with desperation as he thrashed around, eyes pleading for salvation. I felt sick to my stomach, but knew I could do nothing to ease this man's suffering. Although the Chief Heretic spoke in English, his pronunciation carried the distinct inflections and cadence of a German accent. Azazel yelled at the old man, urging him to stop praying to a futile God.

"Shut up, weakling."

The speaker's eyes glinted with malice, sneering with the

391

words, his face twisted into a mocking grin.

"Your God can't save your disgusting soul now."

He spoke in English because this castle wasn't in Germany, and the old man only understood English. The castle's unique architecture made it apparent it wasn't in England either. The guards formed a tight circle, still kneeling, their eyes fixated on the Chief Heretic as he performed the unholy satanic ritual. Raising their arms in unison, chanting, "Lu-ci-fer, Lu-ci-fer, Lu-ci-fer, we honour thee."

It was terrifying watching this evil rite. With a swift and merciless motion, the hooded man leaned down and slit the old man's throat from ear to ear. The old man screamed, jiggling with fright, but as soon as the knife cut the jugular vein in his throat, his scream ceased, and the twitching stopped, replaced by an eerie stillness, as though a puppet with severed strings.

I clamped my hand hard over my mouth to nullify the scream which threatened to erupt from the back of my throat, as I watched the horrific murder take place.

The group stood still as the blood, his life force, drained from the old man's neck, collecting within the channels of the hewn-out Sigil shape on the floor. Crimson red rivulets sank into the hole in the centre of the symbol underneath the man's body.

The sound of the man's blood dripping into a bowl below broke the silence. A dark offering to a darker being. The murderer's eyes gleamed with an icy intensity as he issued his chilling command.

"Let him drain. Once we have done this, only then will Lord Lucifer be satisfied. Then we will return to Prague."

"What do we do with the body, Azazel, Oberster Ketzer?"

"I don't care. Bury it in the woods. The damp soil and decaying leaves can claim the body."

The guard's voice trembled as he uttered the words, "Yes, Azazel, Oberster Ketzer," his voice laced with reverence and terror.

How sad. No one would mourn the old man's passing at his last resting place. His body was to be discarded like waste.

My vision blurred, a darkened scene, and I struggled to stay upright. The eerie glow in Himmler's eyes revealed the sinister presence of Azazel, casting a haunting aura. I realised that he wanted me to see the vision, and I knew that he knew we were aware of Himmler's plot for a new faction. Azazel was taunting me. This was madness. I tried not to see, but the vision kept coming.

Suddenly, like lightning bolt, I remembered seeing this man in a vision before departing Ireland for England in 1947. Back then, eight years ago, I was oblivious to the sinister presence of demons lurking in the shadows. Brutal hierarchies structured the demons' relationship with displays of aggression and dominance. Azazel was exercising his power in an evil display to me. Thankfully, after a few minutes, the vision fractured, but I remained traumatised from what I had seen.

Although I did not recognise the castle, I realised it was another portal, similar to the one we sealed in the Buenos Aires cathedral. With Azazel's Prague comment, he gave himself away. Now we had sufficient information to follow him and seek out the new evil faction.

Azazel was one of the fallen angels, with his own legion, and he sat as an important leader within the unseen realm. He was the demon which had visited me in my nightmare, and I realised he was the demonic link to all the interference the Deliverers and myself had suffered to date, revelling in our horror and fear.

His intense desire for retribution on the Deliverers became clear. We belittled Azazel in front of the devil by casting out many of his minion demons. We upset the status quo of the dark realm by removing the demons from the Nazis, which he and his legion utilised to bring evil to the earth.

I felt Azazel was planning a terrifying new era of chaos and harm, perhaps summoning an arsenal of new evil entities to unleash upon the world. Would we soon be on a new perilous journey to save our loved ones?

Then thoughts of Maeve, my daughter, flooded my mind, causing my heart to skip a beat. Was she safe? What had happened to Andrew, my best friend? So many questions needed answers.

My journey was incredible, evolving through people, lineage, and a calling. My trip wasn't over just yet. I had no choice but to accept change, as the future was inevitable. I could not stay rooted in the past.

Our main spiritual battle was yet to come, which would test our strength and resilience. However, with courage and determination, the future would be what we made it.

It is true that I no longer felt connected to the Catholic Church, because I felt religion used God to justify division, whereas, thank God, our diverse group stood shoulder to shoulder, a tapestry of distinct backgrounds and beliefs, ready to confront any challenge which lay ahead. We, the Deliverers, would stand against the darkness together, a beacon of inclusion and light.

Conclusion

LIFE SEEMED SIMPLE AND STRAIGHTFORWARD with Bruno. Living together as we were in Birmingham, in a comfortable home, it was hard to believe what we had been through. He was, the love of my life, and I was happy.

My journey to becoming a lightworker was a transformative one. I learned so much from Bruno. His experiences throughout the First and Second World Wars taught him how to remain calm and composed in the face of adversity. He was brave beyond belief, and I wanted to mirror his bravery.

My admiration extended to my cousin, Patrick, who suffered great harm at the hands of the demon Azazel, but whose solid faith in God, meant he triumphed over malevolent evil, closing the portal to hell under the Buenos Aires Cathedral, entombing both demons and elementals. He never wavered in his belief, and he taught me the value of faith.

I benefited from an introduction to the spiritual world by Angelina, a child prophet, showing me the extent of the light energy gift, and psychic powers. She helped me to believe in my gift and guided me in its use. I looked forward to gaining further understanding through positive interactions with Angelina, to fine tune the wielding of my gift from God.

Clara, Bruno's sister, showed me the importance of historical knowledge and the lessons it could teach us, to be important. Her providing the group with holy relics was incredible. Her demise through demonic attack was heartbreaking and salutary but I was determined to honour her memory.

Instinct always drove me to confront problems directly, ignoring logic and nuance. No longer willing to stand by and watch evil attack those I loved. Instead of being always on the defence, I wanted to move forwards and be the aggressor.

Learning and understanding the importance of love, light, and friendship. Banding together as the Deliverers, supporting each other, and never giving up. Our group worked closely together to defeat evil, fulfilling God's will.

We as Deliverers going forwards would adopt the Templar motto, *Non Nobis Domine, Non Nobis, Sed Nomini, Tuo Da Gloriam*, which translated as, n*ot to us, Lord, not to us, but to your name give the glory.*

Epilogue

WHAT NEXT FOR THE DELIVERERS? There was no doubt in my mind we needed to continue to pursue Himmler and eradicate his demonic infestation before he could influence others to join his evil quest. We didn't know where to find Himmler, but I was certain that God would find a way to help us.

At the back of my mind, I was concerned for Maeve, my daughter, continuing to have vivid dreams nightly in which a young child appeared, pleading for my help. Who else could it be? I had to find her, but Himmler needed dealing with first.

I did continue to wonder about Maeve, however. What kind of person was she? What did she think? Was she okay? So many questions which needed answering. I was happy to carry out my destiny and God's will, but I desperately wanted Bruno, Maeve, and me to be a family. It was my personal ambition, and the depths of my determination to achieve it knew no bounds. But my senses told me Maeve was no ordinary child, and that tracing her and recovering her would be no easy task.

My mind reverted to the people we had encountered, and the experiences gained on my transformative journey. Where was Andrew? What had become of him? The question stabbed at my heart. Leaving him with Andrea, emotionally unstable, still haunted me. I knew it was essential I went to Argentina to eradicate the evil from the Nazis, but at what price? If only I knew if he was safe and well?

Himmler, Maeve, Andrew... so many loose threads. But one thing was certain. Azazel remained a thorn in the side of the Deliverers, and we were a constant irritation to him.

Inside, I knew I had changed. I was no longer the young woman who thought herself 'bad' from childhood. I was 'good'. Nothing would stop me from bringing light to the dark. Bring on the battle. We were ready for it.

Appendix

We had encountered so many demons I began to understand why they had shown themselves in certain situations and possessed certain humans.

Lucifer/Satan/The Devil – Pride – Lucifer was the highest angel. Lucifer and all the angels were continually in God's presence and knew the glory of God. There was no excuse for rebelling or turning away from him. The fallen angels seem devoted to opposing God and attacking God's people. They will not repent, and God does not give them a chance for redemption.

Satan would not bow down before the newly created Adam and incites humans to sin by infecting their minds. He is God's adversary but is subservient and cannot defeat God. He is not omnipresent.

Azazel-One of God's fallen angels, a demon with an ordinary man's hands and feet. Possessing twelve wings attached to his back, with six wings on the right and six on the left. With red skin, a barbed tail, and yellow glowing eyes and skulls and goat bones attached to his body. He teaches man how to make weapons and the art of warfare. He acts as the Devil's right-hand demon and sits at the top of the legion of demons.

He leads a group of two hundred fallen angels, called Watchers, who descended to earth to take human wives. They taught forbidden knowledge and corrupted mankind. Azazel leads them. Their offspring are the Nephilim, who are fallen angels who lay with human women.

Beelzebub/Satan- Gluttony - This demon is the Lord of the Flies or Dung. representing gluttony and pride. He is a powerful demon who is high in hell's hierarchy. He gets humans to believe in false gods and promotes war. Beelzebub possesses humans to conduct sadistic acts on other humans. Hence, he was the ideal demon to inhabit a Nazi SS Soldier. In appearance, he is typical of demons. He will have purple or red skin, horns on the top of his head, typically ram's horns, a long tail, and a long-forked tongue. He has wings in the style of a large fly.

Mammon– Avarice - This demon is another fallen angel who represents the greed of man, wanting more possessions, money, and general wealth. He creates obsession, which leads to envy and temptation. He looks like a wizened old man, or a red-skinned creature of colossal size.

Agramon–This is the demon of fear. He will play on a man's fears or phobias. With red glowing eyes, arms of a bear with taloned fingers, legs of a goat with cloven feet and a snake adorns his body. He has four horns protruding from his head. He often changes his image to create the most fearsome appearance possible.

Leviathan– Envy - The Leviathan portrays itself either as a mammoth serpent or a dragon. The Leviathan is the embodiment of chaos. This spirit is frightening, as it is a formidable and destructive spirit. He breathes out fire like a dragon and has sharp teeth. It is impossible to fight physically, as it has impenetrable scales. He especially hates humans who follow God, such as a priest. He is more of a foot soldier of the legion of demons.

About the Author

A mother of two grown-up daughters, based in leafy Surrey, UK. Married with two husky dogs, which dominate my world. My mother passed away, and I felt driven to write my first historical fantasy novel. There are two follow on novels on the way, and ideas for many more. My hobbies are singing, dancing and having fun. It would be an honour for me if you accompanied me on my writing journey.

You can connect with me on:

🌐 https://www.maisiemoonbooks.com

🐦 https://twitter.com/@MaisieMoon53998

📘 https://www.facebook.com/maisiemoon

🔗 https://www.linkedin.com/in/kristina-lushey-5b4016314

🔗 https://www.instagram.com/maisiemoonbooks

🔗 https://www.threads.net/@maisiemoonbooks

🔗 https://www.youtube.com/@maisiemoonbooks

🔗 https://www.tiktok.com/@maisiemoonbooks

Subscribe to my newsletter:

✉ https://maisiemoonbooks.com/mailing-list

Also by Maisie Moon

I like to mesh historical fiction about powerful women within a supernatural background. I have enjoyed writing the Sisterhood and Guilt, and look forward to your feedback at info@maisiemoonbooks.com.

If you enjoy any of my work, please do submit a review. It really helps independent authors to become better known!

Love, Maisie Moon x

The Sisterhood

You can listen to this as an audiobook on Spotify, Audible or Googleplay. Also available as an e-book download or paperback from Amazon and various other outlets.

It's the precursor to the first of the Nancy Flanagan Chronicles, Guilt. It tells the story of four kick ass women who face the challenges of the centuries they live in, from Medieval France through to Ireland in WW2.

They are gifted with an ancestral light energy weapon, and use it to fight evil wherever it manifests itself. An uplifting and inspirational read.

It won the International Firebird Award for Short Stories.

Printed in Dunstable, United Kingdom

DARK SISTERS

BOSTON PRETERNATURAL
INVESTIGATIONS UNIT

AOIBH WOOD

ISBN-13: 979-8-9921061-0-7

Cover Art By Rebecca Frank

For all of us, may our power shine in times of darkness.

To all of my Trans Friends who gave me the courage to press on.
And to you, my lovely readers. I pray to Mother Morrigan that you have a happy life.